In the Beginning the Dance

Autumn & Craig

My hopes for the future
ride with you. Each of you
shine a light in my heart
— but together you blend
me. You inspire The
rest of us w/ your love
and sense of community

Larry

In the Beginning the Dance

a novel

Lanny Cotler

Democracy Dancing Press

Published by
Democracy Dancing Press
1517 Casteel Drive
Willits, CA 95490
707-459-9550

A division of the Intergalactic Society for Humanics

This is a work of fiction. While, as in all fiction, the literary perceptions and insights are based on experience, all names, characters, places, and incidents either are products of the author's imagination or are used fictitiously.

Cover painting by Pierre Delattre, "Dancing for Mother Earth", Ortenstone Delattre Fine Art, www.ortenstonedelattre.com

Library of Congress Cataloging-in-Publication Data

Cotler, Lanny. 1941–
          In the beginning the dance / Lanny Cotler. – 1st ed.
          Pg.cm
ISBN 978-0615497525

     1. Poetry—Fiction. 2. Native American—Fiction. 3. Community build-ing—Fiction. 4. Nuclear storage—Fiction. 5. Medicine—Fiction. I. Title

10 9 8 7 6 5 4 3 2 1

This book is dedicated to all those intent on
completing the American Revolution

"Torus"

The Universe is a doughnut
Come and take a bite
No inside no outside
No day no night

Only a rolling roaring silence
As it seeks to understand
How it popped from God's mind
Into your open hand

~Lanny Cotler

"There were no even surfaces. The walls rip-
pled around as in a cocoon softened and re-
newed by the annual caress of a woman's
hand.... I felt how safe and warm I would be to
sleep in such a place."

~Peter Nabokov, as quoted in Healing Spaces
in the Tewa Pueblo World *by Naranjo &
Swentzell, describing the sensation of a traditional Acoma Pueblo house.*

Prologue

The Indian in question was from the Pueblo nation. He'd been arrested in New York City a week ago. At the time of his arrest, he was on the steps of the New York Public Library, standing between the two looming stone lions, pouring gasoline from a can onto his clothing, intent on immolating himself. His clothes were traditional Arabic—*keffiya* and *thawb*. Two dark complexioned men carrying sturdy walking sticks were holding the gawking public at bay, stopping anyone from interfering with the doings.

When his clothes didn't catch fire (the gasoline was merely a weak infusion of Celestial Seasons Sleepytime Tea), the Indian, ranting and raving, then took off his Arabic clothing only to reveal underneath the clothes of an Orthodox Jewish Chasidic rabbi. He quickly exchanged the *keffiya* for a *yarmulka*. Again, he poured liquid from the gas can over his clothes and attempted to light himself on fire.

The gathering crowd oo'd and ah'd, some crying that he stop, others urging him on. Cellphones and video cameras were sucking it in.

"Not till the sons of Abraham come together as the brothers they are shall there be peace in another land they call holy. Israel out of Palestine! The USA out of everywhere it doesn't belong! Light! Gimme a light that works! I'm ready to go! I long to be reunited with my Buddhist brothers. Light! Damn you! Carry me away in the smoke of justice, in the love of justice. And that is all I'm going to say."

One of the men keeping the public at bay pulled another lighter from his pocket. He tested it, showed the crowds it worked, and handed it to the Indian who now with reverence took off the rabbi's vestments and revealed a war-painted body wearing only a leather breechcloth. In his belt a tomahawk smoking peace-pipe. He took the lighter and lit the pipe. Great puffs of smoke circled round his head.

"Abraham, call your sons back together! Abraham, bring your women to the river. Sarah and Hagar. Let them cleanse each other. Let them heal their hurts and bitterness. Let them wash away their jealousy. Let them forgive each other. For the sake of their sons and daughters. For the sake of their descendants!"

With that, his two attendants quickly made a bier, a stretcher, with their two walking sticks and a serape or poncho. The loud Indian lay down on the stretcher. The two men poured the last of the faux gasoline on him and attempted to set him on fire.

That's when the police arrived. They took the Indian away without a word. The police would have released him the next day, but the Indian kept making trouble, acting out, taunting the cops, breaking things, threatening anyone who came near him.

Today, in his holding cell, he calls out: "You can lock me up, you colonialist pigs, you can keep me for days, for weeks, hell, I don't care. Well, a week, anyway. I have a gig in the Village in ten days."

～

Act I

Up from the Underworld

Go to sleep my daughter
Go to sleep my son
Once the world was water
Without anyone
        ~Bert Meyers

1

GRANDFATHER SNAKE

Sunrise in Northern New Mexico. Between the abrupt and implacable Sangre de Cristo Range and the chasmic Rio Grande River Gorge. Upon the flanks of the second-tallest mountain in the state. There sits San Lucas Pueblo as it has for eight-hundred maybe a thousand years.

In a two-acre field, on the lower outskirts of that reservation, an old Pueblo man is on his knees inspecting closely the exposed root ganglia of his struggling corn stalks.

"Too dry. Not shiny enough," he grouses to himself. "Gray. Should be brighter yellow right there. Them cracks—not good."

September, and his yield has been puny and scant. Dragging his hoe with him, he crawls to the next plant and traces his fingers up a stalk, down a leaf. He shakes his head again and spits.

Come in closer. Look. He has broad shoulders, a bit of a belly, and his black and gray hair is shiny and tied with a colored-faded cloth in the traditional single chignon. Cautiously stiff from a fugitive back pain, he pulls off a piece of root and chews it, spits again. As he moves forward, he hears the snake's warning and freezes. Instinctively he relaxes, smiles, and turns slowly. He speaks gently in the language of his people.

"Grandfather, have you come to help me?"

The diamondback starts to unwind and leave, but something bothers it back again to hiss and rattle. Like a cobra, it rears over itself ready to strike. Simon Zamora reaches deeper, finds love and aims it. Angry or threatened, the snake backs away slowly. Simon's smile now fades. He's concerned by the snake's behavior.

With the help of his hoe, Simon stands and opens a dike, a levee the size of his arm. Water flows into an irrigation ditch. He rests his chin on the hoe-blade and ponders.

Know this: his grandmother had taught Old Mirriamma how to make pottery. His father had been a well-respected medicine man. His grandfather was elected by the Council to be War Chief and then Governor, many times. His great-grandfather was known to all the kiva boys as a fierce fighter against Navajo and Apache raiding parties. But for years Simon has had little to do with his clan or his tribe. He keeps to himself, quiet and respectful, and un-talked-to mostly.

Twisting his mouth, swallowing, spitting, as if something doesn't taste good, he slouches toward his village—past shaggy-barked juniper-pole fences, some new, some fallen, past scattered flat-roofed adobe houses with round roof-supporting viga logs protruding like cannons, past a boy riding a horse chased by a dog, past two teenage girls who hide their eyes. A run-down pickup truck bounces by with two men laughing stupid drunk in the back. A woman gracefully pulls bread from a traditional beehive outdoor oven. She waves to Simon as he turns a corner and disappears.

～

Two-thousand miles away in New York City, a member of an even older tribe is struggling to make his grandfather understand that blood may in some cases *not* be thicker than water. In fact, the equation and the wisdom behind it may be changing, radically.

"—Zeyda, I hear you. I swear I understand what you're telling me. But you're not hearing *me*. I'm Jewish because you're Jewish—because my father, your son, was Jewish. And my mama, you've told me, was one of the most beautiful, wisest Jewish women that you've ever known. I'm not denying my heritage, fercrissakes—I'm Jewish culturally, and by blood if you insist, but that's about it."

"Don't talk like that," says his grandfather on the telephone from even further away—from Israel. "What did I do wrong? Tell me, Favileh. I'll fix it. I'll make amends. I'll never make you eat Brussels Sprouts again. You don't want to wear a yarmulka—so don't, big deal. But you're at a crossroads in your life, and that's exactly when these things must be considered."

"Grandpa, listen. I'm almost 29 years old. I'm a medical doctor about to start practicing. So let me get a little practice in before I move halfway around the world to a country I am not at peace with. Israel is not my—"

"Stop, please! You'll do what you'll do. But you are Israel and Israel is you. Israel is the home we Jews have waited almost two thousand years to return to. It's bigger than me, bigger than you—. It's like you say, you're about to really start your life, as a doctor, okay, so these things seem a little remote to you now. But some day—and soon I'm telling you—this is the destiny of all of God's people."

"God's Chosen People, Zeyd? You know how that drives me crazy. It's wrong to say that. It isn't true. It can't be true. And it's immoral to say it. It's unethical. At the very least, it's silly and counter-productive to say it. It will only make people hate us."

"Hoo-ha! This is news? Okay, okay—so when are you coming if only for a visit? I miss you."

"I miss you, too. Look, I finish my residency here in a few months. I'll come then and help you find a new apartment—because I think I'll start my new job in June. Hey, did you get that computer set up yet, so we can talk and see each other at the same time?"

"Your next job? So you've decided? Wasn't that hard to figure out—like I told you."

"No, Zeyda, I haven't decided yet, but I'm close. I'll call you next week."

The young man kisses the mouthpiece tenderly and hangs up the phone. He looks at himself in the mirror next to the door to his apartment. "You're Jewish. You've always been Jewish." He looks away, then back again quickly, his eyes narrowing. "What makes you Jewish? You look like a Jew. No, I don't. Yes, you do. What is a Jew?"

2

Grandmothers Gather

Tonight the grandmothers meet again, as they have on and off for the past three weeks. As they have, when the situation demands it, for thousands of years.

Tonight, in an old adobe house on the high side of the village. From here, one can see the entire pueblo, how it is divided by a little river, and far to the southwest the deep gorge of the Rio Grande River.

Inside the room is bare. No right angles anywhere. A few benches along the walls.

Shelves and niches built deep into the adobe walls, fashioned by hands two hundred years ago. Kachinas fetishes feathers stones seeds dried flowers—carefully and sparingly placed. An old yellowed envelope, a bold 1953 cancellation mark canted across the stamp. Three large copper Mexican coins. A stuttering line of strange capped jars containing various plant or mineral substances. Other than this the room is fairly bare.

Three weeks ago Renata "Tall Gal" Obregon died. She was 89 and took with her many good stories. They grieved at her passing and they grieved at the passing of her stories. During the days that followed the grandmothers gathered at night and talked about the stories Renata had told.

Anyone may come and sit quietly and listen. But only a few do. Tonight, all women, except for one man, Sotero Lujan, in his 90s, who sits and listens with a simple smile, a slowly bobbing head, and sleepy eyes.

Those who come listen with quiet and serious intent. In between the stories there is peace and reflection. There is beauty and patience.

There is loneliness in the smoky air, an unspoken sadness, a voice without words, and words without voices. There are many good stories told. They are told so they can be remembered. If someone remembers a story differently than the teller—so be it; no one offers corrections.

There is stillness, too. Stillness is created, welcomed, and well-oiled. Stillness is revered almost as a deity. But those gathered care less about the deity than what they feel when they come together like this.

It is productive. It is what their elders told them to carry down through the generations as important. And it is. And so they do.

They sit on simple chairs or stools around the center of the room where there is a hole in the floor. A fire pit. Sometimes they sit on the benches along the wall. They sing quiet, uncomplicated songs that express their humility before each other, the fire, and the earth beneath them.

The breathing. The hiss and crackle of the fire. Outside, a nightbird. Once, the quick passage of wings. And then the wind through the cracks around the windows and doors.

Past midnight those on stools stand and move the stools away. Two pick up brooms and sweep the hard adobe floor. With corn meal from a soft, white leather pouch, a woman draws the lines of the Four Directions around the fire-pit. The old man remains on a bench in the corner, possibly asleep.

Finally, one woman crosses the floor to the shelves and selects a few specific things. This is Mirriamma Moya. An unassuming woman in her eighties, she is a repository of her tribe's knowledge of plants, animals, rituals, clans. She's also a potter who is perhaps unaware that an elegant New York City art gallery is currently selling one of her pots for $2300.

This is her house.

Sixty-three years ago, when her husband was still alive, Mirriamma's brother-in-law had come back from World War II with a blond bride from Brooklyn who unwittingly named this important shelf when she said, "This certainly is a lovely knick-knack niche", and the alliterative name stuck and everyone has called the shelf the knick-knack niche ever since.

The youngest woman in the room, Gladys Bernal, is 67 years old and by far the most limber. She follows Mirriamma around the fire-pit agilely placing items on the floor that Mirriamma hands her, adjusting them according to the slightest movements of Mirriamma's eyes, lips and head. From time to time someone acknowledges the significance of the placement or the relationships and grunts approval or understanding.

It's a process. A single process. The many have functionally become one.

This gathering has no recognized power or authority. The Tribal Council will meet when it meets to decide the "important matters" of the tribe. The division between the Old and New Ways is clear.

There are no women on the Council. Nor do they have the right to vote for who sits on the council. On this pueblo women do not vote—but on half of the 19 pueblos the women can vote.

This, among other reasons, is why women have been meeting like this for thousands of years.

Perhaps there are six or seven things ranged around the fire-pit.

Mirriamma turns and inspects the set-up: "Mother Earth gave birth to us here with all the other animals. But She gave us one special gift. She gave us the ability to think about what we are thinking about. What other animal thinks about the fact they can think? Oh, well, it's what we are."

There is silence in the room after that. For a long while.

One woman clears her throat, very loudly. Then another, younger, in her seventies, clears her throat but much softer, as if teaching a lesson about good manners.

Then Gladys breaks the silence. "Our medicine isn't as strong as it used to be, is it? Men blame us for what they have caused. We don't have the influence we used to have. The men of our tribe don't listen to us anymore. Have we forgotten what women are supposed to remember?"

Then Twayla Rafael, who hasn't said a word all night, or the night before, "The connections aren't there anymore. They've been broken. You think?"

Mirriamma stands and like a sumo wrestler raises one knee quite high and drives it down onto the floor. "We can reconnect them. But it's going to take a long time. We may not see it. But our grandchildren must. What we do here these days may not succeed. But it will be felt. Our people will feel it. Mother Earth has already felt it."

Twayla reaches for a piece of apple next to her but decides against eating it right now. "There have been many original peoples who have died. Hundreds, maybe thousands of tribes and peoples and cultures—old people, and their stories, have just disappeared. Some killed. Some just died out of loneliness maybe. It's a mystery. Everyone in their tribe, gone."

Mirriamma, under her breath, "It's not a mystery."

"You know," says Gladys scratching her head, "we're thinking about what we're thinking about, just like you said...." After a silence of 15 seconds, she adds, "Are we looking for something in particular tonight?"

"I can feel it," says Mirriamma. "I can sense it. But I cannot name it, or even describe it to you. I close my eyes and all I can see and hear—are the dancers doing the Turtle Dance."

"The Turtle Dance?!" says Lita Castillo with surprise, a thin woman wearing a blue scarf. "There are not even women in that dance—."

"Yes, but it is an old dance, an important dance. The men do it so that women can think about other things. It's like that. We all have our parts to play. The men may dance it, but the women—*ay-yai!*" She stops and tries to think about what she is thinking about. "There's something else here, but I cannot see it or hear it clearly enough."

"Something else?"

"Part of the song, part of the music, some of the steps are missing in what the men do today. I can almost see it when I close my eyes. But it slips away. I think it is important."

"How do you know it's important if you don't know what it is?"

"Because when I close my eyes I can also see my grandmother, and I remember how during the Turtle Dance she always would touch my shoulder or squeeze my hand in the middle of that dance so many years ago, and it was always at a certain point in that dance, some-

11

thing, something special would happen. It was strong medicine. But I forget what it was."

Ethel Goodmorning, a short, round woman, turns to Gladys. "Your father was in every Turtle Dance—ask him. He'll know."

"My father," sighs Gladys, "is in Santa Fe now, at Kalinda House. He hasn't spoken since Easter. Lung cancer, you know."

Ethel nods dolefully, but then more animated to Mirriamma, "Your niece, Anabelle, she used to help him with the costumes and teach everybody the songs. Her father, Hector, he was a war chief. She knew everything about that dance."

"Anabelle, yes, she would know, but you remember she died, 12 years ago. I close my eyes, and I can see her. Even only back 12 years we had forgotten so much. But Anabelle had a great memory. And her mother, Cora, yes, and then—but Anabelle had a daughter who used to listen carefully. Do you remember, eh? Remember we were impressed with how well Anabelle's daughter listened?"

"Wynema was the daughter's name," adds Ethel, "but she went away after her mother died to be with her father. He was Sioux."

"Yes, he was from a far-away tribe," Mirriamma points to the northeast. "But still, she was taught. Could it be she remembers?"

"She was only a girl, maybe fifteen," mumbles Ethel. "Too young."

"Maybe. She was quiet, but she was quick—."

"Anabelle might have passed what she knew on to her."

"You think...?"

~

Later that night, Mirriamma steps outside. It is cold, clear, and dark. The stars are still there. Hah! She smiles and feels small. She laughs again quietly, takes a deep breath, and feels huge, as large as the Universe.

"I think you'll be coming home, Little Sister. I don't know why yet, but I'm curious to find out.

3

LITTLE SISTERS

Two years ago, Little Sister was restless. She was angry though she didn't know it. She had graduated college with honors and then, in the summer before grad school, had gone to the capital city of Brasilia, deep into the Amazon, for an International Indigenous Peoples Conference. But she had gotten separated from her colleagues on a river-boat tour of the deep rain forest. They had taken off down river thinking she was aboard.

She didn't panic. She sat and waited. The water in a nearby creek that fed the river was quick, clear, and sweet. She had a few apples and almonds in her day-pack.

Four days later, a Search & Rescue boat found her sitting quietly on a fallen log where the creek runs into the river. One of the professionals noticed the cast off crayfish shells next to her feet, but said nothing.

It was during her wait that she realized she had been restless and angry for years.

Today, she extends her arm—a curious, innocent snake—and touches the rough bark of a tree as she passes. Seems hard and lifeless, she thinks, even for November.

Memories of other trees in other places flood in, trees that make her smile, then disappear into the shadows of her mind. She takes a deep breath as if to hold onto them, but lets them go with a sigh. They are gone. Again.

She sniffs the air and catalogues the smells. Some of them do not belong here.

The first snow of the year begins to fall. She listens to the sounds. She not only names them, she indicts them, near and far. *The snow will change everything, especially the sounds.*

She looks down and picks up a handful of Earth. It's beautiful, crumbling in her hand. She wants to understand the personality of this particular soil, the components, the virtues.

She smiles and smells it. The smile quickly fades. Becomes a frown. Analysis sets in. She pokes at the earth in the palm of her hand. What she finds makes her growl: the indestructible filter of a cigarette butt. She throws it down, aware that she is desecrating the Earth. *It is cooling off now*, she says to herself. *Maybe the Earth can rest awhile from the onslaughts of humans.*

She disappears inside herself. She pulls the collar up against the chill and contemplates another winter here. *When can I leave? I want to move on! Soon. Soon.*

Her face is the color of adobe. Light reflects from her edges in purples and golds. Her eyes are the color of the high desert where her mother came from, a very light hazel. Her clothes the color of the trees and lakes of her father's country. Her name is Wynema Mondragon. At 27 and an accomplished solo traveler, she knows she doesn't belong here. She leans back against a tree and closes her eyes.

She opens them with a start and looks at her watch, then turns and walks onto a path where the snow is catching. A few seconds more, and she pushes through some bushes and steps out onto the sidewalk of ground zero for American Chic—Central Park South, New York City—mainlined.

She takes a few steps, looks back, smiles grimly. "I don't belong here," she says under her breath. "I do not even belong here." She is barely whispering. She cups her ear so she can hear herself better. "I don't belong here." Then changing the words, but not the music, "I be Long-Hair-Maiden-Weeping."

Horns, ambulance siren, passers-by arguing, the audio amperage of the Big Apple—assault her, anneal her.

With her teeth she pulls the nipple of the plastic water bottle and squirts a jet down her throat. There's no turning back. Next stop Cambridge, England. Let's do it.

Her grandfather was a well-loved Sioux leader. Her father, the first of his tribe to earn a Ph.D. degree, teaches engineering at Wake-sh'ti Community College in North Dakota. He is quite proud of her and prays for her every day.

Her mother's mother: Mirriamma's sister.

She herself is a Ph.D. candidate in Native American Studies and Linguistics at Columbia University. She finished her dissertation two weeks ago and is now waiting to hear from her dissertation committee.

In an email to her father upon the anniversary of her mother's death twelve years ago: "Dear Dad, am I really descended from a long line of Indian princesses? And just what is 'an Indian princess' anyway? There was never royalty. There were the clans. And stories about brave or compassionate women and grandmothers. So, Papa, my rebellion is complete: I'm abdicating the crown. If you want to give me a title, please call me the Queen of Curiosity. It's a little lonely out here. There aren't a lot of Native American explorers. But there are a lot of wise women. Thinking on this day of your Anabelle, my Mom. Your one and only, Wynema"

When she reaches 59th Street, near Columbus Circle, it's five-thirty and she plays hell hailing a cab. Finally, one stops and she jumps in, dumbfounded to see that the cabby is wearing a Plains Indian war bonnet. Like a screech-owl, *This isn't happening!* stabs through her head. She rolls her eyes and opens the door to find another cab.

"Hey, don't be freaked," the driver says through a cracked-tooth grin. "Settle back, where're ya going? I ain't no whacko, unless having seven kids can make ya a whacko."

She throws herself back into the seat. "Thirty-third and 8th, okay? What's with the get-up?"

Her cabby is the classic New York Don't-Tread-On-Me aggressive driver, darting and dodging down Seventh Avenue, a master of the articulated horn. Grateful to be asked, he responds, "I'm actually Native American—well, part—and I'm celebrating my heritage."

"What tribe?" she asks. "Let me guess. Hmmm. Cherokee?"

"Omigod, you can tell?! I mean, you can see it in my features, or what?"

"Not exactly." She sighs.

"But you knew!"

She looks intently into his mirror. "Whenever someone tells me he's Indian, it's usually Cherokee. That's right, three out of four. Like Jordan, Mackensie, Tiffany, Brandon—you know the tribal name-flavor of the year."

"Nyeah. Come on. Don't shit me. I ain't shitting you, kid. My father's father's mother was a full-blood Cherokee. I could claim tribal status if I wanted to."

Wynema bursts laughing. "Believe me, you don't want to. I thought you were Italian."

Bobbing his head, "Well, yeah, everybody else in da family is Italian, but still—." He is hoping she will say something while he scrutinizes her through the mirror. He has to ask: "Say, I don't believe dis. Are you an Indian—I mean, Native American—or what?"

Wynema points ahead with her hand, as if to say, Just drive.

"C'mon, lady, I got you there, ain't I? You are! My lucky day!"

"Anishebegwe."

"Beg yer pardon."

"My tribe. We're called Anishebegwe." She lies.

"Is it part of the Iroquois Nation?"

"As a matter of fact it is," she says, knowing full well it isn't.

"You from upstate?"

'Yeah, like Montana."

"We got parkways around here with names that sound just like that. I never heard of your tribe, though."

Wynema settles deeper into the seat. "That's because we haven't been featured in a Walt Disney or a Western movie yet. But we're working on it."

"You laugh, but it might happen. Western movies are definitely making a come-back. And they're very influential on culture. Wonder why Cherokees are so popular then."

"Trail of Tears."

"Is that a movie or a well-known ritual dance or something?"

"Oh, yeah."

The cabby has to slam brakes, pound horn, swerve. "Watch it, ya sonuvabitch! Yeah, and your mudda's mattress!" He turns to Wynema. "Sorry, kid, I—"

She puts on a thick New York accent. "Yeah, shua, your mudda's mattress, no problem."

She wonders whether she could have walked the 26 blocks and one avenue over in the time it took the cab to arrive at front of a brownstone converted into an off-off-Broadway playhouse. As Wynema pays the man, he asks, "You wouldn't happen to know what style, I mean, ya know, what tribe this particular head-dress comes from, wouldja?"

Wynema bends forward, her eyes scrutinizing the war bonnet. Finally her head nods. "Cherokee," she says, "definitely East-Western Cherokee."

"Ya really think so?! C'mon, you're jivin' me. You serious? I mean, that would be great, cuz, East-Western Cherokee, ya know, my great-grandmother...I mean, cuz I just bought it in a pawn shop and I was hopin'—"

She is out of there, gone, dust. He'd have given her her money back if only she'd elucidated with a little more detail.

4

PRIESTESSES OF SAÏS

"A pawn shop," she mutters balefully, as she enters the theater, merging with many other arriving women.

They are young and old, white, brown, black, yellow, red, purple, pink. A diversity of humanity's women, converging. But they're here for a purpose. They know what it is. It's on all the faces. She adds herself to the mix.

The stairway is crowded. Only women here. For a brief moment, a dark but exciting fantasy possesses her. A secret meeting of the high priestesses of Saïs. Women who can communicate by telepathy. Women who are keenly aware that only they perpetuate the mitochondria. African. Asian. Australo-aboriginal. Middle-eastern. Scandinavian. Slavic. Amharic, Hispanic, Melanesian.... Though they'll never use the word Shamanic, they know what kind of conclave this is.

Her fantasy is broken by the sole woman fending her way down the stairs. She is Hispanic, possibly Puerto Rican. Wynema notices that the woman carries an unlit cigarette in her mouth and another between her fingers that flutters like a wounded bird above the rising waters.

"Do you have a match?" she says to Wynema as she passes.

"I don't smoke," turns Wynema with a gentle smile.

"I don't either," swipes the smoker, "my cigarette does. Get a life." The rising tide that sucks the woman down the stairs buoys Wynema up. She laughs to herself—*Okay, these might not be women of the Shamanic Way, but they do have a purpose and a passion.*

The theater serves as a lecture-hall today. Every seat is filled, and a few younger women sit on the steps in the aisles. These are women who have created a space in which no man is welcome. Let him come just out of curiosity and see how fast he is flushed to the street. Women wearing beads and power symbols. Feathers and favorite clothes. Clothes and trappings invested with special energies. The women sense and appreciate these things.

One woman touches the pendant she wears, thinking, *The power of this flows from a woman in Ghana, through me, to all my sisters. Our power as women is needed at this time.*

Wynema is exhilarated by the unspoken bond and energized polarity. She smiles, and yet parts of her are still uncomfortable, unconnected, tentative. *What is the framework in which all this is happening?*

Then she remembers the cabby's headdress. *It was real. That cabby—he was wearing a Nakota chief's war-bonnet that was fucking real, and from the looks of it, quite old and true to tradition. To whom did it once belong? There are those who can tell from the pattern of the colored cloth windings at the base of each feather who made it and even when. Someone who knows. Living knowledge now paleologic. That war-bonnet was never made for a tourist. It was made for a community, by an elder, to be worn by a man much younger, who was prepared to give his life for his tribe, his clan.*

There's no turning back.

She listens to a woman speaking from a podium, a short, thick woman with fuzzy grey hair. But Wynema hasn't plugged into her yet. Her mind wanders like an ant disconnected from its colony.

Then something the speaker says makes the crowded room burst out in approval, and this focuses Wynema's attention. The speaker goes on about how the time is now and how there's power in numbers. But again the war-bonnet steals her concentration. *How did it lose its family, its maker?* She's not so much asking how and why; she's condemning it, and grieving after the fact.

Now another woman is speaking, tall, elegant, soft-spoken. "... And we want to stop using the terms 'feminist' or 'feminism'. They've served their purpose. Now it's time to move on. And if that doesn't get your panties all in an uproar, then this will. I want us to reach out to our sisters on the right. Yes, you heard me!" She points through the walls to the street below. "There are women out there on the political right who are disaffected with reactionary conservative, especially neo-conservative policies and, even worse, neo-conservative practices.

"They're tired of being ruled by the 'strict father figure'. Been there, done that. The promises of community, love, and a simple, just, spiritual life in their terms, in women's terms, haven't been fulfilled, and they're starting to see that at their own spiritual core—they are starving!

"Listen sisters, we are so self-righteous in our progressive outlook that we risk losing a great opportunity. I tell you there are women on the right who know that the hard times are only going to get worse. Well, we want to be able to go out there and talk to those women about it. They might understand. Some will surely understand.

"Women from all walks have more in common with each other than men and women from the same culture. Think about it. They might appreciate other women simply putting out a helping hand, a communal hand, a knowing hand, saying 'Hey, what do we have in common?'

"Let's go with that for a while and forget about our differences, our culture-taught, catechismic differences. That's right. Maybe what we share in common is more important than where we differ.' This is the wisdom of Native American women. This should be the wisdom of women in general." She paused for a moment. "Are there any Native Americans here?"

Wynema arches her eyebrows and tries to smile as she slowly, humbly raises her hand. Only one other woman does in this room of two hundred, and she's even shier than Wynema. As she lowers it, another hand touches gently down upon her shoulder. Bronze and black. Alána. She slides into a seat behind her.

5

Earth Fusion Jazz

Out on the street, turning up Fifth Avenue, Alána Mdibweh looks Nubian or Zulu, but she is Ngoro from Zaire, the Once-and-Future Congo. She is the first child born in America to a Ngoro warrior—physically strong, socially important—now a wealthy business man, Tangaro Mdibweh.

Says Wynema, "You know they made some very important points back there. I'm glad I went."

Alána throws her a withering stare that says, *Like are you serious?!*

"Well, yeah, I mean, sorta, yeah."

Alána's look shifts to a gentle *Spare-me-the-bullshit.*

"Okay. You're right. What are they missing? What are *we* missing?"

Alána doesn't hesitate. "Traction, my love, universal connection. Look, my mother told me stories of my great-great-grandmother—all on the woman's side—who was able to speak to the women of our village and make them all understand what was at stake for any issue before them. I know, now you're going to ask me about what's at stake. Okay. It's always the same thing. It's simply the knowledge of what it takes to survive the times we're in and the men who bully us. My great-great-grandmother could make herself almost invisible and still communicate and inspire, and each woman would walk away thinking that she—not my great-great-grandmother—had just thought of something profound. Let the other person think it was her idea— that was my great-great-grandmother's secret."

Wynema touches Alána's cheek tenderly. "You're talking about leadership."

"Yes, but much more than that."

"Like what?" Wynema stops and turns.

"C'mon, keep walking," says the warrior's daughter. "I'm cold. Look, the trouble with your so-called democracy is that you only get to choose from candidates Big Money puts up. The decisions they make for you just benefit Big Money. We talked about this. Your political representatives should do what my great-great-grandmother did—and that is to find out what's at stake for any issue and tell the People, and then listen to the People, and then and only then vote on this or that."

Two exceedingly tall and nattily dressed women-shopping black athletes stop in their swaggering tracks and watch the two women approach. "Hey, yo, my sleek panther-women," says one, "stop and stare, take the dare, do you know who we are?"

Alána, her neck long enough for ten or twelve Masai rings, slows, turns but keeps walking. "We noticed but—bells and whistles?—sorry, nothing."

"That's cool. But you noticed. That's important to us brothers. But don' box me out, noamsayin?" He reaches into his shirt pocket, then snakes his long powerful arm over the heads of the passers-by, who instinctively duck though there's no need to. He hands Alána his card.

She takes it and straightaway picks her teeth with its corner. The women keep walking, barely missing a stride.

"Whozat?" asks Wynema as she lightly shop-grazes the window to her left.

"Oh, you know, whats-his-name, from the Knicks, their starting point guard–."

"Tito Kajemba!?"

"That's the one. He supposedly going for the record of fucking more than one thousand women in a single year. Gettin' all sorts of help from his fan clubs with this. Can you imagine?! I mean, shee-it. Kinda geekish, though, if you ask me."

"Tito Kajemba geekish?"

"Yeah, to me he's kinda geekish."

"Nah, you're just not into men."

"Not right now, I'm not. Hell no. But forget about those assholes. I want to get back, uh, to when you raised your hand in that meeting as a Native American. Did you, I mean, did you feel like you were like representing your tribe and your blood, you know?"

"Hey, I'm barely representing myself, let alone my tribes."

"That's right, your parents come from two different tribes. Me, too, actually. That's why we had to leave Africa. Yours really are different, culturally I mean. But my two are the same—only different in name, and competitive to the death."

The taller Alána leans and bites Wynema's neck, But the Indian is unresponsive. This doesn't bother Alána who just raises her eyebrows and accepts it as a future challenge. "Oh, come on woman, I know, you're just feeling nervous. They're gonna accept your dissertation! Nobody's done anything like it, and you know it. They gave you that fellowship at Cambridge because they know your Ph.D. is in the bag. It's obvious. And the grant you didn't get, you'll find another to apply for, and you'll go on and continue your research—you know, where you said they have a sign language that was really unique?"

"Mongolia. Unique and efficient."

"Right. Always wanted to go there. But that's not the only reason I'll visit you. You know, maybe we'll start our own tribe there. Okay, seriously, maybe I can come film you doing your thing and, you know, we'll make a documentary. I have all the equipment. And maybe we'll find a third—you know, I can picture a three-way, you me and a beautiful Mongolian—"

Wynema stops dead in her tracks and begins to sign. They're both fluent in signing, their movements definitive and dramatic.

"*Why?!*" Wynema asks with graceful hand and arm movements. "*Why film my work?*"

Alána signs back, "*Because your work is important. Wanting to give the gift of sign-language to women everywhere, to be able to talk, to share—to share the common wisdom that women all over know: that violence among peoples is less than useless. And it's women going to bring this to the world. Not men.*"

The people on the street who pass them slow momentarily, move on. It's like a dance, signing, and, depending on the signer, mesmeric.

"Then why didn't they give me the grant?"

23

"Because you not perfect to them. Only to me."

Wynema's signing becomes less dramatic. "*What's that supposed to mean?*"

"*That you're still missing one piece of the puzzle.*"

"*What piece is that?*"

"*Ah, that's what we're about to figure out.*"

Then, after a few steps, Alána adds: "*I read your dissertation. I think it's great. But I have some questions.*"

"*What questions?*"

"*You write about signing becoming the universal language. But aren't you compounding the difficulty by suggesting that it happen through women?.*"

Wynema's signing becomes even smaller, 'quieter'. "*Yes. But it won't happen through a mass movement. It will happen in little pockets, enclaves—here and there around the world.*"

"*And how will that come about?*"

"*That's what I'm working on now.*"

And with that both are again walking down the street, gracefully slicing through the liquid of passing people.

It was sign language that brought them together, just before they started grad-school. They met in Paris, at a conference discussing the merits of the various signing languages used around the world, and instantly became friends.

Alána and her whole family had learned American Sign Language, sometimes called ASL or Ameslan, when her sister was born deaf. Alána took it a bit further; to delight her sister, she became a dancer. That led to her becoming a choreographer and videographer. While music-videos are the rage, Alána is doing her best to raise the status of dance-videos. She has made award-winning videos and documentaries of deaf women dancing.

Wynema as a child was taken by stories and movies that invoked Indians using sign language. Innocent enough. But when she moved to Montana to be with her father and became close friends with a girl who signed because her parents were deaf, Wynema decided to learn ASL. To ease the pain of missing her family and friends at the Pueblo she threw herself into signing.

Wynema and Alána remained best friends all through grad-school, and for three summers have taught jazz and modern dance to deaf teenagers. Last summer they choreographed dances that included signing in the dance itself.

"*Feel,*" they tell their students in sign, "*feel inside yourself, your heart beat, and then a bit slower your breathing—the inner rhythms, the pulsing rhythms of life itself, dancing—feel the dancing, the rhythmic waves, the opening and closing, the beats, the bonding, the celebration. Put the pulses of the movements of life into your body dancing, and feel the dancing of your partner or the dancer dancing by you as you pass. Feel it, right to the edge...*".

Simultaneously, they plop onto a bus bench and speak out-loud again.

"...and you still got your job teaching right now, so you got nothing to worry about."

Wynema isn't convinced. "But I wrote a great proposal, one that deserved that funding, especially these days—I mean, look what's going on in the world!"

"The only 'fun-ding' you're gonna get around here, sistah, is sex, dancing, and racquetball. You want to go to the club and play with those walls?"

Wistfully, "No."

"Okay, then let's go get jazzed tonight, I mean, into some slithery Earth-fusion jazz!"

"No," sighs Wynema, "I just want to stay home and read."

Alána stops and pulls a DVD out of her bag. "Okay, a friend just loaned me this. We could snuggle up."

"What is it?"

"It's called 'Reel Baseball'. You know, like silent films about baseball from the early 20th century. I mean, it's supposed to be hip. And it has great old organ accompaniment."

"Are you out of your mind?"

"No, check it out." Reading from the back of the box: "'The cruelest tale is the crude 1909 baseball Western called *His Last Game*, the story of a Choctaw Indian athlete star who on the day of a big local game kills a gambler in self-defense but is allowed to play the game. And then is executed.' Hey, woman, this could be the key to the universe. Nothing changes, does it?"

Wynema gets up and takes ten steps down the street. "I'll take the Earth-fusion jazz?"

"All right! I saw it, it looked cool, was at The Blue Note or maybe that other place around the corner, the Stalactite."

6

AH, YOUR FIRST MAN!

The Stalactite Jam Joint is smoky, with incense, but not tobacco. Tables ring the room on consecutively raised terraces giving every table a good view of the stage below. The walls, the ceilings, the chairs, the tables, the floor—everything is painted in flat dark earth tones.

The waiters and waitresses uniformly wear tan Cossack shirts with the flag of their country of origin silkscreened on the front and backs. Somehow all the patrons here know to wear something dark as well. Alána is wearing dark purple trimmed in black, and Wynema, dark green, with a sheer black silk scarf at the neck, and square coils of thin, pounded, dark patina'ed silver pendant earrings.

A janitor in black tattered coveralls walks on stage with a broom and quietly sweeps it.

Wynema bends to the woman sitting at a nearby table. "Is there dance in the performance tonight?" The woman doesn't know. "Thanks."

"Hey," pops Alána, "did that check from our last teaching gig come yet?"

"If you need some money, I can cover it until—."

On the extreme right side of the stage something the size of a Volkswagen bug is covered with a black cloth. The janitor pulls off the cloth, revealing what has to be called a "contraption", a cross between a pilot's cockpit and a drummers trap set: an electronic console on a heavy articulating jib-arm mounted on a motorized dolly and stabilized by out-rigger feet.

The audience reacts with movement and murmurs that express their surprise and curiosity.

The janitor in one deft move slides up into the cockpit seat, flips a few switches and takes command of the lights and sounds in the room in an expressly kinesthetic way. In a few seconds the audience knows they are already watching the performance. The show has begun.

This is Chumba Ito—half black African, half Japanese, short and powerfully built, shy, reclusive—a master of computer graphics, lights, audio and video. He is a one-man band and light show, a multimedia fighter pilot, who begins his attack by moving into an intriguing, fugitive percussive formation. With speakers all over the room, he controls where the sounds are coming from. He makes the sounds and images dance and morph, confusing and delighting the senses. He uses his arms, his feet, his knees—his entire body squirms in the chair to adjust the controls.

Alána slowly softly touches Wynema's arm and with a seductive look suggests that what they're about to experience is going to be—

Wynema with a look tells her to be still and pay attention, as she points to a matrix-array of flatscreen monitors that begin to flicker upstage, behind and to the left of the pilot.

But Alána cannot contain herself. She pulls Wynema's ear against her mouth. "That dude's music makes love to this space. A thick jism creaming the air—."

"Stop it. Let me listen."

"While his right hand freaks out on a synthesizer, his left hand tortures a computer for effects—one creating the throb, the other the jism." She slides her hand onto Wynema's thigh and slowly inches it upward.

Wynema smiles slyly. Alána's hand stops then slowly pulls away, its job done. Chumba make them feel their female.

Wynema reaches into her handbag. "Would you like a brownie to go with your Irish?"

"High-essence?"

"From the Mendocino Kush."

Alána answers yes with her eyebrows. Wynema places a brownie on a coaster in front of her.

Alána arches her long neck and takes a quick sip of her Irish coffee. "That's real down, sistah," she says fluttering her eyes.

The music fades until it floats pulsing just below the surface. Everyone becomes quiet. Into the silence, the lone plaintive call of a flute, then a shaker, then as if lost within a deep mountain cavern, soft incessant aboriginal drums. As the houselights dim, the hanging grid of 20 flat video screens laid out 5 by 4 begin to pulse, synchronized to the slow thrusting downbeats, revealing finally a scene from somewhere in the Southwest. Adobe, adobe, only adobe shapes and colors gathering themselves in the preternatural glow of a high desert dawn. Two elders wrapped in blankets climb ladders to the highest roof of an ancient pueblo.

Wynema's eyes widen then sharpen as she grabs Alána's arm and squeezes it fiercely.

"Wha–?!"

Whispering: "That's San Lucas! My home! I swear it!"

The audience oohs and ahs. Now Chumba floats in men's voices chanting.

"What are they doing?" Alána asks, impressed by how charged Wynema has become.

"Those are elders of the Turtle Clan. They're gauging the sun's ascension. They...they do this every morning. They've done this for over a thousand years. I used to watch them. Never spoke to them. Wasn't supposed to. They're watching where exactly on the mountain the sun comes up, and because that point moves south in the winter and north in the summer, they know without a calendar whether to plant corn or harvest it or get ready for the Deer Dance or San Lucas's Feast Day or—"

"Cool. But that's your village? For real? I mean, you showed me pictures once, but—"

Breathless: "It is! I was born there!"

The multimedia scene shifts and swirls, now a close-up of the rough weathered dark hands of an aged man whittling with a small pen-knife. Chumba feeds in an underscore of strains from Johnny Whitehorse's Native fusion...

"What's he doing?"

"Carving the leg-bone of a wild turkey, turning it into a whistle."

A slow knowing creeps across Wynema's face. Alána is enthralled and keeps looking quickly, surreptitiously at her friend.

Lights on the stage come up half and a spotlight now follows a man, a wraith, stalking across the stage in Indian-biker black. Tattoos. His arms taunt the screens, then individual members of the audience. When the scene behind him becomes a wide shot of an Indian in silhouette herding his sheep into a corral on top of a ridge-line, he and the audience become enthralled with the long slow zoom into the weathered and sad features of the Indian.

Wynema points silently, incredulously, to the performer. "That's Frank Zamora! I know him. His family's the same clan as my mother's. Did you know he was going to be here tonight?"

"I did not. Never heard of him."

The performer turns menacingly on a white woman in her eighties at a table next to the stage. But the woman isn't frightened. She's turned on.

"The buffalo are gone now," he hisses. "We got postcards for a while, but then they stopped entirely. We tried to trace them down... but the trail ended out on the West Coast in a trailer park below Ventura and we never could get their forwarding address."

He spins. Spittle and sweat fly off. Exploding rings of Saturn. The white-haired woman feels a drop of it hit her lips. To her, he is fiery, predatory, and she loves it. He delivers not poems but fulminations. Chumba's score makes Frank all the more reptilian.

Alána is impressed: "This is one wild, possessed, angry Indian."

He pauses, works his audience. He wheels, then leans close again to a table of Afro-Americans. Chumba dips the background audio levels when Frank speaks.

"I am an Indian because that's what you call me. I have a tribe, but in that simple word we of many Nations are combined and split into bingo-spinning casino-rich dirt-poor data-based caricatures of ourselves.

"I am a Native, in a cocoon." He leans quickly to one side as if listening for something faint and fugitive in the distance. Then back darkly with a harsh, menacing stage whisper: "Does the lowly caterpillar thick with itself know that someday it will fly, light dazzling and dangerous?"

The audience loves being lashed by his accusations. They yell and hoot and grunt and whistle. Frank snaps his finger and the audience, suddenly well-trained, shifts quickly into silence.

"'*Ecoutéz*!" he rasps. Chumba's music pulses not louder but more incessant. His left hand the bass and the right the percussion. His hands take up a duel. Frank dances, spins, devilishly whirling.

Alána leans over, bites Wynema's ear. "How well do you know him?"

"I know him."

Alána pulls back, raises an eyebrow, demanding details.

"It's been more than ten years—"

Alána looks harder at the man, discerning, divining. "I'm listening."

"He was the one—."

"Tell me more. The one who—?"

"You know, he was the first."

"Ah, your first man."

Wynema nods diffidently.

"One of those, with the gift of seduc—."

"No. He was gentle. And I was curious. And it felt right. I was totally...willing."

The two women turn to the stage and give it their undivided.

7

THIS ONE IS CURIOUS

An hour later, the audience is still clapping even after Frank and Chumba have left the stage for a break.

Wynema turns and leans slowly towards Alána's ear. "I know it's hard to believe after this performance, but he was—well, sort of sweet then, as I remember."

"As you remember, girl?! You just oh-so-nonchalantly happen to remember, do you?"

"Okay, he was magic, even tender, a myth among my people. He had a book of poetry published by the time he was twenty—and he chose me. And I gave myself to him. I more than gave myself to him. I gave myself to the ancient universal all-powerful imploding act of fucking—two human missiles of hormones connecting in that way. Yes. I did, I totally did. He more than fulfilled my fantasies. What can I say?"

"Oh, yes, I see. You had a good beginning as a woman. Sweet. That's rare, you know."

Chumba and Frank return. The music swells; jamming jazz and Native American modalities forced together in counter-intuitive ways that somehow work. The music arches, explodes, and falls in shards around the tables and chairs, leaving Frank, almost solo, continuing under with a didgeridoo. The tricks and strange sounds he makes with his circular breathing serve to intensify his anger.

He sweeps to the other side of the stage and looks with longing at something flying off into the night sky. Then turning back quickly on the audience with portent:

"It will take only three generations after the Indians are gone for you to feel us. Only three generations? *Ai*, only three. You won't have to wait seven generations. You will look at the red sunset and the music will come back to you and finally you will study the Trail of Tears and say I'm sorry, we're sorry—forgive us Ancient Ones, we knew what we were doing and didn't care. It won't happen again, you say. Hah! You destroyed our world, now you're destroying your own. But not to worry, we will come back from the dead to save your sorry asses."

The audience starts a slow pulsing applause and reaches a crescendo as Frank becomes the quintessential predator, stalking. He pantomimes taking an arrow from a quiver on his back, nocking it to an imaginary bow, then fires it point blank into the heart of a handsome man sitting at a table nearby. The young man's eyes go wide when the imaginary arrow hits.

"Don't worry. It's not about who's the spider and who's the fly. It's about harmony and balance and cooperation—you dumb, arrogant fuckwits."

The word "fuckwits" gets a huge laugh. He walks with a slight limp to the other side of the stage. The downbeat of the next tune breaks the moment and Frank pulls up an electric guitar and joins the melee. There are abrupt, momentary, shattering pauses in the music, and in those breaks, immediately felt, are the soft, faraway sounds of a community chanting, intoning collectively...somewhere.

Alána's vibrating cellphone draws her away.

Wynema doesn't notice. She simply stares at the stage, remembering.

Eleven years ago, at sixteen, she graduated with honors from a small, Northern New Mexican high school. Then, suddenly, she was moving away from the only place she called home. It was a momentous choice, but the right thing to do. Everything conspired to tell her so.

Her mother had passed away the year before. Her father had moved back to Montana, to the land and village of his Sioux tribe, and earned a graduate degree in engineering. Wynema had been living with her uncle, her mother's brother, but had missed her father a lot.

She had done her senior-year science project on wind-generated electricity. She had found a ravine half-way up the mountain behind the pueblo that she noticed was a constant funnel for wind—enough to pump water up to the highest corn field, the one maintained by the war-chiefs for hundreds of years. The spring that fed that field had dried up years ago. Now the wind would bring it water again.

Her father now wanted to work the winds in Montana so that his people could generate their own electricity. He begged his daughter to join him in this effort. You can't survive, he had told her, using more energy than comes in from the sun or the Earth's core. Wind and geo-thermal—they can help achieve this goal.

She said yes and agreed to leave. It amazed her. And it amazed and deeply saddened her friends. She spent a whole day saying good-bye to her family and friends at San Lucas.

She would leave the next morning. Her uncle would drive her to the airport in Albuquerque.

She was remembering but trying not to remember at the same time.

The night before she left the Pueblo, as she and all her friends who had come to say goodbye were leaving the plaza, Frank Zamora was sitting in the shadows of a drying rack, sitting on a beat-up motorcy-cle, watching her leave. He lifted a pint of brandy to his lips and drank her a safe journey. Then, taking in a couple breaths of night air to cool his blood, he fired up his bike and roared towards her.

He cut the engine and coasted the last hundred feet. He smiled and just looked at her and handed her a silver bear on a silver chain. "I carved it, then cast it, then polished it for you. The Bear, your mother's clan, you dig?"

She tried to smile, told him how nice it was, and that she wouldn't see him for a very long time.

He said, Oh, I'll see ya, I wanna see ya, I gotta see ya. And with that he looked at her in a way that riveted her to the spot, and then he was gone.

Later that night, she was trying to relax into sleep. Long day to-morrow. The June night—the air was soft and pushing in all direc-tions. The coyotes in their play on the flanks of the mountain made her ears buzz and itch. She rubbed and poked them, but it didn't help.

She frowned and touched the silver bear now at her throat and closed her eyes and opened them and sighed and tossed and turned—.

And then he came to her window. He had climbed three stories and no one had heard—like a gray-ghost, he peered in and whispered. She saw him and her heart beat faster. He wore no shirt, but across his chest was tied a blanket of many colors. He pointed to the roof and was gone.

She didn't think. Didn't think anymore. She slipped out of her room and passed her mother and her grandmother's room, and the room in which her two uncles slept. And then all the children sleeping peacefully. She had to pass through her great-uncle Delfino's room to reach the ladders that led to the roofs. His snoring frightened her, sounded like a wounded bear.

She knew what was coming and was rising to it with a gathering abandon. No, with a sharpening purpose.

She climbed the gray, weathered ladders. Her flannel nightgown caught a night wind and touched her in a way she never felt before.

On the roof, Frank stood looking out over the pueblo.

She was frightened. She was not frightened.

Frank heard her approach, but he didn't turn. As the wind was at his back, he tried to catch her scent. *There! That's it. Come, little sister. A little closer.* His nostrils flared. He inhaled the universe. *This one is special,* he thought. *This one I will take my time with. I won't push. I won't have to push. She wants it. I will let her find her way to me.*

She wanted to say something, to whisper, *I am here.* But she said nothing. She took a few steps closer. *He will hear me and turn. I will see if he is kind, if he really cares. I will know if this is right. I think it is. But I will know. He will not have me against my will.*

She saw the way he kept looking out. What was he looking at? She saw him untie his hair and let it fall on his bare shoulders, catching the moonlight. Was there moonlight? Not much. Half. But it caught a haze in the air and diffused and spread out around them. His skin looked pale and almost turquoise. Turquoise? His skin shone. She walked up softly behind him and put her arms around his waist,

35

her head against his back. She smelled him. Mesquite brush, red river earth, wine, horses, leather, vanilla, sweat. She liked it.

He touched her hands. He scraped the backs of them a little with his nails. Lightly. Scraping. He turned slowly, inside the circle her arms made around his waist. He turned around to face her. Her face now on his chest.

I have come, she said. *Did you think I would?*

No, he said. He lied. He knew she would come.

I want this, she said.

I know, he replied.

I don't want to get pregnant.

I won't come.

But I want you to. My moon will come tomorrow. It will be okay.

It will be good, he whispered.

He took her face in his hands and smoothed her brow with his thumbs. He wanted to lick her eyes and nose, but he didn't. He smelled her and she smelled him. They did this until they heard a rooster crow.

Go way you silly rooster, he whispered into the night, *it's hours before the dawn.*

Kiss me, she said.

I was hoping you would ask, he answered.

☙

He kissed her so tenderly. She became instantly hungry for another. He gave her all the kisses she wanted. But he kept slowing her down. He felt her give herself to him. *This one is special. This one will remember how slowly I have gone with her. This one will teach me things I haven't even dreamed of yet. She is unaware of what she is going to teach me. If only I let her. I must just go slow. Can I go slow. She is so sweet. So delicious.*

He reached down slowly and let his hand come up her thigh slowly. He drew up her nightgown as slowly as he could. He would take forever to reach her place, but he would get there. He felt her quiver and he stopped.

☙

Her fingernails dug into him just a little.

His hand continued the journey. When he first felt her woman-hair he almost lost control of his thoughts, got dizzy, had to breathe in very deep. Her hair against the nightgown against his hand, it made a sound. No, not a sound but texture, a texture he could hear, no, not hear, but sense beyond just the touch. Now his hand was over her entire place. This was sacred ground. This was a sacred opening. This was *nansipu*, the door on the floor to the center of the universe.

For a moment he hesitated. This was too good for him. Too sacred for him. He was an outcast, no good, a drunk, a lost soul. He had no business here.... But the smell of her brought him back, grounded him, disappeared all thoughts. This was all there was. All there ever was. All that will ever be. She was biting his chest softly. She was moaning. She was praying.

She was making soft sounds she had never made before. She wasn't listening to herself. She was listening to his sounds. She would let herself go only as far as felt right.

She remembered her grandmother teaching her to listen to the sounds the horse made as she lunged him on a line in a circle in the corral. Push him, but go slow, all according to his sounds and his breathing, her grandmother said. Watch the way he holds his head and looks at you.

She looked up into his eyes. There was a question in them. Yes, she whispered as she took the blanket from his shoulders and let it spread out there at the top of the tallest building in the village. She didn't know nor did she care that there had been others, countless others, young and hungry and full of life, who had been here before. Who knows how many have been here, for the same reason, for the first time, right here, in the last hundred, in the last thousand years?

He was naked now. She was willing to take off her nightgown, but he wouldn't let her. Let me find you slowly, he said. You will hide from me but I will find you.

His hand again rubbed her place. Then something happened and she let out a high-pitched sigh, almost too loud. And she felt a flooding of energies run through her. And he did too. He made a soft sound of knowing as his hands traced the curves of her body slowly towards her breasts. She wanted to hurry his hand, to touch her breasts. No man had ever touched her breasts. Her mother had taught her to be modest, but she loved her breasts. Books she'd read from other native cultures had taught her to think of her breasts as sacred.

Yes, even so. Did he know this, too? His touch told her yes.

She wondered if she changed her mind now, could she stop him? If he changed his mind, would she let him?

Another sound escaped her as his fingers touched her nipple and all thoughts flew away. She saw them fly away with two ravens that flew over head and made some soft sawing sounds. He made those same sounds. Then she did. Then he was kissing her breasts, her nightgown raised to around her shoulders.

He took her nipple in his teeth as gently as a catamount carries her newborn cub to a new den. He raked her tiny nipples with his teeth. He pulled them with his teeth until she whimpered, then licked them as if to sooth the wound.

Suddenly, he felt her hand. She had found his hardness. Had she ever felt this thing before? No, he was the first. Aye, so sweet. He wanted her to grab him and pull. He wanted to tell her to pull. But he caught his breath and waited to see what she would do. He tightened himself and pulsed his blood down there and he knew she felt it. He waited.

There. She squeezed just a little, exploring. He squeezed back. Then she started to explore, taking her time. He buried his mouth into her neck. Slowly, she started to pull and push. Ai, this one is curious—.

～

Alána returns with two tall tropical drinks reeking of coconut. "Here!"

"Oh!" Wynema is startled.

"Where you been?"

"Right here, listening to the mu—" But Frank is gone. Wynema sees the stage is empty.

Alána smiles. "Remembering were you? Just remembering? I don't wonder what. You wanna stay for the third set? Twenty minutes they be back maybe. Then, maybe, you'll want to go backstage."

"No. I'm ready to go."

As she drinks deep from the tall tropical, Wynema's cell flashes. "Hello?"

She almost drops her drink. Her eyes go wide and she looks shocked at Alána. Then she speaks in a language she hasn't spoken in over a decade. It is guttural and halting. She bends to allow Alána to lean over and listen.

"*Ya tihk a'we'enah. Tur'or m'Wynema, zeekh kalu Mondragon.* ...Yes, yes...I'm sorry, I've forgotten. *Ya ma'thik en koyuu.* Sorry. ..."

She looks again helplessly at Alána, until someone else comes on the line.

"Oh, hello, who? ... Jolene? Yes, Jolene! I remember you. This is Wynema...yes, Mondragon. Yes, she said she was Mirriamma...My great auntie...Of course, but it's been so long. ...Oh, sure, well, okay I think I understand. I guess I don't remember our Pueblo dialect very well. ..."

She nods her head attentively, taking in the details.... "But, Jolene, isn't the Turtle Dance danced only by men? What—what can I possibly know about it? ... And it's been years. ... Well, yes, my mother and grandmother did, but I think I've forgotten. I probably have forgotten. ... Okay, well, I'll think about it." She looks at the number on her cell. "Yes, I have it and I'll call you tomorrow, Jolene. *Mitocoya-hundt.*"

Closing her flip, she can't talk. But Alána wants to know. She still can't talk. She looks to the stage, to Alána, to her cellphone. She's incredulous and drains her tropics in two draughts.

"What language was that?"

"Pueblo. My mother's tongue." She raises her hand and waves it at the stage. "Wow. There was my own Pueblo village up on the screens. And then Frank. Now this strange call. This—this has become a very strange day."

"Who was that first woman you spoke to? I could feel her voice from here. That woman had juju!"

"The voice was...the woman calling was...it was Mirriamma, my great-aunt, and if I remember her, my memory is pretty vague. Then she handed me to a younger woman, Jolene. And I do remember her. She was in my high-school class. She said Mirriamma was trying to do something very important, okay, but.... *Ai yai...mitocoyahundt.*"

"Yeah, I heard you say that. What's *mitocoyahundt.*"

"You pronounce it very well. It means something like, uh, 'We are all one' in Pueblo."

"What did she want?"

"I don't know. I mean, I'm not sure. She knows that for the last eleven years I've been living with my father's people on a reservation in Montana. Different tribe. Different culture. Different world. Why would she ask me that?!—

"Ask you what?"

"Wait a minute. Before I left my mother's pueblo, they gave a ceremony for me, for safe travels, and—it was Mirriamma who came and did the ceremony."

"So she needs you, whoever she is."

"She said she'd been thinking about me—can you imagine?! And she wanted to know if I could come home and retell some stories. Me?! Then I spoke to Jolene and she said something about my mother telling me stories about the origins of the Turtle Dance—that's a dance we do only on the first day of the year. She said that Mirriamma's younger sister was my grandmother, and she didn't have sons, only daughters, and so my grandfather told her daughter those stories—the ones that are so important for the Turtle Dance. Her daughter was my mother and, it's true, she told those stories to me, to put me to sleep at night, or so I thought. And I guess I still remember those stories and told her so—Mirriamma, I mean—and she was so happy and—. Amazing! I must not be understanding this. I mean, I gotta work this summer to go to England next fall. The teaching fellowship doesn't pay all that much—but England, I mean, that's an opportunity I can't pass up. She drums her fingers back and forth across her forehead. *'Tears of rage, tears of grief, why must I always be the thief? Life is brief. Life is brief.'*"

"What's that from?"

"I don't know. A Joan Baez song, I think. It just popped into my head. I'm going crazy."

"Sweet darlin', life is long. Think 'Life is Long'. It's a better way to spend the same time."

"No, wait! That Joan Baez song. It was Jolene who always played it. I visited her one day. She was playing it over and over. She was raped. That's right! I remember now. She was raped by some relative.

She was into boys a lot then, but she was only 13 or 14. It happened off the pueblo, so the municipal court tried the case. The judge came down heavy on the rapist. 12 years imprisonment, or something like that. And his friends and relatives packed the court, and when they heard the sentence, all hell broke loose. The judge threw them all in jail for a night. But she—from that moment on, she changed. I'd always been into books and taking care of my mother who was long suffering from emphysema, asthma, and diabetes. But from then on, Jolene and I connected on books. Then mother died, and my dad moved away, and so did I."

Alána touches her friend's hand. "Hey, if you go before that check from our teaching gig comes, can I send the money to you on the rez?"

Wynema grabs a coaster from their table and writes on the back. "That's easy. I haven't forgotten that address in ten years. Just send it to me care of San Lucas Pueblo, 87526."

Alána picks up the coaster, memorizes it, touches it to her forehead, and throws it down. "Got it now—maybe forever. Let's get out of here."

"Geez, the way you can remember numbers."

"Yeah, I should have been a mathematician or a bookie."

"Hey, what makes you think I'm even gonna go to New Mexico? For a Turtle Dance?"

"I dunno. Could it just be that I know who Queen Curious is?"

Wynema waves her head in the air challenging her best friend to divine her future. "Hey, smell that?"

"Yeah, but what is it? Cedar?" asks Alána on the fly.

"Frank must have brought Piñon incense with him. Big on the Pueblo. I mean, that's what we used to cook with. But there's also some good ol' marijuana slicing through that, from over there. And that tall blond that just passed us, she's wearing 'My Blessing' by Madonna. Yuk. And the woman who was sitting next to me, she—" Alána grabs her by the hand and pulls her towards the exit.

8

THE JEW AND THE JAMAICAN

Across town and an hour and a half earlier, two doctors, senior residents at Mount Sinai Medical Center, have just finished a complicated C-section on a Chinese woman. Satisfied, they turn the close over to second-year residents and allow themselves to step away and end their 18-hour day. They visibly breathe deeper and pull off their bloodied gloves and throw them into a canister labeled "HELL". One of them is happy to be thoughtless now, empty and spent; the other is lost and desperate in his ruminations.

The happy one is a Jamaican built to play muscular forward on his country's Olympic basketball team. They placed fifth in the world that year. He's 6' 6". The desperate one is built to be the first Jew to take home a ribbon in the National Fencing championships two years in a row. He is 6' 4". They are in their prime. It's downhill from here on out, the Jew constantly reminds the Jamaican.

They're good friends. Their pantomime shows it. The dark one turns and faces the operating room and smiles broadly with the pride of a job well done. Expecting his friend and colleague to take this all in with joy and satisfaction, he sees that the other is lost in his usual obsessive introspection. So he smacks him.

The other, perturbed but unwilling to break the code of the pantomime, screws his face around into utter annoyance and asks without a sound What the fuck's with you already?!

The basketball player shoots a three-pointer then quickly spreads out his arms taking in the entire beautiful gloriously-equipped operating room, as if to extol it, praise it, to show deepest gratitude for it... after, "...well, you know, a job well-done by you...and me."

The fencer acknowledges it with a short shtick of heroic indulgence then uses his whole body to portray annoyance at the other's insensitive intrusion into his quiet, sincere, and necessary moment of introspection.

A nurse passes by without stopping. "Why don't you guys take up ASL, you know, American Sign Language? It's a lot more elegant than you spasmos."

Both surgeons feign shock and indignation as they start quickly for the showers.

Physicians' locker room. This place can feel one of two ways depending on whether you're coming or going. That is, are you cautiously approaching work? Or recklessly fleeing from it.

The stainless steel door is 48 inches wide but still not wide enough for two nearly 30-year-old doctors who, so full of themselves and in sync, find themselves stuck shoulder-to-shoulder in the doorway.

"You first, oh Great One!"

"No, you, your Majesty!"

"Oh, no, I insist."

"Au contraire."

"After you, my dear Alfonse."

"No, you, you're white, thus deserving."

"No, you, you're black, thus deserving even more."

—until the shorter one, Will, falls headlong into the locker room, blaming without a sound the taller for the near catastrophe.

To which the Jamaican, now pulling off his light-cerulean-blue scrubs: "I miss you already, man." Dirty and bloodied as his scrubs may be, he folds them respectfully and then places them carefully in the wash basket.

The Jew, "Hey, I do, too, like yesterday, bro." He crumples and stuffs his scrubs.

"No, I'm a lot more serious than that, mon."

"Okay. I hear ya. Thanks."

"I mean, I can feel the void forming, the gap, the hole, the emotional lacuna—"

"The 'emotional lacuna'? Okay, you win."

"—The emptiness as a result of your going away and my missing you in my life. We've been through a lot. Kicked some ass. Topped some peaks. Took some falls—"

"You ever think of going into acting?"

"It's like a part of me, mon, a part of my very being will be missing. Seriously, I never had a friend as good as you."

"Or maybe becoming Jewish. We could convert you. That'd balance you out."

"That's sweet, mon, 'cause I'm really going to miss you."

"Yeah, well, okay, now that we got through that, what do you want to do tonight?

I dunno. What do you want to do...?"

William Kornfeld son of Yitzchak son of Avram son of Nusan son of Tudris...and Jahbig Trenchton of Jamaica, son of Jahbig son of Jahbig son of...have been best friends since they began medical school at Harvard seven years ago. Both will be certified surgeons when they finish their residencies. Will is heading into Family Practice with a strong focus on Epidemiology; and Jah into Obstetrics and Gynecology. Will also has a Masters in Public Health that he did while in Med School. Jah will return home to Jamaica but only after acquiring a broad set of modern medical skills and certifications. His country needs this of him.

Will's grandfather Abraham was born a hated creature on the border of Germany and Poland. But he escaped to New York and married Rosa Chasen. They had one daughter, who died in her teens, and one son, Isaac. Isaac fell in love with Devorah and had one son, William Nathan, who was born in the Harlem at the Lutheran Hospital on the corner of 146th and Convent Avenue. He is among the first generation of Jews (after how many generations?) to find peace and freedom, health and happiness, and not be afraid. He, to many old country Jews now in America, was and is, because of this, an extraordinary blessing, a miracle. There are other miracles, these Jews will tell you, but more on that later.

Abraham was ten years old when the Jews of Germany experienced *Kristalnacht*. He was twelve years old when his parents were trapped, humiliated, and murdered. At thirteen, instead becoming Bar

Mitzvah, he was forced to work carrying dead bodies of Jews. He escaped; his first miracle. Some kind Christians took him in as their own. It's a rare but well-known story.

Jahbig was luckier. Some ambitious Jamaican government official, high up in the Education Ministry and looking for a showcase good deed he could pin up on his office wall, one day discovered Jahbig in a rural school and, impressed with the boy's intelligence and the respect his teachers had for him, decided to make an example of how well poor children from the villages can succeed if only they are given the proper guidance by the proper professionals charged with taking care of the people. They put him into the finest private schools and saw to his every need—as long as Jahbig did well. And Jahbig did very well. His father, the fourth Jahbig since slavery was abolished, was a sugarcane farmer. He never learned to read. But some say the man was a genius, the way he could fix things, even things he'd never seen before.

They lunge for their lockers about ten feet apart along a long maple bench. Jahbig is bouncing as he undresses and heads for the showers. Will immediately falls back into his deeper thoughts. Jahbig keeps looking over at him, concerned again by this interior turn. Just before entering the showers, he turns, big black and naked, to his ruminative friend. "What the fuck's with you?"

"Huh?"

"Where you at?"

"What do you mean?"

"You sure as hell ain't here, mon."

"No, this is exactly where I'm at. Right here right now."

"Your ganja's gone gray, mon."

"Hey, you had my undivided back there. The C-section."

"No, no, right here right now, just like you said."

"I'm saying it was cool what you did with that C-section."

Jahbig throws up his hands, but follows him in. "That's true."

As he adjusts the temperature, "I particularly was impressed with the way you were able to move the baby before you cut. I mean, you hardly touched the uterus and yet—you knew just where to touch to get that baby to move. How'd you do that?"

"Ah, well, that you don't learn in medical school."

"Okay, maybe not. But it can be described in medical school and you're about to translate it for me into its full and detailed medicalese glory."

"No I am not, because I can't. Like I'm trying to tell ya, it has nothing to do with medical school. How do you think I got through medical school? I'm not as smart as you. I don't have the education behind me that you and the others do. C'mon, what you got comes from the culture, you understand, the magazines, the TV, the conversations, the parties with other highly educated sons and daughters of brains or big bucks. That's where you're coming from, and med school is rigged to advance those who master those things. You hearin' me?!"

A few minutes later, as he reaches for his towel, Will stubs his toe. "Ow!"

Jah glances at the toe. "No blood. So, when you don't have those...those goodies to count on, you move forward by grabbing onto something else. Something else, mon." Jah grabs his towel and heads back to the locker room.

Will is left hanging, unsatisfied. "C'mon, give! The C-Section, like the C is for Chinese." He follows, like a giraffe from watering-hole to dust-wallow.

Their lockers are large and contain many changes of clothes to wear. The Jamaican pulls out a dark turtleneck. The second-generation Jewish immigrant pulls on tie-dye underwear. "So, c'mon, man, finish the story."

"Okay, okay, if you think you can handle it. So, just before I make my cut I force myself to stop thinking. That's right. I know what I have to do, so I don't have to think about it, right? I know it already. So I stop thinking for just long enough for me to feel the energy of what's going on down there. But not with my head."

Jah bends towards his friend, looks left and right to make sure no else can hear this and whispers, "I just feel the energy that is coming and going between my fingertips and that woman—and voilá! I let myself touch the uterus just there, and—I think it was the back of the baby's head and he, I mean, she—she felt me and pushed against my fingers and I gave her just the right amount of back-pressure and she—" Jahbig interjects a Jamaican exclamation for happiness! "—*Ir-ie!*—she moves herself around so that when I cut the head will be just at the right place for my cut to be as small as possible and—. Hey, mon, am I getting through? Can you see why medical school has nothing on the coming or going of what I'm talking about? *Fi mi dey nuh odda way.*"

Will's head spins and he can only speak slowly and haltingly. "Uh, yeah, I guess I can see what you mean. Whew! Jah, that description was as good as what I saw you do. You did it and you described it and you said it would have nothing to do with med school and you were right. Goddamn it, you were right. That blows my entire confidence in what I learned at med school. You fuckin' took two-hundred thousand dollars worth of med school education and you tossed it out the fucking window. So cavalier. So insensitive to all the struggles my family and I made to pay my way through med school and now you just destroyed it. *Bumboclot!*"

"Good, mon." His shoes on, he blasts for the door.

As they cut back past the O.R., a new surgical team is already at work. Will pauses and looks back, listens. The muted intensity. The precision. The expectancy. The complex, computer-assisted, beautifully high-tech, pastel colors, the impenetrable chrome and stainless, the aseptic, germ-free implications, the sanitary state-of-the-art glory—especially the soft, fugitive, intricate post-modern sounds, the delicate composition and clarity and continuity of the hums, clicks, pulses, beeps, and the other-worldly intercom and cellphone ringtones. Unobtrusive, but incessant. Any shift in them and the educated ears of those who monitor these sounds are immediately alerted.

Jahbig steps back and grabs his easily distracted friend by the sleeve, "I'm not even going to ask what you're doing. Let's get out of here."

They step from the corridors of professionals into the large foyer of this great hospital where the public mixes and moves, always with a little awe and trepidation in their step.

They are moving faster now, in sync'd stride, making for the large glass servo-assisted doors. They understand the terrain. They're careful not to acknowledge any of the many people known and unknown as they leave the hospital. They do not want to get waylaid.

Nor do they notice as they step out into the November of New York how underdressed they are for the first snow, how cold they are as they lean into a raucous dusk wind and walk quickly along 49th Street.

"Why don't we take a cab?"

"Okay."

"Where are we going?"

"I don't know."

"!"

Jahbig holds open the door of a cab, laughing.

"What's so funny?"

"Nothing. Just life, mon. "Third Street and Sixth," he says to the driver. Then poking his friend with huge, balletic, darting fingers, "Hey, your gran'fadda come to this county, escaping the Nazis and all that, and he was a success here, right? He worked hard and made a lot of money, and you told me when he went away to Israel you gave him your blessings to spend every damn dollar of his money on himself, because you didn't need it, and you didn't want it, and that you'd be okay without it. Ain't that right?"

Will wags his head cautiously, suspicious of where this is leading.

Jah thinks he's onto something. He scrunches his head down between his shoulders. "But you, you think you still got some years of indeterminate specification ahead of you. You still have some generic dues to pay, you think. You worry where you gonna work. How you gonna pay back your college loans? What you gonna specialize in? How you gonna sharpen your blade beyond sharpness? You don't know. But I say that's okay. Because it's something you gotta figure out without handholding your gran'fadda in the Promised Land. Say yes!"

"Look," grumpfs Will, his patience growing thin, "I don' wanna talk about this all day. I just wanna move, a little dancing maybe, get out the kinks with a coupla drinks. We been working eighteen. Let's go listen to some music! Or, let's go to the Harlem. Turn the fucking cab around! Let's go do the Def Jam Slam Poetry thing up-town."

Jah motions the cabby to continue on course. "You can run, white man, but you can't hide. Let go of Israel, mon, it ain't your thing."

"I know that! You know that. We've been over this 47 times."

"How's Grandpa doing? You hear from him lately?"

"This morning. I called. He's doing okay. He's learning how to compose music on his Mac."

"Cool. You had three choices, now you have two. So if going to Israel's not an option, then you gotta choose between doing research at one of the most prestigious places in the world, or...or go do bandages and C-sections, dialysis and diabetes on an Indian reservation. Big choice. Hard choice, I know—."

"C'mon, Jah. I'll figure it out. I got a few more days."

"If you go to U.C. Med at San Francisco, you'll be right across the bay from me, Jahbig Trenchton! We rule out there, mon!"

Since many Jews think out loud in a friendly crucible called *argumentum gratia argumentum*, Will holds up a finger. "Look, I'll pay off my loan a lot faster if I take that job with Indian Health Service. I mean, that's the deal: they pay off the loans, and I won't have many expenses there." Off Jahbig's look of incredulousness, "Okay, faggedaboutit. Am I out of my fucking mind? You're right. I'll go to Frisco. You know about Andrew Wheaton—new book out on HIV vectors. He works there."

Jahbig slaps his friend on he knee. "Now you're talking. Yo, in Frisco never say 'Frisco' because they'll know right away that you're not from there. You gotta say San Fra'cisco without pronouncing the 'n'."

Will doesn't reply. Once again, he's lost in thought. *He's right: three choices narrowed down to two. Hallelujah! My friends feel like relatives, always weighing in, and they know which are the hard choices, and they zero in on them like smart bombs. The same conversation. Twenty times. Fifty times. But I have only one relative. Just one. Hitler killed almost all the rest. Mom and Dad died in a car accident, and Mom's parents died a long time before I was born—in Turkey or Iraq or Palestine, nobody knows—and I don't know if they had any siblings. No, just my grandfather, who escaped, miraculously.*

'It's a miracle!' His grandfather had always told him. 'You gotta respect miracles. You and me together, after everything—we're living miracles!'

                          *

Before he took his grandfather to Israel, almost a year ago, they had an argument.

"My miracles don't own me, Abba."

"That's a *shanda* to say," his grandfather hissed.

He had heard his grandfather say this many times, whenever he even hinted at not being grateful beyond his ability to express it, for just being alive and given the holy task of rebuilding *Am Yisrael* and *Eretz Yisrael*, the People and Land of Israel.

His grandfather had many ways to say the same thing: "To suffer for so many thousands of years and then to be exterminated—almost a third of all Jews living, to almost disappear, what would that say about our gratitude to God, *baruch sh'mo*? But you, you just want to dissolve into...into—"

"The Great Unwashed? The Goyim?"

"Goyim, shmoyim, I'm not talking about them. I don't trust them. And you, big shot, in spite of your great achievements—of which I'm so proud, it's true— you shouldn't trust them, either. Trust your own. *Shema Yisroel*, kid, and I'm not kidding!"

"I know, Abba-Zeyda, I know. You want the world to work that way, to make sense that way. But it doesn't. Good times, bad times. We're sailors. We play the winds as they come. It was bad yesterday. It's good today. It'll be bad tomorrow. But this is where my life is now. Maybe when I'm your age, I'll come to Israel. Maybe it'll make sense then. If you gotta do it, do it. We'll visit each other. We got the money. But Israel isn't my country. And today it's an apartheid state. And I know you don't want to hear it, but it's true. I don't like it. I'm ashamed of it. This is where I'm going to make my home. I don't like Israel today. I did when I was a kid and you sent me to Zionist camps, and I had a great time. But I grew up. I read books and talked to people, and I learned the truth about Israel. And I'm ashamed, Abba, of what they're doing to the Palestinians."

Abraham had a good sense of humor, even though he didn't want to have one right now.

"If you weren't so big, Favileh, I'd slap the crap out of you for saying that. Israel is an ancient dream and a promise. You don't talk bad about her. But I...I still have good sense. You? I'm not so sure of. Come to Israel with me. It'll be good. Zeyda and son. Son and Zeyda. Two of us they couldn't kill."

"You are such a romantic. I mean, you still like to watch cowboy movies. You think going off to Israel is like being a pioneer. The kibbutzim are dying, I'm telling you. It's not the same country it was in 1948. Everything changed in '67. I'm sorry to tell you that, but it's true. You're lucky to be able to do what you do. Me, too. But—so we gotta fulfill ourselves, each in our own way."

"We're all we got, Favileh."

Will stepped to the little table by the door and brought him the latest issue of *Ha-aretz*. "I'll go to Israel with you, set you up, check it out, make sure everything's kosher, and then we'll be in touch, constantly, Papa, or we'll come visit each other, and you can afford it. And what else should we do with it? Don't save your money for me. Spend it on good deeds in Israel."

"For damn!" Jahbig jumps when a big truck almost collides with the side of their cab. "Crazy bastard!"

"Don't worry," says the cab-driver, "I saw him coming, had 'im edged."

Jah takes a deep breath. "Will, okay, so you made up your mind. You're going to San Fra'cisco. Hey, this is America where to be rich you gotta have lotsa, lotsa debt. Fuck the Indians. I'm an Indian. I know what I'm saying."

"You're no Indian."

"There are two kinds of people in this world," says Jahbig with deep seriousness, "Whites and Indians."

"I'm not white. I'm Jewish."

"Yah, well, never-mind because I'm not white, either. But I make my point. We're out here, mon. This is it, cabbie. Out!"

The cab pulls up and they jump out somewhere in the Village. Within ten paces they're dodging haymaker snowflakes and flying down a brick stairway into a subterranean bar.

It's a dark and gloomily lit and rather monochromatic bar. Gray, gray, gray. Almost oppressive. Looking up through long horizontal translucent bulkhead windows just below the ceiling, Will sees ankles and feet of people walking by outside on the street above. And the entire decor is monothematic: WWII German submarine. Music comes from little gray sqawk-boxes everywhere. Music from the European 30s mix with the lonely rhythmic pinging of sonar, searching, always searching. Almost inaudible beneath all the sounds is a track from the intercom of a submarine underway, on the hunt...in German!

Jahbig sits comfortably at the bar sipping scotch-and-sodas. Will is spooked by the environs.

Jahbig speaks first. "I'm not hungry. Are you?"

"You're not hungry? I'm not hungry either. We should be hungry."

"We should be very hungry, mon. What then are we living on then?"

Will takes a sip and a deep breath. "We're living on hopes and dreams and lusts and passions, the promise of an excellent medical career and," pointing to the scotch in the soda in the glass in his hand, "on the calories inherent in the C_2H_5OH dissolved in this CO_2-charged H_2O. Liquid sunshine, you beautiful child, the renewable resource and biofuel!"

"What'd you just say?!"

"The alcohol. We're living right now on the calories in the alcohol."

"No, not that. About renewable resource and biofuel."

"Just a joke."

"No, those are hot topics right now. They're important, pressing, topical topics right now."

"Okay, so?" Will forces himself to focus. He sets his drink down on the bar. He bends over and looks at his friend more closely.

Jahbig puts his drink down and slowly lowers his head onto this hands. "What's today?"

"The 4th, Tuesday."

"I phoned in my acceptance at Oakland General over a week ago. Way ahead of the deadline, which isn't for another week. Tomorrow is the deadline for Watts."

"What the fuck are you saying?"

"You sure I'm sure that *I'm* on the right track in *my* life?"

"Of course I'm sure you're sure," says Will a little surprised. He looks hard into his friend's dark eyes. "Me? Maybe I worry too much. But you?! You're always so sure about what you're doing. Hey, come on, we've had this conversation before."

"Yeah, I know. " Jah stands to leave. "I may not be Jewish, but this place is weirding me out, too."

"Sit down. Talk to me."

"Tell me anyways," say Jahbig, blinking his eyes. "Pretend I'm very insecure."

"But you're not insecure. You're the securest person I know." Will sighs. "Okay. Fine. You're finishing your residency and worked hard, and you are going to step onto, at a fairly high level, onto the medical staff of one of the finest hospitals in the world."

"Yeah, mon, but I could have taken that job in Los Angeles—"

"—in Watts, right, developing a much-needed program for delivering babies to—"

"To—yes, you've told me—to AIDs afflicted black women who are desperate and suffering as only the poor can suffer."

"Well, those are important, pressing, topical issues right now. Hey, I'm just thinking—."

Two women, out of nowhere, step up and stop directly in front of the two doctors now standing, leaning back against the bar. Both women look back and forth slowly from one man to the other, taking them in, enjoying their fantasies, their probing curiosity, their appreciation of these attractive men. Faint smiles creep into the four faces. But Jah and Will, with only a gentle acknowledgment, continue their conversation.

"Well, don't think," Will says, "leave that to me. Go with the gut. Trust the Force. That's what you're good at. More important than nobility of purpose is precision of purpose, strategic purpose, because—"

The two women nod, turn, sigh and disappear.

"—because in Oakland you will be working with some of the finest doctors from whom you know you need to learn if you're ever going to take back to Jamaica the skills you need. You dig?"

"Are the skills I need for Jamaica the skills that sophisticated Oakland General can teach me, or the skills the desperate women of Watts can teach me?"

Will grabs his drink and sits down on his stool. "C'mon, man, this is crazy!"

"Renewable resources and biofuels."

"Huh?"

"They triggered something in me."

"You've worked all this out. You made the right decision."

"You're right," says Jah easing himself onto his stool. "I did. Wow. That was strange. For a second I felt like I had not made my decision. I forgot in the moment. But I'm back now, uh-huh. You reminded me. Thanks, mon. I have a plan. Now you need a plan! You took your gran'fadda to Israel, you looked around and saw that Israel wasn't what you wanted, and you left him in good hands and came home to do what you want and need to do. You had three choices," Jah intones as he moves to go. "But it has now narrowed down to two. You have only to decide between—"

"UCSF Med and some Indian Health Service clinic in the middle of nowhere. I know, I know. We've been here before"

"Sounds similar to the choice I had between Oakland or Watts, does it not?"

"Yeah, okay—so what? The deadline for letting them know is two weeks for Public Health and three weeks for San Francisco—."

A woman wearing a scant sailor's uniform offers them hors-d'oeuvres from a glistening tray. Four sailors aircraft carrier insignia walk up and wait their turn at the tray.

"I'm glad I'm not on a submarine," says one of the sailors to the others.

"Wouldn't you want to be on a submarine with me, pupkins?" the waitress asks in a Betty Boop voice.

Jahbig, loyal to their conversation, leans in closer. "Okay, so tell me about that Indian Health Clinic thing. How many doctors are there, what are their specialties, and what would you hope to learn there that might be unique, in all fairness to that situation?"

Will laughs ruefully. "One. Me. That's it. I'd be top dawg there. It's a solo gig."

"You gotta be pullin' my leg, mon!"

"Nope, one small adobe medical out-patient clinic that serves two Indian Pueblos, San Lucas and Santa Carmina. Population thirteen-hundred thirty-three. But I'll have an NP, or maybe a PA, a couple of RNs, a lab tech, a computer geek, a loyal staff or two, and, oh, a dentist twice a week."

"Okay, that's it! You think you're Doctor Livingston?! Albert Schweitzer?! I'm calling your grandpa, your academic advisor, your rabbi, your shrink, and that woman, what's-her-name, Carmen, the Puerto Rican who taught you the Puerto Rican Water Trick last week who made you think you were Zeus in the Saddle—I think I got you figured out! The Messiah Walks Alone!"

"Hey, why'd you want to go to Watts anyhow? Because there's an idealism there, a purity of purpose—."

"We're outa here. Let's go."

"How deep in this submarine did we just dive?"

9

CARE OF SAN LUCAS PUEBLO, 87526

The Stalactite is around the corner. A Mongolian woman wearing a yak coat and holding a penlight holds the door open for them.

Two minutes after Wynema and Alána leave the Stalactite, enter Will and Jahbig. They pull almost as many looks as the women did. Jahbig heads straight to the table where the women had been. Will is trying to ask everyone they pass who's playing here tonight.

"Two double Lafroaigs, soda back," says the Jamaican to a blasé waitress as he unties his dreads and lets them fall. They both settle into the chairs.

"Umm, my chair's still warm. Why didn't we go to The Blue Note?" asks Will.

"I saw this woman going in the door, a patient of mine actually, who's got this insane crush on me. Forget about it. I gotta stay professional."

"You mean to tell me that there is no woman you've known, or know now, or ever dreamt of knowing—that couldn't, if she wanted to, ravage you of every vestige of professionalism that you think you cling to?"

"No. No. Absolutely not." His thoughts run away from him. "Well,—" He thrusts his nose into the air and sniffs, to the left, to the right. "No, not here, not tonight at any rate."

Will picks up a coaster and places it neatly in front of his friend. He picks up another coaster and—"What the fuck is this?!"

"Whazzat?"

"What were we just talking about back there in that submarine?"

"About Carmen who did the hot water trick and kept you hard all night long?"

"Noooo! About my future."

"That's what I said. About your choosing between working at UCSF Med or, you know, at that Indian clinic on that pueblo out in the middle of—"

"And what the frak was the name of that Pueblo?" says Will with a dumbfounded look.

"Santa Lucille? I don' remember."

"Well, look at this—a coaster with my name on it and the name of that other pueblo, San Lucas." He hands it to Jahbig. "Is this spooky, Jah—or are you fucking with me?"

Jahbig takes it warily and reads: 'WM, care-of San Lucas Pueblo, 87526'. "I swear I didn't do that. Juju, mon. And besides, you didn't say anything about no zipcode." He thinks about it for a second. "Is that the right zipcode?"

"Actually, I think it is."

Chumba mounts his console. He becomes a fighter pilot shooting his twin machine-guns at Frank slowly being lowered head-first through a panel in the ceiling, suspended by a thick hemp rope tied to just one ankle.... In a Tarot deck: the Hanged Man.

They watch the same set the two women had just seen.

Now, at the end of their last set, Frank and Chumba are persuaded to encore.

Chumba pulls a lever and his rig rises and turns, the lights change, and the air is filled with the sounds of wild creatures, then combined with the chatter of children pulling their parents this way and that in a zoo.

The video matrix comes alive with the dying sad light in the eyes of various caged animals. Frank ranges the stage, the LCDs, the audience. He sets, wheels—

"Claws dulled by dull concrete, he has no teeth, but children squeal when the great bear stands and moves heavy to the edge of the trench and bars that separates them from the beast. He is fat from soft food doled out by whiskey keepers believing him content—"

He pauses for a moment then turns with the audience to watch a particularly sad sequence of a great Grizzly shifting back and forth on a rock.

"—with his step-and-step world, walled by white men holding the keys. He once roamed and ruled and hunted and sired great sons and daughters and roared at the clouds in a furious exultation to life."

For a few moments he looks away and breathes heavily and swallows hard. As does the audience.

"But now he walks from the back wall to the rim of the valley of cement, stands, scares little children, then walks back again on a reservation in a zoo."

Will and Jahbig are stunned into silence. For a time they can only look into each other's eyes.

Then Will picks up the coaster again and turns it over and over.

10

SPOONING

A week later, early morning, in the apartment they share, Wynema stands naked before the bathroom mirror. "I don't know who I am," she says softly to herself.

"Sure you do," says Alána just as softly from the bathroom doorway, shower-beads glistening.

Wynema starts and reflexively covers her breasts with her hands. "You startled me."

"Of course I did. For an Indian you're easy to sneak up on. Stop looking and telling and talking and gawking. Just breathe. Close your eyes."

The Indian obeys, drops her hands, closes her eyes and breathes deeply.

"There you are. Back again." Alána glides across the tile in bare black feet. "I'm your panther and you're my eagle, my forward scout, my radar. You just tell me what you see, and I'll tell you who you are and where you are and—." Standing behind her, Alána's hands slide up her waist and cup her breasts like the petals of flowers closing for the night.

"I'm serious."

"You're the most serious person I've ever met in my life."

"What a horrible thing to say about someone." She slips out of Alána's gentle grasp.

"No, it is not. It's tender."

"Maybe serious people don't know who they are."

"Let's watch Ladyhawk again tonight," says Alána putting bounce and excitement into the air. "Who do you want to be, the hawk or the wolf? I still have a bit of Godsganja left."

"Did you forget, I'm flying out today."

"No, it's tomorrow!"

"The redeye, tonight."

"Oh, don't go." She goes to Wynema, opening up her robe as she goes. Their nakedness unifies them as they take turns nosing the other's ear. "Come back to bed." "I gotta pack." "In a bit." "But now is forever...."

An hour later, lying in bed, the African is spooning the Indian, the former awake, the latter barely. "Why do I have the feeling that I may not see you for a long time?"

Wynema stirs, smiles, pushes back in deeper. "Oh, stop it. It's nothing. I'll be back soon. A week. Two weeks. What could it be? But I gotta go—you understand that. I mean, she called me. That means something."

"Oh, yah. A shift in the polar axis. The Mayan calendar clickin' in earlier than expected. The birth of a New Age originating from San Lucas's umbilicus *ki-vé*."

"*Kíva*," she gently corrects. "There are two kinds of people: Old Age and New Age. The one is cautious and conservative, the other curious and progressive. There's a time for each."

"You're curious. Do you remember you told me how when you were lost in the Amazon you were able to dissolve away your anger?"

"Yes. We've talked about it. No?"

"Tell me about it...again."

"Well, for four days I waited to be rescued. I gave myself a week. I knew I could take care of myself for a week. After that, I told myself I was going to do something, you know, proactive, about getting myself out of there. I suppose I was starting to think about building a raft or something. All rivers lead to the sea—and other people. So, while I waited—and I'd recommend getting lost like that to almost anyone—I had time to think about things. I thought about how angry I'd been all my life, and just stuffed it. Didn't deal with it. Didn't take it apart. Or look at it closely. I didn't know just how much it possessed me, controlled me, made me who I was. I was angry about being an Indian. Angry about what this country had done to the Indian. And in many ways what it's still doing. And then anger that had nothing to do with being an Indian. Just the injustices, everywhere. It became clear to me that I was angry at the injustices that didn't have to be, and that I'd been ignoring these feelings. So for a while there, lost in the Amazon, I got really angry. But I experienced it. I saw it come, I saw it hit me, I saw my reactions to it. And when I saw them in relation to the situation I was in, alone in the jungle, anger no longer could be either the cause or the effect of my feelings and thoughts and experiences. Same perceptions; different reactions. Does that make sense to you?"

"I do understand. How come they took four days to rescue you?"

"I was a loner. I didn't know anyone at the conference. I was invisible to everyone. I kept to myself. When I disappeared, no one noticed. No one noticed until I didn't file some report, or, I don't know, submit a survey about our trip. It was in all the newspapers down there."

Three hours later, on the curb, saying goodbye next to a waiting taxicab, Alána has tears in her eyes. The cabby is patient, his meter on. The two woman stand in silence, looking into each other's eyes. Finally, Wynema reaches up with her two hands and pulls Alána's face slowly down to hers. They kissed softly.

"Everything of mine is boxed and labeled. If I'm not back by the time you find a new place, just pay someone to help you move my stuff and I'll pay you back."

Alána can stand it no longer. She opens the cab door and guides Wynema in. Through the open window their fingers touch.

The cab disappears. Another aboriginal ghosting from sight.

11

HE DOESN'T TRUCK WITH IDIOTS

The airplanes come and go. Will stands near the security gate saying goodbye to Jahbig, on his way to Jamaica for a week to be with
his family at the memorial of his favorite uncle, Daddy Joe, who died
last week in a spew of bullets—bullets from the guns of goons sent in
by developers to clear a few villagers from land they "weren't making
productive use of". Joe was married to a woman from that village and
had come to help her family negotiate with the developers.

"Don't do anything foolish while I'm gone," says Jah as they hug
and part. "I'm with your Zeyda on this one, bredda. Take the job at
UC Med, and we'll be across the Bay from each other, and you'll be
cool, and I'll be cool, and we'll rule the Bay."

Will lowers his eyes—inhales, exhales, then pulls the Stalactite
coaster from his shirt pocket, flipping it with his fingers like a gambler
would the Jack of Diamonds.

Jah's eyes widen, fix, then soften. "Damn, you didn't do that!
Why'd you do that? I know why you did it, but, really, why?! We had
it set out there, you and me. Step by step, we do it together. I know
eventually I have to go back home and work—that was the deal. But
you ain't locked into anything. After San Fra'cisco, you might even
have come to Jamaica, foot loose and fancy free, and be top dog in
epidemiology and—"

"Jah, I know you're disappointed. First Zeyda and now you. I'm
sorry."

"What happened, mon? I know it ain't just the magic of that
coaster."

"I want to work at ground level before I shoot for the stars."

"What the fuck does that mean?"

"Renewable resources and biofuels. Tell you the truth, I don't know."

"Hell of a time to tell me, as I'm stepping onto an airplane. How can I have your back if you don't—"

"Maybe it has to do with that C-section we did a few months back."

"What C-section?"

"The last one we did together. The Chinese woman? The one you told me the story of about how you turned the child so you could get the best cut. The way you—"

"Fercrissakes, mon. What's that have to do with anything? Shit, I knew I'd regret telling about that."

"No, man, really, it was good. I've never forgotten it. Fact is, it haunts me."

"What's that have to do with going to Indian land?"

"Nothing. Everything. I don't know. They live in the same room in my head. I don't know."

The alluring, futuristic woman's voice on the airport PA system: "Last call for United flight one-seven-seven-six to Miami, Florida, and Kingston, Jamaica, now loading at...."

Jahbig grunts and growls and grabs Will into a fierce hug. "Okay, then, do it! If you be trusting my crazy stories—who knows why?— then I gotta trust you. But as soon as you hit New Mexico and I San Fra'cisco, we're going to take flying lessons and buy a plane and visit and visit each other and—. Shit, what am I saying? We ain't gonna be able to afford jack-shit for years. Gotta go—."

Will, over the heads of the masses: "I'll be here when you get back. Call me. I'll pick you up. We'll talk about it."

Over his shoulder as he steps into the electronic terrorist-sniffer, "Sounds like it's a done deal to me. Blessings on you, brother!" Gone.

Will watches his buddy go. *I feel like a damn fool. He knows I don't know what I'm doing...or why. Or maybe I do. He even looked like he had confidence in my decision. Was it a real decision? When did I make that decision? Last week. Last night. Five minutes ago. Let's run down that logic again. What logic? I don't remember a damn thing. What did that C-section have to do with anything, any-*

how? I'm an idiot. No, I'm not. Jah doesn't truck with idiots. There-
fore, I'm not one.

12

The Future Thinks Mirriamma

"She's coming. Anybody else coming?"

"Gladys' sister, with her two sets of twins."

"Anybody else?"

"Victor is taking some Washington big-wigs to some doings over to the Mirabals."

"Governors do this. They aren't the real doings anyway."

"Who else?"

"The new doctor. We're gonna get a new doctor. I'm happy about that. For all my grandkids, you know."

"The new doctor. Yes."

"An' you say she's really coming. Soon, you think? Anabelle's daughter. Anabelle was my cousin, on the good side."

"Wynema. Yes, she's coming. I always liked her. But I couldn't always figure her out. Lot of people coming. Better than a lot of people going away. How many of us are there left anyway?

"I hope my son brings me that toilet paper. I'm addicted to it now."

13

SISTER MOUNTAIN TO MT. EVEREST

There's full-full-moon directly overhead, which can only mean it's around midnight. It's brighter tonight than a dark overcast day. She's walking by herself around the pueblo's plaza, past the church, the courthouse—across the simple foot-bridge that spans the little river that flows through the village. Wynema is on the phone, speaking to her advisor at Cambridge, England.

"...I'm surprised and happy and very grateful. I know it's a strange request—"

Her advisor, an Irish woman with a lilting accent: "When we finally understood the kind of work that you were doing there, well, we feel it's in everyone interests for you to pursue it, as you say, a bit longer. I hope when you come to us next year, you will be the better for it and share with us what you can."

"Thank you, Miss Danforth. I really would only do this if you gave me your blessings. I shall take good notes. I believe I can relate it to my work at the fellowship—"

"We're hopeful, too, and want to express our confidence in your work, there now and when you join us here. Congratulations on the positive report from your dissertations committee."

"Thanks."

"Good-bye then."

The digital air goes dead.

The midnight air at the plaza comes alive. Deep alive. Colors shoot through the moonlight and bounce softly off the round corners of the adobe buildings. Fireflies. *There are no fireflies in northern New Mexico.* Soft distant music—drum, rattle and gourd. But she knows there is nothing but silence here. Everyone is asleep, and she is cold.

She shivers. But it is hot tonight, almost humid. She turns with a start. Someone. Something. An animal. A wolf. Slowly approaching. She stares at it. *There are no wolves in New Mexico.* It is nothing. Even the air is still. She smiles. She feels for her pulse at her carotid. She can't find it. Wait a minute! Is that it? That slow? A heart doesn't beat that slow. But it is. Her breathing is long. Her heart is slow. She is cold.

So she sits down on a log bench. Her eyes slowly look up at the moon. Finally, she smiles and lowers her eyes.

June 20. Months later, not weeks. She isn't restless at all. She doesn't know it, but now she can quiet herself, make herself small, and fly. She is two thousand miles from New York City—*Alána, you were right. I miss you. I miss you*—and walks with her great-aunt out onto the low hip of the mountain that protects the Pueblo from the harsh northern weather. They peer down upon their village, on the multi-storied adobe building complex that had no architect, no plans, no permits, no red-tags. Maybe two-hundred rooms in a hundred distinct structures. Perhaps another hundred in the surrounding, outlying houses—*the middle class.* They see the yards and corrals, the gardens, the irrigation canals that have withstood a thousand years of Utes and Comanches from the plains to the east, Navajos from beyond the gorge to the west, Spaniards from the south, mountain-men from the north, the Euro-American land rush, and the seductive gifts of modern science. *Were they gifts really? What is the nature of a true gift?*

Wynema turns and speaks. "I came here for a week."

Mirriamma touches her hand. "Seven days, seven years, seven decades—they all go by so quickly, you know."

"It's almost seven months. Are you holding me here against my will—you know, by some magic?"

The old woman laughs. She points to a man far-away and tiny below, near the outskirts of the village, shuffling along with a stitch near a corn patch.

"Who's that?" asks Wynema.

"Oh, that's Simon."

"Of course. His is the last cornfield over there. From up here, I—"

"His corn is weak again this year. He's very worried." The old woman shifts her weight then leans on her walking stick.

"Do we know why his corn is having trouble?"

Mirriamma's hands are remarkable. They are always moving or her fingers intertwined, like antennae—she senses with them. She doesn't speak with them, but she listens with them acutely. She laughs again, then answers:

"There are things we can know. There are other things that—well, that never become knowledge. Only experience. Like love affairs." Again she laughs, as if she were quite taken with herself.

The two women sit now upon their haunches and look out across the ten-mile expanse that reaches to the deep canyon carrying the Rio Grande River at the bottom. After a while, Wynema asks, "Is there mullen hereabouts?"

"Mullen? *Doesn't grow here*. But a woman doctor from—" She tries to remember. "—from Wales, maybe. Anyway, she visited me once and brought me some of that. I used it twice. Works good. How come you want it?"

"Margaret Tafoya. She has a cough she can't get rid of. Thought I have her make a tea?"

"Have her smoke it."

"She has a cough and you want her to inhale some smoke?!"

Mirriamma takes forever to turn her head and look at her great-niece and let a little smile creep out.

"Okay, okay, I'll have her smoke it, but only a little."

"That's all it will take."

They turn to the west. They see how the mesas ride in crisscrossing like waves pummeled by competing winds. How they approach the heartland where the Pueblo lies at the foot of the tallest mountain in the region. Mirriamma points with her thumb up over behind her. "They ever tell you the name that mountain behind us?"

"Walker Peak? I know it's sacred to our tribe. And our name for it is...*Mon'gatcho*. Is that right?"

"*Mon'ga'ticho*. Your mama taught you that. Good."

"Actually, Mama taught it to Beaver-Goes-Backward, my father, and he, with his crazy Sioux accent, told me its *Mon'gatcho*."

"That name is way older than our tribe. Way older than any tribe."

"Let me ask you this, Grandmother. Is it only a coincidence that the sister mountain to Mt. Everest—"

"In Tibet, yes, I know—"

"...it's called by the Tibetans *Mahn'gatchu?*"

Mirriamma has to stand up and stretch herself out. "You're sayin' that's kinda strange, huh?"

Wynema stands. "Well, it's a heluva coincidence."

"As my grandfather would say when I discovered something wonderful, '*Ya-na-neh ha-way-yo*'."

"What's that mean?"

"'This is connected to that.' Big mountains like to talk to other big mountains. Like that."

As they start their trek down the slow slopes of the mountain, they see Simon disappearing into a grove of willow that grows thick besides the water canals, the *acequias* and the smaller *sangrias*.

Mirriamma points with her mouth. "That's Simon. Now you see him, now you don't."

⁓

When she goes to bed tonight, Wynema will call Alána and try to explain how it is that she's remained here so long. At least she'll try. It will be harder to explain why she spoke with the officials at Cambridge and got them to defer her Fellowship one year.

"Are you mad, my darling?! Should I immediately come out there and save your ass?"

"No, just be patient. Something's unfolding."

"Unraveling?"

"No, revealing itself. It's more interesting than I expected."

⁓

Young woman and old pause at the last promontory before the steeper descent on a path that narrows as it enters a cool stand of trees next to a creek.

"*This should be enough*," says Wynema in her mother's tongue. "*Why am I restless? Nervous even sometimes.*"

"*It is good*," says Mirriamma softly. "*Alert, like the owl at night.*"

"*Takho?*"

"Alert."

"Alert!? I feel confused, small, empty—"

"Ah, 'empty', that's good, too."

"Good!?"

"Empty is a good place to start," says Mirriamma in English. "Be sure and pronounce the *tuó-makh* for 'empty' with the accent on the 'o'."

Wynema nods, locking it in. "If I had stayed here instead of leaving ten, eleven years ago, you would have taught me these things—"

"You've forgotten nothing. We taught you the beginnings of these things. They are just hidden—" Mirriamma taps her head. "—Like some boxes in your garage. But they are not gone. And you had other things to learn in other places. Ten years. It's nothing. It's good." The older woman moves gracefully down the narrow path into the trees.

When they exit the trees, they find their banged-up pickup and get in and just sit there for a while listening.

"Sometimes we learn things before we are taught them."

Wynema's eyes narrow. "Tell me why you really called me back here."

"It is good to clean one's tube no matter what you decide to do."

"I came for a week!"

"That's how long you thought it would take."

"To do what?"

"Whatever you thought you wanted to do."

"But you were the one who called me! Well, you were right, somehow I did remember how my mother described the colors and the textures of the costumes the men wear in the Dance. And with a little help from you I was able to describe it in the old language. Amazing."

"You can't describe the same thing twice in two different languages."

"I'm sure you're right. It's just that right now my brain hurts. This is harder than grad-school."

"*Ya-na-neh ha-way-yo.*"

Wynema laughs once hugely to herself. "There's something happening here, Grandmother."

"Yes there is."

"My mama died when I was fourteen. I finished high-school as fast as I could. And then I left. My papa needed me and I left the Pueblo never to return. How did you know you even wanted me to come back."

"You told me."

"What?! I? How? When?"

"In my dreams. Was there a big elm tree maybe not far from where you lived, right?, that you like to climb much higher than you knew was safe?"

"It was an maple tree. You saw that?"

"Only in the morning. During my morning naps. That was my best time for making contact."

"Contact?"

"You talked to me."

"I did?"

"Well maybe you were talking to the tree, I don't know."

Wynema scrunches down with a lot of concentration behind the wheel and holds on for dear life and remembers many things.

Five minutes later, Mirriamma: "We can go home now."

14

WHO OWNS THE LAND?

On the other side of the village, a dusty silver-gray BMW sedan rolls slowly to a stop across the street from the old woman baking. A man gets out. He is very tall, a European-American as young as his smile. He points to her oven, then makes the universal gesture for eating.

The woman doesn't smile but she nods and holds up three fingers. She picks up a loaf of hot bread and hands it to the young man who finds it very difficult to extract three dollars from his pocket and express his gratitude while holding a hot loaf. The woman is awed by the man's height.

Back at his car, he tears off a piece, still juggling the hot loaf, and eats it immediately. Finally, he gets back into his car and sits there with his eyes closed and smells the bread and eats another piece with great joy and pleasure. Will Kornfeld, M.D. has made his decision with the help of a good friend and a bar-coaster found in a Greenwich Village jazz joint, and he's here, to start his first post-residency doctor job. *Halavai!*, as his grandfather might say—Behold!

As he savors the bread and looks out at everything: *We are all just dreams in a bigger dream. We dream our dream as the big dream dreams us. We cannot know the big dream's dreamer, no more than the red blood cell coursing through our veins can know us. We cannot know the Universe, the One that contains us all. But as the red-blood cell is a part of us, just so are we a part of the One. We are among the tiniest shards of a hologram. As above, so below, but with greatly diminished clarity or resolution. Still, it's all there. So...blessings!*

He reaches quickly into his pocket for notebook and pen. "I gotta write that down." It will take him forty-five minutes to write something down. And then he will crumple it up and throw it away into the little black nylon trash bag hanging from the cubbyhole lock.

⁂

At a break in a piled-stone fence, Simon stops and squats, his back to the wall. He takes the turkey-bone whistle from his shirt pocket and blows the sound of a hawk. Seconds later, Rio Ortiz, six-years-old, and another little boy pop up from behind the wall, looking skyward.

When Rio sees Simon, he reaches out for the whistle. *"Please, Grandpa," pleads the boy in Pueblo, "let me try. Let me try it."*

As Rio blows on the whistle, three teenage boys, too happy not to be stoned or drunk or both, bounce by in a dilapidated station-wagon. The boy riding shotgun, Dayone Moquino, Simon's grandson, is sixteen and brandishes a small, aluminum baseball bat out the window like a sword.

Dayone and Simon's eyes meet and lock as the car passes then skids to a stop.

Ruben Montoya, the driver, is Dayone's best friend. "Dayo, I want to try that whistle."

"Aw, man,' wines Dayone, "I don't want to talk to my grandfather. Le's go."

"C'mon, *coyo*, I never played one even when I was a kid."

Dayone sticks his arm out the window, slowly waving a red pack of gum. Rio runs quickly to the window whereupon Dayone grabs the whistle and gives up the gum. Dayone makes the whistle scream, then hands it to Ruben. The teenager in the middle lets out a howl.

Ruben tests the stops and the angle to his mouth and he gently blows. He doesn't make it scream at all. Dejected, Simon turns away just as *his* best friend, Teo Vigil, steps through the fence.

"I heard your whistle. But who's that?" he asks, pointing to the station wagon with his chin, listening to the sounds of drumsticks on the dashboard and tentative riffs from the whistle. "Your grandson?"

With his shoulders and a sigh, Simon says "I don't know and I don't care".

"You comin' in to have some chili, ain't ya?"

Simon nods wanly and follows.

Teo is a quiet man, thinks Simon, *but there is a fire in him. He talks to the Grandfathers, I'll bet. I wouldn't wanna get him angry. His anger is a just anger. And nothing's mixed in with it. It's good to learn from younger men. And he doesn't shun me. If he judges me, I don't seem to mind. When my Dahyanee died, he was only a boy but he stayed at my side and shared my grief and my fear and my need for someone.*

Teo wears a well-worn, black-watch wool shirt and a big Zuni silver in-lay buckle to protect his navel. They are like brothers separated by enough years to make people wonder how fertile and strong the woman who birthed them both must have been. But they are not blood. Same Pueblo. Same time and space. Deepest trusting clan-brothers. Teo knows this. Simon knows this. Teo is Rio's grandfather.

Teo likes it when Simon comes for dinner or to watch DVDs. Teo thinks that when he is around his friend he reaches deeper inside himself. He knows that Simon is a wise man inside a crushed man. So Teo is patient. He waits because he knows his friend is suffering and is going to take a long time to heal. But heal he will. Teo knows this. Simon does not know this. But he is about to learn. When he does, Teo thinks, they will celebrate for a week!

He and Simon look up as a big black sedan pulls up slowly not far away.

"C'mon," Dayone shouts, "my father! Ruben, le's get outta here!"

This time he rolls out a maniacal riff of warning off the dashboard. The station-wagon's tires spin and spit back gravel from which everyone has to protect themselves with hands and arms.

Rio runs to Simon, feeling awful for losing the whistle. Simon and Teo just look from one vehicle to the other.

"Victor's back," says Teo flatly.

Simon doesn't even look. "He's got a new muffler. Can you hear?"

The driver is Victor Moquino, the current governor of the pueblo. He is thickly built, powerful in personality, charismatic, wary. He wears a clean white shirt, a narrow yellow tie, and sunglasses. There is an open briefcase beside him and the news is on the radio. He points with concern to the disappearing station-wagon. "That my son in there! Was that my son?"

But he doesn't wait for an answer. Like most politicians, he is more interested in compliance.

"Hey, you know, Teo, the Mescalero Apaches, I visited them on my way back from Washington. They got another $200,000 dollars. Just for doing that government study."

"I heard," says Teo turning to Simon with disgust. "For storing nuclear waste."

Victor's smile disappears. "No. It's good you don't know. Because now as a Council member you must understand. Here's what's so interesting. It's only a grant," he intones, emphasizing certain words, "to study the feasibility of a potential site for nuclear waste. It's free money. We can design in good faith the study so it goes our way. We can do or not do whatever we want with it. Twenty-four other tribes have already applied. But we have a better chance than most of them. Do you know why?"

Simon answers quickly. "Because we are Borg and resistance is futile?"

"I like that show, Simon. No. Because our land is stable."

"Our land is holy," hisses Teo.

Victor is unfazed. "For years they took from us. Now it is time we took from them." Then, lying, he says, "After years of bingo, we fought for and obtained the casinos. We thought we'd make lot of money with them. We made some, I admit that, but not what we thought we would. Not what we thought was ours."

Teo isn't impressed. "Free money, huh? One or two of these reservations is gonna 'win' some radioactive poison for their land. Goody."

Victor taps the windowsill of the passenger's window. "We've had this conversation before." He drives away.

Teo spits and watch his spit hit the ground and raise a puff of dust. "Victor's gonna run for Governor of the Pueblo again next year—."

"Maybe the state," cuts in Simon.

"You can smell it."

Simon kicks up a little dust with his boot. "My son-in-law is ambitious. Very popular these days to be ambitious."

Rio and his friend stuff their mouths with a second piece of gum then run through the opening into the backyard. Simon follows Teo onto his two acres of land. Five hundred yards away the pueblo rises up through the dust like a cubist scarecrow.

᳇

There are dirt roads running down the flattened land that spider out from the large, central structures of the pueblo, that divide up the village into irregular, mostly one- or two-acre parcels. They are not owned exactly; they are not rented. They are given to a family by the Pueblo Council to use so long as the family stays in good standing with the tribe. There are responsibilities and traditions....

Two acres is a lot of land, if you work it.

A hundred years ago almost everyone lived in the main structure. Only during the summer months did people venture away to their outlying parcel, up to ten miles away, where they kept horses, cattle, and sometimes sheep in simple corrals, and especially where the family garden was. Families with a little more means tend to live on these plots permanently now, in adobe houses that are simple, but not primitive by any standards.

Teo's family hasn't lived in the main structure for fifty years. His father built the three-bedroom adobe house that he and his family now live in. He has added a good-sized workshop off to the side of his house. Half of the workshop is 'outside' under a corrugated fiber-glass roof. A ramada. The other half is lockable, where he stores his tools and supplies. This is where Teo crafts ritual drums and traditional instruments, not as mere tourist items, but for serious traditionalists from tribes all over the United States, Canada, Alaska, even Africa. His work is highly respected and brings the best prices. He has a website.

᳇

Near a picnic table under a large piñon tree not far from the backdoor of the house, a middle-aged woman slowly brushes flies away from the food that is laid out there. Teo's daughter and Rio's mother, Jolene, in her mid-twenties, carries a heavy crock pot filled with chili and places it on the table. Jolene is six-months pregnant and very happy about it. Now Rio will have a brother or a sister. This is good. No woman on the Pueblo more than Jolene dreams about fantasy worlds of wonder, paradises blessed with every sweet thing, places you run and laugh and dance through without a care in the world—pictures of health and harmony and joy before the happy fact of life itself.

That's Jolene. She doesn't talk very much. But people like to be next to her. Sometimes they bring over their sewing just to sit quietly and work next to her whatever Jolene is doing. And sometimes Jolene will read favorite passages from her books on fantasy if you ask her. Young girls have started to come by and sit right next to the older women, listening to the stories. When she's not here or at her home with her husband Jerry and their son Rio, or dancing in the plaza, she's helping out with chores at Mirriamma's. That's Jolene, pregnant with their long-awaited brother or sister for Rio.

Not far from where Teo and Simon sit, Sotero Lujan, slight, angular, unassuming, closer to a hundred than ninety, rocks back and forth in a rusty and creaky garden chair. He's telling two girls a story in the old language.

"...They couldn't help themselves. They were too heavy now to move. So one by one the giants popped them into their mouths and ate them. But Wakhmatu, who hadn't eaten a thing, quietly slipped away."

Rio and his friend, eager to listen, run up and give sticks of gum to the girls and Sotero. The wizened man with wild almost goofy eyes motions the kids to come closer, to hear the end of the story, a secret story and meant for nobody else's ears. "*Come, sit, hurry, be still....*"

Teo shows Simon a drum he has just completed. Simon inspects it carefully showing it respect. Not far away, Jerry Ortiz, Jolene's husband, is stretching a deer hide on a well-worn willow frame his grandfather, a Diné, had given him.

Teo points again at the drum. "That one came out good. You know who ordered that one? Somebody from the White House. I'm not kidding. The President, what's-his-name, his assistant in charge of decorations, he ordered that one."

Teo knows the names. It's just his way of maintaining the distance, with unfamiliarity.

"What you think about that?" asks Simon.

"Yeah, right," muses Teo. "Damned if you do, damned if you don't. I am ashamed to tell you how many hundred percent more than regular retail I'm charging him."

"Teo, come! Simon, good to see you!" Tessie, Teo's wife, is calling them from the back door. She wears a colorful skirt she bought at Wal-Mart and, with praises to White Buffalo Woman, is as pregnant as her daughter Jolene.

Teo and Simon join the others at the picnic table. As always Simon sits farthest away from everybody, whatever the situation. People often make sure the furthest away seat is left for him.

Teo still nurses his disappointment and bitterness. He leans towards Simon. "Victor's 'free money' is a bad thing, ya know that."

"You're bitter."

"Duh."

"Maybe we'll survive," Simon says, "Pueblo roots go deep."

"Yes of course," admits Teo, "but there are changes. They make me worry."

"No, they make you think. When things change, someone better be thinking."

"Yes, okay, but look at our youngsters." After a pause. "Your grandson, Dayone."

Simon cannot stop his face from darkening. He nods. They sit. Teo silently offers Simon a jar with a spoon in it. "Chokecherry jam. Delia Armijo made it. Good."

Thinking of his grandson, "He's an angry boy."

Teo is sorry he brought it up. "Hey, what about your cornfield? Any better?"

Simon grinds his thinking around, until, "The right moon. Summer rain. I didn't dance but I prayed. I shoulda danced. And Grandfather Snake came to me today. I usually know what my corn is trying to tell me. It grows, it talks, I listen. But...something's wrong. Even Snake wouldn't tell me."

"You'll figure it out."

"No!" Then more softly. "This is different!"

Surprised by the outburst, Teo offers Simon a doughnut. Simon declines.

"Hey, how about coming to Council meeting and stand up with me against Victor?" There is a long silence. "I'm asking."

Simon slowly puts his palms face out in front of him. "Not my way. Not my road."

Teo's thoughts drift...until with pursed lips he points to Sotero. "The children and now even Jerry, who doesn't speak our language, listen again and again. Heh. That story Sotero is telling them, he told that same story to me almost 50 years ago. I was Rio's age. It's a classic all right. If it weren't for the old stories, our language would blow away in the wind."

Both rise and slowly walk over behind the eager listeners.

With a gesture, Sotero draws the children in closer. "*But these Ogres, these T'ai-kár-nin, were big as giants, stronger than five strong men...and they had an appetite only for human babies...baby young, baby brown, and baby very fat. And when they came, they took away the babies to their caves far to the west in the hills of Kú-Mai. The babies cried so loud, even the moon turned to listen. But—that wasn't enough. Tomorrow I will tell you how a very clever mother saved all the children, so that the T'ai-kár-nin began to starve and wear their belts so loose that their pants fell down.*"

The children laugh. Jolene brings Sotero chili, fry bread, celery and peanut-butter, and iced tea. Rio runs to Simon, who ruffles the boy's hair.

*

A few minutes later, on his way to the bathroom, Simon notices mother and daughter in the kitchen. Tessie is cleaning up at the sink. Jolene steps up next to her and they both look out the window and find themselves taking a deep sigh and rubbing the small of their aching backs at the same time. They catch each other and burst out laughing.

*

At that very moment, in an open space between the Plaza and the entrance road to the Pueblo, next to the bridge that crosses the creek that runs down from the flanks of the mountain and through the plaza, three teenage boys are shooting a basketball into a basketless hoop. Not far away standing next to his car Will watches with interest. With pluck and enthusiasm he asks with a gesture if he can play.

Before the older and shyer of them can turn and leave, the youngest runs up to Will indicating that now the teams are even.

They play. Will is amazed how he can feed the ball to the 13-year-old in a way that baffles the older boys. More amazing is that the kid then has just enough time to shoot and if he doesn't make it Will is there to tap it in. Will thanks the kid each time for the shot or the assist. They take turns hammering each other's fist in celebration. The two older boys don't know who's more amazing, the white giant or their little brother.

Teo and Simon approach the benches in the workshop area. Teo sighs as he picks up the core of another roughly hollowed drum-to-be. But his thoughts are elsewhere. Suddenly, he sets it back down and rushes off. "I forgot something," he says, ae goes to a wicker table nearby and retrieves a parcel. But before he hands it to Simon, he asks, "But what if Corn is trying to tell you to come back to your people? That happened to my uncle Tenorio once."

Simon's jaw goes tight. "Don't get ahead of me, little brother."

Teo stiffens then softens then hands Simon the package. Simon slips out a book and reads the cover.

Teo's apologetic. "Post Office got that over a week ago, all ripped open. You never go there so Sally down there asked me to give—"

Simon reads from the title page. *Smoke Poems: a Book of Explosions by Frank Zamora*. "Is my son getting more famous?"

"Guess so. Teenagers here sorta idolize him. You seen the book yet anyway?"

Simon shakes his head and slips the book into his shirt. "My son says he's fighting for the old ways. I don't know about that. How he can do that in New York night clubs—how he gonna do that? I dunno. Maybe my son's a ghost dancer who fights with magic words. You read this yet?"

Teo nods solemnly. "I did. Jerry bought me a copy. Good title."

Simon pats Teo's shoulder as he gets up to go. "Guess I better get back to the Clinic. Got some shrubs to plant there."

Simon drives slowly in his rusted-out Chevy-6 pickup. A huge jackrabbit bounds across the road in front of him. A coyote hot on the chase. "Heh-heh-heh. You never get him unless you got friends over there waiting in ambush. Heh."

15

FEDEX FROM ISRAEL

At the edge of the reservation, the Wind River Trading Co. More for tourists than locals, more of a gallery than old-time general store. This rustic, reservation-rough boutique is situated where the state highway passes the road onto Indian land: five miles to San Lucas, another ten to Santa Carmina. Here at the trading post, Indian, Spanish Colonial, vintage western or pioneer paraphernalia have been carefully placed inside and out for effect. Everything is for sale. The trader told his coke dealer that once, and the dealer said he pay for half the trader's mustache and laid down a benjamin on the counter. "A hundred bucks? Done!" And he took out a straight razor from the cabinet and cut off half his mustache. It was months before that grew back in. He kept asking people if they'd pay, even 50 bucks, for the other side, but no one took him up on it.

Will stands next to his vehicle, looking up the long, narrow dirt road toward the Pueblo. He is happy, he's stoked. He can hardly contain himself. Patting his BMW as if it were a horse, he heads into the trading post. Next door, adjacent to the trading post, a sign: U.S. Post Office, DOS PUEBLOS, N.M. 87526. He pulls the coaster from The Stalactite out of his shirt pocket. *Yup, 87526. This is the place.*

Inside, Will is impressed by the dark oiled or sun-bleached grey wood everywhere. Old glass-topped display cases filled with guns, knives, pottery, jewelry, *santos* (religious statues), *retablos* (painted icons), medicine bundles, fetishes, kachinas, moccasins, etc. Will glides through, enthralled, silently whistling. Behind the main counter, polishing a concho belt is a big, burly, thick-bearded man, the owner, the trader, Martin Phipps, closing in on 40. His clothes reflect cowboy, trapper, biker influences. He's an elusive, competitive, not-altogether-reputable Anglo, but a helluva survivor, and raconteur.

As Will wanders the shop, Phipps tracks him with a keen eye. Will examines things closely, appreciatively. Self-confident, almost swashbuckling, Will picks up a white-and-black-on-red pot. "Does each pueblo have a unique style?" he asks the trader.

"Yep, mostly. That's an Acoma pot. 'Bout 1910. Maybe ought-nine."

Will points to two small black-on-black bowls. "San Lucas and... Santa Clara?"

"Not bad. But just the other way 'round."

Will laughs, flicks his head, and saunters to a gun case. "Tell me something. Do Navajos come up here to trade...or sell their goods?"

"Sometimes. You lookin' for Navajo?"

"Nah...just lookin'. Whoa!" Will points into a showcase. "That one there is beautiful"

"Yup. Winchester '73, octagonal barrel. Carbine, with the original saddle ring."

"You mind if I heft it?"

Phipps opens the case ceremoniously, hands Will the rifle.

"You really a trading post?"

"All depends, pardner. What ya got?"

Will hands the rifle back to Phipps, holds up a finger, exits, the screen door creaking and slamming behind. Phipps turns his back and opens a tiny brown bottle with a tiny silver spoon attached to the cap. He quickly snorts a bit of cocaine into each nostril. He hears the door open and wipes his nose.

Will returns with a soft leather long-bag that he lays on the counter. He slowly draws out two ornate swords. "Sabers...Seventh Cavalry. 'Bout 1910...maybe ought-nine."

Knowing he's being twitted but impressed nonetheless, Phipps steps around the counter and picks one up. Hefts it, extends. Will picks up the other and steps into the opposing position. He salutes Phipps, then extends. Self-conscious, Phipps withdraws—then suddenly extends and lunges. Will, with a small, deft, lightning motion, parries and lays the flat of his point on Phipps' cheek. Phipps whistles out a breath, but is too macho to move. Simultaneously they become aware that someone has entered and now stands awe-struck just inside the door staring at the tableau.

Phipps slowly steps back. "Hey Doc! You're just in time to sew me up. This guy is dangerous."

Dr. Stephen Cutter is in his mid-fifties, a cardiologist by specialty, and soon to be Will's first Indian Health Service boss. He laughs. "That man can sew up anything he cuts."

Wheeling on Will. "I knew it! You're the new bandage-man."

Cutter rushes in to shake warmly Will's outstretched hand. "Hi. Steve Cutter. No jokes about my name from now on and we'll be cool. You're Will Kornfeld? Am I late?"

"No, I'm early. Drove through the Pueblo, you know, just checking things out before anyone knows who I am. Bought and ate a whole loaf of hot bread." He reaches for the saber. "I guess I'm not ready to trade yet."

With a slick move, Phipps hands it back, pommel first. "Slippery bastard."

"Watch out for Martin," drawls Cutter, "he's an outlaw. But every town needs its outlaw. Why don't we drive back to Panchita's and get a bite, then I'll introduce you at the Clinic. They're open today from two to five."

"Bullshit!" bellows Phipps. He sticks his head into the back room. "Put two more steaks on the fire, Sally."

Cutter looks from his watch to Will. Will shrugs, smiles.

Half an hour later, outside in a patio area behind the trading post, Phipps, loudly laughing, is turning steaks on a barbecue with a 14-inch bowie. Cutter, tibbling his margarita, eases back in a weathered, homemade juniper-stick garden chair.

Will, too energized, paces, drink in hand. "You know, there's an online network now that can connect me to epidemiologists all over the world. Wham! Info and data at the speed of light. Crucial. I—"

Phipps interrupts. He isn't hampered just because these men hold advanced medical degrees and he never graduated high school. "Hold on! I didn't ask about computers. I just want to know why anyone who just graduated from one of the best—"

"*The* best," Will corrects him, feeling the first effects of the tequila.

"—medical schools would come to a place like this."

Will stops pacing. The doctors, mellowed now, look blankly at each other.

Using his fingers to count the reasons Phipps continues, "There are only three, three possible reasons: One, to run away and hide. Two, because you have an intensely trendy interest in Indians. Or three," as he eyes Will keenly, "because like yer boss here you wanna be a big turd in a small latrine. No offense."

Phipps looks from one to the other, then bursts out laughing. Will smiles broadly, wryly, then starts to pace again. "That's good, Mr. Phipps. Who knows, maybe all of them. Or—maybe there's a fourth lurking that you...will...never know."

Outside, an hour later, Will exits with his sabers' long-bag. Cutter goes to his Lexus SUV and takes out a big manila envelope. Will stashes the long-bag in the BMW's back seat. Phipps, lingering in the doorway, barks to Will, "You're heading into Injun country now, Doc. Any relatives I should contact...if'n you're never heard from again?"

Ignoring him, Cutter hands Will the envelop. "Here's all your mail's been forwarded. And after you see the Clinic and meet the staff, I'll show you your condo in Santa Fe. It's primo. Way better than what I had when I first came here twenty years ago."

"Santa Fe?" Will is taken off guard. "But I thought I was going to live—"

Phipps claps his hands together loudly, then shouts into the store. "Sally! Don't you have an FedEx or some kind of overnight letter for Doctor Goldberg here?"

"Kornfeld," says Will. "I know, sounds a lot like Goldberg."

Cutter gets in his car and Will into his. "Follow me on in!" he shouts, as he takes off.

Phipps lumbers up and hands Will another envelope. "Hey, in your copious free time, stop by and I'll show you the real stuff." He pats Will on the arm and points after Cutter.

Will takes off.

"I think it's from outa country," shouts Phipps unheard.

Five miles from the Trading post, just past two adobe pillars that flank the road like sentinels guarding a great estate, the road T's—the right hand goes to San Lucas, five miles ahead; the left, to Santa Carmina, ten miles. San Lucas is closer to the mountains. Santa Carmina closer to the Rio Grande.

Cutter, then Will, turns right and disappears over a rise known to locals as Stop'em Hill.

After four point five miles of narrow but paved road, on the left, is San Lucas's new casino, called Lucky Lucy. Half-mile further is the Pueblo proper.

In terms of Indian casinos, Lucky Lucy is small. The parking lot here holds fifty cars, with room for five RVs. By contrast, the casino at Pojoaque Pueblo holds 300 vehicles and 25 RVs.

A little further on the right is San Lucas's Indian Health Service Clinic, a modern adobe designed with simple, functional charm and a newly paved parking lot not far from the main steps. A driveway through ancient elms leads to three older adobe buildings at the rear. Over a dozen patients—on the front steps, by their vehicles, in the shade of some cottonwood trees—wait for the clinic to open.

On the side of the Clinic, next to the driveway, Simon, who part-times as the Clinic's gardener, is on his knees, struggling to pull up a weed's thick root from a flower-bed. Tugging, he watches Cutter's Mercedes, followed by Will's BMW, drive past to the staff's small parking lot near the rear of the building.

Cutter steps out and stretches and waits for Will. He knows that the Clinic staff are waiting inside, all eager to see the new doc for the first time.

Will turns off his motor and opens the FedEx letter. His expression falls abruptly.

As Cutter steps over, "Bad news?"

"My grandfather. He's been diagnosed with a brain tumor and this is the report from his doctors in Israel. Dear God. Why didn't they call me?!"

Reaching through the open window, Cutter puts his hand on Will's shoulder. Will, his vibrancy fled, turns his gaze from the papers to Cutter. He speaks softly, mostly to himself. "He just moved maybe less than a year ago. He begged me to go with him. And now I've been on the fucking road for a week taking my own sweet time. Oh, shit! I know why they didn't call. I changed my cell carrier before I left and didn't tell anyone!" He looks back at the letter. "Ah geez, this doesn't look good!"

Cutter is truly moved. "Then there was no way for anyone to get hold of you, Will. You know, if you don't want to start work for another week, you can fly over there—someone'll cover for you. At least call." He points to the papers in Will's hands. "I'll bet there's a number in there somewhere."

Will looks again through the papers, thinking, not really thinking, feeling, not really feeling, imploding—.

16

BEING IN THE MOMENT

Wynema sits at Mirriamma's pottery-making table. She's on her cell.

"...Papa, you're saying Alána called you out of concern for me?! Why didn't she call me?!..." Wynema pokes at the lump of clay on the wheeling, wet and waiting. "I explained it to her, and I explained it to you. Do you think I made a mistake? Is that what you're saying?..." She unconsciously rubs her cheek, leaving a streak of clay that will dry hard and white. "I've been reading, and thinking, and corresponding with other women all over the world. Everything seems to be telling me to stay here a little bit longer. Can I call you tonight? I'm in the middle of something...." She smiles and pats the clay. "... Okay, thanks, Papa. I love you, too."

She sits there thinking....

Now she is rolling out the clay into long lengths she will soon coil up into a bowl. But the clay "ropes" are uneven and soon break. Wynema groans.

"Imagine," says the old woman approaching, "right from the beginning, that you got the tiniest speck of fire in the palm of your hand—" She puts her own hands together and rubs one slowly in circles against the other.... "—and you feel something grow all around the speck, but always in the middle you keep that speck of fire. If you don't—the clay won't know what you want." Mirriamma eyes the fallen mass. "No center."

Wynema sighs as she crushes the clay to start over. She wedges it again and takes a deep breath and relaxes her toes and finds the center. "I see the speck."

Will sits hunched in his car. He has someone in Israel on the phone. He listens, face contorted. Cutter stands close by the door.

Will hangs up. Can barely speak. "His system crashed—all of a sudden. Pressure on the medulla. He's in a coma, for the second time now. They think he will regain consciousness. The tumor is inoperable. Radiation out of the question." After a long pause, "He's been dreaming about going to Israel for fifty years. And now, nine months later, my grandfather is in a coma in his beloved Promised Land."

"Will, I know it doesn't look good, but think positively."

"You're talking to another doctor, Steve, not a patient. We know what this means."

"Follow me to Santa Fe, I'll show you your place and—"

"He's all the family I have—and he's eight-thousand miles away."

"Go to Israel. We've waited for you all through med school. We're lucky to have you. But we can wait another week, ten days, whatever it takes."

Will slowly pulls himself out of his car. As he stands and reveals his height, Simon, whom no one has noticed, on his knees and still pulling weeds, looks up...and up...at the young doctor's height, towering almost a foot above Dr. Cutter. Suddenly, the root of the stubborn plant he's been pulling breaks loose. Simon falls backward and winces in pain. He's cut his hand and it's bleeding. He picks up the cause: a long-buried arrowhead. He knits his brow and sucks a tooth. He looks from Will to the arrowhead then takes the bandana from his head and wraps his hand with it.

Will looks but doesn't really see Simon. All he sees is a bandana being wrapped around a bleeding hand. "But I can't do that to you," he says turning back to Cutter, "I'm supposed to start work—"

"We have five doctors working in Santa Fe. We'll each fill in for you one day during the week you're away. You can fly from Albuquerque, maybe one stop somewhere—Atlanta, New York—to Tel Aviv. You'll be there tomorrow. Go."

Will's head is spinning. "My God, how long have they known about this? How long has Grandpa known? Why didn't he tell me that something was wrong? A mid-stem tumor. Oh, Christ!" As he puts the papers back in the envelope, "No need to mention it to any-body here."

Cutter arm slowly arcs as he points to the Clinic. "Will, if there's one thing they understand better than anyone—"

"What? What's that?"

"—Grief."

Cutter waits patiently. Finally, Will turns and sighs. Cutter smiles softly, puts a hand on Will's shoulder.

"Either you're going to Israel, going to work right now, or taking the day off. What do you want to do?"

"I'll go and unload my stuff in Santa Fe and—" then indicating the Clinic, "—you tell them whatever you think is best. Israel. Oh, man, the continuity of Israel, from him to me—I let him down. He's been worrying this from the first minute he arrived—"

"Will. I don't know what you're talking about. But go. Be with him."

"The discontinuity. The differences between us. About the place of Israel—for Jews. He'll never forgive me." He looks down into Cut-ter's face. "I'm sorry, I—"

"Go."

⚜

Inside the Clinic, waiting impatiently, excited, even giddy, the staff cannot contain themselves. They've been waiting for weeks for this moment. Who will the new doctor be? What will he be like? Will he like us? Will we like him?

The clinic is bright and white. Everything is white. Fresh white. Patinated white. Repainted white. Peeling white. But there are colorful works of good Indian art placed neatly on a few of the walls. There are many healthy potted plants and hanging vines, all cared for by the dental assistant.

Lola goes to one of the front windows and peeks out, in spite of the loud whispers urging her not to. Lola Martinez is an LPN from neighboring Santa Carmina Pueblo, in her thirties, neat and attractive, short and stately plump. Not dumpy at all. "He's leaving! He's not coming in. He's going away! Here comes Dr. Cutter. Quick—"

"Quick what!? Oh, stop it everyone," says Louisa, as she opens the front door, but only a crack. "Why are we being so silly. Let me see what's going on."

Louisa Moquino is Victor's wife, an RN and the Clinic's Director for many years. She is graceful yet professional, and her eyes dart, indicating a cautious nature. She is decisive—except where her family is concerned. She is also Simon's daughter.

Rebeca Rael, the receptionist, is at her desk on the phone, talking under her breath to her counterpart and friend at Santa Clara's Clinic, expectantly waiting to describe the new doctor as he arrives. She is young, half Hispanic, and loves wearing her white uniform. Lola's "quick" forces her to hang up and step around her desk to see what's going on.

Cutter comes in, takes a deep breath, and looks at everyone in the room.

Rebeca gives Lola a little nudge and urges with a gesture to do something.

Lola in turn bends to Louisa who snaps a look urging Lola to be patient, but then quickly to Cutter, "Doctor?"

At first, Cutter is lost for words. "I, uh—I want to tell you that the doctor—you'll like the new doctor—but he just received—just a moment ago—some really sad news about his grandfather, whom he hasn't seen in a long time and who lives now in Israel. Well, Doctor Kornfeld was all fired up to meet you today and start work, but I gave him—I suggested that, uh, he hold off and go immediately to see his grandfather."

Everyone is moved. Louisa, swallowing hard, speaks for the rest. "Yes, yes, of course. Is he going to be all right? His grandfather?"

"His grandfather was just diagnosed as having a mid-brain tumor that's inaccessible, inoperable."

Rebeca rushes to Louisa's side to comfort her quietly.

"Listen," says Cutter, pointing to the patients waiting outside, "I can probably call my office and—that is, if you want me to stay and doctor today."

Louisa rushes to Rebeca's desk and looks at the schedule, considering....

A few minutes later, behind the clinic, Simon opens a garage door, full of gardening equipment and supplies. As he drags out a wheelbarrow filled with tools, a pain spikes him sharply under the ribs in the back. He steadies himself against the doorjamb. He hears Louisa's voice calling from the back door of the Clinic. She is putting out some trash.

"Papa! Don't move the heavy stuff. I want someone else to do that."

Simon straightens smiles and waves.

"Lot of patients today. Gotta go, Papa. Hey, is that your hand bleeding? Come in here and get it dressed. Right now."

Simon keeps on working.

"If you come in, I'll let Lola bandage it for you."

Simon drops his tools and brushes off his hands on his pants. "Why'd the new doctor drive off like that?"

"Doctor Cutter is covering for him. We'll be fine."

"You can tell me."

"He's afraid his father is dying. Brain tumor. I mean, his grandfather."

&

The sun is directly overhead. Mirriamma and Wynema sit in the shade of a ramada and look out over the Pueblo and the high desert beyond. The younger woman reaches for her black hemp shoulder bag and pulls out two Japanese folded fans. She snaps open one and hands it to Mirriamma. She opens the other for herself. As they fan themselves, the old woman stops and looks at the fan. "Pretty good." Then resuming fanning, "You were a 'feminints' or something. What's that mean?"

"Oh, feminist. It simply means fighting on all levels for equality between men and women."

"Oh, you mean like Sofie Naranjo at Santa Clara."

"Do I know her? I know the Naranjos. I wonder if she's related to Luanne."

"We're all related." She bursts out laughing raucously for a moment. "Luanne makes better pots than I do. Anyway, probably a cousin. She and her mother Nina convinced the Council to give women the vote on that Pueblo."

"Women here still don't vote, huh?"

"On Isleta and Laguna, they do. What time is it?"

Wynema looks at her watch. "Almost one. Why?"

"This time next year women will vote here. You watch. More changes coming. Some good ones, too."

"You're just saying that so I'll stick around. I told you, Grandmother, I have to go. They gave me a year to put it off. But a year—that in itself is amazing! I'll be the first Native American woman to ever get such a fellowship—at Cambridge—never been done. And for me, it's all aimed at getting women to be the main force behind making sign language the universal language."

"You mean like everyone in the world?"

"And it's going to happen through women. All over the world."

"Good idea. Somebody should do that."

"That's what I'm saying—I want to do it." Wynema is whispering loudly. "Sign language into the world of the hearing, the non-deaf! And it'll be the roots of feminism doing something else concrete—you know, not just protesting. Think of the benefits of a universal language that doesn't take away from anyone's spoken language. Imagine what it would mean to us! We could teach and speak our Indian among ourselves, learn English if we want to, but always have a way to talk to everyone, anyone!"

"Be nice on the ears. What's feminism have to do with signing?"

"I'm still working on that. But I know it's there."

Mirriamma suddenly laughs and looks at Wynema. "You know, if what you say happens there will be a time, maybe, when only women, all over the world, will be able to talk to each other this way. Only women. No men." She laughs again. "That will be a lot of fun."

"Yeah, could be cool."

"But it's only natural."

"Huh? What is?"

"I'll tell you a story about Beaver-Goes-Backward."

"My father!?"

"He had come to see my mother, to get some medicine for you."

"Me?"

"You were young, just having your first moon, and your mama, Anabelle, wanted to strengthen your blood. He came and got the medicine, and I asked him about a book he was reading. He was always reading some book. It was about evolution. He opened the book and found a place and read to me. I remember because it was about how humans learned to speak. Anyway, it was about how it was women around the campfire who learned to speak language first, you know, among themselves while the men were out hunting or something. I thought it was funny then, and I think it's funny now. Women speaking among themselves maybe for a thousand or ten thousand years, only them, not the men. Ha-hah-ha! I like that. Sorta, kinda like what you're talking about now with sign language, ain't it?"

Again, the two women look out across the desert towards the Rio Grande, fanning themselves slowly.

"You know," says Mirriamma, "we forget to remember the things we told ourselves never to forget." Then after another pause, "You know what good medicine is?"

Wynema turns and asks with a glance.

"Tricks to make us remember."

It takes a moment, but Wynema gets it. "What's great medicine then?"

Without missing a beat, Mirriamma replies, "Being in the moment."

"Sounds pretty New Age," says Wynema smiling.

"Sounds pretty Old Age to me."

Wynema takes a deep breath and closes her eyes.

Wynema opens her eyes. "How long have I been sleeping?"

"You weren't sleeping. You were traveling."

"C'mon, how long?"

"Maybe ten minutes."

"Just ten minutes?!"

"Did you dream?"

"I don't think so."

"Okay. How you like to drive up the canyon? Walk around a little. I think some friends of mine just showed up there. What you say?"

"Friends?"

"Flowers—and other creatures."

As Wynema stands her legs buckle, just a little. "Whoa! What happened to me. Feels like I've been asleep for days."

"Like I said, you been traveling. Wears a body out in no time."

Wynema rapidly shakes her arms, legs, neck—stretches. "Okay, I'm back. Let's go."

Mirriamma is jealous. "Kids. What strength. Recover so quickly. Not fair. I forget what it was like." She smiles, reflects, "But I think I liked it."

17

KEEP ALL THE OPTIONS OPEN

As soon as Will touches down in Tel Aviv, he calls the hospital.

"...Yes, this is Doctor William Kornfeld, Abraham's grandson. ... Yes. I just arrived in Israel, five minutes ago. ...He what?! ...That's great! When? ...My God." He looks at his watch. "...I'll take a taxi as soon as I pass through Customs. Thank you. Oh, God, thank you!"

Will has no difficulty in finding a taxi. He steps in and sees that the taxi-driver is wearing a cowboy hat, a well-worn but once fairly good one. "Ramat-Aviv Medical Center, please."

As they blast away out of the airport, the driver asks through the rear-view mirror, "You a gringo?"

"You mean an American, a Yank? Yes. But I imagine you get a lot of us here."

"Well, we shore do. Get a lot of greenhorns from all over the world."

The driver has that unmistakable Israel accent when speaking English. No one pronounces the word "world" in quite the way Israelis do. It's unmistakable. But it's tortured even more by his attempting a 'cowboy accent' at the same time. "I'm Israeli by birth—never been to America—but both my parents were American, from Texas. I could claim American citizenship if I wanted to."

Will isn't charmed at all. "I don't know, these days, it's not what it used to be. Maybe Sweden or even Costa Rica, which has weather a lot like Haifa. No, maybe more tropical. Let me ask you something, Tex, okay? How do you feel about what your country is doing to the Palestinians?"

"Whoa, pardner! You go right for the jug'ler there."

"I don't have much time. A week maybe, and I want to know how Israelis feel and think about the situation. Is it inappropriate to ask?"

"You're going to die in a week?! What you got?"

"No, I'm not dying! I'm only going to be in Israel for one week. Then I have to leave. It's all the time I seem to have...for finding out."

"You want an answer to that question and everything else to happen all in one week? Fair enough. Settle back. In this traffic it's going to take forty minutes to the hospital." He is forced to brake and swerve and rolls out the expletives.

Will cocks his head. "That sounded like Arabic. Was that an Arab back there?"

"No. It was an old Jewish lady. Idiot! But I don't curse in Hebrew, and my cowboy cussing is pretty limited. Teach me some."

"Does everybody cuss in Arabic?"

"'Fraid so, whippersnapper."

"Sounds racist to me."

"Ain't sayin' it ain't. I don't mean nothin' by it though. Lots of my friends are Arabs."

Will thinks for a moment, then offers, "A cowboy would say 'A-rabs', like the letter 'A' sounds." Will shakes his head—at himself. He doesn't believe he just told him that.

"A-rabs. Yeah, that sounds good. Much obliged."

"So you don't mind if I ask?"

"About the Palestinians?"

"Well, really more what you think about your government's policies."

The driver is silent for a while.

"You're asking the wrong person. I'm you could call schizophrenic."

Will says nothing. The driver continues.

"Well, maybe I'm multi-personality disordered."

"Go on. The meter's running."

"Some days I wake up and I'm a Jew with a history. Other days I wake up and I'm a Jew with a future. When I'm this way, I look back. When I'm that way, I look forward. When I look back I'm afraid. When I look forward I'm also afraid."

"So what's the difference?"

"Ah-ha! You see, it all depends on what I fear. When I look back, I want to have a strong military presence, lot of muscle, the power to say 'what you do to me to hurt me, I will do to you a hundred times worse, and will continue to do that until you stop hurting me'. When I look forward, I want to have faith in democracy, that people can live together in peace and justice. But no matter which way I look, I'm afraid. *Fershtaist?*—as my grandfather would say."

"*Ya, yich fershtaien,* as my grandfather would say."

Will is silent for a while...until, "So tell me, which way makes you feel better? Looking forward or back?"

"Are you a lawyer?"

"No, a doctor."

"Good thing you're not an Indian chief."

Will laughs courteously. "Why you say that?"

"Because then probably you'd scalp me—hah-ha-ha!" The driver quickly becomes serious. "All right, I'll tell you. I wish I could believe in democracy. But our elders who are older and wiser, they carry the burden of protecting *Eretz Yisrael*, the land of Israel."

"They may be older, but what makes you think they're wiser? Couldn't it be that they're so hurt and afraid and angry themselves that they've become irrational in their hatred for what was done to them—to us, the Jews?"

"Listen, my friend. You ever been to Israel before?" He sees Will looking in the mirror.

"Once. For a few days, about nine months ago."

The driver shakes his head. "Then what do you know—what do you really know—about the Arab—the A-rabs? You don't. You don't know much. Isn't that true?"

Will doesn't answer. *If I answer that,* he thinks, *I admit to him that I know nothing. As Jah says, 'When in doubt, think about the question while looking the other guy straight in the eye.' So that's what I'm going to do. Ah, there, he sees me in the mirror.*

"Are you trying to point out how much I know or how little?" Will asks gently. "All I suggested was that those in power today suffered so much in their lives that their suffering has—well, has warped their wisdom. And the proof? It's clear that what they're not doing does not serve their long-time interests. What was Einstein definition of insanity?"

"And all I asked you was how well do you know the Arabs."

For five minutes neither speaks.

Will is imagining two lines in space—two lines that will never meet. Now he sees two lines meeting head on, and stopping, and never moving again, until they turn blue, then gray, then nothing. He sees two lines that do meet, then combine, then move off in a new direction, somehow merging together—

"You working, or going to a conference or something, at the hospital?"

"—Huh? No, I—my grandfather is a patient there."

"I'm sorry, okay. I hope he's better soon. Oh, and you should know that you're driving with a person who knows more about Hollywood westerns than any other person living in Israel today. What was the name of Tonto's horse?"

"No clue."

"Little Beaver."

"Well, that changes everything," says Will as he pays the man and steps out in front of the Ramat-Aviv Hospital.

The driver reaches into the cubbyhole and pulls out a little white cloth bag and hands it to Will.

"What's this?" asks Will.

"A bit of *Eretz Yisrael*—some dirt from the Wailing Wall. For you, nothing, a gift. Keep your powder dry, *compañero*."

"*Todah rabah*."

"*B'vakashah*."

Simon is sitting on his haunches at the edge of his cornfield, a brown paper bag on the ground next to him. He picks up a handful of dirt and smells it.

As he walks down the hospital corridor, following a woman in a pink uniform, Will is trying to read a text-message from Jahbig on his iPhone: 'Questions to ask'. "Right on, Jah."

They turn to the left down a long and busy high-tech corridor.

Will's thoughts shift—to the promises he made to himself about what and what not to talk about with his grandfather. He shakes his head. *How do I avoid talking about Israel in Israel?*

She leads him to the ICU, to his grandfather's private room. Since the curtains are drawn, most of the light in the room here comes from all the instruments connected to a man who just came out of a coma.

I wonder, thinks Will, *if the word 'coma' is a cognate to the word 'cama' meaning bed.*

The nurse leaves the doctor to be with his grandfather.

He moves next to his Zeyda. *Sleeping so peaceful*, he thinks, *not in a coma, but relaxed and letting the body heal itself, always seeking to heal itself, homeostasis, a return to balance.* His eyes trace all the wires and tubes back to their command centers. He knows what each one does. *They're all here. All our tools. All our tools.* That phrase echoes in his head.

He puts his hands out in front of him. About a foot above his grandfather. He looks at his hands, he turns them over, he stretches and flexes his fingers. He moves his hands back and forth slowly above his grandfather's body. He smiles and closes his eyes and feels peace towards his grandfather he loves so much—.

"What are you doing?!"

Will looks down at his grandfather whose eyes are open.

"You're a faith healer now?!" says Abraham. "That's what I spent for your education my money on?"

∾

Simon is still squatting at the edge of his cornfield. But now, empty paper bag next to him, he is reading his son's book.

From Kansas to Iowa
Nebraska to Ohio
the corn-gut of America
stretches green patience
enslaves the Earth

Run your hands in it —
mechanized motorized
chemicalized pesticized —

we force our Mother to produce
whether she wants to or not

If this or that
ten thousand acre
plot does well
your commodity futures
are assured

But a master corn grower
among native peoples
growing a native plant
for native reasons
all interconnected
in a fabric
like a living book
tells us
how to live better
braver wiser lives

To watch a native
corn grower work
you must get down
on your knees

Simon rocks his head back and forth slowly considering the poem.
The rock shifts to a nod. "On your knees...and pray," he says out-
loud. *Not too angry, that one,* he thinks.

Will quickly pulls his arms away. "You're awake!"

"Why shouldn't I be awake? Favileh, it's you! You've come! I told
Dr. Grossman, just a minute ago, that you'd come and we'd figure
this out."

Will bends over and they kiss each other on the cheek. Abraham
can use one arm and holds Will to him.

"I'm so glad to see you," the grandson whispers. "I was worried."

"I know, boychik, but don't worry."

101

"They told you about your brain tumor?"

"Yeah, sure, never-mind. Listen. You should see my house. Are you in a hotel?! Get out. Get into my house. It'll be your house some-day. It's not so small. It'll be perfect. A good ender for me. A good starter for you."

"Zeydaaaaa...."

"What are you talking? We're keeping all our options open, right? Like I always taught you, right. KATOO!"

"Yeah, 'KATOO', Zeyd."

"'Keep All The Options Open'. That's all what I'm saying."

"Right. So, when I go back, I start work. My first real job." Will laughs almost derisively at himself.

"Why you laughing? I don't want you to go back."

"I say my first real job, but—you should see this place."

Abraham says nothing. He just looks quizzically at his grandson.

"It's very primitive, Zeyd."

"So, right now you're expecting me to ask 'If it's so primitive there, why don't you come here, and work and live here, where they have the best?'. Right?"

"No. But I was thinking about—the detour, after Harvard Med and Mt. Sinai in New York, through a poor reservation of 1300 Indi-ans in the middle of the—the most beautiful country I could ever imagine! Zeyd, it's gorgeous! It's breathtaking! It's magic."

"You stand on Mount Zion or Mount Horeb at the top of Jerusa-lem. I won't say Mount Moriah because I don't want you to beat me to that place, because I haven't been there yet. We Abrahams have a destiny there, you know. Or better yet, go to the Tayelet, just to the south of Jerusalem, and look out to the north—such a sight, such a feeling, such gratitude, Favileh, I can' tell you."

"So you like being here, uh? That's good. I think I'm going to like it there—"

Suddenly, he notices his grandfather is asleep or—. He quickly but gently reaches under the chin to feel the carotid pulse. For a moment, he can find nothing. No pulse. He reaches for the Emergency But-ton—

"What's with you!? I was resting my eyes."

"Sorry. I—. It's really good to see you, Zeyd. I'll let you sleep."

"Nonsense. There's plenty of sleepy-time coming, I can tell you that. You meet Dr. Grossman?"

"No, not yet. But I will. You sleep and I'll go see if I can find him. Then I'll be back and we can talk about how to deal with that tumor."

"There's no dealing."

"Wait a minute. Who's the doctor here?"

"Who's the patient? The real question is, How patient am I?"

"Zeyda, lie back and relax. I'm here. Let's talk. But let's talk easy, okay."

"I told Dr. Grossman I'm doing nothing that dulls my brain, even if it extends my so-called life a week, a month, or a year. I don' care." He tries to hold both hands up in front of him, but he's too wired in. "Look. Over here is sharp as a tack. Over there is borscht. Strict orders, I gave him. Nothing that moves me in the direction of borscht. He made it clear from the start that the tumor is inoperable. So why mess around with this technique or that technique? I'm gonna take my time and make the best use of it. *Fershtaist?*"

"Rest, Papa. I'm going to find out what's going on."

Abe thinks, *What's going on is over here, not over there. I can tell you that. Why we want our kids to be doctors, I don't know. I used to know. But I don't know anymore.*

꧁

Wynema scoots around the back of Mirriamma's old Ford pickup to help her get out as Mirriamma's feet are caught in the baskets on the floor in front of her.

"Sally told me she saw the new doctor fighting with long-knives against Mr. Phipps."

"What?!"

Mirriamma chuckles. "She lives down the hill two houses with her mother, Bertha, and she works at the post-office out by the highway."

"Oh, next to the mountain-man's boutique. That man makes my skin crawl."

Mirriamma bursts out laughing. "I have some salve for that, made of beeswax, lard, and *Diyuo-ma-jii!*—'ants-crawling-plant', that's what we call it. Stinging Nettle, I think. That's funny."

"Long knives meaning swords?"

Mirriamma nods. "Yep. With swords. Scared Sally to death."

The younger woman reaches for some sage on the dash and rubs the leaves between her fingers, closes her eyes and inhales deeply. "Tell me about Simon, the man whose corn is weak."

"Same thing."

"What do you mean?"

"It's a fight, with knives that go deep."

In Dr. Grossman's office, Will waits while Grossman looks over Abraham's charts. Grossman seems to be having a trying conversation, silently, with himself.

Will waits as long as he can. "So tell me what kind of tumor my grandpa has."

"Glioblastoma"

"Glio. Not good. Is that type primary to the brain, or is it metastatic?"

"Starts in the brain itself. He doesn't appear to have another primary that could have spread to his brain, such as lung cancer. The bad news is it can run in certain families.

"I know. And glios are usually rapid. What do you make of his recurrent comas?'

"There are some indications that it's bleeding periodically, but we haven't localized it. This could produce edema in the adjacent brain such that the normal brain tissue becomes swollen and inflamed. When this happens, coma could be the result."

"Has he had any seizures?"

"No. And to tell you the truth, that surprises me."

"He's on steroids now?"

"It's the only thing we can do to shrink the swollen tissue."

"And the bleeding?"

"Not much to be done there, really, without doing more harm.

"What would have to happen before you'd send him home? And, of course, I'd make sure he had professional care there."

"Well, another MRI every time he lapses into coma isn't going to help."

"How do we account for the speed with which he enters and, even more perplexing, exits the coma?"

104

"The tumor may also be affecting his hormone levels quite suddenly as it puts additional pressure on his hypothalamus and pituitary. These changing levels could explain why he has such a dramatic shift in consciousness."

"Grandpa has made it clear that he wants no heroics."

"Well, there might come a time when he needs an external ventilator. I mean, certainly his ability to breathe will become progressively compromised as the medulla is affected by the tumor. As his heart and lungs are good, this will only prolong the inevitable."

"I understand."

"At some point we may have to feed him through a tube into his stomach."

"Dr. Grossman. The doctor in me and the grandson are going to be in conflict. I don't know what that means. And I'm afraid. Sounds very unprofessional."

"Not at all. Sounds very human to me. Take it step by step. We'll work it out together."

⁓

Will reenters his grandfather's hospital room. "I'm so happy, Zeyda! Dr. Grossman's happy."

"I got a tumor and you're happy?"

"Doctor Grossman briefed me. He said we'd talk later. But he did say that certain things are looking good."

"And certain things are not looking good."

"Yeah. Hey, I brought us a little tuna salad." As he adjusts Abraham's bed, "You're not in a coma and I'm happy!"

"Did I tell you that when I wake up from the comas, I feel great!? When I wake up from sleep, I feel terrible."

"That's unusual. I'll ask Grossman about that."

"You see what I told you: It all depends on point of view. You live here, *b'Eretz Yisrael*, where our ancestors lived—you breath the air they breathed, you smell the earth they walked on and you—"

"Abe!"

"You're calling me 'Abe' now? Not Zeyda? Now I know you're about to hit me with a good one."

Will just stands there. Biting the inside of his lip.

"Give it your best shot, buster!" Abe looks at him. He really looks at him.

"Zeyda, stop. I'm not going there. I don't want to go there. So stop asking."

"Who's asking?"

"I can see it in your eyes."

His grandfather laughs. "I can't keep it from my eyes. Nobody can. But I wasn't going to say a word."

"You didn't have to. Look, I just came to see you. I mean, if this was it, if you were—"

"I know. It's good. I'm so happy you're here. But you can't blame a guy for wanting—. It's only natural. But, listen. What I've discovered in nine months here, I'm telling you it's incredible—"

"Zeyd', you're sick. I came. Let's be together."

"What do you mean 'sick'? I have a tumor. I'm not sick. Big difference. It's going to kill me. But not today. Everybody dies sometime of something. Big deal."

"A tumor is a very big deal. I'm a doctor, I should know."

"Hey, hot-shot, listen. I'm going to think of it as an idea—yes, as an answer even. My tumor is the answer to the question I've been asking all my life. And the day I die the answer will be made known to me. And then I'll know. And it'll be great. Who doesn't want to know before they die? Not everybody has a tumor with an answer at the ripe old ago of—how old am I?"

"Eighty-eight."

"—at the ripe old age of eighty-eight. The answer of answers—at eighty-eight. Pretty good."

"I know. But it's not about numbers. Eighty-eight...ninety-eight...even seventy-eight, can be a good life. If you did your best—and you did, Zeyda—and you followed your conscience, you were a mensh. Right?"

"Yeah, yeah, all that. You'll teach it to your grandchildren. But I'm talking here something else. I'm talking about—" He beckons Will closer, then whispers, "—keeping the tribe going!"

"Well, Zeyda, listen. Please. The tribe will keep going—if it keeps going. If it does the right thing to survive. We've done a great job of surviving so far—"

"But at what cost? With what pain?"

"I know." Will takes a deep breath. "But we're not unique in that way. There have been others who—"

"We are! Don' say otherwise! We are unique—."

Will tries to interrupt, but Abraham won't let him. "Maybe there are other peoples who are unique as well. Okay. But whatever it is it's something to hold on to—to make grow—for our children—for our great-great-seven-times-great-grandchilden."

"Papa, that's interesting. Seven generations. That's what the Indians say—"

"Indians, shmindians! I'm talking Jews who suffered and held on and kept the faith so that me and my Yitzchak, your father may he rest in peace, and now you could...could, eh—." With his one free hand, he points up and punctuates the air and searches and searches. "—So that you could—. Goddemmit, I get so close—I can almost say it. But then—" The old man is having trouble breathing. "—I'm not sure whether it's to praise God and be grateful, or reestablish the Temple, or bring back all the Jews to a place called home that can never be violated like we were violated. I get right there and—zetz!—the road splits into three and I'm not sure again."

"Zeyda. Lie back and relax."

"I know this tumor has the answer. There's only one problem."

"Nu?"

"When I find out the answer from the tumor I won't be able to tell you. I'll be dead. Let me work on this a little. There's got to be a way."

"Papa, cultures stay strong because they put forces to work to correct what could be fatal mistakes. Sometimes they come from without, with no love, only violence. But sometimes they come from within, from someone who loves them, who cares and who refuses to deny ugly truths, even about oneself, about one's own."

"I don't know what you're saying—Mr. M.D. with a MPH—but you wanna know how a culture stays strong and survives? I tell you. If you're forced to move around, because people are jealous and mean and kick you out, and you're always afraid for your life, and you can't always take all your things with you—you travel light. That's right. A suit of clothes, maybe—" He lowers his voice. "—and The

Torah. It's just a book. Doesn't weigh that much. And if they take it from you, you know there's another book just like it, waiting for you somewheres, and you'll get to it someday. And you do. And you do. Over the centuries, you do. That's what holds us together. We didn't have land. You can't carry land. But a book—."

"Maybe there was something else—along with the Torah."

"You think? What could it be? What else is like The Torah?"

"An idea. A dream. A purpose. The pursuit of justice."

"Hah! Not bad. A good answer. I'll have to think about it."

Abraham turns away, but just for a moment. "I thought about it. They're the same thing—Justice and the Torah."

"Okay. The Pursuit of Justice is the idea, the dream, the purpose, and the Torah is the physical manifestation, a reminder of that. Whenever you forget, read the Book."

"Not bad."

"But the land, *Eretz Yisrael*—Zeyda, how does that fit into the equation that you're willing to do immoral things to protect it?"

"When you say 'Never again' and you mean never again, you do what you must do to protect it. Security. It guarantees we Jews will have the freedom to remember or be reminded—Never again."

"It doesn't—it can't guarantee a damn thing. Military might, financial growth—without justice, they can cause more pain, more suffering than they can protect—"

They are interrupted. Grossman steps into the room. "Uh, excuse me. And you two are out of your minds! Mister Kornfeld is supposed to rest and otherwise avoid stress. And Doctor Kornfeld—what kind of doctor did you say you were?"

Will's embarrassed. "Yes, of course, I'm sorry." He turns to Abraham. "Zeyda, he's right. We shouldn't be talking about these things."

Abraham throws his head back with disappointment. "So Doctor Khokhum—what things should we be talking about? Or when should we be talking about these things? Some other time? Like I have a lot of time left." He flails one hand in the air. "Hello!"

Will turns to Grossman. "He's right, Doc. When is there time? Whatever time we have left, we should be free to—." He stops himself mid-sentence.

"Doctor Kornfeld, do you really mean that?"

"No, you're right. You're both right. I'm wrong." Will falls into the chair next to the bed and sighs. "How about you give us both a shot of Thorazine or Percoset and we'll be so mellowed that we can talk about anything without getting stressed?"

"Are you serious?"

"No, of course not." Will turns to Abraham. "He's right, Zeyd —."

Dr. Grossman leaves the room, heaving a deep incredulous sigh as he goes.

Will looks at his grandfather only to find him asleep. He gets up to go to the bathroom—"

"Can I explain myself maybe," comes Abe's voice, "without getting you upset?"

"Hey," says Will turning around, "an explanation is an explanation without any need for me to get defensive." He sits on the end of the bed.

"All I'm saying is, is it such a inconvenience to find a beautiful *yiddishe madel*, a woman with such intelligence, such beauty, such grace, such unspoken, invisible connection to all the stories, all the history of our people—somehow in her young eyes is this wisdom!—is it such a trouble, such a terrible thing to look for her? To find her? To love her? And let her love you—though why she'd want to marry you, I haven't a clue. But of course I do—because you're beautiful, too. And so, then, you make children. And you tell them the stories. And so it goes on. Like that. Not such a bad thing. In fact, a good thing."

Will sighs again. "Not such a bad thing. But, Zeyda, if it's a good thing, and the Jews, all of us, want this to happen, we have to be honest about what the state is doing in our name. Personal...political...it's all connected."

"I'm talking you and babies, and you're talking about Israel and its policies with the Palestinians. Why does it always come back to that?!"

"Because that's what's at issue right now. Right now the state is doing very wrong things. I'm saying very wrong things, Zeyda. And, like it's talked about all through the stories of the Torah, there's come a time when the people have to make a course correction to what their leaders are doing in their name. Read the Prophets. It's happened before. It's happening now."

"But there's only one Israel, Favileh! One! And the land will protect us, as it was promised."

"But not if you do things that will come back and haunt us. I know the stories. God, I know the stories! I'm sick of those stories. There are other stories. Better stories. We don't know all the stories. You don't know all the stories. There are stories all over the world, stories that are right for this particular moment—if only we'd listen!"

"We got the stories! In the Torah! They're all there—like you said—if only we'd listen! But you gotta have a family, that's the obligation—children to pass it on. Okay, that's it. You want me to sleep. Okay. But you—you should go to the top of Jerusalem and sit down and shut up and look out. And then you tell me. Then you tell me. Go. Come back. It's a small country. Zip-zip, back in a jif. I'll be fine."

Will goes up on the mountain in Jerusalem. He climbs to the top of a cliff called the Tayelet. He sits down and he looks out and he waits.

It comes slowly and not without fits and starts. Oh, he can see what his zeyda said he would see. His brain can sort those things out. But the feelings—those are not as linear, ordered, communicable. They cascade and disappear into his mind as he reaches out for them. Did the caravans from Egypt and the Negev once come up on the right through that valley? Did they bring milk and honey? The bee that alights on his knee, an oasis from flight, seems to confirm this.

The heart of Jerusalem on his left. The rolling hills in early summer aglow in greens and golds all dusted with sand and desert and sun-baked Earth. He cannot see the Jordan River, but he thinks he senses it far to the east. *What do I know of these things? What does the bee know? Does it know what it knew yesterday? Does it know what her ancestors knew right here or even way down that valley a thousand, five thousand years ago? What makes a city holy? Can a city be holy? What the fuck does "holy" mean, anyway? The bee is holy. Because it is a part of a whole and it knows this and loves this. It doesn't know it loves this. It isn't plagued with knowing it knows,*

110

but it knows.... Knowing is time conscious. Where is Mount Moriah from here? Did Abraham of Ur know that sending away Ishmael and Hagar would create such problems, such disruptions fercrissake? Did he ever know? Did a bee ever alight on his knee? Did he know the sadness, the regret? Did he look out and divide the land? Did he contemplate separating the bee from its hive? A bee can take a long time to die. The hive takes longer. And the alive connection between the hives even longer. The death of a bee. The death of a man. The death of a planet. The death of a star. The death of the blink of the Eye of God.

I don't believe in God. Parse that. "I" predicates "no belief" in something called "God". Just because I don't believe in God, doesn't mean God doesn't exist. All I'm saying is my concept of God is incommensurate, paltry, it isn't relevant to a goddamn thing. Grow up! I can see what Zeyda means. I feel it. Things come together here, converge, merge, melt, recombine, take forever to explode into the stardust we're made of. Wow. So this is the Tayelet. Okay, some paintings work....

Every atom in a hammer knows it has just been struck the moment the head hits. But does it know it before the strike? Can it feel the deep shift in inertia, the air on its cheeks or horns as the hand drives the handle drives the head to its nail?

Physician, heal thy fucking self.

＊

Now Will sits on a chair outside his grandfather's hospital room. He peeks in. Still sleeping.

Dr. Grossman steps up and hands Dr. Kornfeld a folder. "The readouts are perplexing. The bio-readouts and the brain scans don't relate, don't compute. Never seen that before. It's like we're dealing with two different people at two different times. When he pulled out of the coma, his bio-panels and readouts should have changed, adjusted, but they didn't. When he was in the coma—and the EKG and the scans definitely confirm he was deep and far away—his bios should have chased them, but they didn't. We're working on it. I sent everything to a friend in Berlin, the best. But your grandfather seems to be doing great now, so I'm encouraged. What do you think?"

111

Will is racking his brain. "I don't know, never covered anything like that. But thanks for asking."

The PA system—in Hebrew, of course—softly asks for Dr. Grossman to report to Room 23.

"I have to go. I'll be back."

Will sits in the chair in the hallway and pulls out his cellphone.

Jahbig in Oakland answers his cell. "Yah, mon, howsit? You must be calling from the hospital."

"How did you know?"

"It's three in the morning, mon."

"Here or there?"

"Does it matter? Whazzup?"

"Sorry. Listen. Grandpa's tumor is definitely a glio—."

"That's heavy."

"Yeah. The good news is two hours ago he woke up."

"That's good."

"The weird thing is he shows no signs of having been in a Class 3 coma. They don't understand it. The concomitant bio-stats don't match. Now he wants to hike up the sides of Mt. Horeb. His doctor, Zvi Grossman—I like the guy—is totally at a loss. What you think?"

"How long was he down?"

"About 36 hours. Then, after another 36, he went under again. Days later, he's up and out and looking and talking great."

Jahbig yawns. "What you think?"

"I think this is going to happen again. They don't, not necessarily. Their experience tells them this kind of tumor in this kind of place and these kinds of comas—are quickly fatal."

"What's the correlation between his brain and the bio read-outs—you say they're inconsistent?"

"Totally inconsistent. They're doing diagnostics on the monitors. That's how concerned they are. His delta looks good, going in the right direction, but they won't make any predictions."

"I agree with you. Not them. He's over-cycling. He's looking for himself. He's definitely going to go in-and-out again."

"Wait a minute, Jah! Over-cycling I can get. But what do you mean he's looking for himself? Don't know that one."

"Ah, right. You remember the Chinese C-Section?"

"Yeah."

"The baby was trying to turn. I felt what he was trying to do. And I helped him, with just a little push at, what turned out to be, just the right place. That's what you did by being next to him. From inside the coma he pushed, and from outside you pushed—and he came to."

"And what did you mean by he's 'going to pass through consciousness again', as if he wasn't going to stay conscious?"

"We're all just passing through, Will. Maybe I'm not being helpful. Send me a complete read-out and I have friends in neurology who might have some suggestions. But you know, they got the best there, too."

"I know. Okay. Thanks, Jah. I'll send them. But tell me how it's going there for you."

"I like San Fra'cisco. President Obama came out here and the town put his feet to the fire. A woman, at the Grace Cathedral, interrupted his speech, but he stopped Security and let her have her say. He was so moved by her that he completely switched his position, right then and there, and admitted the reasons why Single-Payer Healthcare has been held up and swore he knew a way to make it work. It was breath-taking. That's the power of San Fra'cisco."

"You sound good."

"Bad like yaz! I am. How's that place you set up in Tel Aviv for your grandpa?"

"A condominium. Think of a small, gated community in Scarsdale or Beverly Hills. Swimming pool. Sauna. Two blocks walking from good bagels at the Wilshire Delicatessen and Organic Brew Pub. Seriously. Google it. Ya know, it turns out we actually have here what we think is a distant cousin on my mother's side. Can't be sure. But he's married to a Balinese woman who is an out-of-work RN."

"A Muslim?"

"Absolutely. She's very sweet and very smart. She's agreed to be here for Grandpa from 7 to 7 seven days a week. And she has a friend who will sleep here on the other shift. All this—if and when he comes home from the hospital. I'll be heading back to New Mexico in a couple of days."

"You still wear that silver medallion, the medal you won in the nationals?"

"Yeah." Will fingers it at his neck.

"It has a bear on it. Put it around your gran'fadda's neck and leave it with him."

"Am I hearing you right?"

"It has ju-ju, mon. I'm working with a Blackfeet Indian. Best radiologist here. He was telling me that for most of the tribes in the Rockies, the Bear is the totem of healing. Especially for the Pueblos"

"You doing Medicine there...or Mescaline?"

"No! I'm nine-thousand miles away. I'm doing the best I can. Give me a break."

Imitating Jah's Jamaican, "Give thanks, mon." And he gently touches the off-key.

&

Will sits with Abe now resting in bed in another room. Not as many monitors. He's holding his medallion necklace in his hands. "So, something else happened to me on my little trip to Jerusalem. You want to hear, Zeyda?"

"But did you go to the Tayelet?"

"You asked me to. I went."

"Nu?"

Will nods, doesn't say anything, just nods. He tries to say something, but he doesn't. Just nods.

"NU?"

"It was good."

"That's it?"

"It's beautiful."

"And?"

"So you want to hear what else happened to me?"

"Oy, we can't all be painters. Certainly. Tell me."

"As I descended the mountain, I walked down through the Arab quarter, and there I saw two young Israeli soldiers treating a very old Palestinian man with such contempt you can't imagine. One of the soldiers kept a German Shepherd on tight leash, but it kept lunging at the old man, until the old man stumbled and fell down against a broken stone wall. The soldiers were shouting questions—in Arabic, I think—and when the man's answer didn't please the soldiers, the one with the dog would halve the distance between the old man and the snapping jaws of the dog. I watched this going on until I couldn't stand it. As I crossed the street and headed towards the soldiers, this is what went through my mind.

"I'll pull out my cellphone and as I step up to them, I'll use the words 'rabbi', 'child', 'emergency', and I'll say to them, 'Excuse me, but Doctor Cohen and Rabbi Hershel have sent me to find an Arab man who lives around here by the name of Ali aka Kahlay—I just made up the name—who's donating one of his kidneys for a Israeli boy, the son of a member of your Knesset.' And I'll keep saying 'rabbi', 'child', 'Knesset', and make a big deal of looking at the soldiers' names and insignia, and describing them on the phone.

"And when I reached them, I said pretty much all that. But the Israeli soldiers probably didn't speak English. They looked at me with leaden eyes and just walked away. That German Shepherd actually snapped at my hand and his teeth were less than two inches away.

"Anyway, I helped the man to his feet and gave him the bottle of water I was carrying, and said 'Salaam Alekum', or something fairly close to that."

With that Will sits back in his chair and takes hold of his grandfather's hand. For a brief moment there is a sad connection, but soon the old man closes his eyes. Conundrums have a way of inducing sleep.

While he sleeps, Will carefully attaches his medallion around his grandfather's neck.

⁂

Two days later, Will sits next to Abraham's bed. There are flowers and a basket of fruit. Only one medical monitoring device.

"I gotta go, Zeyda."

"So go. I'll be okay."

Will bursts out laughing. "Forgive me, Zeyd."

"You're laughing?"

Will immediately drops his head into his hands and tries with all his might to stop crying. But he can't stop.

"Come over here," says his grandfather.

Will hides his face, burying it under Abraham's arm. "How can I leave? How can I go? But I have to. This place isn't for me right now. Can you forgive me, Zeyda? Please."

"Of course. I'm not going to die just yet. I promise. I'm working on something."

"I'll come back. I'll be back in a few weeks."

"A month. Get acclimated. But not too acclimated." As Will stands, Abe touches the medallion around his neck. "What about this, your prize?"

"Just a good-luck charm now."

"From a doctor?"

"Humor me. I love you."

Dr. Grossman slowly opens the door. Will steps over. "You'll monitor the size of the tumor once a week, and we'll see if he has anymore bouts with...unconsciousness?"

"That's all we can do right now. I'll keep you posted."

"Thanks. I should be going. My flight—."

As Dr. Grossman puts his hand on Will's shoulder, "Oh, and I'd like to know more about the outside research you're doing on the Pueblo reservation. I've been trying to help my son, who's an epidemiologist, like you, to do similar research in Gaza for years. But there's no money. Lot of political flak."

"Are you serious?!"

"Hey, some of us do not support the policies of our government. Go. *B'Shalom*. Be well."

18

JUMPING LOCAL ROPES

A river runs through the Pueblo, fifteen feet wide and with great force in the spring. A big cottonwood bole three feet in diameter was split with handtools two three or four generations back and laid opened up to double-plank a bridge from one half of the village to the other. Lovers come here, especially in the Spring, when the water rushes by loudly so no one can hear what they say and promise.

But today, carrying baskets full of small pieces from many kinds of plants, Wynema and Mirriamma stand quietly dead center on that bridge, listening. Two ravens overhead, mates for life, harass each other for the pure pleasure of it. Mirriamma uses her hands to listen. Wynema watches the dance.

Now they sit on a low adobe wall that was built as a bench five hundred years ago.

"I'd like to meet Simon."

"Oh, you will. You will."

"He has a son and a daughter, and his grandson's name is Day-one?"

"*Ya-huh.*" Mirriamma nods as she pulls a stalk with a flower from her basket and shows it to Wynema.

"Ah, that's *kha-mo w'hi-to*, good for menstrual cramps, unless we've just used, uh—what was that?—oh, yeah, *to-ta bikhu-lii*, because it will antidote the *to-ta bikhu-lii*."

The old woman just nods again and selects another bunch of leaves bound by a rubber-band and holds it out. "Don't need the flower for this one. Just the leaves. But look at the flower anyway. See how it goes around, the little paths make a spiral, and connects here where it began. The other flowers are the same, but they're all different. How can that be? If you had a whachamacallit, a microspoon, you could—"

"Microscope."

"Yes, one of those, you'd see how each part connects to every other part. How is that possible? Under, over, around corners and edges, through time, around time, every part talking to every other part, in this flower, in every flower, in all flowers. It's just like that. This flower, you, me, the village...everything."

Wynema is enchanted. Enthused. A little giddy. "There's new science now—Probability Theory, Systems Analysis, Quantum Mechanics—that sorta suggests the same thing. I think. So, maybe you're right."

"I'm right. But not because I know it. But because it's all around. You start to see it all together when you're older. Maybe 55."

"When I'm 55 years old!? I can't wait that long."

"Don't worry, you'll get there. The kachinas will lead you."

"The kachinas?!"

"Yep. Those little dolls. We have four hundred and forty-seven of them, you know. Spirits of all the things. Heaven, Earth, Water Spring. Sacred Mountain. The Zunis and Hopis know them best. But we're catching up. Hah! There's the rattlesnake and even a snake with feathers, like in Mexico."

"I'll never learn them."

"Of course not. Nobody ever learns them. You marry them, and you know by now you never learn anything about who you marry. Getting close to who you marry is only gonna show you how much more you *don't* know. Crazy, eh? You gotta marry a lot of things before you're done. Storm cloud and fire, rainbow and deer and eagle, corn blossom, squash blossom—you'll marry them all, and only then will they tell you their secrets—" Mirriamma is suddenly convulsed with laughter. "They'll tell you their secrets all right—but what good will that do if you don't believe them." More raucous laughter. "That's how you go steady on through, uh, thick and thin, eh? Isn't that what they say?"

"Who says that?"

But Mirriamma just looks into the little flower one more time. "Hey, you know I think I see a rainbow inside here. I'm not kidding.

But, hey, nevermind, now it's time for us to go through all this again, but this time in Pueblo."

≈

Having left his BMW at the airport in Albuquerque, he's driving home on I-25. *Home, he muses—this is going to be my home for two years. Israel isn't home...and yet I felt a connection there. I didn't like it there. But here, I don't feel that connection at all. There is distance, the separation of cultures, of being a stranger in a strange land. But I like it here. Can I judge Israel? I was there twice for a week each. Of course, we must judge. Facts don't lie. Sentiments can...and do.*

≈

He pulls into the doctors' parking lot at the Indian Health Services Clinic in Santa Fe. Central office for all clinics here. He sits looking at a book he's brought back with him—of gorgeous Israeli art work. His eyes lock onto a page. He stops time and steps into the moment.

Creativity. Art. Expression. Synthesis. Evolution. Do I identify with what I'm evolving out of? Or with what I'm evolving into? Is evolution conscious of itself evolving?

Art. Creating something out of the pieces lying before you. Self-consciousness is a vector. It's going somewhere. What's the difference between art and evolution? They're both growing out of themselves into something breathtaking, something new and wonderful, something new and horrible. What is horrible is horrible relative to who- or whatever perceives it as horrible. The abattoir is horrible to a cow. To you, one step closer to your filet mignon. When the coyotes left this valley, the field-mice had a field day for a long time.

He leaves the moment, steps back into time moving forward. *Time to see Cutter. Start work.* He closes the art book and sets it on the passenger's seat.

Inside, a very tall, possibly Scandinavian nurse carrying a bouquet of carnations, plucks one, smiles, hands it to Will, and points to Doctor Cutter's office.

Cutter offers him a seat. Will hands him the carnation and then a copy of the stats he faxed to Jahbig and tells him what he can of his grandfather's condition....

Cutter smells the flower. "What do you make of it?"

"He's in a private room now? If he stops dropping into coma and the glioblastoma settles down for a while, he'll go home. I've set up professional care for him if he does."

Cutter scans the file. "Three times in and out of coma with little to no side-effects? From the point of view of medical science, Will—this is pretty interesting. Seriously interesting."

"I suppose, but—." Will stands, hitting his head on a high-hanging mobile. "Let's talk about my work up there, while you give me a tour of this place. You're my backup down here, right?"

"This place? You should work here for a while. Then you'd know crazy."

"You Jewish?"

"No. Why?"

❧

He and Cutter stand behind a computer tech in the records room. Will points enthusiastically at the computer screen. "There, thanks, if you could print that out." Then, as he follows Cutter back into his office. "That should have something on it. I told you my last paper was about the hantavirus on Navajo after it was isolated. Did you ever connect any deaths to hanta here?"

Cutter opens a file cabinet drawer behind his desk and pulls out a folder. "One. Another's suspected. But—no vectors here. Will, the Clinic's a full-time job. There may not be time to do your virus research? At least not till you get acclimated and get a rhythm going. This isn't uptown. I'm just saying."

"I'll be fine. I'm used to the work."

"Great. Then let's throw in the Tularemia epidemic—. Jesus, Will, this can all wait."

"Umm! Rabbit Fever. Good. Yeah, that'll fit right in."

"Damn it. You're going to be their doctor there. It's more than a full-time job. It's gonna be a sea-change for you! Until further notice I'm *your* new doctor, and I'm telling you don't rush it. Take the time to...get the lay of the land, so to speak. Trust me on this one."

"Steve, I hear ya. I swear, I do. I'll do what you say, but I told you I've already laid the groundwork for a data collection network. If I'd gone to U.C. Med on that fellowship, I'd be drone number ten on a nine-man team studying something someone else is interested in. Here I do my own work. And I'll write the paper on it."

Cutter looks out the window. "Yeah, you can make a reputation with a virus, all right. Go for it. But Clinic first. And don't push it to-day."

"Of course. You're right."

"Goddamn, I wish I was your age again. Or do I? Ha. Okay, I'll call and tell them you're coming. The nurses and staff have been wait-ing for this day for weeks. You sure you're ready?"

As they shake hands, Will hesitates. "Do me a favor. Let me just go to the Pueblo now without—well, without your calling them. Let me go and meet them and introduce myself—to each of them. I think I can settle in and learn the local ropes better that way.

"The 'local ropes', huh? Think you can just learn them like that, huh? I like that expression, 'local ropes'. Oh, yeah, there are local ropes all right."

They reach Will's BMW.

"What about the keys to your new townhouse? Want me to have someone drop th—"

Out the window as he drives away, "We'll talk about it tonight."

"But—! Where're you going to sleep—? You go, Doc."

As he passes the Wind River Trading Co., he notices there's a stretch-limo in front. *They come from near and far to get Phipps to show them the "real stuff". He's inside and dealing.* The chauffeur is leaning against the fender, talking to two local teenagers, who are try-ing to sell him something. *Is everything for sale? The trader: an an-cient trade. Phipps should change his name to Buylow N. Sellhigh. If I asked him if he'd sell a ceremonial object he knew was old and stolen, would he sell it or try to find its owner—what would he say? "Does a bear shit in a buckwheat patch?"*

Will sits in his car in front of the Clinic, both hands still on the steering wheel. It's Saturday and the Clinic will be open from 2 to 5 this afternoon. There are the patients milling about outside waiting for the Clinic to open. *My God,* he thinks, *there sure are a lot of pa-*

tients! We can't see that many patients in three hours. What am I getting myself into?

He steps out and puts the laptop bag over his shoulder. As a UPS man carrying his own packages walks by, Will picks up a thin hangable clothes bag and a thick, well-used briefcase, and follows the UPS man in.

As Louisa signs for the UPS, she double-takes the strange sight near the door. "Doctor Kornfeld! You're back!?" She hurries over to him, and shakes his hand, and would hug him if he gave the slightest gesture.

"Hi, I'm Doctor Kornfeld—Oh, you already said that. I'm sorry to surprise you, I should have called, but—well, I thought it best I just get back here and get to work. I hope that's okay."

"Of course. Your grandfather—?"

"He's okay, thank you. Well, he's stable and not in pain and he may be going back to his own place soon—."

"Good. I'm glad. Everyone is very anxious to—"

"You must be Louisa Moquino."

"I'm sorry, yes, I'm the Clinic's Director. See." She points to her name-tag and giggles slightly. She points to what he's carrying. "Let me show you to your office, then I'll introduce you to everybody."

Will likes his office, even the post-modern Indian art on the wall opposite the window. He points to the Exer-Cycle next to the window.

"Oh, that belonged to Governor Lujan who died five years ago. He left a note saying that our doctors should exercise more. Kind of nice of him, don't you think?"

"Absolutely. Thank you both."

There's a knock at the door. Louisa opens it. It's Lola. She's able to convey her impatience and the impatience of everyone else with a single gesture.

"Doctor, it's time to introduce you to everyone."

Lola steps up, blushing. She keeps looking back at Rebeca who's peeking around a corner."

"This is Lola Martinez. Lola is an R.N., and we're proud to say, she's also...."

...And the introductions continue. He meets everyone there.

~

Louisa gives him a complete tour of the facilities.

~

Back in his office, Louisa places a fresh bottle of store-bought water on his desk. "You really want to begin working today, not Monday?"

"Absolutely. It'll be a short day. On the other hand, it might be a long day."

Louisa doesn't understand.

"There are a lot of patients out there."

"Oh. Not really. We could do twice as many."

"You could? I mean, we could?"

"You'll get the used to us pretty soon."

He steps next to his desk. "Thank you. I feel good about everything I've seen. I feel I'm in good hands here. You'll turn me into a good physician."

For a second, Louisa looks uncertain, then gets it, then laughs.

"I guess I'll change into something less comfortable." Will laughs shyly at his own joke and waves to Louisa.

He looks around his new office. He imagines Cutter talking to him in front of all the staff. *You guys are pretty lucky. I think this new doctor's gonna be a good one. Knows his stuff. It's been a long, rough day for him. A rough week. How come you didn't wait till Monday?*

And now, out loud to himself: "Yeah. How come I didn't wait till Monday?"

~

Out front, there are patients and families seated comfortably. Each patient brings at least three or four family members. Ah, that's why…. Children run around more than their mothers appreciate. A mid-aged man and woman, sitting on a padded bench along a wall, attempt somewhat awkwardly to read the same magazine. There are pamphlets on tables, filing cabinets everywhere, wall charts, hanging plants, skylights, a flat-screen TV, and Rebeca's desk always neat: Reception.

Rebeca calms a boy's fears while the boy's mother deals with his colicky infant sister. Two kids play on the floor. A woman embroiders. Lola dispenses at a pharmacy window to an older couple. Will, wearing his white lab coat, comes out of his office. The room quiets.

Louisa approaches carrying a lot of charts. "Here's your patient load. We'll keep them for you here at this station." She moves around Rebeca's to a tall narrow table along the wall. The Doctor's Station! She puts the charts on the counter. As she takes the first patient's chart, "If you have trouble communicating, you know, to anyone, I'll—"

"Do some people not speak English?"

"Well, not exactly."

"I think, Mrs. Moquino—"

"Call me Louisa, everybody does. It's just that there might be a cultural difference in the way that English—. I know you're very well trained, Doctor, but...yes, I'm sure you're right about that. If you need anything, just call. Just jump right in. And she taps the rest of the charts on the table."

Will looks at the schedule. "Wow! The first five patients are 'Sandinos'. One family?"

"Not exactly. We have a lot of Sandinos here. I'll show you to the first exam room."

Louisa opens the door for Will. "Hi, Jack, this is Doctor Kornfeld. He's our doctor from now on. Doctor, this is Mr. Sandino. He's been here since five o'clock this morning, sitting under the water tower."

"Five o'clock? Didn't you have an appointment?"

"Well, yes and no," puts in Louisa from the doorway. "He did if his fishing trip fell through. And it fell through—right, Jack?"

"I think my fishing buddies were just hung-over and slept on through."

"It was a tentative appointment, Doctor." She adds, a little embarrassed, "Depending on the circumstance. Doesn't happen that way too often."

"Well, doctor," says Jack enthusiastically, "I had time because I was out there trying to write an essay about why I want the job as jailer over up in Jemez working with the Marshall there, you know, Billy Cheatwood. He don't need no essay, but the County bureaucrats do. Because Marshall Billy's a good guy, but he can't find no qualified help there. I have experience, and he knows it."

"I see. Great. Thanks."

Jack Sandino points to a leather bag and an old fishing pole tube closed at one end with a red handkerchief. "Didn't catch a damn thing yesterday either, Doctor, and probably won't for another month. Anyway, I got itches in places I don't even want to talk about. But you're the doctor—." He taps Will's name tag. "—or so it says."

"That's great, Mr. Sandino. If you'll just have a seat on the end of this table. Itches, uh?"

19

DO ALL INDIANS KNOW SIGN LANGUAGE?

Mirriamma stands bending over the wheel next to where Wynema has sat for the last two hours. Pushing against a wall, Wynema stands and stretches the long muscles of her back and the back of her legs, unwinding from the tension of coiling up that bowl.

The old woman carefully tests for variations in thickness. "Pretty good. Pretty good. Let's fire it and call it your first!"

Wynema is reenergized. "Really?!" Then the irony hits her and she laughs loudly. "Right, let's get my first one out of the way, you mean."

Mirriamma repeats herself but with a different inflection. "Pretty good, eh?"

"No, it's just that—I mean, here I am making beginner pots for you and not doing that teaching fellowship at Cambridge. There's an irony there and—" She puts one hand above the other, and then switches back and forth. "—and somehow it's okay."

Mirriamma screws her mouth this way and that and asks without a word for Wynema to continue.

"Well, I don't know but it's really rare for a place like Cambridge, you know, to offer you a fellowship and then you turn around and ask them for a year's leave of absence before you even start and they say okay." She takes a deep breath. Mirriamma does the same. "I mean, they happily said okay, that I can have the fellowship in a year and I won't even have to reapply. That's kind of amazing, you know."

"You feel okay, uh?"

"Yeah, I do! I can't believe that I do but I do. I mean, it's still there as a possibility for me, Cambridge, you know. But this—you—I think this is what I need to be doing right now."

"Me, too."

"Good. Then it's settled. I think. For a while. To go on ju—just like we're doing. Of course, I don't know how to describe what I'm doing like to any of my friends. I tell them I'm studying Native herbs and remedies."

"Not pottery? Pottery is very important. Brings the spirit of the Earth into every home that uses it."

"Right, but, uh...they tend to think of pottery either as a serious art form that you dedicate your life to or as a...a hobby."

"I see."

"Into the *hands*

"But look, I don't have to describe what I do to anyone. Not really."

"Good. Probably better like that for a while."

Mirriamma's daughter comes over with a teapot and two cups on a tray, and sets them down on a bench. Her name is Pabepa, and she has a nervous tick in the way she holds her head. She's continually making soft sucking sounds with her tongue and teeth. Challenged, but pleasant to be around. Many have asked: if Mirriamma is a medicine woman why hasn't she treated the problem? Answer: she has, to great effect over the years.

Mirriamma thanks Pabepa with a soft touch to the hand and turns to Wynema. "Tea, m'ija?" using the Hispanic expression for 'beloved younger woman'. "What's that other thing you study big? Linguinis?"

"Hah. Linguistics."

The old woman leans forward and affects a serious mien. "Tell me more."

"The scientific study of language and its structure. Including the study of morphology, syntax, phonetics, and semantics. Pretty thick, uh?"

"Oh, I understand some of that. What's that got to do with why you're an Indian?"

The younger woman is taken off-guard, completely. "I don't understand."

Mirriamma breaks out laughing. "Oh, never-mind. I don't understand, either. You're learning our language again is very strong. That's good."

"I thought I forgot most of it," says Wynema almost embarrassed. "I mean, when I sat down at first to write down the ways we speak, I couldn't do it. It wasn't there. Now it's starting to come back."

"To write it down? That's funny. We never wrote it down."

"No, of course not. But it's just a way for me to think about it."

"Talk to the children. Sit with them in the plaza or down by the river."

Wynema smiles. "That's what I do!" The smile quickly fades. "You know, a lot of the children don't speak it very well anymore. I'm not surprised, but I am concerned."

"One of the reasons we called you home."

Wynema sits up, leans forward. "It wasn't just about the Turtle Dance, and getting it right?"

"I know, I know," says Mirriamma, "you have questions. It's not easy to explain."

The younger woman begins to fret. Has she been tricked?

"There's an old story—"

"There's always an old story—."

"The Dance is important. Very important. But once you got here, we saw other things. You have connections—."

"Connections? To what? To whom?"

"To a lot of things. You are like Sipapu, the entrance to the underworld, our connection to Mother Earth. But you travel a lot. You take your Sipapu with you. You connect to other native peoples. Something like that."

Wynema, gently sarcastic, "Oh, now I understand everything."

"You do? Then you better explain it to me." Mirriamma is serious.

"No, now I understand even less."

"I don't know when, but it will become more clear to you soon. Right now, I need to ask you another question. How good a sign language talker are you?"

"Third-best non-deaf signer in the United States and Canada, in 2008."

"Really? How you know that?"

Wynema is instantly embarrassed by her bragging and deflects the question. "Oh, there are conferences and workshops and—and they feel competition and acknowledgement are good. But, hey, sign language can become the universal language, for everyone in the world in the world to communicate, without losing their own dialect, and—"

"You think that a good idea?"

"I do."

"Okay. So, can I see you sign? Do white people still think that all Indians know sign language?"

Wynema chuckles. "I don't think so. What do you want me to sign?"

"Oh, everything I'm about to tell you now. I want to see, not just hear."

"Okay."

Mirriamma takes a deep breath and begins: "So, my grandfather told me of our long-ago ancestors, the Anasazi, who almost disappeared. Their great cities fell apart. Maybe it was great changes in the weather or water. Maybe it was their leadership who grew arrogant and blind."

Wynema listens intently and signs simultaneously. At first she is awkward, jerky...but soon she's into it with all the embellishments that enhance the meaning.

"My grandfather said if the people die, their ceremonies will die with them. So it was a time of great changes. It was the end of a time. It was a time for everything to die. Almost everything, he said. You see, a few people wandered away. And they wandered for many generations. And even they almost died. Their ceremonies died, and they were almost like stupid people. But slowly, very slowly, new ceremonies were created, because the urge for ceremony was still a spark within them, and so ceremonies grew again. They tried to remember the old ways, but it was no use. New ceremonies that had some echoes of the old ones brought the people back into harmony with the land once again, and with their ancestors. And so, it's like that. What goes up, goes down. It's the way things are." And she starts bouncing up and down in her chair again.

Wynema's intense concentration in signing suddenly collapses inside her. She lets out a deeply stressed breath then turns to Mirriamma with wide questioning eyes.

"I don't understand at all. Somehow this has to do with me and why you phoned."

"Very good. But that's enough for today. We'll see if you can sign from Pueblo on another day. Can you teach sign language to every child in this village? Oh, never-mind, I'm tired. But we could go to the river and swim." Mirriamma laughs heartily. "Who wants to see an old woman swimming in the river?

It's 5 o'clock at the Clinic and the end of a long day. The room is almost empty. Victor enters, happy to see his uncle Ray and wife Tonita among the last patients of the day. Then he waves hello to someone else, whose name he won't have to remember, because he's walking out the door.

Not far behind his father, Dayone, exaggerating his angry slouch. He wears dirty jeans and a black sleeveless Green Day t-shirt with 'American Idiot' emblazoned across the front and back. He steps over next to Rebeca's desk and shifts back and forth like a caged feral cat.

Rebeca looks up at him from her desk and thinks, *he is so socially awkward and passive-aggressive around authority that he makes people nervous. Poor Louisa. She looks over at Victor and secretly suspects it's Victor's fault.*

Louisa enters, tired. "Hey, Victor. Hi, Dayone. What a day! New doctor—."

Using only gestures, Victor asks if the new doctor is in his office. Louisa points 'out back.'

"I'll wait in his office, okay? When you get a chance, ask him to come in."

Louisa nods and heads to the back door.

She exits the building and walks toward a small, run-down, two-bedroom adobe, separated from the Clinic by an overgrown lawn and parking area. This adobe casita is where the doctors used to live when they lived on the rez. But today—centralization, privatization, outsourcing—most doctors live in town or the encroaching suburbs, upscale.

Unseen, Simon works on his knees in a flower-bed just around the corner of the building.

As Louisa crosses the driveway separating the buildings, Will exits the old physicians' residence, holding a folder, startling her and himself. "I'm going to live here...I—"

"Oh, but the doctor's townhouse in Santa Fe they have for you is so beautiful. This is the old living quarters, and we just use it for records now. Hasn't been lived-in or cleaned really in five years."

"And this room next door?"

"Oh, it's a garage we use to store some tools and things."

"Well, I think we could take the records and put them in the garage and then—'

'But Doctor Kornfeld—"

Will smiles and puts his whole heart into convincing her how much he wants this. "You know how much time I'll waste commuting from Santa Fe? An hour maybe—each way. Okay? And I wanted to talk to you about—well, some research, because I have some extra work on my own that I'm going to need your help on—if you're willing. But it's important work, Louisa. And I came here to work." He points to all the unused buildings. "This still belongs to the Clinic, doesn't it?"

"Well, yes, it really belongs to the Pueblo which leases it to IHS, so you should probably talk to the governor, and you know—he's right here right now to meet you, Doctor. In your office."

"The Governor?"

"Victor Moquino."

Louisa blushes. "You know, like we told you, my husband."

"Oh yeah, right, okay." Handing her the folder he's carrying, "Here's the latest prescription protocols and patient progress forms from Public Health in Washington. Some new guidelines and procedures. You know the bureaucracy."

Louisa takes them uneasily. Will straightens his lab coat, his hair with his hand, and heads into the Clinic.

A few minutes later, Louisa stands next to Rebeca's desk, reading the Public Health papers he gave her. She doesn't believe the complexity of this stuff and turns from one page to another. "Why do they have to duplicate what they have over here with what they have over there?"

Rebeca steps up mouse-like next to her. "You want to go over any of that with me? Maybe it'll be easy with both of us. I know how you hate it."

Louisa nods and points. "Look at this. Who created this? Do they hate us out here?"

*

Meanwhile, Dayone, master of invisibility in spite of his carefully constructed rebellious appearance, looks down the corridor towards his mother's office. He moves quickly, quietly.

Inside the office, he is opening his mother's purse, withdrawing her wallet. He takes two five-dollar bills—just as Louisa enters, still reading those papers.

"Dayone! What are you doing?!" As if she didn't know.

"Aw Mom, I just need a few bucks...and you said when I cleaned—"

"You promised me you wouldn't go into my purse again. If I can't trust you—." She is reserved but angry as she takes back the bills.

Dayone hangs his head.

"I'll give you five, but you promise, remember?—"

Dayone doesn't move.

"C'mon, here. What's the matter?"

"I just needed ten dollars."

She gives him the other five. He takes the bill and speedily disappears.

She sighs.

*

Victor sits in front of Will's desk pretending patience. Will stands behind it and returns some documents to Victor. "This is interesting, Governor. A detailed survey would give me insight into the tribe's health in one fell swoop. I did a post-grad fellowship in Public Health. Maybe I can assist in some way. Why exactly do you need this report now?"

"Well, Doctor, we did a survey a few years ago. But it's really out of date and what we need now is a little different. I appreciate your willingness to help. It will prove most useful."

Will persists, innocently. "What's your study going to be used for?"

"We intend to apply for a number of federal grants. This may identify some areas that are strategically important for the Pueblo."

"Might I be able to use the data in some of my own research? I'm fulfilling a research grant myself, for the Dept. of the Interior. An epidemiological study."

Victor is never willing to give away anything unless he understands the terms exactly. "Perhaps."

Will follows Victor out of his office into the hallway. "Oh, Governor, I forgot to ask you. The house out back where the physicians who worked here used to lived—I'd like to live there and not in Santa Fe at the, uh, government compound."

Victor is taken by surprise. "I've seen the townhouses you doctors live in down there. They're quite nice." His first instinct is to ask himself what the red flags are if any. He looks up the hallway and then behind. No one. He takes a little longer to think about the request. He thinks about the health survey that is absolutely needed to apply for that Federal grant. He thinks about the shifts in relationships, lines of command, influences it will strengthen or weaken. He thinks about the benefits of knowing exactly where the players in the game are and what they're doing. He makes his decision. "Well, it's been a while since any doctor lived here on the Pueblo—"

"I really just want to focus on my work here. And the commuting—."

Victor smiles to hide the instant anger at having been interrupted. But then says, "I suppose it would be okay then. Yes, okay."

"Thanks, I, uh—can I hire someone to help me clean up the place?"

"I'll have people here tomorrow to do it. But I really can't imagine why you'd want to live out back when you could live in Santa Fe at—. What's the name of that compound?"

"Actually, I think you *could* imagine."

"How's that?"

"I mean, thank you so much. I simply want to devote my time to my work. Thank you."

The Governor smiles as he shakes the doctor's hand....

Will's head races, *I hope I don't shake his hand too long. I don't want him to think of me as a complete asshole. They know grief. They're used to it. Know how to show it. Know how to hide it. It'll be good here. The closeness of things around me, not the openness of the road and a cold townhouse unattached to my life work here forty miles away. No, a place like that would be an open blatant invitation to other upward-mobile professionals to call on me all the time, I know the scene, and invite me out for drinks or dinner or parties or to a play or, my God, go to the Opera! No, I have work to do and a new life to learn. Where the action is. Time to focus.*

He lets go of the Governor's hand. "Thank you so much. I like to work out in the morning, so can we do it after lunch? The clean-up."

Victor nods solemnly, affecting great concern. Will senses this and is immediately self-conscious. Victor, more like a big brother now, places both hands on Will's shoulders. "We have heard about your grandfather."

Taken off guard, "He's okay—well, not really. It is an inoperable brain tumor. But—well, we just don't know."

"I understand. Well, I wish him the best. And you."

"Thanks."

Victor looks closely to read the other's state. He finds the ways elusive or unsteady, thus strange and disconcerting. Will retreats towards his office trying to hide his uncertainty.

In the reception area Victor is with Louisa confirming his sense of the suppressed grief the doctor feels for his grandfather. Louisa looks towards Will's office. She touches her husband's cheek and moves quickly to a scheduled staff meeting.

Outside, Will is indeed containing his grief. The weight of the day. Of the week. He steps across the driveway to his home-to-be. He opens the front door, but it is stuck. Some junk has fallen and now blocks the door. But he pushes hard and it opens. He steps inside and closes the door and leans his head against it. His mouth opens in racking silent pain. Zeyda, I'm sorry I can't take care of you. He doesn't see the scorpion that scuttles over his foot and slides into a fissure at the bottom of the cracked adobe wall.

20

The Bear Takes Us in a Circle

Done for the day, Simon is two hundred yards away, walking home—when he stops, turns, not sure if he heard something. Looking back and forth from the arrowhead in his hand to the Clinic, he walks on.

It's dusk. An unseen dog barks stupidly as Simon approaches the central plaza in the middle of the Pueblo. One guttural sound from Simon quiets it. When he isn't at his summer house and garden, he lives here, in a small room tacked onto a large, very old three-story communal dwelling. His family had lived for generations in this and five other rooms on the other side of the wall, but now this is all he needs, all he is given. It's easy to close up a window or doorway in adobe, or open one up.

Inside, he lights a couple of kerosene lanterns. There is a fireplace set for cooking. There is a small pantry and table beneath the only window. Against another wall, a stand-alone clothes-closet made out of rough-sawn cedar wood and a cot and a bookcase with boxes and a few dishes. A nightstand with two candlesticks and a basin. A few woven rugs on the floor.

Simon pulls Frank's book out of his shirt and sets it on the nightstand next to a small portable CD/DVD player. On the other side of the cot is a small workbench for the silver and turquoise jewelry he makes from time to time.

He sits at the table and polishes a turquoise bracelet with a cloth, occasionally looking at the book. He pushes a button on the CD player and listens to Robbie Robertson and friends sing a peyote water-drum prayer song—from a CD his son Frank had given him.

Above his head on the wall an old handmade bow and two crossed arrows probably made a century ago. On the bed is a copy of National Geographic with a cover of a Native American kneeling, reverently pouring cornmeal on the ground in a circle before a killed elk.

After a while he turns and picks up Frank's book. But he doesn't open it. He just looks at it and feels its weight in his hand. *I don't have to read this anymore,* he thinks, *I know what's inside. His anger and stories of all his women. And his accusations and his terrible longings, all wearing colorful clothes and masks to hide behind. If he yells at an old broken down tree, I know he is yelling at me. If he spits on the ground, I will feel it hit my shoes. If he taunts his enemies, he is blaming me for living among them for so many years.*

He is about to throw the book against the wall, but he doesn't. Then out loud, "They say he writes pretty good."

Outside, the light has changed. The last sun sits low and now slices in across his knees. He sits on his bed, immobile, wearing only shorts. Now he leans back against the wall. His eyes close just as they see the dust jacket of Frank's book. A colorful butterfly poised on a bleached buffalo skull.

He dreams. Of when he was ten. Before the government took him away.

Simon, go slow.

Yes, father.

The people will have meat if we go slow, and your mother will have a warm blanket.

Look, Father, the bear takes us in a circle.

Simon relaxes as he dreams of his father placing his hand with love and pride on his shoulder. All around him the forest is sweet and sparkling and alive no matter where he looks—the air, the light, the colors. He sees a huge bear crashing through the trees, then disappearing.

Hmm, yes, you are right, my son. This is strange.

But what then is at the center of the circle, Father?

The smile on his dreaming face changes to a question then to a concern.

Good thinking, son, very good. A circle, hm, always around a center, hm, then let us go see.

They move quietly after the bear. His checks his rifle, then they veer off at right angles to the flight of the bear. They pass an outcropping of rocks among some trees. As his father moves off, Simon is drawn to look behind some huge boulders. He whispers loudly.

Look, Father, a den...and a mother and her little cub!

Get away from there! Behind me! Something is wrong with the mother! She is sick or poisoned. Oh my, she is in pain. The male will come.

Father, will she die?

The sound of a male bear growling loudly covers sleeping, dreaming Simon like a blanket of fiery noxious smoke. He sees his father wheel right and face the male bear.

Get behind me, now!

He sees his father quickly raise the rifle in defense. But the rifle disappears and becomes the bow and arrow hanging on his wall over his head. His father releases the arrow and he hears the arrow hitting the bear and the bear's loud mortal gasp which becomes Will's cry of *Goddammit, Papa!* Simon's dreaming face winces, twitches, then relaxes. He dreams on....

He's kneeling next to the fallen bear, his great mouth open, his great tongue hanging limp upon the ground. But immediately, almost out of the bear's mouth, a small tree is growing, growing so fast he can see it grow and branch and leaf out. A little cedar tree. He grabs the top branch of the tree, as his father shouts, Don't touch!

Too late, his little hand has bent and broken the main branch, the tallest.

I broke it, Father.... Father? FATHER!

The boy looks around. He is alone...and instantly terrified! He calls to his father again—.

Simon starts awake, staggers up out of bed in a daze, knocking Frank's book onto the floor. He takes a few steps, changes direction, opens the door, exits...and retches in the moonlight. Two coyotes in the distance laugh at him.

&

At this very moment, Will is sleeping in his sleeping bag curled up on the roof of his house-to-be.

As the sun rises Simon, sweaty, is finishing filling his old truck with a load of firewood. The first sunlight hits the top of his summer hut.

He drives his pickup slowly, deep in thought. He passes Sotero sitting on a stool against a wall fast asleep in the morning sun. He passes two small boys scrambling agilely down one ladder and then another, and he remembers doing this as a boy. But they're going to kiva to study with the old men. He didn't do this as a boy. Circumstance and government policy selectively intervened.

He drives up a narrow dirt road behind the Pueblo, up the flanks of the foothills that keep rising towards the mountain—to a small adobe house, separated from its closest neighbor by a 100 yards downhill. There's a beehive oven outside. A goat pen. A '37 Dodge truck that hasn't been moved in decades. Chickens and a coop painted purple. A garage with no doors. In it an old man sits on a lower bunk, quietly smoking tobacco rolled in a cornhusk. On the other side of the house is a big ramada shading a long workbench, some traditional pottery equipment, and a few chairs and stools.

In a patio area still in the shade, Simon unloads the firewood. Through her window, Mirriamma studies him. Behind her, Wynema in jeans and a t-shirt enters data into her laptop, occasionally looking up at her mentor. More attuned now to the ways of the old woman, Wynema lowers the volume to some Johnny Whitehorse flute music coming from her computer. She rises and stands next to Mirriamma at the window. The old woman heads for the door.

Simon is neatly stacking the wood. Mirriamma appears at the corner of the woodshed. "Okay, I appreciate the firewood. But what did you really come for, anyway?"

"Not because of your cooking, old woman."

"Then how come you always eat so much? You bring me some early corn pollen? Nah, way too early, I know."

He shakes his head. She leads him to her work-table. They sit. Wynema silently appears holding two clay cups which she then fills from a hanging water gourd. Simon, grateful, takes the cup.

"Hey, how you doing Miss Mondragon? Say, you know I remember your father. I once drove him to Albuquerque where he was going to college. Nice fella. And I remember you. You remember getting into a fight when you were thirteen or fourteen? That was my cousin Ernie's mean and stupid daughter, Linda. She's still mean and stupid. She's blind in her left eye now. If you have to hit her, get her coming at ya from that side." Simon laughs.

Wynema nods, smiles, says nothing. But she remembers. Then, to be polite, "How are you, Mr. Zamora?"

"Me? Oh, you know. Gonna be late this year. Corn's having trouble...'n there's little pink worms in the roots I never seen before."

Wynema takes a step away as is proper when she sees Simon lean closer to Mirriamma, almost whispering. All she hears Simon say is, "...In the old field, not the new one. Shouldn't be. That was the first sign."

She watches Mirriamma tilt her head back and forth, weighing his judgment. A wind comes up. Unconsciously, she puts her nose into it, sniffs.

Simon is lost in his own thoughts as he gulps down the water and reaches into his pocket for the arrowhead. "Then I dug this up, and it cut me."

Mirriamma takes the arrowhead, nods. Wynema's curiosity gets the better of her, so she steps over offering to fill Simon's cup again.

Simon continues. "Then I had a dream."

"Let us go inside. Dreams can fly away too easy in the open air, and I want her to hear." She indicates Wynema with her lips. "She will join us." Simon just grunts okay.

Most modern Pueblo homes don't have rooms with fire-pits in the middle of them anymore, as their fireplaces are on the side or corners, and many use electricity or propane for heat. But here the room is swept clean, except for two bags of beans and a pile of clean, used clothes in a corner, and two bear rugs. On one bench, someone has laid out some little leather bags and the kachinas and fetishes—some Zuni or Hopi, some Santa Clara, only one from San Lucas—none from Santa Carmina.

Simon squats by the fire and feeds it dry willow sticks. Mirriamma approaches him, carrying a shallow, black clay pot with a long handle. In the pot, some smoking Mugwort leaves. Simon sits on a stool. With an owl's wing, Mirriamma smudges the smoke all over him. With another motion she pulls Wynema out of the darkness to sit next to Simon and fans smoke all over her, too.

The three of them sit there for a long time. Simon reaches for his cup again but it is empty. Wynema is there before he can put it down.

Then he tells her about his dream, the bear, his father, himself as a boy, the little tree.... Then silence again.

Finally, Mirriamma: "Go to the next Tribal Council meeting."

Simon is stunned. "Me? No way. Why you bring that up?!"

"Is your life open to your clan or tribe?"

"You know it's not."

"Bear's great circle in the dream is the tribe. It needs you. Even as a boy you knew that the circle always points—well, it points to its center."

The intensity of the moment somehow is too much for the younger woman, and she quietly excuses herself and goes to a small table and sits down slowly on a three-legged hand-carved stool. She breathes deeply to calm herself. She's confused and doesn't understand her reactions. She tries to release the tensions gripping her by brushing down her own arms with her hands. She pulls a handkerchief from her back pocket and blows her nose hoping it won't bother the other two. It doesn't. Her head moves back and forth from thoughts about herself to thoughts about Simon and Mirriamma...and the process...the healing process. She knows she's supposed to understand what just happened—not just to Simon, but to herself. Why is her heart beating so fast? Why is she confused? Something is threatening. Threatening what? It must be a way of thinking, of reacting, of finding her center. She tries to express these things to herself, to talk to herself; but her thoughts jumble.

She can neither see herself, nor talk to herself. This moment will pass. But she will not forget it.

Simon speaks again taking deep breaths every few words. "The Council is men like...like Victor, not me. Like Teo...not me. You have always understood this."

Mirriamma steps over to a shelf with various fetishes and human-like figures. Her hand glides near them...until she selects one. As she returns to Simon, she passes by Wynema and shows her which one she has taken.

"Not talking about the Council, old man. Talking about your people. Victor's not bad, but he is not a good father to his people—."

"Or to his son."

"—Because he doesn't know how to listen. But you can teach your son-in-law this."

Mirriamma places the fetish in front of Simon who eyes it suspiciously.

"Victor won't—. No." Simon stops himself.

"Won't respect you anymore than you respect yourself? That's true."

"Always it comes back to me, don't it?"

She reaches out gingerly, takes the fetish and holds it out in front of him.

"Your grandmother gave this to me when I was sixteen."

She takes his hand and closes his fingers around the fetish.

"Woman, please, this is not what I come—"

"Listen to it. Learn what you must do to carry your words to the Kachina world."

"I'm with the way of the Taos. They don't do Kachina, and I don't do Kachinas anymore. Don't know if I ever did."

"Simon, stop. You know that tree, that little tree in your dream? It's the connection between the Earth and the Sky, between mother and father. But with you, more like between father and son, I think."

Simon stiffens. Mirriamma softens, closes her eyes, visualizing.

"I see the tree. Top of the tree is bent, you say? I don't know this tree, but maybe, maybe I think your son, Frank, is coming home for a visit soon."

Wynema's eyes jerk open with a start.

So do Simon's. He sees a big motorcycle roar out of the darkness and run right over him. He jerks back reflexively.

Wynema goes interior trying to figure out what this means to her, emotionally, intellectually. She realizes quick enough that it has nothing to do with her, but for Simon. She can feel him. She breathes easier.

Mirriamma taps him on the shoulder and he jumps. "Good, good," she says, as she reaches into her bosom and with a demure smile withdraws a small leather bag. She offers it to him. Wynema leans forward. It's difficult in the shadowed light to see.

"Well, for some reason, today is a day for giving corn. This corn-meal here came down from corn you gave me when your woman, Dahyanee, was still alive. You will find use for it."

At first Simon recoils but he catches himself. "Okay, okay, I will take it. You're messing with me now, I know it." Nervously he faces the younger woman and points to Mirriamma. "Yeah, she's messing with me. But I deserve it, I guess, all the years I picked on her."

He takes the little bag and rises. Very emotional now he turns to go.

"Oh, by the way," she says as he reaches to the doorway, "that old arrowhead you found. What you think?"

Simon looks at his bandaged hand, then reaches into his pocket. It's not there. "Oh, I left it at my room.'

"So what you think?"

"Yeah, yeah, an old arrowhead, an old wound still bleeding, I know."

Mirriamma raises her eyebrows as if to say, See, you guessed it on your own, didn't you? Simon grunts and nods fatalistically, then glances at Wynema, who's sorting herbs and quietly entering data into her laptop, thinking, *Isn't sometimes a shoe just a shoe?*

21

Falling Out of PickUp Trucks

The next morning at the La Posada Hotel in Santa Fe the late breakfast tables outdoor are filled. It's an upscale mainly white world of power and money. Mariachis play softly. Tourists ask a waiter to take their picture. Champagne brunches. The sun is shining on the New World Order.

Victor and a hired professional enabler, an executive consultant in his mid-thirties named James Manley, sit at a table. They wash down the last of it with champagne. Manley's expensive ring and Rolex watch sparkle. He speaks in low careful tones as they slowly sip their lattes and let their eyes wander.

"To get your tribe's application on the docket for consideration at D.O.E., I've got to get your grant application in before the 25th of next month."

Victor winces but recovers quickly. "That means I'll have to convince the Council in only one meeting. How many other tribes is your firm consulting for?"

"Only one. We believe you both can succeed."

"I want to see spelled out in black and white the difference between what the feasibility study will cost us to produce and what the total grant monies will be. No hidden costs. Blow the fine print up into something a man can see."

"On your desk by Monday, Victor. Oh, and I'll get you a video of all the things the Mescaleros have done with the monies they already received. What about that health survey?"

"I've got it under control. We just got a fresh new doctor at our Clinic. He's eager to...fit in."

Across town at the Santa Fe Inn, in the health spa, Will is grunting hard as he does lateral dumbbell lifts. An insignia-shirted instructor for the spa approaches. With a huge grunt, Will holds his arms straight out, trembling, straining, until the weights fall and crash together, and he cries out in agony.

"Excuse me," asks the instructor. "Mind if I ask what's your plan? I mean, what're your goals? I like pain but not torture."

Without responding, Will swings the weights outward again, his face contorting into an ugly grimace as he stares the man down.

Later that day, between the Clinic and Will's house-to-be, Will sets grocery bags on the roof and leans a new mop and broom against his BMW. Pensive, he takes a potted dwarf Lebanon cedar out of the back seat. Its top is bent 90 degrees. Heading to his house, he almost bumps into Simon, who's carrying a shovel from the tool shed.

"Hi, I'm Doctor Kornfeld. What's your name?"

Upon seeing Will's potted tree, Simon recoils, "Ay-yai!" *That tree. I've seen that tree. From my dream. Bent like that at the top.*

"Didn't mean to frighten you. Won't need the shovel. I wanna start on the inside."

"On the inside?"

"General cleaning. Over here in my house. I'll show you."

Dwarf cedar in hand, Will moves quickly. Simon follows cautiously.

It's a dust-laden mess. Will sets down potted plant next to the front door and enters, looks around for Simon, then exits.

Simon, still holding a shovel, is mesmerized by Will's little tree.

"Come on in, or are you waiting for the other worker?"

"The other worker?"

"Let's bring all the junk outside."

"Outside?"

Will suspects feeblemindedness. "Before we can clean we gotta empty the place."

"Okay, doctor, I can help, if that's what you want."

"Good."

But Simon, still perplexed, doesn't move.

"Are you going to help me...or what?"

144

Simon points to Will's tree. "Is that for the Clinic?"

"No, no, this is mine. I don't know what I'm going to do with it. I brought it from Israel. My grandfather's idea." Will now moves his little tree into the shade, but then quickly picks it up places it in the sun. "Maybe it would do better in the sun. I don't know."

An old pickup arrives with two men and, in the back, a woman and a lot cleaning materials. The driver sticks his head out the window. "You the new doc? The Governor says you need some cleaning help?"

Will looks at Simon, then at the cleaning crew, then leads the crew into his house.

Simon slowly squats next to Will's cedar, looking at it carefully.

The next day is Monday. Back to work. In the patients' parking lot, a man and his pregnant woman and two small children climb down from their pickup. Two older children are in the back calming down two excited, tethered goats. The mother lines up and inspects her family, then ushers them in a file toward the front door.

Inside, the reception area is full and busy. Will stands in the hallway surveying the waiting room. He doesn't see Sotero, who is fully 13 inches shorter than he, standing right next to him, also looking out at the waiting room. Sotero tugs at Will's sleeve. When Will looks down, Sotero is offering him a stick of gum. Will declines then motions for Rebeca.

"Yes, doctor?"

"I've asked, but none of my scheduled patients is here and yet the waiting room is full. Where are my patients? And who are all the people who are here?"

Rebeca is somewhat flustered. "Dr. Kornfeld, most of our patients who have appointments only come in if they are sick or hurt. So if they don't have an appointment, then they won't come in unless they are sick. So the ones who are here don't have an appointment."

Will stares blankly, then looks down at Sotero, who smiles broadly back at Will and now points to an orange, lidless, empty pill-bottle in his hands.

Inside an examining room, Lola holds open the door as Will enters and stops abruptly. The small room is jammed. Will looks with a gathering perplexity from infant to 16-year-old mother to 33-year-old grand-mother to 49-year-old great-grandmother to 66-year-old great-great-grandmother to an 85-year-old great-great-great-grandmother who is Navajo and drop-spindling some yarn.

When Will's head reaches the oldest woman, Lola speaks, pointing to the 85-year-old woman, "Doctor, this is Ana Tenório. She insisted on meeting you before she would agree to your examining her great-great-great granddaughter."

All six generations smile at Will, who bows to the oldest woman who looks up briefly, then nods, then greets the doctor in Pueblo, thus expressing her approval. For a moment Will just stands there and marvels. To himself, *Here is proof of the fractal nature of space: people coming out of other people, one after another and after another after another…. Birth, a singularity, at the event horizon. Wonder if Jahbig has thought of this.*

In another examination room, an hour later, Will and Louisa are treating the multiple contusions of a shirtless man who is clearly inebriated. The man is in a daze and doesn't respond.

"Doctor, this is Martin Montoya, Ruben's father—you know, my Dayone's best friend."

Will thinks he remembers. "What happened? Some kind of accident?"

Louisa speaks to the man in Pueblo. "*He wants to know what happened.*"

The man answers drunkenly in kind. "*My wife beat the shit out of me for drinking.*"

Louisa thinks about it for a moment and then says to Will, "He fell out of a pickup truck."

Will looks up from the man's chart. "What's this in his chart a year ago? 'F-O-O-P-U-T.' Fooput? And I saw it in someone else's chart yesterday."

Louisa rolls her eyes and with a sigh explains nothing at all. "That would be, uh, Fell-Out-Of-Pick-Up-Truck."

Will looks at the chart again, then at Louisa, then at the hapless man…and chuckles once as if he gets it.

He doesn't get it.

It's sundown. In between the Clinic and Will's bungalow there's a rusty basketball hoop, sans net, that hangs on the garage. Wearing athletic shorts and shoes, Will plays hard against an imaginary opponent. He talks out the game, and not for fun.

"He fakes out professional advice—drives his grandfather crazy by coming here—does the work-ups, shoots—"

He doesn't even hit the rim. "—And misses! Air-ball! He takes a feed from the clinic nurse who's been in the key forever—shoots, and—"

He makes it. "Yes!"

Simon, rake in hand, stands, almost hidden at the corner of the Clinic, watching.

Will dribbles left and right, as fancy as he can, unaware of Simon. He dribbles off his foot, grabs the ball and blurts, "Fancy dribbling past the Governor of the Pueblo, he sets—"

He shoots. "—for a three-point health study—"

He misses but grabs the ball and rushes in for a hotshot lay-up. "And the treatment—"

He turns it into a slam-dunk. "—saves the patient! Yes!"

Simon, still unnoticed by Will, is standing closer now, next to a decrepit, '56 Cadillac ambulance completely, charmingly, overgrown with weeds and almost hidden beyond the garage.

Will chases a rebound and almost bumps into Simon! Will is speechless, then recognizes him, embarrassed, out-of-breath. "Ah, I get it, you're the gardener."

Simon nods.

"You're Louisa's father. Simon, right? I owe you an apology. I thought you were supposed to help me, so I...probably was a little rude."

Simon resumes his raking, so Will turns back towards the hoop.

Simon stops him before Will can shoot. "I remember you asked me to help you. That doesn't seem rude to me."

"Yes, but I wouldn't have asked if I'd known that you were the wrong person."

"How could you know if I was wrong person?"

Will scratches his head. Then, an idea hits him. "Wait a sec! I know what you're the right person to ask. Don't go 'way." Will dashes into his house. Simon resumes work, almost laughing.

A few seconds later, Will hurries out, carrying the potted cedar with the bent top. "Should I keep this inside...or bring it out...in this climate, I mean?"

Upon seeing the plant, Simon reacts again. Will notices his anxiety. He puts the plant down. "What's wrong?"

"Where did you get this plant?"

Will becomes somewhat off-balanced himself. "Well, my father, well, actually, my grandfather, he—"

"Your father?! Ai! This has to do with your father."

"He...he...gave it to me because—yeah, my grandfather."

Both men look down at the tree, then, at the same moment, back at each other. When Simon says nothing more, Will slides away, hiding his rising emotions. Simon stares at the tree, then snaps awake, calling to Will.

"I will help care for this...your tree."

"Well, thanks, I appreciate that."

"I'm sorry about your father."

Will nods and fidgets an adjustment to the potted tree. "My grandfather, thanks. I'll just set it here and you can think about what to do with it."

He goes into his house.

22

The Sound a Deer Makes

A week or two later, late afternoon, and Simon is at his daughter's house unloading grocery bags from Louisa's car. Victor pulls up speaking on his cellphone. Simon goes into the house with the bags.

In the kitchen, Louisa is quick-fixing dinner. Everything she unpacks, puts-away or pops into the microwave is refined, processed, or pre-packaged. She moves unselfconsciously to the bass-thumping hip-hop music coming from Dayone's closed bedroom. Simon enters, puts more bags on the counter, then sits at the kitchen table and looks off at the news on a small TV.

Louisa notices him. "It's not a bad cut, but it should have been better healed by now. Too late for you to get a tetanus booster. The new doctor could give you a checkup, you know."

Simon, toying with the arrowhead, looks at his cut hand and shrugs. After dishing a portion into a plastic container from a previous package, Louisa puts the instant meal on the table in front of her father. Victor enters, nods curtly to Simon, and heads to the corner of the room that is his office. It includes a computer and an all-in-one fax machine, scanner and printer. Pointing to Dayone's bedroom, Victor turns on Louisa:

"The sun is down, Louisa! Time for that noise to stop."

Louisa opens Dayone's bedroom door. The music falls silent. Moments later, Dayone enters and sits at the table, wearing an iPod and, with his drumsticks, tapping on everything. He stashes his sticks just in time, as Victor, checking his mail, eyes Dayone, who is still grooving to the earbuds music.

As Victor approaches the table, his patience snaps. "Dayone, take off those things!"

Louisa deflects. "Victor, tell my father how many jobs you figure will be when you build that Government storage thing on the rez."

Wrong! Victor rolls his eyes and sits down. He knows Simon's been influenced by Teo. Louisa hands him a plate of food.

"A lot of jobs. And things would be a lot better if my own son could hear what I say to him. Dayone! For the last time, take off those damned headphones!"

Simon quietly rises and takes his plate outside.

Dayone, tuned out, just widens his uncomprehending eyes. Reaching across, Victor yanks off the earbuds. Dayone reacts quickly, jumping up and falling backwards over his chair. Embarrassed, angry, he grabs his drumsticks and bolts, yelling, "Just leave me the hell alone!"

The door slams; he's gone. Stony silence.

Victor starts to eat, then pushes away and leaves. "A Governor of his tribe, who cannot control his own son. Maybe it's in the boy's blood."

Louisa's face shows pain at the insult.

It's twilight at the crease where the high desert meets the distant mountains. Clouds and setting sun. Cinematic vistas. Maxfield Parrish blue-violets shading the golds. And yet, close by, beyond the small now-deserted gas station at the edge of town, where the highway runs past the turn-off to the Pueblo, at the rear of the property, there's a filthy, trash-strewn dumpster against which sit three teenage boys. One reaches for a 40 oz'er of cheap beer and guzzles it. Another with his grimy hand pours the last drops of carburetor cleaner, a deadly solvent, into a plastic bag containing a dirty rag. The third is tattooing a stag onto his arm with a pen-knife and a ballpoint pen. "Hey, save some for me!"

On the left is Jesse, 15, a hell-raiser, a lost child, an alcoholic. His brother, in circumstance and blood, Armand, 14, takes the plastic bag, carefully jams his face into it, and inhales deeply. The third, forever holding his battered drum-sticks, is Dayone. Their talk is slurred and disjointed, but they obviously understand each other.

"Yo," burps Dayone, "leave some for later, okay, PeeWee?"

Armand inhales after each word. "Don't...call...me...PeeWee, you fu—"

Dayone dutch-rubs Armand hard on the head. From the other side, Jesse digs into Armand's ribs and takes the bag. He sniffs hard... until his head drops heavily. Dayone grabs the bag careful to preserve the fumes. Jesse starts, gulps for air, takes a swig of beer. Dayone inhales deeply, his eyes rolling in drugged ecstasy. "Hey, man, you know why I like this shit so much? 'Cuz it's the cheapest way to kill the mos' brain cells."

Jesse looks confused, but Dayone laughs bitterly and shakes his head. He hands the bag away, then takes his drumsticks and begins to play a complicated paradiddle.

"You goin' home t'night?" asks Jesse.

Dayone spits. "Nah, my dad's a flash bully and wants to kill me like yesterday."

Jesse laughs with Armand. "You could go to your grandfather's."

"He ain't no help...a dirt farmer with no moves, *coyo*."

Ruben Montoya arrives, a scruffy daypack on his back. It's clear he's their spiritual leader—tall, gaunt, poetically handsome. Though he looks like hell right now, there is a vitality and radiant beauty about him. Squatting down, he takes, sniffs, and drinks. Grinning mischievously, his eyes narrow as he looks at his friends.

"Hey, hey, hey! Powwow heaven!" Ruben makes the sound of a monkey as he tries to pull everyone into one pile. Groans and complaints from the others until Ruben makes a show of drawing out from his pack two fifths of cheap whiskey. Wide-eyed awe, then a big shout from the boys.

Armand tries to stand. "Now we can get serious wasted."

Somehow, Jesse remembers. "Aw, man, no. Cuz we gotta go. Mom's going to the hospital, remember?"

Armand looks pitifully at Ruben. "Can we take one of those bottles?"

Ruben hands him one without a thought.

Dayone stands and dances. "Gonna get real bent." He rides his drumsticks off everything and everyone. "Yep, gonna be a spiral by the time we get done. Where'd you score such a beautiful score, man? I know you didn't buy 'em."

"Yeah, right, got 'em from my sister's crazy boyfriend, you know, Mingo...the guy who broke Johnny Tafoya's arm."

"No shit! You ripped 'em off that big dude?"

"Well, he was passed out, and I figured, hell, I can just bring back the empties, and he'll think he drank them."

Everyone laughs. Armand and Jesse stand up shakily. Each takes a huge gulp of whiskey. Then, leaning on each other, they wander off into the closing darkness, swaying, swigging, giggling.

Dayone can't help but take one poke. "Later, man. Later, Pee-Wee."

Armand, from out of the shadows now, "Don't call me...(he burps)...PeeWee!"

"Lay off him, Dayo." Ruben takes the bottle. They stand. Love and friendship. Pass the bottle. Ruben throws his arm around Dayone's shoulder—silhouettes next to a two-lane road that vanishes to a point at the end of the desert.

"C'mon, Dayone, tonight we go on an adventure, a great journey...."

"I'm in there."

They're walking down the highway, heading for the vanishing point. Dayone is thwapping his thigh with his sticks as he walks and wobbles. The sun slips away but the rising moon fills in with a sadder light. The road is deserted. Dayone and Ruben share that wonderful, lucid drunk—no hostility or pettiness, just the clear, charmed reality of poets and saints. Gradually, unselfconsciously, as their pace slows, they begin to dance. For young and gawky, macho young men, their steps are quite delicate and gentle, almost feminine. They dance alone, they dance together, their rhythms connect and their steps become stronger and simpler. They push against the Earth, with every intent to make the Earth feel them. They dance and pause, as if waiting, just long enough, to feel the Earth push back at them. Move and pause, speak and listen, act and react—it was a conversation. And their faces showed how they felt. Ruben's eyes are feral and his tongue an ogre's, he pushes his face into Dayone's.

Dayone growls with each breath, rough, loud, and rapidly. He becomes a shivering gargoyle.

And they dance. And the grotesque sounds they make. And the soft sounds, too, the moaning.

Dayone swoops low, leaps high, and falls into a crouching position beneath Ruben. He watches Ruben and plays his drumsticks off the pavement.

Ruben dances and chants—sounds with meaning, not mere words—until he wheels and freezes and looks Dayone in the eye. He points this way and that. "You know what?" he rasps, breathing heavily. "I think I kind of understand, now."

"Understand what?"

"Why I was born an Indian." His breathing slows.

Dayone takes a big swig. "What do you mean?"

"To be a witness, man." He takes the bottle from Dayone, holds it as an offering to the moon, then drinks long. "It's like all this stuff that's happening, everything that's been going on—it's all leading to something, like, you know, how people ask you what you want to be when you grow up and you never know what to say because you know you aren't gonna grow up—that there's just not enough future left."

Dayone begins leaping up and back into the crouch, again and again.

Ruben shifts his weight from one foot to the other. "You know how when you look into a mirror and you don't see anyone. But you're not afraid. And then just as fast, the guy you're looking at in the mirror, he's looking everywhere but at you. He won't look at you. His eye will never look into your eye, because he is afraid."

Dayone punctuates the moment with a feverish riff of sticks on asphalt.

Ruben throws himself into his dance.

Suddenly, Dayone stops. He's yelling but his voice isn't loud. "Yeah! So what!?"

Ruben slows, stops, and faces his friend. "Well, I think—I know I am here to witness all this—to be here, to see it, to remember it—like, maybe I was here 500 years ago. Before the white man, maybe I was living right here—being a Pueblo, but free, alive, on the Earth, under the sky, not separate, not lonely—just fucking alive in the world."

"Yeah, I know what you mean. I almost felt like that once or twice, when I was a kid."

"Right, yeah, me too—that's what I mean. But now, it's so different, that world's not here. I don't think I can be *in* the world anymore. I can only walk around on top of it. So that's why I think I'm here now. It's like the old part of me—almost remembers—wants to have, like, a last look, you know, a last look at just the world, like, take a last look around and then—BAM!—I'm outta here, catch a bus to California, get rich and famous, beautiful women all over me like your uncle Frank, man."

Dayone remembers eight years ago. When they were nine. A tribal cop caught them for breaking into Sally Archuleta's house to steal an elderberry pie. "We weren't going to steal it. We were just going to eat it," Ruben said to the cop, who took them to the tribal police office anyway.

While they sat there, waiting for Victor and Ruben's mom to take them home and beat the crap out of them, they overheard the Governor talking to the police chief.

"Those FBI guys are here again, trying to find out who Frank Zamora's friends here are—you know, if they're into AIM or that new protest group, Dead Indians for Justice. Could mess up all those annual grants we apply for. They're gonna come talk to us eventually, you know. I wished I knew what were really looking at. We'd know better how to deal with them when they come."

Dayone remembers how then he and Ruben two days later, playing in the plaza, overheard the feds talking and comparing some photographs with what they were looking at. When they walked away, Ruben followed. Dayone followed Ruben. They played…and they listened. Wherever the feds went, the two boys followed. Ruben not only listened—he remembered. The boys knew how to do this without drawing anyone's attention.

The next day they went to the governor's office. Ruben innocently recited everything they had heard—word for word. Dayone couldn't remember a damn thing, except his uncle Frank's name. But he vouched for the accuracy of everything Ruben recounted.

The Governor was dumbfounded. And very pleased. When he turned again to the boys, they were gone.

Dayone is yanked out of his revery by Ruben whooping once loudly, only to be answered by distant coyotes. "I'll send for you, *coyo*. You come and live with me in my big mansion."

He laughs hysterically, wheels around to embrace the night, then takes another swig. Suddenly, he touches his hand to his forehead, looks at the ground all around him, behind him. He looks up into a black sky getting blacker by the sinking of a sad moon. He reels. Melancholy floods his face. He wants to speak, but cannot. Emotional vertigo. Both boys sink slowly onto the littered shoulder of the old two-lane highway.

No movement, no other life on the road, Dayone touches the knee of his best friend.

Ruben inhales and spits, then drops his head. "Shit, dude, I don't know. We're between the ways. The old ways and the no-ways. We're just hanging, like, what do you want to do later, you know, like, when you're 30, or some shit—it's always going through my head."

Dayone coughs a hollow laugh. "I don't know. Probably be dead by then."

Silence—then Ruben jumps up and spins around. "Hey, hey, hey! Watch me do my big deer dance."

Still holding his bottle, he uses his other fingers to make a semblance of antlers. He dances in the moonlight, drunk, powerful, and graceful, elevated by some ancient memory. Slowly he becomes the deer, and the world around him changes. The air becomes thicker. Dayone efforts just to breathe it in as he rocks back and forth to the rhythm of Ruben's steps. The sounds of the desert congeal around a low thrumming far away.

Ruben's footfalls change pace, and he's dances in earnest now, bending low, then raising up to sniff the air for danger—a young buck on the edge of the road. In the moment, so alive, Ruben spins, spins, then suddenly flings the bottle. It cartwheels in silhouette against the moon, through the thickness of the air and the raucous sounds. Ruben stands immobile in the middle of the road, head flung back, both arms out-stretched, howling, exultant.

Sometimes when the panther comes, the deer gives himself to her—the big, black beast, *AI-AI-AIAIIIII...!*

Suddenly, glaring headlights, and then that thud—the sound a deer makes when hit by a heavy high-speed vehicle—followed by the sound of a bottle breaking—then the sound of an 18-wheeler roaring off into the night.

See the frozen face of Dayone, seeing all, incapable of understanding, yet hit again and again by the horror.

Towards the vanishing point, the fancy taillights of a semi-truck fading to black.

Dayone is running. He sees nothing. He hears nothing. Only the vanishing point in front of him now. Whichever way he turns and runs—the vanishing point.

Last year Ruben and Dayone were at a party. Dayone was drunk. Ruben was not drunk. Jack "the Hulk" Munoz was there and very drunk. Jack wanted to pick a fight with Dayone. Ruben stepped in and said, "Don't do that." Jack turned and took a swing at Ruben. Ruben just moved his head away, and Jack missed and fell over. But he got right up and took another swing. Another feint and another miss. Again and again, Ruben just dodged those bullets, without hardly moving a foot. Until Jack was too tired to stand and so sat down in the dirt. Ruben stepped closer and looked down at him intently, curious about something. Jack looked up and softly called Ruben names—the worst he could think of. Ruben kept inspecting the creature sitting on the ground. Dayone finally came over and pulled Ruben away.

"What the fuck you doing, man? He's gonna fucking knife you. You crazy, or what?"

"You ever notice that he has two different colored eyes?"

Dayone is running. There is nothing...until he falls into the arms of his father sitting on the side of his bed. Gasping, crying, in deepest pain: "They took him. The aliens. Ruben, they came and took him. He's gone."

It is morning, and a few late mourners are hurrying into the old Catholic church that presides over the plaza. It's long and narrow, and a waist-high, thick adobe wall surrounds it. For centuries, lovers have leaned against it at sunrise.

Inside, the priest sings prayers for the dead in Spanish. Colored light from stained-glass windows. Simple wooden pews. Women in shawls, men in clean shirts, children trying to be good. Overwhelming, emotional pain. Louisa is crying softly. Will, in a suit, his own losses merging with those of Ruben's family, cannot hold back his tears.

Lola, sitting with her large family, one of whom was an aunt to Ruben, stands and steps over to Will and hands him a candle. "It's okay to light one for your father. I'll show you."

Will shakes his head and turns away, then quickly turns back and nods. He follows her to "the sandbox" where congregants can place their personal candles, a direct communication from them to Jesus, Mary, the many and diverse saints.

He's never stood this close to one. Cautions run through Will's head. *A Jew doesn't light a candle in a Catholic church. It just isn't done. There's no law among the 619 laws in the Torah that forbids it. It must be more of a directive from the collective Jewish gut. Is it a prohibition taught unconsciously, by sensibility or tribal aesthetic?* Will feels queasy doing it, but he breathes into it. He lets go of himself and thinks of the Montoya family. The queasiness dissolves away. He relaxes. He doesn't realize that in this simple act, the entire village has halved the distance between him and them.

Ruben's house. Amidst a grouping of old rustic adobe structures next to a sprawling garden surrounded by vehicles long ago deserted. People enter and leave, some bringing food.

Inside, Ruben's mother is crying, with occasional high outbursts of grief, surrounded by other women. Ruben's body lies on an old be-decked pallet, dressed in leggings and a ribboned shirt, and partially covered with a blanket. Ruben's father, Martin, is in a circle of men. Teo steps over, shakes his hand, offers the traditional envelope, containing support money. Two women enter carrying more food. Victor sits stolidly along a wall with other men. Louisa is in the kitchen. There are various quiet conversations here and there. Jolene sits quietly in a window's alcove, surrounded by four six-year-olds, loyal to her for the fairytales she's read them. They just look at her and say nothing. She reads to them, but she is far-away.

One man, "—and someone told me he was sleeping in the road."

Another, "No, I heard he was drunk and dancing."

His wife, softly, "Not so loud."

Another woman, "Ruben would have gone to college. I know his teacher who told me he was very smart—very smart and—."

Victor, speaking softly, has Teo and another man cornered. "With the grant money, we could build a teen center. Things like this wouldn't happen." Then to Louisa as she passes, "Where's my son? He should be here." Then quickly back to Teo, "Look what we have to gain. For our children."

Teo takes a deep breath, "Our land is our life—our children's life. The world is going crazy. Do we have to follow them?"

"Who?"

"Those who go in stupid directions."

For a brief moment, it seems that Victor is registering and reacting to the insult. But his almost expressionless face slowly fills with a soft but wry smile. He nods and gracefully slides away.

Simon enters, goes to Ruben's father and hands him another envelope. Eyes down, he quickly exits. A few eyes follow him out.

Ruben's younger brother, Tony, helps old Sotero Lujan manage the uneven steps, as they follow Simon out.

Simon stands by a fence. As Sotero passes, he pats Simon on the hand.

Simon grunts a respectful greeting. *It could have been my grandson. It could have been me as a boy. Simon looks up and sees Will leaving. It could have been many of the boys here. The young women aren't doing any better. I really would like to know what would change things. Money? The Indian doesn't understand the concept of money. Victor thinks he does, but he doesn't. Dayone doesn't have a clue. Me, too. Ruben had a lot of clues. Always liked that he was close to Dayone. I know what he offered Dayone. What did Dayone offer him? Dayone doesn't know. Nobody will know now.*

Louisa brings Simon a plate. She, too, pats his arm then re-enters. As Simon eats, something draws him to look up into a tree next to the window. Hidden from view and hiding, curled up and gripping the trunk—Dayone. Without thinking, Simon reaches out towards him—just as Dayone looks down and sees, then turns away. Simon slowly lowers his arm, his head, and puts his plate and fork down.

23

OF THE 432 TREATIES THEY MADE

Days pass. Wynema finds a root that turns red when cut and exposed to air; it smells sweet but puckers her mouth when licked. Mirriamma accepts a visit by two medicine-men from a coastal tribe in Washington state. Louisa all day Sunday, from sunrise to sunset, cleans her house. Teo rebuilds a sweat-lodge with new willow branches and new rug remnants. Will hires Jerry to help him repaint his kitchen. The Pueblo resets itself as it has done for centuries. Such is the virtue of a continuous contained community.

In the Clinic reception area, Simon carefully carries the potted cedar tree from Will's office towards the rear door. He passes Will, who doesn't see him. Will moves quickly through the busy Clinic, absorbed in a patient's chart. Though Will stands head and shoulders above everyone, the patients are now more comfortable with him.

A young boy, with his mother, father, and older sister, opens his mouth and points to a new bandage as Will passes.

Will, charmed, stops short and stoops. "Yeah, it's going to be all right. I bet it won't hurt a bit by tomorrow."

The boy sticks out his hand and solemnly shakes the doctor's. Will stands deeply moved, then rushes off casting one last look and a wave.

Will enters one of the two examination rooms. A small, delicate woman, Mrs. Rojas, mid-thirties, is seated on the end of an examining table. Her little boy watches.

"Hello, I'm Dr. Kornfeld. How can I help?"

The woman is shy and lowers her head.

"I...I feel some way."

"You feel some way? Which way?"

"I feel some way now."

"Can you tell me exactly how you feel—?"

She looks down again and shakes her head. Will purses his lips, pulls at his chin. "Hmm. Excuse me for a moment, please." He exits the room holding up his index finger.

A moment later he has Louisa there, standing next to the woman. Will watches.

"Mrs. Rojas, could you please show me *where* you feel some way?"

Louisa puts her hand into Mrs. Rojas' hand which the woman guides to her pelvic region.

Tapping his forehead as if to ask, Hello, is anyone home? Where?! Of course. I should have thought—. "Okay, now let's get to the why and the what we can do about it. Okay?"

It's a late afternoon, behind the Clinic, as Simon locks up his tools and walks away. The pain in his back is clearly bothering him, but when he hears Will and Louisa around the corner, he turns to listen.

"Doctor, shouldn't we do those biopsies before you even suggest it might be cancer?"

They're at the back door. Will's locking up. "Don't want to lose precious time on something like this. I did the panel, double-checked and correlated the stats over the Johns Hopkins med-line. It is a cancer. But it's early, and we can get it." Then softly as he offers his arm down the steps. "That boy will grow up *not* without his mother."

Will is strangely grim and pleased. Louisa, genuinely concerned.

"Is your mother alive?" she asks.

Will shakes his head. "She and my father died in a car accident when I was nine. My grandmother died of—I lost her when I was—. I'm sorry about your son's friend, Ruben."

"Did your grandmother die of cancer?"

"My grandmother? Yes. I was sixteen when she—"

"I was fifteen."

Will turns with a look of question.

"When my mother died," Louisa adds softly.

"Of cancer?"

"No."

Will stops, reflects, releases a huge sigh. "'It only takes a moment to die.' She told me that—my grandmother did—just before she—. It's the one thing I hate about being a doctor."

Off her look of question.

"Death."

They each lose themselves in their own worlds for a moment.

"And my brother Frank—he was only nine when our mother died. I think it affected him —well, forever"

"My grandfather—I call him Zeyda—he, uh, is the only family I have left." Will goes interior, momentarily shifting his weight and his eyes from one side to the other.

"Doctor?"

Will returns to the moment. "How did your mother die, Louisa?"

Simon, unseen by Will and Louisa, is intent on her answer.

Will is starting to break apart inside. Louisa senses this and changes the subject. "Is that why you decided to study medicine? Your grandmother dying, I mean."

They walk slowly towards Louisa's SUV.

"It makes no sense now, but at the time I thought I should've saved her. I actually believed that for years. She told me I was always too serious. My grandfather always said I wasn't serious enough. Can they both be right? I remember her very well. She laughed a lot. She told me that being my grandmother was the best thing in her life. Her last words."

"I would be proud if I could say that."

He lurches away to his house, hiding the emotions that threaten to overcome him. Louisa stares sadly, nods, then gets into her car. Simon sits on an stack of old adobe bricks, then turns and stares into the setting sun.

More days pass. More weeks. What's happening at the Wind River Trading Post? Teo pulls up. Two elderly Indians in blankets sit on the porch and smoke. One of them is quietly pulling on a beer from a bag. A hippie-wannabe-Indian squats in the shade, stitching leather, apparently very at peace with the world.

Inside, Simon sits on a stool next to a glass-topped display. Phipps has a dirty welder's hat on. "Simon...Simon. All you'd have to do is come and tell stories. We'll set up thirty, forty chairs. That's all. Some stories your grandfather told you, or maybe something personal about what you and your father or uncle did when you was a boy. They'll eat it up, and I'll give you a hundred bucks."

Simon shakes his head, then looks to the door before it opens. Teo steps in. "You ready to go?"

Outside, Simon and Teo head for Teo's van. Phipps exits and locks up.

"I got cleaned up," says Simon, "but I guess I really didn't want to go."

"Simon, please, this has been your way for 30 years. That's long enough. The tribe needs you. You did what you had to do. Now it's time to do what you have to do. Times change. It's that simple."

"You are closer than my blood, but go slow. We'll pick up my truck on the way back, okay?"

Simon winces in excruciating pain as he steps into Teo's van. He looks to see if Teo saw him. He didn't. Suddenly, a commotion breaks out from behind the post-office. A group of teenagers spills into sight, two of them fighting. Teo quickly gets out. Phipps comes barreling out of his truck and breaks up the fight. Dayone and a bigger, older boy, Domingo, are dirty and bloody, wasted, tired, and feeling no pain.

"I warned you guys about this shit at my place!" shouts Phipps, as he grabs both boys in a headlock and squeezes. "Wanna see what I did when I was a bouncer on the Sunset Strip?"

The boys scream until Teo steps up and Phipps eases up.

A third boy in the shadows, a friend of Domingo's, points at Dayone. "He started it. Mingo din't do nothin'."

Dayone, slipping out of Phipp's grasp, charges his enemy. "And I'll do it again if he says anything against Ruben!"

Phipps, now helped by Teo, keeps the fighters apart.

"All I said was that he stole from me," says Mingo, nursing his upper thigh.

"Ruben was no thief!!"

Mingo sneers. Teo, with only a look, orders Dayone away to his van.

"You guys are lucky there weren't no customers out here, 'cause I'da stomp the bejeezus out of ya. You ain't warriors...you're punks!"

Teo to Dayone, "I'm driving you home."

When Dayone reaches the van and sees Simon, he bolts, shouting, "Just let me go! I can take care of myself, 'cause I ain't riding with him!"

As Dayone runs off, Mingo flips him the finger.

Simon looks from one boy to the other. "I wonder what Ruben stole." Off Teo quizzical look: "Domingo is stupid. But he was telling the truth."

They drive slowly onto the Pueblo. When Teo sees a dead dog in the road, he stops and puts it gently into the back. "That's Ramona's dog. Now she has no one. I'll bury it for her." As they continue, "Boys can be stubborn."

Flatly, Simon says, "He gets it from me."

Teo snaps a look at Simon. Simon turns and they lock eyes. Teo turns away first, then wearily, "That's bullshit."

When Simon says nothing, Teo softens his voice. "Why does your grandson reject you?"

Simon says nothing.

They pass two men unpacking a new freezer-chest from its cardboard box. Then a young man fixing the stainless steel flue to his fireplace, his hands black with the patching compound. Then two magpies taunting a dog on a chain, while a dozen other magpies plunder the kibble from the dog's bowl.

Teo answers his own question: "Because he knows you know him, and he is not ready to know himself."

Simon changes the subject. "The Council meeting we're going to. I am not my grandfather, or my father. I'm just the next stepping-boulder down the creek." As the van winds through the Pueblo towards the meeting, Simon adds, "I'll listen, but I will not speak. I have my reasons."

"Your reasons are not reasons. They are old ghosts. Let them go."

A few hundred yards down the biggest roadway leading away from the plaza and across from the Tribal Courtroom are the Government Tribal Offices, including the Council Meeting Hall, a tall, flat-roofed adobe with a portico along the front. Some people mill about. Children play. The dirt street is wider here. Under the portico, there are two rooms or stalls that serve as a pottery and a jewelry shop.

In front of the jewelry shop, Phipps worries his beard but talks confidentially to Will. "Nah, I never been in one of them meetings, but I know what goes on. You're special, you're the doc, so you gain entrance." He stops talking, but his mouth keeps moving, as if he were silently talking to himself. "You gonna talk about your health survey thing, right? Well, give 'em the facts they want and don't go acting like you understand the Indian. They hate that."

He pulls at his beard again. "You see, they got lotta secrets, things that you and I ain't never gonna learn. I mean, you're their doc, but I bet you don't know who their real medicine men are, the religious leaders who hold the real power. Hell, I don't either. But the tourists, and there's a lot of 'em, are hungry for magic and mystery. So I get medicine men, the real McCoys, from other tribes. And I set up, ya know, seminars. I want to do one on the rez, you know make it more authentic, but the Council don't buy it. So I'll do it again this year in Santa Fe. Might be interesting, ya know, as a doctor, for you to come to one."

Will's interest has shifted to Wynema, who's crossing the street, carrying a cardboard box. Phipps tracks his gaze. Wynema briefly glances at them but quickly lowers her gaze. She enters the pottery shop.

"Good eye, doc. I know her. Works for the best potter on the rez. College girl, too. But don't get no ideas. The last thing you want to do is be nailed for nailing the locals."

Several men pass close by and enter the Council building.

A patient from the clinic waves to Will, though he doesn't remember his name.

Will, thanking Phipps with a shake of the trader's thick hand, enters the building.

Across the street, Teo is parking his van.

A Indian who shows Phipps a silver concho belt draws him away.

Inside the Tribal Council Hall there is a circa-1900 painting of a tribal Governor holding a silver-tipped cane. That cane is mounted on the wall behind the Governor's chair. A villager, serving as sergeant-at-arms, instinctively raises his hand to stop the white man—until he understands that this is the doctor whom he's been told to let pass. He points to a row of chairs off to the right of the raised dais.

The meeting is underway.

Will's senses are heightened as he takes his seat. He hears the coughs, the moving chairs, the muted whispers, the rattling of a slow-moving electric fan. Will has kept his eyes down, but now he slowly takes in the room. It's dimly lit and there's smoke in the air. Will doesn't like that, but this is a different culture. The curtains are half-closed. Twenty men sit at tables arranged in a U. Four chairs are empty. More chairs behind and then benches for villagers in the center of the room and around the perimeter. Half the seats hold villagers, mostly men, only a few women, and no children. All avert their gazes and show no impatience—except Victor, who sits in the center as Governor. His eyes and fingers give away his stony anxiety.

There is a microphone on the circular table in front of every Council Member's chair—all except Victor's. He doesn't use a table mic; he alone wears a wireless lapel mic, as he often stands and walks as he talks.

Council member Clarence Pino is talking. He's in his early 40's, heavy-set, and wears a wide-brim, Montana-bent cowboy hat. He sits next to Victor and looks at each seated Council member as he speaks. If there is a generalizable Native American accent, Pino has cultivated it. "So I guess what I been trying to say is, well, the government has always taken from us and now we can take back. Legally. We deserve it. That's what I'm trying to say." He sits down slowly.

Victor picks up the slide projector's remote. "On my recent trip to Washington and Raleigh, North Carolina, (click) I toured some nuclear power installations. (click) They showed how the government transports spent fuel rods." (click) He looks at an empty seat near him and then around the room. "Council Member Vigil should be hearing this. Anyway, I sent a complete set of the important documents to each of your homes yesterday. I asked you to read them and think about them. This is an important moment for us. Do any of you have any specific questions right now?"

Council member Churino stands up, a document in his hand. "What's the main difference between a "permanent repository" and a "Monitored Retrieval Storage" facility...this MRS?"

In slow motion, Victor slaps his hand down on the table in front of him. "An MRS is temporary. Only used for 40 or 50 years. Then the rods get moved to a permanent place, like what they're trying to build down in Carlsbad and another over under Yucca Mountain in Nevada. Those facilities are built to last ten thousand years."

Council member Reyna stands. "How much of our land they need?"

Victor answers. "Only about 200 acres. Built above ground. I got a slide...(click, click, click) Here. It looks like a low-rise industrial park. Blends into the landscape."

Teo and Simon enter. Teo goes to his chair on the dais, Simon to a side bench in the back. Council members, including Victor, are surprised at Simon's presence.

"Ah, good, good...I see that, uh, Council member Vigil is here."

Simon tries to be invisible, breathing long, slow, and contained.

Victor is reasonable, committed, confident, and subtly works his people. "Please don't get me wrong. I'm not saying we should build a storage facility on our land at this time. Maybe later. Maybe never. What I *am* saying is—and listen carefully, please—if the government is willing to pay us a hundred thousand dollars just to study the possibilities, I'm willing to look into it—if there are no strings attached. But they must give us the money first, which will go to our own people, create jobs, teach our kids how to use computers. So I say we will learn a lot, without promising to build anything, maybe ever." Satisfied with his explanation, he sits down.

Teo rises. "You say we can claim this grant money even if we choose later not to build?"

Victor nods.

"No tricks? No Catch 22's?"

Victor shakes his head.

Teo looks left and right, smiles grimly. "You talking about the same Federal Government we all know? Of 432 treaties they've made with Indians, they've broken all but two."

A few wry chuckles. Separately, Simon and Will gauge the room until their eyes meet.

"We can stop—." Victor holds his reply until the room quiets, then regains control of the discussion by making the men wait an uncomfortable moment longer. Finally, "We can stop negotiations at any time. No penalties. I've had lawyers check into it. We do our 'study,' we can keep the money...no matter what we do after that. They know some of us are not going to build anything. They're willing to lose that money. I'm willing to take some of the money they're willing to lose and spend it on our village. Aren't you?"

Teo is unconvinced by Victor's confidence. "There is more at stake than money."

"Like safety," says Victor swiftly. "The money will pay to study these things."

Teo presses. "A hundred thousand dollars is not much money for the whole tribe. What if they paid us to study the "feasibility" of selling our tribal lands in exchange for a hundred thousand dollars to every man, woman, and child of our tribe? Just the *feasibility*—would you be for that, too?"

"No!"

"How about three hundred thousand? Five hundred thousand?"

"I get your point. This is different."

Clarence rises with passion. "Yes. It is completely different. We need economic development. And we must vote as a tribe to get what we can."

Council member Churino slowly stands. "I was opposed. Now I am in favor."

In the momentary silence, an on-looker stands. "I need a job."

Another Council member: "I am ready to vote with Governor Moquino."

Teo looks to Simon for help, but Simon lowers his head.

Victor whispers to Clarence. "One more vote and we have enough."

Victor stands. "To the Council I say, I have looked into every aspect of this. I have sat for long hours with President Chino of the Mescalero Apaches, and he has told me of all the benefits. Phase One is only the beginning. Phase Two is an additional two point eight million dollars. There are technicalities, but we will still be under no obligation to build a damn thing on our Pueblo. They're trying to lure us. They are desperate. But there is no barb on the hook! Time for us to step out of the Stone Age."

Suddenly, from the plaza outside, the sound of screeching brakes, vehicular impact, glass breaking. Pandemonium inside...outside. Most of the people in the courtroom rush to the windows or the doors to leave.

～

As Mirriamma, at home in her kitchen, reaches for a box of herbs on a shelf next to the sink, she stops suddenly and listens. Wynema, washing dishes, notices this and pulls the iPod's earbuds. "What's up?" Mirriamma just shrugs and takes a sniff at the little box.

～

Outside, next to the collision, two men hold Dayone as he struggles to reach Mingo, the boy he had fought earlier and who is now struggling to get out of the old Datsun he's just crashed into the corner of the pottery shop. People from everywhere, including Phipps, converge on the scene.

Victor sees Dayone and moves quickly. The crowd separates and lets him through. He is furious, larger than life, and with a look commands the fight-action to cease. Mingo is bloody, drunk, and dizzy. Will starts to step in as a doctor, but Simon gently restrains him.

Mingo wipes the blood from his forehead. "He threw a fuckin' rock through my window!"

"And he tried to run me over!" Dayone raises his fist, but Victor grabs the hand and bends it backward, forcing Dayone to cry out and fall to his knees.

"You've embarrassed me for the last time." As Victor bends his son's hand even further, Simon, out of nowhere, lightly touches Victor's arm, causing him to release Dayone.

169

Though Simon is embarrassed for interfering, he speaks. "Let's let the police take care of this. You want to finish your meeting. Let's slow everything down, as is proper."

Teo is upset by Simon's trying to restart the meeting. "We don't have the votes, Simon."

"We may lose the votes this round, but it is Victor who holds the power. Let's give him some rope."

Dayone bolts. Victor glowers at Simon, then shouts to his deputy. "Call Tribal. Tell 'em to take both boys into custody." Then to everyone, "The best thing to do now is get back in the meeting and complete our business."

As Victor passes Will, in a low and strained voice, "We won't speak about your health study today. But we are going to do it."

Inside, a few minutes later, Victor, jaw clenched, is quietly counting heads. Clarence surveys the room and nods to Victor. Will stands off to one side, swept along.

Teo addresses the room. "All the members are not going to return. We'd better postpone—"

"We have a quorum," says Victor breathing heavily through flared nostrils.

When all are seated, before Victor can set the vector, Simon rises.

"My grandfather, Valentino Zamora—." He pauses, takes a deep breath, reticent and awkward. The room quiets. He continues, "Many years ago he was a Chairman of the All Indian Pueblo Council. He told me the story about Blue Corn Girl and Coyote, the one where Coyote seems to be in a big hurry like that and asks her to fill his jar with corn. Blue Corn Girl thinks it's a little jar because she only sees the top of it sticking up above the ground, but underneath the ground is—the rest of the jar, and it's big."

Excited sounds of recognition and understanding by a few people.

Council member Churino is impatient. "Yes! We all remember. She had no idea what she was really promising to do."

Laughter, grunts, other human but inarticulate sounds are released by various people, all expressing relief from the previous tensions.

Simon, "There are things we can do if we own the land. There are things we can do if we protect the land for our grandchildren. They are not the same. Does the land belong to us the living? We have votes. Yes. But I say the land belongs to the dead and those not yet born. They do not have votes. We must check for the 'big jar'."

Will is fascinated with Simon.

Churino attempts to recover his power. "My grandmother told that story to me, but it has nothing to do with—"

Teo stands. "Is there nothing we can do to raise money in a way that doesn't dishonor or endanger the land?"

More mumbling and grumbling from community members.

Victor rises as he sees Council Member Reyna returning. "I think we can vote now. We can work together on this. Our grandparents worked together."

Simon, still uncomfortable, assesses the faces of the council. He starts to say something else, thinks better of it, sits down.

An old man, standing next to Teo, elbows his friend in the ribs, "Maybe your grandmother, Victor, 'made bread' with Simon's grandfather."

Everyone bursts out in laughter...even Will gets the off-color joke.

But Teo doesn't want the frivolity to take over. "There is wisdom in our stories. Let us wait and look deeper...as is proper."

Something about this turn makes some of the Council Members nervous. Reyna and two others voice agreement with Teo. They rise to leave.

Clarence is furious, but Victor restrains him and whispers, "There are many stories where Cougar beats Coyote. We haven't lost. And, please, don't look like we've lost."

Clarence nods.

Outside the Tribal Courthouse, the setting sun casts that unique New Mexican earth-and-rosy glow on all vertical surfaces. The villagers spill out. Simon avoids people. Several council members draw Teo off to talk privately. Teo suddenly stops, as if what they are saying 'proves' his point, then with pursed lips indicates Simon, who stands alone by the truck. They all look and reflect for a moment. "Ever think you'd see him do that?" Teo says with wry grin.

Jesse, Dayone's friend, runs past Will who's walking away towards the clinic. "Frank is coming! Frank is here! I saw him off the plaza!"

Two more teenagers run by shouting. Heads look up the street. A mid-70's, battered Ford 4x4 pickup, carrying a big camper and pulling a trailer-mounted Harley-Davidson chopper, rounds the corner and heads towards the Courthouse. People shout and scatter. All except Simon, who doesn't move.

Frank pulls up sharply, coming within a foot of knocking down his father. Frank leaps out, wiping his nose and loosening his jaw as if he just snorted cocaine, happy to see everyone, including Simon. He is carrying a long, thin, dark purple velvet bag and accompanied by two young women. One is Asian wearing a sexy woman's version of what Frank wears. Her hair is short-cropped and dyed metallic bronze. The other is an Indian from the plains wearing biker black leathers and mirrored glasses, beyond cool. Frank, as always, is in costume, but a bit on the scruffy side.

Frank rushes to Simon, taking his hand. "Hey, Pop. Where's Victor? I mean, you knew your neon redskin was comin' home, didn't ya? I'm askin' the Council to sponsor my next tour. It's a money-maker and I got the numbers to show it. How the hell are ya?"

Simon tries to hide his discomfort. But Frank is famous and his fans crowd around him to welcome him home.

Will is drawn back, but stays in the background, watching.

Jesse rushes up to Frank. "I saw you on MTV, *coyo*, doing that rad-rap poet thing. You were smoke, man!"

"Thanks." Even flying, Frank can sense something. "Is the meeting over? Simon? Where's Victor? What's going on? Let's go get a drink together afterwards, on me, just like new times."

Simon takes a deep breath. "It's good to see you in one piece and happy." He pulls away and heads towards Teo's van.

Teo and fellow members of his clan watch as Victor exits the building, clearly upset with the meeting, accompanied by Pino, Churino, Reyna, and others. Frank heads to Victor, pulling himself together as they meet. Victor knows how popular this anti-hero is.

Galantly extending the velvet bag, "Hello, Governor. This is a Governor's Cane, stolen in the mid-eighteen hundreds from Pojoaque

Pueblo by the grandfather of the grandfather of a lovely Chicana I met in Los Angeles. She gave it to me to liberate it from her father who's a racist and abusive and—." Frank steps in closer to Victor. "I thought you'd like to be the one to return it. I, uh, hoped to make it before the end of the meeting because I have a money-making idea that can get some righteous respect for our village and your attempts to—"

"Your timing is bad, Frank." Victor takes a deep breath, more for all the villagers circling them round. "But I'm grateful for the...for the repatriation of this cane. Quite a story."

He takes one step away then quickly steps back and speaks flatly. "But your sister and I welcome you. You can park at our house tonight, and I'll talk with you tomorrow. Meeting's over."

Victor walks off before Frank can stop him. Frank's fans crowd him.

Simon sits in Teo's truck, lost in thought

Teo gets in. 'Preciate your story in there like that. 'Preciate it a lot. Damn. You hit the nail on the head—drove it deep with one little blow."

Teo drives off slowly through the dispersing villagers. They pass closely by Will who's walking home. Simon and Will's eyes connect and then disconnect.

As Will turns away from the receding truck, he is face to face with Phipps. "Now din't we catch a little action here on the rez this morning, eh Doc?" asks Phipps with a know-it-all look. "Heh-heh. There ain't many people gonna see what you'n me'll see over the next few years."

Will immediately knits his brow. He hasn't a clue what Phipps means by this.

24

HE AIN'T NO CHICKENSHIT SUICIDE

Early the next morning, three elders, as is their way, are gauging the sunrise and the season. Unseen by them but on another roof no more than a hundred yards away, Dayone. He's slept the night there. He stands, stretches, grabs his blanket, and descends quietly.

In front of the Moquino house half a mile away is Frank's camper. Inside, it's messy, clothes strewn everywhere. An AIM poster on one cupboard, a Jimmy Hendrix on another. Empty bottles, chips bags. Frank is sleeping between the women. Outside, the sound of two dogs momentarily fighting. Frank groans into half-consciousness and tries to swallow the foulness in his mouth. He reaches for a quart of whiskey and peers out through the curtain.

Dayone comes around the corner zipping up his pants. He is immediately attracted to Frank's Harley. Putting his drumsticks on the seat, he runs his fingers along the chrome valve covers. Victor exits his front door and Dayone tries to hide down behind the Harley. Too late. Victor sees him, motions him not to move. Dayone, slouched and ready for hell, beats his drumsticks into his hand.

Victor is soft and lethal. "In two hours, you and me are taking a ride to Albuquerque. If you aren't here when I get back, and if we can't work out something with the counselor at Group Home, you're going to St. Mary's in Omaha. You understand what that means?"

"What would you do if they called your best friend a chickenshit suicide?"

"You shamed me."

"He's dead! Don't you understand?!"

Frank exits the camper wearing only jeans, carrying a big sauce-pan that he fills from a faucet then pours over his head. Dayone starts to bounce and move backwards.

Victor tries to soften, but he's awkward. "Look, I know it was a tragedy. But if both of you hadn't been out drinking and lying around in the middle of the road, none of this wo—"

"It wasn't like that! You're such a big tribal chief, but you don't know what's happening. All you care about is your power-trip. Well, don't worry about me. I'm gone!" He wheels and he is...gone.

Victor fumes and sputters and congeals to a point. He quickly recovers. "That's it. Nothing more to do. It's Omaha."

Frank is pulling on his boots, forcing his head to integrate. "Wait! Victor. He's on fire. Don't do anything yet. I'll bring him back."

The wind from the motorcycle fills his lungs like a sunrise. Up and down the crooked paths and rutted roads, his long wet hair flying, sans shirt, Frank sees Dayone ahead and pursues. Catching up, he cuts the boy off. Neither of them move. Both just stare ahead. Finally, Frank coughs and grunts. "You get that poster I sent you?"

Dayone cavitates, he's stuck, and yet his body is moving in a thou-sands directions at once. For a few moments he breathes fast and hard. Then with one deep breath, he stills and nods his head.

They still don't look at each other.

Frank is fiddling with the tassels that hang from the end of his handlebars. "Fathers can be sonsabitches, you know?"

Dayone nods slowly in blind and numbing anger.

"Dayone. You're a good man. But Victor, and maybe you neither, don't know that. You know, sometimes it's like walking a fence. You don't know whether to trust them down on that side or this side. And if you slip, they hit you in the balls."

"My best friend died. He's dead, Frank, dead."

Frank, moved, nods, then draws in and releases a big breath. "I know. I lost a best bud last year when Billy-Free Begaye died." Frank is suddenly emotional and fragile. "He sure as hell fought for his peo-ple over at Big Mountain. He was a warrior, man, a dance-all-night Diné. He wasn't afraid to die and he knew what for."

"I know what you mean."

"Do you know what I mean?"

Dayone is alchemized again, into pure anguish. "I know what you mean, shit!"

Frank reaches in his saddlebags and draws out a half-empty pint of Wild Turkey, takes a swig and hands bottle to Dayone who chugs until Frank pulls it away.

"I heard you trashed Mingo for payin' Ruben no respect."

"I can't believe he's gone, man. I turn to talk to him. I—I can feel him right next to me, man!"

"Hey, it's all right, man. Think about it. He's free now. No more hard times, no more pain, just one big easy smoke. Look, his spirit, it's here now." Frank bends over and picks up a handful of dirt and extends it to Dayone. He lets it pour out into the boy's hand. "You carry it with you wherever you go. But you gotta tell him, man...you gotta tell him that you're okay."

The boy is big-eyed and credulous. "What!? Why?"

Frank steps off his bike and spreads his arms wide. "So he can pull on his mocs and go on. His spirit just needs to know you're okay. Then he can go on."

"Where?"

"Who knows? Only way to know that, man, you gotta go where he went. Everyone's gonna know sometime. You just gotta not be afraid to learn."

Both of them go interior with their thoughts.

Frank flashes back two years when he, thirty miles outside of Phoenix, at the edge of the Pima reservation, was attending an all-night peyote church meeting. Suddenly, their ceremony was crashed by the cops—deputy Sheriffs from two counties. Heads were cracked. Blood was spilled. Many were arrested. The revered teepee was destroyed, and objects sacred to the religion confiscated. Frank went crazy. He was hit and rendered unconscious for two days.

Dayone remembered how naturally and gracefully and unselfconsciously Ruben assisted the birth of calf. Dayone wanted to go for help, but Ruben insisted there wasn't the time and that they could do it. Dayone remembered how Ruben's father had berated Ruben for not going for help, especially since the cow belonged to a prominent

Spanish family that paid the Montoyas for grazing rights. Dayone's anger at the injustice builds....

We fear for Dayone, but it's Frank who starts to hyperventilate. He jerks for another snort, but it's empty. "Fuck it! When you don't have your mother and father...when they're just not there...you can miss your brother a lot."

Frank starts to fall sideways, off-balanced.

Dayone steadies him.

Frank regroups. "I know and you know and there are a lot of brothers and sisters out there, living in the death of their ways, looking for home. I miss him...I miss Billy-Free a lot. Ah, Jesus, I miss a lot of things, *coyo*!"

He needs a drink. Throwing down his empty bottle, he jumps on his Harley and revs it, fishtails, then tears away across the desert through the mesquite and sage.

Dayone just shakes his head in despair and watches. 200 yards away, Frank swerves to miss a tree and goes down. Dayone plods towards him.

⁂

The Tribal Office is neat and spare, unpretentious and somewhat dark. Deeper into the complex, Victor's office is somewhat brighter. There's more glass here, more metal, more Indian art nicely mounted. Victor sits behind his glass-topped walnut desk. Councilman Clarence Pino is kneeling next to a lockable file cabinet, ordering some papers into a pendaflex. He knows these papers must not be seen by anyone, including secretaries. He must do this menial work himself. He is nervous about what he is about to suggest to Victor.

Manley, ever the consultant, looks calmly from Victor to the colorful LCD of his PDA upon which he writes with a stylus.

Clarence stands. "You could call a special meeting, Victor. Or just sign the damn order and we'll pull the votes later. The Council will back you when it's time. They will, Victor."

Manley deftly slides the stylus into its integral scabbard. "Governor, executive orders like these are signed every day, at every level of government—"

There's a quiet knock at the door. Victor's secretary sticks her head in, but Victor waves her away.

Manley continues smoothly. "Let's face facts, Governor. Twenty-four out of the twenty-nine 'communities' that have applied for this opportunity have been Native American tribes. It's a competition, plain and simple, and the most together tribe is going to win. And win big."

Victor ruminates and pours a coffee refill and sips. He looks at Clarence then at Manley. Then coolly nods. Manley has a pen out in a flash.

Victor signs. "I have the authority."

25

A Doctor but No Healer

The door to Exam Room Two opens and Tessie Vigil pulls her daughter Jolene out into the hallway. In their last trimester, both women waddle as they escape the room quickly. Frustrated, pleading, Will's voice calls from within the exam room, trying to stop her. "Mrs. Gomez—I mean, Mrs. Vigil, would you just wait a minute? I know I can explain it to you."

Will steps out into the hallway, but the women disappear around the corner. Lola exits the exam room carrying the charts. She follows Will who's following after the women.

Outside, Will bounds down the steps and reaches Tessie at her car. "Mrs. Vigil, let me just explain. The pills I prescribed...you have to—"

Tessie is in tears. "We have our ways—I do the best—you say I will kill my child—"

"No, I meant nothing like that—all I mentioned was what could happen if a woman your age didn't watch her diet, mixed up medications, and didn't take certain preventative—"

The car starts. "You are called a doctor, but you are no healer. You cannot help me."

Will shouts after her, but Jolene's husband, Jerry, is already driving off with the women.

Get real!—you ignorant, frightened, narrow-minded women! You're still frightened of white man's ways—after how many centuries!? Become the warriors you once were! The world has changed. Learn the terrain and you'll move through it as easily as you did...the forests. Take from us what is good. Take from us what is good for you. Take from us this goddamn...cup of redemption!

The government is not going to say: 'We're sorry for what we've done to you.' It'll never happen. But there are people, millions of people, all over the country who say every day: 'I'm sorry.'

Modern medicine that's based on good science is good. Let it give you what it can. Learn how to take it to make yourselves stronger and healthier.

We know how to turn technology to good advantage. Whose good advantage? Whoever takes advantage of it.

We're the invaders here. Turn us back. Not by brute force. No, we understand brute force all too well. Turn us back with your wiles, your wit, and the best of your traditional ways. Win us over with your beauty, grace, and honesty.

We're as desperate as you.

Overcast. Dark at the horizon. In the distance, across the gorge, the mountains are suddenly attacked by summer thunder and lightning.

Under his breath, Will says, "I can too help you! Goddammit." Then weakly, "I am a healer."

Louisa steps up next to him, surprising him. He faces her. "Her blood panel reads exactly like a woman I lost to an amniotic embolism last year. And she, Mrs. Vigil, isn't following my perfectly clear instructions. She has edema and I—"

He kicks a dirt clod angrily as he returns to the Clinic.

A few minutes later, in his office, Louisa is seated. Will paces behind his desk.

"I *was* talking with her."

"But you're not talking *to* her."

"I'm not here to tell them stories and wave feathers. What I do is cure them, fix them up, make them healthy. Haven't you people had real doctors here before?" He walks out of his own office.

Real doctors sometimes take a long time to make, she thinks.

Simon is working his fields. His horse is grazes nearby. The *thrum-bub* sound that only a Harley makes pulls him around. Frank, battered and disheveled, wheels up, followed by his women driving his camper. Dayone sits sullenly behind Frank. For a moment, Frank just watches his father working. The women get out to pet the horse.

Frank speaks first. "I swear, you can grow anything anywhere."

"Not this year. Anyway, the soil grows the plants. I just grow the soil."

"And I just came to, uh...are you okay? You look bent over. Just came to say g'bye, you know."

Father and son look at each other. Awkward.

Frank jumps off his bike. Dayone slides in behind the handlebars.

From the saddlebags, Frank takes out a copy of his book. He is calm. "The Council turned me down—the Neanderthals. I get more help from other tribes than I do my own."

"But they care about you more than other tribes."

Now he is not calm. "I do what I do, Dad. And I'm good at it, bein' a drunken poet."

The silence slowly crumbles into awkwardness again. "Well, I guess I'll go. Hey, did you get a copy of my book? Maybe I sent you one." Off Simon's nod, he adds, "You didn't read it, though, did you?"

Simon says nothing, picks up his tools.

Frank, in the middle of this wide-open field, begins by poking the air. "Yeah, well, you missed some good stuff."

"Maybe we should talk...or pray together."

As if at a horse-race, urging on the horse he bet on, Frank whips the air with his hand. "You're a colorful old shit. A real inspiration. You haven't prayed in a thousand years. So, no trips on me, okay? We can talk next month in Albuquerque. I got a big club gig there. I'll send you tickets. I want you to come. How many tickets you want? Okay? What a trip."

As Frank turns to go, Simon ventures, "Some things in my life are changing—" But he dodges the truth. "The tribe's trying to decide how to deal with this offer by the government to—"

"This tribe, like all tribes, is finally falling apart, and you're just growing old and scared."

Neither of them notice Dayone kicking down a stack of firewood next to the fence and walking away, heart-broken.

Frank circles Simon, "Afraid you're gonna die before atoning for your sins."

Simon doesn't fight. He speaks matter-of-factly. "That wouldn't be good, would it? What you say is true."

Frank climbs on his bike and lets loose: "Don't die, Simon, not yet. And don't try and change me. I need at least one parent who doesn't give a shit about me. So's I can drink. So I can write!"

Now Frank sees nothing. *Use the hurt to focus. But it doesn't focus. It blurs. I can't hold onto it. If I hold onto it, and he holds onto it, nothing moves. Nothing explains itself. A tug of war. Cross the line. You lose. His love hasn't fallen as far as mine. If he isn't as sorry, what good does it do? No justice. Just hurt. Turn it into something useful. Art stands alone. Art transforms. Art is lonely because it is art. The world creating itself is a lonely world. You're a dumber fuck than I am, Simon.*

As Frank slowly drives away, Simon unconsciously takes a few steps in that direction. Frank's women follow in the camper. Simon looks off at Dayone, disappearing into the rise of piñon and juniper behind the ramada. He tries to continue hoeing, but cannot. He leans on his hoe for a second, then lets it drop and walks dejectedly into his little house.

Simon stands at the window looking out, a glass of water in hand. He stares.

At the far end of his corral fence is the path to the Pueblo. He sees a young pregnant mother leading her six-year-old son back to the village. It's Jolene and Rio. They wave to Simon.

But Simon doesn't see them. What he sees takes place 33 years earlier. The woman outside is Dahyanee, his wife, in her late 20's, pregnant with Frank. The child with her is Louisa at six. Mother and daughter are having fun, and a little difficulty...with their pony.

Louisa looks at Simon and calls out lovingly: "Please, daddy, come outside and help us teach my pony good manners."

When Simon doesn't answer, Dahyanee, disappointed and perhaps a little fearful, speaks sweetly, "Oh, really, Simon, put away your jealousy. I know you're in one of your jealous moods, so come outside and be with Louisa and me."

He remembers himself then: The younger Simon, holding a glass pitcher of water and a glass, paces by the window, torn up inside by anger, guilt, and the ravages of clawing jealousy. He stomps to the door and roars: "Where were you?! I'll kill you if you lie."

Louisa grabs the pony's neck in reaction to her father's shouting. Dahyanee stops and turns and shakes her head. "I told you. I was with Gloria, not her brother, helping her with her dance costume. Her brother wasn't even there. He was in town and besides I think he's a jerk, an idiot, a nobody. I haven't seen her brother in days and he's never so much as—"

Young Simon explodes with rage. "Not true!" He smashes the pitcher sideways into the doorjamb, cutting himself.

The sound breaking glass brings Simon back into the present. He looks at his hand with its agéd scar, then down to where the glass he was holding lies broken. He looks around, goes to his cot and lies down. He takes hold of his fetish bag and closes his eyes.

Outside, the air is cooling. The gibbous moon, having waited until the sun had set, now rises, its light eerily neon. An owl opens the night. The air is soft, almost still. Suddenly, the hazy metallic light is cut by a brief eruptive chorus of coyotes which though distant is clear and concise and crystallizes the air.

Simon is sleeping. He starts into full wakefulness. The coyotes are silent now. He sits up and puts his feet on the ground, alert. Something is wrong. He stands abruptly only to get hit with a sharp pain in the middle of his back. Shaking it off, he moves silently to the door and opens it slowly.

The moonlight shades his face with greens and oranges. *What is it?* Those are the only words he hears inside his head. Then the words cease. Now there is only a drawing out, a pulling, as he puts on his boots and steps out into the night. The sound of flapping wings turns him in a direction. He follows, drawn to something.

When he reaches his corral, his horse turns away and walks briskly to a far corner. Simon follows that lead then continues on in the same direction into the hills.

He finds himself in an arroyo, kaleidoscopic in the moonlight. He moves silently, sensing, not thinking...being drawn. The arroyo bends...until he can see further up the gully. He stops and moves forward cautiously. Then he hears the sobbing, and recognition fills his face. One step further and he sees the boy leaning against a boulder, tears streaking his face, moonlight glinting off the pistol he clutches to his chest.

The terror in the boy's eyes, the pain, the despair. Simon hand slowly reaches for the leather fetish bag around his neck. He inhales as if to call out, but sinks down quietly onto the ground and begins to chant softly, way up raspy-high in his throat.

Dayone hears nothing, except the pounding in his head. His face is wild, fighting off nausea. He cocks the gun, drives the muzzle up under his cheekbone, gashing himself with the front sight. One word escapes his throat, "Ruben". His body, his arm, his finger slowly contracts to pull the trigger—when suddenly he hears the unmistakable deep threatening growl of a bear. It startles him and instinctively he wants to turn the weapon towards the sound, but it is too late. His finger has pulled the trigger.

Simon's mouth is wide open and horror fills his face. He runs to the boy as fast as he can.

But until he reaches him, Dayone falls into the fireball he's become: *I see you, Ruben! But I don't know how to reach you. I can't move. The light hurts my eyes. Where did you go?! I'll get my mother. She'll help you. Help me, Mom! Mom! Mom, I didn't take anymore money from your purse. I promise. Tell Ruben's mom that I see him. He's okay. He knows how to be okay. Man, does he know! I can, too. I'm not afraid. Not a kid anymore. Fuckers won't let me be an Indian. They don't know. I'll show them. Ruben showed them.*

In his bungalow, Will, wearing only sweat pants, is staring intensely into a wall mirror as he tries to mount one of his U.S. Cavalry sabers above it. Finally, sick of his own image, he turns away, stepping first one way, then the other. Unable to remain caged, he charges out into the night, a saber still in his hand.

Behind the bungalow now, he stalks away from the buildings, through the knee-high sage, finally stopping to slash a cactus with the saber. On the outside he's slashing. On the inside, the same. *I told you. Why I came here. I'm not here to play culture games. You didn't go to Israel to live. You went there...to die! I'm doing what my people never did. And never America! Would have made things so much simpler. Seen us for our feelings, our regret. Don't suffer too much, or they'll never believe you. Can't pass through a white forest unless you dress in white. And that won't happen until their bones bleach. Everybody's bones bleach white.*

He exhales with a growl, lowers his blade, and stirs the cactus debris. His cell rings.

It's Jahbig. "Your email sounded depressed, mon. I'm just getting off. You got a minute?"

"I am so happy you called. Shit, am I happy!"

"Hey, I love you, too, mon. Should I be worried about you?"

For a moment, Will cannot reply. He shakes his head, No. "Maybe a little. How can it be so damn different, what you're doing and what I'm doing? You finding the education we got standing you in good stead? I'm not."

"You knew it was going to be different."

"I did?!"

"We discussed it."

"We did?!"

"You're supposed to be shocked. Well, at least a bit. Enough to pull the veil from your eyes."

"The fuck you talking about?!"

"You've seen the veil, mon. The good news is you've pulled it off! If you've made it to talking about it, you've already pulled it off. Rejoice!"

"Jah, shut up. Listen. I don't know if I can make it. I mean, this is fuckin' nuts here. It's another world. Discontinuous to ours. I respect their culture. Damn. I should have held her hand. Not judged her. That's what my mom would have done. Just taken her hand and listened and—she's right."

"Who's right? What are you talking about?"

"A patient. Who doesn't know how to meet the medicine halfway, doesn't know how to bring herself to the medicine we bring her. They need a fucking course in what the modern world is all about! Am I a healer or not?"

"Oh, my dear, you poor sonuvabitch. *That's* where you're at. That's why you're down. They got you there that quick, huh? I don't know whether to praise you or praise them—.

"What do you mean that's where they got me?"

"At the bridge. My sympathies. You want me to come on out for a few days? I just did a colleague here a big favor. I think he'd cover me, no problem."

"What bridge?!"

"When the doctor becomes a healer."

"What's the difference?"

"That's the right question. Would you rather have type AB or type O blood? If you had a choice."

Frank walks around the cactus debris. "Well, AB, of course. You can receive blood from anyone, any type. No, wait. Type O, the universal donor, can give to anyone. Okay, so that would be better. You saying the healer is type O. Right?"

"I ain't saying nothing yet. First the differential, then the diagnosis. Noamsayin?"

"Who the fuck do I think I am?! You know if you asked me why the fuck I came here, I honestly wouldn't be able to tell you."

"The patient will live—. Oh, shit, they're paging me. Gotta run. Love on your Jewish ass. You tell me if I should come out there. Don't fall off the bridge."

He felt the sound of the owl's wings flying past him, but he didn't hear the sound of a car stopping. Nor the backdoor opening. Simon's voice gets through: "Gunshot!" Simon stands in the shadows, blood on his hands and face. "He's bleeding bad—in my truck."

Will jams the saber into the ground and runs. The saber waves goodbye.

In the Clinic hallway, Dayone is on a gurney. Simon holds an IV unit in the air as Will, bare-chested, works intently to stanch the bleeding. "Damn, it broke open again! The BP can't drop anymore. Hold it up higher." He feels for pulse in Dayone's neck. "He's lost so much. Here, gimme that. Go call Louisa and Victor! C'mon, c'mon... Okay, okay. C'mon, Dayone, keep pumping. No more leaks. You're not leaving us yet." Into Dayone's ear, "This is not how you want to die, boy! Not where you want to die! You can do better. Dayone! Dammit! I think I lost him."

Just as Will sets himself for CPR, Dayone gasps.

"Yes!"

A few minutes later, in front of the Clinic, a paramedic loads Dayone's gurney into an ambulance. Will helps Simon into the back. Victor and Louisa follow in their car.

26

TO WEAR ISHI'S CROWN

Somewhere else, in some jaded urban city that keeps alive its dingy night clubs in order to expiate its collective sins, Frank is near the end of his act. Chumba is lost in the shadows where he plays synth sounds and swooping water-drum as an eerie aural pad, and Frank, on one knee, warms his hands at an imaginary campfire at the bottom of a bole of light. On the multimedia screens behind him, a still image of a cavalry saber lies in a bed of cactus debris. As the point-of-view zooms in, we see the saber is engraved "U.S.Army." Frank cranks his face up and around slowly until he sculpts his face just right in the light.

"He was the last of his tribe and he didn't know it. If he had known would he have done anything different? Would he have made videos of himself, drawing pictographs, chipping obsidian, singing his last chants into some basement podcast? An embarrassing desperate attempt to document his heritage his tribe his life. Or would he just go on being the same old same old, a beer a screw a ham sandwich, memories of precision-colored sand-painted nightmares of jail cell dumpster dinners, cold rain in big city alleys?"

He stands and lets the waves of the music float him closer to his audience.

"Each child born, each sweet as fresh milk baby, is another candidate in the silent unknown competition to wear Ishi's crown."

He leans into a table, his hands on his knees.

"It's this simple: today, somewhere," he leaps into the audience and moves like a wraith among them, "the last person who knows how to speak in his own language has already been born, is walking around now just living day to day. Because of course if it were you, if you knew you were the last one, how could you go on?"

Frank and the audience are quiet and still, until the audience erupts into an emotional applause. But we hear nothing. Silence. The moment freezes. Time stops as Frank looks off and listens for something he, too, cannot hear.

⚘

Inside the jouncing ambulance, Simon and a paramedic sit holding onto opposite sides of the gurney. Both looking at Dayone, who is barely conscious of the excruciating pain he's in.

⚘

Act II

The Dreams Have Eyes

If I can't dance
It's not my revolution
~Emma Goldman

27

Now You're Ready to Play

In a part of New Orleans that wasn't destroyed by Katrina, in what remains of a huge plantation's carriage house, there is a blue's joint, a nightclub that brings great music to below sea level. On Thursday-nights, they venture a-field. Tonight, Frank Zamora and Chumba Ito perform. The first set is already in progress. No blues tonight, Margo.

As we peek in, the spotlight is holding Frank on a stool, smoking a cigarette, extemporizing, coolly setting the audience up like frogs for a sneaky slow boil; they can't get rid of their fascinated smiles.

Chumba's music dips down and gently scoops Frank up with a Kiowa modal scale and muted, but thunderous drums. Behind him the 12 screens create a matrix that dissolves, morphs, swirls...and finally becomes a series of jump-cuts of a ghost of a young woman moving through the plaza of an eerily deserted Pueblo. The sounds, however, are robust, of a plaza full of loudly-talking energized people, of kids shouting and babies crying, of dogs barking, of snippets of conversations of tourists bargaining for Indian artifacts and trinkets, of a drum beating in the distance. And yet you see no one, the plaza is empty—except for the ghostly young woman, alone, searching. She sees what the audience only hears. Frank and the audience are mesmerized by her every move, her gracefulness, her sadness.

With Chumba's Native Trance Fusion pumped up soft behind, Frank slowly points to the screen and the young woman, remembering. "The first time I saw her was ten years ago in a crowded bar in Omaha. It was just a flash but I never forgot. Then again in one of those edge-of-town honky-tonks outside of Abilene, must be three years back. She came right up and asked my name. Said she was Corn

Maiden. Wanted some quarters for the jukebox. Slipped away into the crowd with my dollar-fifty...."

The screen-matrix alternates between scenes of the on-coming traffic of a super highway at night and pulling into one truck-stop after another.

Frank takes a long pull from his tall scotch-and-soda glass,

"Last night I was twenty miles east of Flag, driving that midnight cobalt glide and there she was standing in the headlights making me brake swerve dead-stop right flat there onto the desert. She looked the same of course, white buckskin dress and wrapped leather leggings. Her face smooth Kabuki blue in the moonlight. She held her digging stick and wore an iPod. Said she needed a ride to some Pueblo. Said she was going home 'cause her momma was sick and might not pull through. She looked worried. So I punched it on the straight-aways and greased it at a steady 85 till we stopped for coffee at dawn out at the big truck-stop just north of the turn-off to Española."

The image freezes, but without missing a beat Corn Maiden turns into camera and lip-syncs perfectly what Frank is now saying: "She must have disappeared while I was filling up. Left me blue corn on the dashboard and the smell of burning sage. Her voice still echoes, 'Live, be happy, it wasn't you who killed me'."

Later that night at the Indian Hospital in Santa Fe, Dayone is in bed, bandaged, IV'd, and restrained, looking ghastly, his attitude flipping from sullen to wide-eyed lost. Will bends over him, testing pupillary reflex with a penlight. Louisa is seated and Victor is pacing. Simon stands at the foot of the bed his eyes averted.

Will indicates the bullet's path on himself, "Luckily the bullet passed between his upper arm and his ribs. Bruised bones, triceps, but nothing broken. The artery sewed up nicely. Muscle damage, maybe a little concussive trauma to the lung, but—" turning to Dayone, "—if you don't run around, it'll heal."

A nurse enters with new bandages. Will moves to check the wounds.

Dayone doesn't want to be bothered, "I'm okaaay!"

Victor turns abruptly. "You're not okay, and you'll stay here until the doctor says so."

"Yeah, yeah...."

"Victor, come here," says Louisa gently patting the bed. "Sit on the other side."

Will heads for the door. "I'll finish my rounds, and check back."

As Will and the nurse exit, Victor looks at Dayone, almost softly, then his jaw tightens again. Simon stares outside. Dayone gazes at his own fingers rubbing his mother's wrist.

"I had to lie!" hisses Victor. "I told Tribal Police that I took your .22 away, and that you—Look at me, Dayone!—you took my .38 to go hunting! Hunting?! Shit, that makes no sense. Tell me what was going on up there."

Drawing her hand away from Dayone, Louisa touches Victor. "Can't we talk about this later? He's all we have, Victor. Thank God he's all right." She gives her hand again to Dayone.

Victor turns slowly to his son. "Don't you understand my position?"

Dayone groans softly and rolls his eyes. "We all got positions."

"Where's the fun in shaming your father?"

"Yeah, it's a lot of fun."

"He's not telling me the—. Did somebody do this? One of your friends?"

"You think I'd rat on my friends?!"

"You weren't hunting rabbits!—not with a .38 Spe—"

"Tell your father the truth, Dayone, whatever it is. He will understand."

Victor leans in quickly, soft but focused. "There was someone else. Who was it?"

Dayone has to lie again. "There wasn't."

"Was it that Ojeda boy you fought with, what's-his-name, Domingo? Were you dealing with drugs?"

Simon stops the conversation. "No drugs. It was an accident. I was there. I—"

Dayone cuts him off. "It was Simon! I was hunting and he grabbed at my gun and it shot me and I—"

Simon wheels, roars, grabs Dayone by the gown and hair and pulls the boy's face up off the pillow. "That's a lie!"

Surprised, Victor quickly moves to restrain Simon. As Louisa clutches at Victor, Simon collapses, his spirit broken, and crumples onto Dayone's legs.

As Dayone arches to push Simon off, he strains against the straps to tear his IV out, but can't. "What are you doing?! Get off me! You're as dumb as my old man. Leave me alone! I coulda been outa here!"

But Louisa gets it. She understands. "Oh, God! I know what happened! He was going to—. Oh, my child!"

Imagining that Louisa believes Dayone, Simon stands, wobbles, and exits. Louisa is overwhelmed, paralyzed.

Outside in the hallway, Simon shuffles away. Pauses. Stares at an old photo on the wall. Of dancers outside the old clinic building that burned down 30 years ago. Underneath the photo, a caption: "THE DANCING HEALERS."

Louisa steps out, wanting to call him back, but there are too many people and he is so far down the congested corridor.

Victor steps out, puts his hand on her shoulder, and looks accusingly into her eyes. He has always felt Louisa's side of the family was deficient in genes. Remembering the most horrible of skeletons in her family's closet, "Another accident, Louisa? Is your father at the center of another accident?"

Louisa collapses inside herself. "Oh, no, Victor. My God, don't you understand? Our son was trying to kill himself. Papa saved his life."

They look at each other for a long time. Her eyes say 'I'm sure'. His that he isn't sure yet. He exhales heavily, then crumples a little. She touches his arm.

"Our son," begins Victor in a soft, leaden voice, "is more lost than I thought. I know you don't like to talk about it, but you gotta admit that this kind of depression and behavior runs on your father's side of the family. You're the only one who isn't hit by it."

"Victor, if you think it's important to blame my family, go ahead and do it."

"We'll do everything we can for our son."

"Yes, but before we treat it, we must diagnose it. I may be a dumb Indian, my dear, but I do run a Health Clinic."

She touches him again, reenters Dayone's room.

Victor leans back against the wall. *Got to be ready for these events in my family. Got to isolate them. Help them to see themselves. There's cowardliness. They have no vision. They see a blank wall. They cannot help our people. Therefore, they cannot step in and do the dirty work. But it's gotta get done. The real hero is the one who gets it done. My turn to try. I've done everything a good parent does, and more. And everybody knows it.*

Get it out of the way. Like Simon never could. Ever since I knew him, he's been somewheres else. Maybe Louisa, too. Sure as hell grabbed my son by the throat. Holds him down. But he's my son, too. If I woke up, so can he. He's my son! Holding him back, that side of the family. Gotta do the work for two. I'm not afraid. I can do it. Why would he want to kill himself? What the hell were they really doing out there?

A few minutes later, Will is at the Nurse's Station notating a chart. Dr. Cutter approaches and picks up another chart. "The kid all right?"

"Just a flesh wound, Kimosabe."

"You're too young for the Lone Ranger and Tonto."

"Me watch DVD Oldies, $4.49 at Marl-Wart."

Cutter shakes his head in mock-disgust. "That's sick."

"Sick good or sick bad?"

"That data the Governor wants you to put together. It could get involved and messy, and we—"

"What he wants is right in line with my previous Public Health work in epidemiology. So, maybe I can help him with the Federal grant he's going for. If I can do the man a favor—."

"Yeah, no, yeah, I understand, but these things just don't work out that—"

"Are there any recent long-term longitudinal health studies of the Pueblo available?"

Cutter is matter-of-fact. "Sure, hell yes. Lots of surveys and records—all kept impeccably. But no data extracted or made sense of. No budget. There was some narrow-track work done on specific problems like TB and diabetes—got those in my office. Shit. When you give me your quarterly, I show you."

"Thanks."

As Cutter steps away and grins, "I heard you were 86'd."

"Excuse me?"

"Walked out on by an OB patient last week. Dr. Patel, the dentist told me. No biggy."

Will is taken off-guard, flustered.

"Happens to all of us. Cross-cultural thing. Good to get hit and bleed and get it over with early in the game, like a nose tackle on the first snap. Now you're ready to play."

As Cutter smiles, grunts, sweeps away, Simon lurches by, stiff, hunched-over, and withdrawn. The doctor in Will is instantly aware. "Mr. Zamora, is—are you okay?"

"Um. An old back pain. I got pills."

Simon walks away. But Will watches him, concerned.

Later, in the moonlight and greatly agitated, Simon walks alone through the sleeping Pueblo. He approaches one of the kiva mounds, lowers his head, touches his forehead, and begins to chant a prayer, soft, raspy, high-pitched. But his voice cracks, trails off, and he shuffles away, unnoticed.

A mile of walking brings him to his field. He pushes through his cornfield, troubled. He stops, whispers in the old language, "*Snake! This corn is sick. Grandfather Snake...I know you are sleeping but I need your help.*"

28

The Sound of a Door Closing

A few days later, closing time at the Clinic. Another gaudy sunset paints the clinic in red. Rebeca exits the building, wearing a rainbow-colored jacket. She gets into her car and drives off, just as Simon comes around the side of the building, carrying the little cedar tree in its pot. He sets it down on a bench to catch the last rays of sunlight.

He bends closer to it. *You come from too far away to know what's happening here. Are you in the dark, too?* He turns the pot 90 degrees. *Maybe if we keep the sun always on this side we can get you to chase the sun and straighten up some.* Pulling clippers from his pocket, he starts to prune a dead sprig—but stops abruptly; he's bothered, looks around, mumbles again, then moves away a few feet and stares back at the plant. *Okay, maybe you don't want to get clipped. Maybe that twig ain't dead. Maybe that part is just hibernating. Or getting ready to grow again. Louisa and Victor—doesn't matter what they think of me. But they should know what happened. For the sake of the boy.* He squats again and looks hard at the plant.

The sound of car doors opening and closing pulls him around. Two women with infants get out of a station wagon driven by Wynema.

Wynema takes one of the foam-core posters she's brought and balances it against a stair-railing: 'Well-Baby Clinic: Good Food & Good Health—sponsored by San Lucas Indian Health Clinic.' Then, as she lifts a 50-pound box full of workshop materials from the back of the vehicle, she asks, "You really don't mind staying in this car while I help with this class? Why don't you come on in and I'll make you a cup of tea?"

"This car is cozy like a coffin, a kiva, a coccoon" yawns Mirriamma. "It's comfy and there's a beautiful sunset and I have tangerines and this CD ol' Peter Abeyta sent me. And when that's done I'll just be here with myself."

"A CD?"

"Of their new recording of Turtle Dance Songs."

Wynema is amused. "From San Juan?"

"Yeah. They rock."

"They 'rock', do they?" Wynema just shakes her head, chuckles, and struggles the box into the Clinic.

⁓

Inside, in the reception area, other young mothers with babies are seated and waiting. Louisa, helped by a husband of one of the women, arranges chairs into a semicircle, then moves an easel into place:

The door to his office wide open, Will sits at his desk, working with concentration at his computer while talking on the phone crooked into his neck. "...Okay, Doctor, thanks. Are the Hopis as affected by this kind of virus as the Navajos?... Right. I didn't so...."

His computer screen presents a form layout for 'Pueblo Health Survey.'

"...Yeah, there it is. I got it. Thanks. After I plug in your data on the family relationships, I'll send you the whole spreadsheet.... Yeah, the bailouts won't help, either. Hey, those forms I'm creating for our Pueblo's health survey will work for this, too, I'm sure. I'll send you a set.... Okay, thanks. ...Bye."

⁓

Mirriamma looks out the back window at Simon now replastering the wall at the end of the building. Her husband, dead now many years, taught her how to whistle like a cowboy.

Simon recognizes the whistle. He doesn't flinch, no sign that he even heard the whistle. *I'm just going to continue my work,* he thinks. *She can whistle all she wants, I'm not going to jump and come running.* He waits for her to whistle again. But Mirriamma doesn't. Simon instantly realizes he's lost to her again. *Damn! She knows I heard her so why would she whistle again? I'll have to go to her.*

He walks over not too quickly. Looks in.

Mirriamma smiles. "You look pretty upset. You upset?"

With minimal movement of the muscles in his face, he nods, yes, solemnly. Mirriamma, wrapped in a dark shawl, sits in silhouette against the sunset. "I have a couple of hours to kill. Get in."

"I'm dirty."

"C'mon."

Simon sets his tools down, laughs coldly, gets in.

"What's so funny, old man?"

"You. You can't kill time. It goes on forever. What you doing here?"

"We were late. The tall one has to teach something."

"The doctor?"

"No, Wynema. No time to take me home. Anyway, where you been? Thought you'd come back to see me."

"I don't trust myself around people."

"I'm not afraid of you."

With a look, Simon communicates he's not ready to talk about whatever it is. "But I got that tree, right over there, of the doctor's that was in my dream. Want to see it?"

When Mirriamma pats him on the knee, he takes it as a 'yes' and gets out of the car.

He brings it back to her open window. He's repotted it.

She leans to look closer. "Never seen that kind before. Get me out of this car. I want a close look."

Simon quickly opens her door. She motions him to bring it closer. "This is the tree in your dream."

Simon grunts and nods. She leans a little closer to the plant.

"It's the doctor's," he adds. "Brought it with him."

"Only one dream so far, eh?" When Simon doesn't answer, "There'll be others."

"What you sayin'?"

"Let's walk. Maybe we figure it out. Tell me about your grandson?"

This catches him off-guard. He tries but he cannot answer.

"He's the one upset you, Dayone, huh?"

"Found him with a gun to his head."

Mirriamma asks with a look, *What did you do?*

"I heard the great cry of our brother, the Bear, the Bear in my dream. Maybe the boy heard it, too. I dunno. Anyway, he hurt himself. But he didn't kill himself."

"Uh-hummm. Bear Clan mischief."

Unconsciously, Simon pulls the fetish from his pocket, fingers it, then squats, not quite sure how he feels about all this. Mirriamma smells the tree twice. "I never seen one like this. You?"

Simon shakes his head. "Some kind of cedar, maybe."

A young couple, instantly in awe of the two elders, and maybe a little afraid, quicken their pace as they pass by. The young woman, very pregnant, covers her belly with her hands as she continues the conversation with her husband. "You can come into the Well-Baby Clinic, you know. A lot of husbands do."

"No way. Colorado's playing the Giants right now...a double-header on my day off. I got beer to buy and buddies to bet. Call me."

Inside, the reception area is set up for viewing a video. About 20 people, mostly young mothers with infants, sit in the semi-dark room, waiting for the video to start. Wynema is closing the blinds. Louisa stands to the side, preoccupied, exhausted, numb. She bends down and picks up a baseball cap from the floor.

Wynema sees this. "I can handle this. Why don't you go to the hospital and be with Dayone?"

"I called. He's sleeping."

Lola approaches carrying a tray with water and cups. "Louisa? The doctor wants you."

Louisa touches Wynema's hand. "Go ahead and start. Oh, and I think this belongs to one of Dina Baca's boys." She hands the hat to Wynema.

Will is pacing when she knocks and enters.

"Oh, hi, Louisa, thanks. I wanted to show you those health survey forms I worked up."

He gives her a folder full of papers. She looks at them closely then takes a deep breath, "These new forms—they're too much, Doctor, I—"

"I know you don't like it, Louisa, but—"

She steps out into the hallway but turns back towards the door. "Doctor, the staff here doesn't have time. And the patients won't fill them out."

Will takes a step towards her. "None of us has time. And there's no budget, I know. But these are the things that make a difference. Your husband, he asked me, he wants a baseline study done. This is how we learn about the people we serve. We make time, and we don't...."

Wynema has the baseball hat on backwards and is holding an infant. "—So that's about it, I hope you enjoy film." As she's about the start the DVD player, she and everyone else can hear Louisa and Will arguing. Everyone is frozen, just listening. Wynema starts the digital projector, then, baby in hand, disappears down the corridor.

Louisa takes a deep breath and smiles. "There are many ways to learn about people, Doctor, but—."

Will tries to smile, too. "But the sooner we have the objective facts, the sooner we can do something. We create surveys now and extrapolators later—and all of it can do a lot for this village."

Louisa turns to go. "Yes, facts, extrapolated facts. But you may miss the important things if all you're interested in are facts."

"*But he's right, sister, and so are you.*" It's Wynema softly speaking Pueblo from the doorway, still holding the infant and wearing the cap. Then quickly in English, "Maybe we need better data. Can we get someone with an MPH, then maybe some volunteers who can help?"

Will snaps around, thinking, *Another modern young mother with an opinion about something.* "I *am* an MPH, and an M.D.! Excuse us, but this is a private conversation. You'll find someone to help you and your baby back in the reception area."

"Sorry, Doctor, I really just wanted to close your door because we can hear you, so I—"

"Thank you. Thank you," as he guides her gently by the shoulder out the door and closes it.

Wynema bristles at being pushed. She turns away, her nostrils flared. The baby cries.

Louisa takes a deep, frustrated breath. "Doctor, you don't understand. That wasn't—!"

"Can't you get your volunteer leader to help that woman?"

"Doctor, that was the volunteer leader. The one who works with Mirriamma Moya, the—" Louisa turns abruptly and leaves. *Taos has a surgeon that was born and raised on their pueblo. So does Zuni. Why can't we?!*

Will could kick himself. He sits and tries to unkink the pinched nerve in his neck. "Damn!"

Two hours later, it is dark outside and the Well-Baby Clinic participants are leaving and following the little yellow lights along the path to the parking lot. They pass Mirriamma and Simon sitting on a bench against a wall, wrapped in their blankets, the potted cedar between them. Louisa and Wynema, exhausted and dispirited, trudge to their cars.

"Papa, would you lock up? Everything else is set for the night."

Simon nods, stands, picks up the cedar.

Mirriamma nods and points at the tree. *"Trees talk, you know. They only talk real slow. Just slow down, Simon, and listen."*

Ten minutes later, the Clinic is quiet and Simon peers into the door of Will's office. Empty. He's carrying the potted tree. He looks up and down the hallway. Nothing. No doctor. He steps in and sets the tree on its plate, on a bookcase, by the window and puts his hand on the black pot and waits.

On the other side of the building, in the Clinic laboratory and tech room, Will is assiduously tidying up, angry with himself. He stops and listens and hears a scratching sound. He looks up. It's nothing; he returns to his task. Then hears it again and looks under a counter. Nothing. But there it is again. The scratching around. He opens a cabinet slowly. Laughs uneasily at himself. Then hears it yet again! He ventures into the hall.

Will stops and listens down the hallway. He hears three scratches. One. Two. Three. He follows...past the reception desk...up the other hallway...toward his office.

He slowly pokes his head into his own office. Scratching the pot with his fingernail, Simon stands staring at the tree.

Will is relieved. "Oh, it's you. Wow, that was strange, I heard—. I really want to thank you for helping me with that plant."

Simon turns and steps back.

Will walks to his place behind his desk. "Did you need me?"

"I fed your tree."

"Yeah, thanks. Is there anything else?"

"Your father's tree. It means a lot to you."

Will goes to his computer, searching for something on his desk. "Actually, my grandfather's tree. No, not really, it's just that—"

"Why did he give it to you?"

Will drifts with his thoughts for a second, then repeats mechanically his grandfather's instructions: "This is to remind me of where my destiny lies, in Israel, with my tribe." And then as if shaking it off and more to the point, "It was his not-so-sneaky way of getting me to join him there, someday...soon." Will drifts again, unconsciously picking up a hemostat and opening and closing it on his forefinger. He begins to pace. "Look, it's a long sad complicated story I'm afraid."

"Those are the best kinds they say."

"Huh?"

"The best kind of stories. And now you worry about your grandfather. I'm sorry."

"He raised me. He always made friends with single-moms. So they could share dinners and feel like it was one big family. You see, my parents died when I was a boy."

"And Israel," asks Simon tentatively.

"Israel was grandpa's dream, the only destination that could begin to balance the suffering he and his family went through, to get there, because everyone he knew was—."

"Killed?"

"In Treblinka, one of the Nazi death camps. Only my grandfather survived. There you have it. Fastest I've ever told the story."

"Are you from Germany?"

"No. My grandfather was from Poland. Why're you asking me these questions?"

"Hmmm. He came here after the war?"

"Nineteen-forty-six. Married my mother and had a son, Isaac, my father. Thirty-five years later, he married my mother. But when I was nine, my grandfather lost my grandmother—also called Tessie, by the way—and a year later both my parents were killed in a car accident. After that, all he wanted was to take me with him to Israel. Nothing could protect us like Israel, he said. Nothing could heal us like Israel."

"Why didn't you go?"

Will goes interior, then suddenly snaps out of it.

"I'm an American, looking forward. But my grandfather was a Holocaust survivor looking backward. He stayed with me because I was going to school, and then college, and then med-school. Mr. Zamora, it's been a long day."

"Something you said, that night Dayone got shot, about not dying where you don't want to die."

"Did I?" *The kid, lost, searching, hurting—hell yes, he wasn't picking his time or place. Not like my Zeyda. There's a man who's picked them. Bravo, Grandpa. I never really told you how proud I am of you for that: picking your place. Dayone's grandpa. Simon. Why is he so damn curious about me? He doesn't trust me. An Indian thing of figuring out who you're dealing with before you entrust them with your life.*

Simon waits patiently. *My grandson almost died on his table. Wrong place. Where is the right place? He's too young to know. The doctor, too—does he know? He had a good life with his grandfather. I respect him for that. A lot. Makes a difference. Probably a very big difference. Years ago, I probably would have been jealous of him for that. Too old now. But wait! Dayone picked his spot! Why that spot? Couldn't look important to the doctor from New York. But that place—why that arroyo, that rock? Ai! When he was a kid, a real kid, I took him there, with two of his friends. It was the last place I ever told Dayone a story from the Grandfathers.*

Will returns first: "Maybe I meant before those we love are—are near us. I never got to tell my grandma or my parents a lot of things, I guess."

"So that's why this tree was in my dream."

"What's that?"

"It's about my son! I lost him. Road home is long. But as long as it's circular—. Ha!" Simon heads towards the door with a lighter step. "I hope your grandfather is happy now. Someday you'll plant this tree where it's supposed to grow."

Will stands caught in the confusing wake of Simon's words. A grimace creeps into his face. He looks down—he's pinching his finger hard with the hemostat. Will stifles an involuntary cry and Simon looks back at Will from the door. There is a deep gouge on his finger where he was squeezing. He looks up. The sound of a door closing.

29

Beyond the Clinic

In the afternoon of another day, on top of a mesa that overlooks the Pueblos to the east and the Rio Grande Gorge in the distance to the west, Victor and Manley stand near a new but now muddied Cadillac SUV, looking out over the plateau.

Manley sweeps the horizon with his arm. "Fifty, sixty years from now you may be gone, but that nuclear storage facility will have served its purpose. They empty it, clean it, dismantle it and make it disappear as if it had never been there. That's how good our technology will be. I told you, there's one tribe now that's drawing up plans on how to turn their facility later into a seriously modern, industrial-chic hotel-resort. Very enterprising."

Stone-faced, Victor looks at Manley, then across the plateau. "We've done everything we can to prepare the grant application, except to show that general health here is at or above the national standards—and it is."

"And?"

"And the Pueblo doctor is working on that now."

"Very good."

"Actually, he was working on it before he even came here."

"Huh? I don't understand."

"He's an over-achiever." Victor smiles, but waves away the question. "Never-mind."

It's sunny and hot. About a mile from the Pueblo's center, on a ranchito with a three-bedroom adobe, a large traditional wedding celebration is about to take place. Tables of food. People arriving on foot or in vehicles. Some are dressed in traditional clothes and costumes and they will dance and sing and drum. Against one shady wall are chairs and benches for the elders. The women and men sit separately.

Teo greets Louisa. "I saw Dayone here. He's looking stronger."

Louisa smiles and nods and sighs in relief. Dancers singers and drummers ease into action. Louisa pokes Teo in the ribs and points to the music with her mouth.

Teo asks, "Did Simon come?"

She points proudly. Teo nods respectfully and walks away.

Not far away is the corral where a young man is practicing trick riding. Jesse and Dayone, the latter with his arm and shoulder in a sling, and three other youths cheer from the fence. Nearby, Sotero leans on the railing, happy and eating from a plate.

When the rider almost falls, Dayone turns sourly to his friends. "Listen to them back there, dancing and screaming their heads off in this heat. Dude, they go on forever. Stupid."

"Yeah, man." says Jesse, "all that jumping around. But look at Ricky go. He's back on. Yo, dude!"

The rider jumps on and off his horse, one side and then the other, at a full gallop.

Dayone holds his salty ground. "Ruben could ride."

"Where you think he is...like right now?"

"Probably off in some grassy little valley, next to a stream, dancing and singing, just dancing away without worrying about a thing."

"I thought you didn't like to dance."

"Well, I like to dance, if I'm alone."

"Yeah, I feel ya. Come on, let's get some food."

"Hey, *coyo*, don't you respect no Purple Hearts? I got shot, man. Wounded. Go bring me something, okay?"

Jesse smiles stupidly. "Yeah, hey, that's right! Okay!"

Sotero, still eating, now cheers the rider on with a goofy grin.

Here is a traditional celebration that people can understand and love—comfortably chatting, greeting the bride and groom and the music and dancing. The music is live. Four Native musicians. Young, hip, and, like their music, fused to their Native roots. Two women, two men. Keyboard, guitar, drums, and bass.

Standing behind Jesse in a food line, Tessie and Louisa chat. Wynema, traditionally dressed, helps serve. Jesse is taken by her beauty, and her height, as she gives him two heaping plates.

An older man, carrying a ceremonial drum, walks by, motioning Teo and Simon to follow. He hands Teo two drumsticks. Teo accepts and offers one of them to Simon.

"Come on, take it, sit with us." Off Simon's demur, "You haven't drummed in years."

"When I came back from Korea, that's when I wanted to drum. And even when I was a kid, I—"

"But the elders told us boys in kiva that you had abandoned us, that you refused to go to kiva—"

"They thought I abandoned them?! I was just twelve years old! I didn't know how to 'abandon' anyone. All I knew was how to be afraid and lonely. It was everyone who abandoned me to let the government haul me off to their 'away school'."

"What could they do?"

Simon sees Mirriamma on a bench along a wall, inconspicuous in a row of four other women. Unnoticed by anyone else, she points at Simon with a stick.

Simon returns abruptly to the conversation. "Fight like hell and don't let them take me and their other kids away! Is that too much to ask for?"

"You have a right to be angry at that."

"Angry? Not anymore. Now I am only curious."

Simon looks back at Mirriamma and nods his head and smiles. Beyond her, however, he sees Will, arriving in a Hawaiian shirt. He sees how tentative the doctor is, how enthralled with the festivities. Someone greets the doctor and shows him to the food.

Now Teo is curious. "What you mean 'curious'?"

Simon turns to Teo, closing his friend's hand securely around the drumstick. Teo waits for Simon to finish his thought.

"Curious about my son and my grandson. They are the last of my line. And right now, I am very curious about—well, about a dream I had."

Teo is intrigued, but Tessie drags him off to the food table, where Will stands, nibbling off a plate. People are drawn by Will's presence, his extraordinary height. He is introduced around and he stops long enough to make pleasantries, until he spots Wynema, and then can't take his eyes off her.

That is, until Tessie says, "I want to apologize, Doctor, for running out of your office." She takes his hand and starts shaking it. "I don't know what came over me. Well, yes, I do, because I was talking to—" She follows his eyes to see what the doctor is looking at. *He's looking at Wynema.* "—I was talking to Wynema Mondragon, who you probably have met. Have you met her?"

Will, somewhat distractedly, "No, I don't know her. What'd she have to say? I mean, I'm the one who should apologize—. I'm sorry, what where you saying?" He can't turn his head away from Wynema.

Teo interrupts. "She's very protective," he says and then points to his hand that Tessie won't let go of.

"Oh, that's all right," says Will awkwardly. "I should have been more sensitive. I'm learning." Then to Teo, "What's she protective of?"

Teo chuckles. "She's a *gia,* a mother of the community, so I guess she's protective of everything around here."

"I understand," says Will, not really understanding anything at all. "This friend of yours, Winona—."

"Wynema."

"Yes, Wynema. Please thank her for me, well, for explaining that I'm not really a bad guy after all."

Now Tessie is quite aware that Will cannot stop looking at Wynema. "Well, why don't you tell her yourself."

"Well, thanks, I will, if I ever bump into her."

"Doctor, you're looking at her right now."

Then Teo, urging Tessie, "Go ahead."

Tessie is shy, almost embarrassed. "Well, we want to invite you over for dinner...sometime."

"Sure, I'd love to, that's great." And he's still having a hard time keeping his attention away from Wynema. "Shall we call each other?"

Tessie looks to Teo, not understanding the question. "Okay, that'll work," Teo says as he drags Tessie away. One last word from Tessie: "Doctor!" When Will looks, she points emphatically at Wynema.

Will smile, nods, still doesn't understand. Then he does.

Mirriamma watches everything. The music stops. Her eyes dart from Will to Wynema, who glides about, gracious, self-contained, rarely speaking, helping children with costumes, picking up used plates and cups, watching other dancers. She isn't aware that at each of these stations, Will follows at a distance, drawn to her. The music begins again. Wynema has her head cocked, listening to the music.

She moves, even while standing still, says Will to himself.

Mirriamma, sensuously eating a ripe fig, sees Simon walk over and stand next to Will.

"Ah, Mr. Zamora. This is very nice! Truly festive. May I call you Simon?" Off Simon's nod. "Could you tell me who that woman in yellow dancing over there is?"

Simon looks from Will to Wynema to Mirriamma and back to Will. "An apprentice, to the village witch."

"Nahhh. You're pulling my leg."

Simon's smile disappears, as if he were indignant at the doubting. Will gestures 'no offense'. Simon grins. "Just messin' with you, Doc."

"Now I think I maybe sorta met her, not really, at the Clinic. I thought she was a mother."

Will looks to Wynema as pain suddenly enters Simon's face. Will doesn't see this at first. Simon fights it, but slowly is forced to kneel. His hands reach down to the loose, dry dirt. As the pain increases, his fingers dig into the earth, grounding his agony. Now Will sees!

"Simon, what is it? Where?"

With difficulty, "Nothing, muscle spasm."

Simon tugs a small prescription bottle from his pocket and hands it to Will. Louisa has seen and comes running. Simon's pain passes, and he attempts to stand.

Inspecting the bottle, Will helps him rise. "You've been taking these since way before the other doctor left. That's too long on these relaxants." To Louisa, "I want to see him tomorrow, in the A.M., for a checkup."

"Papa?"

Simon groans at the idea, but reluctantly agrees.

"You come over here and sit down." She leads him away.

People look with respect or warmly acknowledge Will. He looks around for Wynema—and finds her. She's looking directly at him. Now she's walking towards him. He's finding it difficult to breathe or swallow. She comes right up to him.

"Is he all right?"

Will is transfixed. "I, uh, I don't know. I hope so. There was something about the way he grabbed himself, against the pain, and that prescription he had—something about that that doesn't fit. Is he related to you?"

"We're all related, Doctor." She smiles briefly.

"Oh, right, 'O'mitaykwee-asin'."

"Very good. It's true, you know."

"I don't doubt it for a minute. A second. A micro-second—"

"Thank you."

"Do you really believe that? You and I are related? And I don't mean just by the mere fact that we exist together."

"I guess it all depends on what you mean by 'exist'."

"Do you exist here, on this pueblo, now and always?"

"I was born here. I lived here until I was fifteen."

"Then you went away."

"And now I'm back."

"Forever?"

Wynema smiles a sophisticated New York smile. She shakes her head. "I don't think so. There's a big wide world out there."

Will nods his head. Somehow that wasn't the answer he expected or hoped for. If you asked him to explain, he wouldn't have been able.

Wynema looks away and sees Simon sitting now too far from Mirriamma. "So, you hoped Simon was okay—."

"Well, yes, I mean, he's coming in for a checkup tomorrow."

"That's good. But you won't heal Simon in the clinic." Off his look of question, "If you wish to understand the Indian, Doctor, you must go beyond the clinic."

"Beyond the Clinic?"

"Go to Frank Zamora's concert in Albuquerque next week."

"Simon's son?"

"A poet. A performance artist."

"Ah. I met him. I saw him the day of the Council meeting. Saw you there, too, I think, and I talked to him at his father's place, but he was kind of, uh—"

"He's an alcoholic. But you won't know who he is until you see him perform."

"Well, I actually did see him perform. In New York. At the Stalagmite."

"You mean the Stalactite? In the village?"

"Yeah, about seven or eight months ago."

"Hmmm. That's strange because I—"

"Well, I'd like to see him again, but I really want to apologize to you, I mean, for my rudeness in the Clinic. I didn't recognize you, I was upset at, uh—"

"It takes time to settle in, and it's not easy when you're worried about your grandfather."

For a moment, Will is speechless. "Uh, oh, right, my grandfather, yes, well—. You're Wynema, right?"

She nods and they both stare at each other.

Then as quickly as he can, to take the pressure off, "Are you going to Frank's show?"

"Yes. I'm going with friends who've never seen him." She lowers her eyes. "Well, enjoy the wedding." She looks at him one last time, "Bye."

She disappears. Will looks around to see if anyone is watching. Only Mirriamma.

The next morning, Simon sits with his shirt off at the end of a padded examination table at the Clinic. Will has just checked him over and now leans against the door lost in thought.

"Simon, let me say this as clear as I can. I—I don't like it. Something's not right. I know I'm not supposed to say that so you don't needlessly worry, but you don't seem like the type to mince words about—"

"Thanks, Doctor, I appreciate that."

Louisa knocks and sticks her head in. "Doctor, you told me to tell you when Dr. Cutter calls."

"Thanks, Louisa. I was just telling your father that we need other tests. I know it isn't a muscle spasm. Okay?" He reaches for Simon's pills. "No more of these, not until we know what we're dealing with."

"I think it's my corn. Something's not right down there in the *soil...the soil.*"

Louisa is emboldened. "Don't listen to him, Doctor. If he needs tests, he'll have them. Do you think it's something serious?"

"When a man his age has to drop to the ground because of something he's had for more than six months, I treat it as potentially serious."

"Oh, don't worry, he'll go. I'll tell Dr. Cutter—"

"I'll be right there," he says shaking Simon's hand. She exits and Will hands Simon his shirt and notices two abdominal scars, one on the front left, one on the back left side.

"May I ask how you got these?"

"In the War."

"Korea?"

"World War Two. I was 17. Sent to the Pacific."

"Bullet? Shrapnel?"

"Bayonet."

Will winces. Simon puts his shirt on. He is unemotional.

"Probably hard to talk about."

"Don't know. Nobody ever asked."

"Must have been enough to send you home."

"They sent me home, but I went to Texas, to raise horses with...a war buddy. But when the war was over, he, uh...turned out to be not such a buddy."

Will stops writing, muses. Simon turns to leave.

"Your friend was a white guy?"

"Still is."

"He's still your friend?"

"No, he's still a white guy. Bad joke." After an awkward silence, "But then I did a really stupid thing. I reenlisted during the Korean Conflict."

"Wow. What was your job?"

"Taking care of some horses for a general."

Another pause. "Hey, I was thinking about going to your son's show, next week in Albuquerque."

Simon, at the door, turns back. "Whoever suggested that...wants to change your life."

30

My Country 'Tis of Thy People You're Dying

The Nosmo King is Albuquerque's most notorious night-club, located at the southern tip of Old Town. It was an old western adobe two-story brothel, restored with a touch of purple and yellow neon. It's an hour-and-an-a-half before performance and Will is last in a long line of people waiting to get in, half of whom are Native Americans, not just Pueblos but Pima, Piute, Navajo, Apache, Hopi, and others from farther away.

An hour later, inside the lighting is colorful but subdued. The air is clear: no smoking. Everywhere some form of the club's graphic: 'NoSmo King.' And they mean it.

Over a balcony railing, peering down like gargoyles, Dayone and Jesse quietly, but wildly, approve of the table below where Wynema sits with three attractive Pueblo women in their 20s. Two tables away: Louisa, Simon, and Lola.

Will enters, eyes adjusting, looking for a place to sit. He sees Simon and Louisa, smiles, approaches, offers his greetings. "Good evening."

But as he nears their table, he sees an empty chair next to Wynema.

Louisa is quick with the offer. "Doctor, please come and sit with us."

"Uh, thanks, but I...I'll come back, I'll come back."

He glides up to Wynema's table, looks around, then, "Well, I came as you suggested. Any particular place I should sit...to, uh, get the most out of it?"

"You could sit over there," indicating a chair at another table. "Or over there," pointing to a seat even further away, or—", torturing the pause, she indicates the chair next to her, "—or sit here."

Will stretches his neck towards the distant seats. "Let me take a look at those seats over there." He takes one step away, but then, "No, I guess this would be better. May I?"

Wynema laughs quietly, as Will sits down next to her. Neither lets on that they appreciate the little games. What follows is a subtle, tentative exchange of facial and body language, a sensual pantomime: about what they're feeling, their sense of this place, even the pre-show recorded music. Finally, they burst into silent laughter, to enjoy the moment, only to become a little nervous again.

Simon glances at Will and Wynema, then slowly around the room.

Will turns to Wynema, speaking softly. "So why did you say I ought to—I think you said—look beyond the Clinic?"

Wynema smiles commanding loud drum beats to erupt—interrupting any possible conversation—drum beats interwoven with the thread of a high liquid fugitive flute. The crowd settles and the musical pad continues until the house lights dim, revealing Frank, lit now by a single bright spot, standing sideways to the audience in full Native warrior dress. He turns from one side to another, from one persona to the other—because the other half of his costume, stitched together impeccably, is made up in pink-face with a cavalry soldier's uniform. Helped with Chumba's lighting, Frank will flip 180°, back and forth, masterfully.

"I say, 'This land is sacred.'" He turns.

"You say, 'What do you mean by sacred?' He 180's.

"I say, 'This is sacred where we are. We worship here. We bury our dead here. We meet to rejoice in each other here.'" He turns again.

"You say, 'Can you prove this is sacred? Show us documentation. Explain the rituals in detail. Submit letters of reference, petitions and resource materials. Attach jpegs of people praying. Bring your files, to the Courts of Just Us. We will take it under advisement. We will call expert witnesses. We will determine if you have a legitimate claim.'"

"I say, 'You are a soulless people to store the bones of our ancestors in cardboard boxes. I do not know if I should weep for you or attack you as monsters.'"

"You say, 'Can you prove this is sacred? Come now!'"

"I say, 'Calling the Earth sacred is another way of expressing humility in the face of forces we do not fully comprehend. When something is sacred it demands that we proceed with caution. Even awe. Come over here, stand on this rock, look around. Can you prove it isn't?'"

He freezes and the audience takes a moment to express their approval strongly. But they are quickly cut off when Frank turns full-face to them, half-Indian, half-cavalry, and pulls out what looks to be old documents written in parchment.

He peruses them. "Old treaties and promises. In fact," holding up one, "here's a bite right out of the 14th Amendment to the U.S. Constitution."

He shuffles off on the Indian side and speaks like a darkie. "Yassa, Massa Lincoln. You done freed us all righ', and den made us as equal an' free as all da white folk."

He takes the parchment and wipes his ass with it. "Shee-it! The 14th excluded Native Americans! All men are created equal? My ass!"

He wheels and kneels at the edge of the stage, pushing his face towards a big Indian at a stage-side table. "What you think? All men 'cept you and me! You angry 'nough yet? Heap Big Chief Piss-In-The-Wind.

He lets the crumpled document fall on the table, spins, points, and Chumba makes the multimedia screens come alive behind Frank with a torrent of images and sounds and music.

"I am an Indian rifle on horseback, aiming to make a difference, from first war cry to last, loud and serious—like fist-fights and literature ought to be."

He disappears from the stage, but, via one of his favorite toys, a wireless microphone-headset, his voice continues over the images and music.

On half the screens, on the left, B-roll footage, jammed and cut in spurts—quick slow quick quick quick—of Native Americans all across the United States protesting, demonstrating for their rights, angry, outraged. And on the right, modern middle-class Indians in their everyday clothes (slightly Indianized) walking quietly through the main tourist attractions of the United States—from the Washington Monument and the Lincoln Memorial to Las Vegas, DisneyWorld, Hollywood, and a studio set for a western movie. They simply take it all in, calmly, though perhaps tinged with a touch of sadness.

"You say you want to be my friend, share my rage and storm the bastions of imperial expertise who are all too willing to lay waste the remaining Native Peoples—living relics anyway. You say you understand or feel the value of our ways, our medicine, our connection to the Earth our Mother. You say you have freed yourselves from racism and are willing to prove it. Then prove it, I say—now! Just look around and take the hand of someone you've never met before. Hold it up as a sign you're willing to work for justice! Get out of yourselves and into the bald act of action. Look like a warrior and in the eyes of the stranger say: 'It is time...time to act...time for justice...now!...'"

And he repeats it, "It is time...time to act...time for justice...now!..." and repeats it until many in the audience joins him and says it with him. "It is time...time to act...time for justice...now!..." ...until Frank returns to the stage and throws up his arms, and the audience snaps quiet and still.

"It's time for democracy now! If not, wimp out and die again, a third world to yourselves...or worse."

Frank wears a berêt, dangles a cigarette from the corner of his mouth and speaks with Tom Waits' body language. The single big image behind him now is of a narrow nighttime street in Harlem, lit by a single streetlight.

"I saw the best braves on my reservation crawling through the blindingly white handout world, strangling on the bowels of Saturday night, smelling like an angry drunk."

The image behind him shifts to a vast prairie. The music becomes a single native drum. His voice becomes the melody.

"Ancestor, grandfather, to you the Earth did not belong. You belonged to Her! The wide expanse was yours, Grandfather, to shepherd in a sweet-faced wind. But those who think they rule see you small, a savage dancing stone-age infidel—they have no eyes, no nose, no sense, that you were a warrior, a lord of this land, without owning a damn thing."

From the darkness, someone hands him a Wendy's hat and a burger with an arrow through it. "Screw the beef. Where's my buffalo?"

As the lights and screens fade out, the audience laughter swells... until they hear Chumba's mix of a harsh wind in the distance and Buffy Sainte-Marie singing "My Country 'Tis of Thy People You're Dyin'." The screens slowly reveal a group of four destitute Indians passing a bottle as they sit on the littered ground against a graffitied wall beneath the logo of the United Employment Agency of America.

Frank changes costume quickly, enough to become Gen. George S. Patton, in his ribbon bedecked uniform-shirt and hat. Behind him, a large American flag slowly lowers, stripes vertical, covering the screen.

He exhorts, "When you see your people robbed, raped, and tortured. When you see them malnourished in the mind and body. When the lands and culture that made you what you are turn to puddles of polluted goo—you'll know what to do."

He backs up, seemingly inadvertently into the lowering flag which now covers his head. He waves for help and the flag starts to rise. But with a contorted body roll, the flag becomes a noose tightening around his neck. His boots kick in the air—and the life in his body fights, loses, and leaves him. He holds this audience-frightening position a little too long, until the audience fidgets, then he drops, and the act continues—the image up behind him is again the Washington Mall, but this time packed with all-American demonstrators. Chumba kicks in at the keyboard creating a celestial choir.

Sweating profusely, Frank watches the flag disappear and the screens dissolve through a series of photos of Martin Luther King, Jr.

Frank narrates: "I have a dream that one day Native Americans will regain what is theirs, that our spirit, past and present, will bloom again. I have a dream that the wisdom that is held in this land's first people will be the driving force to put us in right relationship with our Earth. I have a dream that the Earth will be cared for by loving children. This will happen long after we aboriginals are all fuckin' dead, of course—but what the hell, it was just a dream."

Frank just stands there mute and blank and listens carefully as first a few, than many, then everyone is applauding wildly.

Simon's face is also blank. Louisa's mouth is partly opened. She's in shock. Dayone, above, is enthralled. Wynema is genuinely still and internal, tears welling.

Will's mind is racing, integrating, disintegrating, reintegrating—as turns ever so slowly until he can see Wynema and is awed by her tears. Only then do his tears come.

Behind Frank, a huge image of Leonard Peltier ghosts but dimly into view. After a few moments, Frank quiets the audience again and, one after another, calls out the names of Native American activists in attendance. They stand for recognition. Instead of applause, the audience finger-thrums lightly on their tables.

Ten minutes later, literally in the bowels of the joint, in the basement, a subterranean hallway that was built for access to the sewer lines, in front of Frank's dressing room, Louisa struggles to pull Simon through clamoring fans. She keeps saying as she goes, "He's my brother. He's my brother...." And people make way.

Wynema and her friends follow. Then Will. Chumba roars on above, a one-man finale.

When Frank—holding very tall plastic cups and surrounded by fans, mostly women—sees his family in the hallway outside his dressing room, he clears the room brusquely. He sees Wynema.

Louisa speaks, "You remember Wynema Mondragon? It's been ten years since—"

"Yeah, yeah, Sis, thanks for—"

"You were terrific, my little brother!"

Frank can't take his eyes off Wynema. "Thanks."

"I thought you were terrific, too." Wynema says flatly.

Frank plumbs for deeper meanings, then abruptly to Simon, "Pretty nasty, huh, Dad?"

Simon is awkward, uncomfortable. "Strong stuff."

Louisa is deeply moved but confused. "She would have been so proud of you tonight! Mom, I mean. Seriously, that you spoke your words. She wouldn't have liked the cussing, but as I sat watching you, I could just feel our mother's presence."

Frank can only marvel at his sister's ingenuousness. "Sis, you, you sweet—" But Frank, he just chuffs and touches her lovingly on the cheek.

Simon and Frank look at each other, freeze-nailed. There is an unquiet silence, until Simon turns to leave. Frank looks to Will, then ignores him.

Louisa notices, "Oh, and this is Dr. William Kornfeld, I mean, I work with him at the Clinic, he's the new doct—"

Frank looks from Will to his sister and speaks in Pueblo dialect, *"Who gives a shit?"* Then in English, "Glad you could come, sis. Who wants a drink? I can fix you up." Then to Wynema, "Good to see you again. I mean, you've grown up since—. Say, what do you think was the racial split out there?"

The door busts open. Fans push in, including the three young women Wynema was sitting with. Frank sensually high-fives each of them, then turns back to Wynema.

She clarifies, "You mean, the audience?"

"Yeah, maybe about fifty-fifty?"

She nods, concurring.

"Good, that's about what I want. I don't know how much the whites really get." To Will, "No offense." Then quickly back to Wynema, "Hey, some friends are putting on a party tonight. Be good if you came." He leans towards her. "There's this teacher, very popular, who's making a lot of money giving seminars and who wrote a book called something like Shamanic Ways: from Rosebud or Disneyland. She'll be there. She's a phony of course, but she actually has a lot of good things to say."

When she doesn't respond, he asks in Pueblo, *"You're not going with this white guy are you?"* But before she can answer, his eyes fill with the feminine presence of the three Pueblo women. "Whoa, but you guys are invited, most definitely—to the party." The three giggle, flush, fidget.

Wynema smiles softly. "Thanks, but I have to get up early tomorrow morning."

A few minutes later, outside in the club's parking lot, people are leaving impressed and provoked by the evening. Simon stands by the entrance, leaning against a wall, gripping his side in pain. As it subsides, he hears Louisa and Will approaching and hides any sign of distress.

"He's like a great surgeon," says Will. Off Louisa's look of question, "Your brother—you come out knowing you've been cut, but you just don't know where."

"He's traveled the world a lot since he was...a boy. My head is still spinning." She turns to Simon. "Does he speak for that many, or is he just a good performer?"

Simon shrugs, turns, then tries not to show the piercing pain again in his mid-back.

But Will sees this one. As he moves towards Simon, Wynema exits the nightclub and converges on them both.

"As of yesterday, Simon, you still hadn't got those medical tests done."

Simon acknowledges this irresolutely. "Okay, Doc, you're right, don't worry."

Wynema steps up. "Doctor, are you going back to the village now?" Will is caught off guard, but definitely interested. "My friends want to party and I don't."

Will nods to Wynema, but to Simon, "I'm serious, Mr. Zamora. Those tests."

Simon nods a promise.

31

IF THE DOCTORS WERE INDIANS

Will drives his BMW intently trying to figure out how to get on the freeway heading north. "I take this one up the ramp to the left, right?"

"Next one." She studies his face, then turns front when he looks at her.

"Did I see what you thought I needed to see there tonight here at Frank's thing?"

Her voice is flat and belies the irony of her answer. "He died again for our sins, right up there on the stage."

"How does Frank's anger help me understand Indians—or Simon in particular?"

Wynema gently laughs. "By just asking that, Doctor, he already has!"

"Call me Will, okay?"

She says nothing. As Will turns away, she thinks, *He's going to figure it out. That I knew I was going to drive home with him all along.*

"You're not into partying?"

"Not tonight."

Will thinks, *I'm not going to tell her how happy I am that she's not into partying tonight. I'm not going to ask her how many Pueblo people intermarry. I'm not going to ask where she went to college and what she studied. I'm not going to ask her what she does with Mirriamma. Why not? Doesn't feel right.* Then he does say, "They always party after those kinds of things, uh?"

She thinks, *Here it comes. He got me.* She blurts, "I had a back-up plan. Louisa. Her car is big. I was going to go home with her."

A few moments later, Will breaks the silence. "Tell me, are your people glad that the I.H.S. provides them with doctors and health care?"

"Why, yes, of course."

Will waits for more.

"But it would be better," she adds, "if the doctors were Indians."

"Well, sure, but—"

Their eyes connect. Wynema makes sure that she looks away a moment before he does.

A little later: "Can I ask you what kind of thing you do with the woman you work with?"

"With Mrs. Moya? Her name is Mirriamma."

Will quick-glances. *Indian women,* he thinks, *are much more inscrutable than Asian woman.*

Wynema lowers her head, *"This isn't small talk. He doesn't know how to go slow. I knew this was going to come up.*

Will suddenly reaches for a CD, which startles her. "Here," he says, "is some great oud music which will give you a nice soft carpet to walk on while you tell me what you do. You already know what I do."

"I just finished my doctoral dissertation."

Will says nothing. He just listens.

"And a few months ago my dissertation committee accepted it and I was granted a Ph.D."

"I shall call you Doctor from now on."

"Thank you, Doctor."

"My pleasure, Doctor. And the woman, Mirriamma, with whom you work—?"

"I'm getting to that. What's your hurry?"

Wynema lets the silence play...until, "Don't you want to know what my doctorate is in?"

"I figured you'd tell me when you wanted to."

"Hah! That's very 'Indian' of you. Very good, Doctor, you're learning."

"I appreciate your seeing that, Doctor."

"Okay, so the title of my dissertation was 'Signing: the Universal Language'."

"Wow! That relates to why you're here so soon after they granted you the degree."

"Not exactly. Stay in the left lane! Good. I only wish that it related more. She says it does but I don't see it yet."

Will doesn't understand anything. "Fascinating. I mean, who says it does?"

"Mirriamma."

"Oh."

Wynema continues. "Okay, I'll tell you this. A few months before I was supposed to go to Cambridge on a teaching fellowship, Mirriamma called me and asked if I could come back to the Pueblo—I thought just for a week or two—because she thought I might remember some songs and things that my mother taught in the Pueblo language, for Godsakes, a long time ago. Does that sound as strange to you as it did for me?"

"I don't know. Did you?"

"Remember the songs? Of course not. Absolutely not. It'd been ten years since I left and didn't speak Pueblo again after that. I learned the Sioux dialect of my father's tribe, and some Ojibwa. I fell in love with languages, actually. But I forgot Pueblo. ...Or so I thought."

"Ah! Enter Mirriamma."

"Right. She either knew I hadn't really forgotten or she knew she could somehow wake them up in me. Had to be."

"Well, that's great! But why did Mirriamma want you in particular to remember these things? Weren't they available elsewhere among your tribe?"

"You'd think so. But I think it had more to do with our moiety."

"Excuse me. Your moiety?"

"A group of clans. But, well, that's something I really can't talk about. Clan stuff, you know."

"Oh. Sorry."

"No, that's all right. But some things—you know, none of it's written down—some things were passed down through the men and some things through the women—.

"Like mitochondria."

"Right. And my mother really did like to teach me things, all kinds of things. Passing things on to her only daughter was my mother's religion. I mean, you can pass things on in books, but it's more likely to grip and grab and become a living part of you if some-one face to face, you know—." Suddenly she becomes self-conscious. "Where was I? Oh, yes, I—"

Will interrupts. "No, really, I get it. I want to know what—"

"Okay. So I thought I'd come back here for two or three weeks at the most and let see how much I could remember. I mean, I'm into linguistics 'n all—"

"So, what's kept you? Ah, this is your work with Mirriamma."

"Precisely, Doctor. I mean—" She fumfers. *How much,* she thinks, *can I tell this guy? How much do I really know, anyhow? I mean, this man is a modern allopathic A.M.A. doctor—a rationalist, a reductionist, a logical-positivist, a natural scientist. He isn't built to understand. It would only cause him a great big tummy ache. Cognitive dissonance.*

Will is patient. He doesn't push her. He's incapable of pushing right now, taken as he is with her face and voice. He thinks, *If only I could lean over a little and smell her. I want to smell her. Right now. But I'm driving. Maybe I could ask her to lean over so I could tell her a secret. Very mysterious. No, that would be stupid. We're in a car driving 85 miles an hour, and there's no one else here. Yeah, that would be dumb all right. Oops, here comes a car. I'll look at her just as the headlights flood her face. Damn! Missed. I'm slowing down to 60.*

Looking straight ahead into the blackness in a matter-of-fact voice, she says, "I think there's work to do right here where I was born and partly raised."

"I beg your pardon?"

"I asked Cambridge if I could put off my fellowship until next year and they said yes."

Will is impressed. "They guaranteed you another fellowship a year in advance?!"

"Yep."

"Wow!"

"I know."

"I mean, do you see it as part of what you're going to teach, you know, your future work?"

"Obviously, Doctor."

"I see, Doctor. I take your point." Will knows there's more to ask here, but something tells him not to push it. So he punts. "Your mother and father were from two different tribes?"

"My mother was San Lucas Pueblo. My father Assiniboine Sioux with maybe a little Ojibwa, like I said. And you?"

"Okay. My father was Jewish, born in New York. My mother was the other kind of Jewish, called Sephardic, born here but with roots going back to Spain...until the Spanish Inquisition.

Wynema wryly brightens. "We have something in common then!"

"What's that?"

"1492."

It takes a moment for Will to get it, but finally, "Bad year for the Indians...and the Jews."

A herd of antelope dart across the freeway unseen, unhurt. The BMW speeds by, disappearing into the night.

An hour later, the BMW cruises slowly by the San Lucas plaza. A few couples are walking around the common space, each hand-in-hand.

After climbing a low hill, Will pulls up slowly next to Mirriamma's house. In the daylight, by himself, he knows he would not be able to find this place.

Wynema turns and smiles. "Thanks for driving me home" then immediately opens her door and steps out. "I have to get up early. Talk to you later. Thanks again."

Will watches her walk away. He moves over to where she was sitting and sniffs the air. Something's there, just the hint of it. He can't name it or associate it but clearly thinks he caught the scent, if only barely. He's intrigued, the scent is intriguing, yes. As he opens his window, an owl hoots. He smiles. If he were Pueblo, he wouldn't.

32

A LAND MADE UNHOLY BY GREED

A few days later, Will goes to Santa Fe Indian Health Service headquarters to see if he can pull up any summaries of data collected by the Clinic over the years. That done, he drives slowly around Santa Fe's downtown plaza, taking in the scenery while checking in with Lola on his cell. "This is like Fifth Avenue in the Southwest!" he exclaims. "Huh? ...No, sorry, Lola, I was—what were you saying? ... Yes, you're right. ...Then write it up for 300 milligrams, B.I.D. ...No. I'm already in Santa Fe.... No. Errands first. But I'll review the lab results at one.... Okay, tell Louisa. Thanks." Suddenly, he spots Wynema entering an upscale Indian Art Gallery and comes alive. "Uh, make that two or two-thirty."

Stoked, he stuffs the phone into his coat pocket, pulls into a "Handicapped Space," and tosses an "M.D." placard onto the dash. He leaps out and crosses the street to the shop Wynema entered.

Will is about to enter Osona Galleries when, at the door, he sees a sign with the shop's hours and telephone number listed. He steps off to one side, pulls out his cell and dials the shop's number.

Inside, the owner, chatting with Wynema, answers the ringing phone, then hands it to a surprised Wynema. A tiny black teacup dog yips at her feet.

Outside, as Will talks, he sees Wynema's image in a tall, shop mirror. What he says 'reflects' her every move and aspect.

"Well, as I was leaving the hospital, I had this vivid image of you standing there, somewhere, just smiling, wearing levis and a red shirt, a rainbow in your hair...and it was strange, because I was in the midst of something, and there was a little black dog, and you looked down and were surprised; then you turned around, gathered your wits about you, touched your cheek and...and I don't know—so, when I had a moment, I thought I'd call you and—listen, I have to come in to Santa Fe today. How about if you show me the Santa Fe that isn't on my map? Could I pick you up at—looking for store's name—oh, I don't know—at Osona Galleries? I love that place. It'll only take a little bit to get there. Don't go away. I'll pick you up."

He hangs up quickly, grins, then settles back against the shop's front, breathing hard.

Wynema is flabbergasted, embarrassed. She turns about in a daze.

Will, seeing Wynema is about to exit, exhales all his breath, and rushes into the shop, jostling her, acting surprised.

He follows her back outside. "'Preciate your taking me around."

She wheels on him, narrows her eyes, then bursts out laughing. "*Coyóte!*"

They sit on a green metal bench in the middle of the Plaza. Will is looking at the Indian women sitting under the porticos across the street selling their wares.

Wynema, out the corners of her eyes, looks at Will. "Pueblos are maybe the only Native nation still living on their original land."

He turns slowly to her. "It's all about land, isn't it?"

Her eyes follow a flock of pigeons, their wings arched back, gliding down ten feet away. "In more ways than one."

"You know, I have no family except for my grandfather—none, all gone. But he's on the other side of the Earth now because of a piece of land. It's all so irrational. And causes so much pain."

"Israel."

"And Palestine. And Judea. And Samaria. A Land made unholy by greed, chauvinism, and separatism."

She stands and stretches like an athlete before a race. Then sits again. "It's in your Good Book, right there at the beginning, I think. 'And man shall have dominion, over the land and the beasts and—"

"'Dominion!' There's the problem. I wonder if that's really the right translation. What if the original version said 'stewardship' instead of 'dominion'? You think that would have changed anything?"

"I don't know. Depends. Remember what Chief Seattle said about—"

"Yeah, I know, he nailed it. Cute. But they'll never hear it. It's so stupid. I don't want to have anything to do with any of them—Zionist Jews, nationalists, Chosen People people." Will drifts away.

Wynema scratches his knee with her finger. "Wow. With you it goes deep. I'm sorry."

"Huh? Oh, right. What was that you said about 'in more ways than one'?"

She smiles and laughs. "Well, most people think about land in terms of ownership and what they can get from it. But if we look at the land as our Mother—."

"Powerful image," says he.

Their eyes connect. They both smile. Become self-conscious. Look away. Go interior....

Strolling now, they look into the window of another gallery facing the Plaza. "I love the way this artist stacks his images and interweaves them, different dimensions, the inside and the outside, the known world, the felt world. And he paints it with mud, dirt, rocks. Literally! The colors, too, no paint, just the colors of the Earth. Dirt paintings. Beautiful."

"Who's the artist?"

"The man standing next to you."

"Huh?"

Standing beside them is an impish, perhaps eccentric 70-year-old man wearing a dark beret, tufts of white hair poking out on all sides.

Will faces the man, smiles, and points to Wynema. "You painted those?"

In a thick French accent, "But of course. You like?"

Will: "She describes your painting very well."

"My name is Pierre. Come in, if you like. I'll show some more." The artist bows with a dip of his head and sweeps inside.

Wynema smiles. "I do like his work. I'm going to come back."

But Will now is only interested in her. "What's the difference between shaman, clan chief, or medicine man...?"

"Those are all...English words."

"Is Simon...anything like one of those?"

"The woman I study with respects him a lot. His grandfather was a leader, a spiritual man...and once a Chairman of the All Indian Pueblo Council. And his father was a healer; his specialty was bones and joints. People came to see him from all over—"

Will's cellular phone rings and he instantly reaches for Wynema's hand—but stops just short of touching. "I have to tell you that that's the last time I shall grab for you without being absolutely sure you want to be grabbed."

"What are you talking about?"

"About pushing you out of my office at the pre-natal clinic.

She shrugs it off. "No sweat."

Finally, he looks at the text message. His expression changes.

"What is it?"

"It's Simon! I got to run."

Inside the Indian Hospital in Santa Fe, Will moves almost at a run. As he careens around a corner, he almost collides with a gurney on which Simon, unconscious, is being pushed rapidly by paramedics running with an IV drip.

"What happened?!"

The lead paramedic answers, "He collapsed outside your Clinic an hour ago, Doctor. Came to on the way down here, but passed out again. Pulse 120...BP dropped initially, but stable now 96 over 69. MRI's in process."

They all disappear into the MRI control room.

A little later, in a six-bed room for men, Simon is sleeping, an IV running to his arm. Other sensors on his chest and fingers.

He opens his eyes. Will is standing at the foot of his bed, writing in a chart. Upon seeing Simon awake, Will sits in a chair and tenderly picks up his hand.

"You look worried," says Simon.

"Me? I exude confidence and great optimism."

Simon beckons Will even closer. "Bullshit."

"Okay. You got an aneurysm, on the aorta, just below the heart. Picture a big bulge, a weak spot, like on an inner tube that—"

"Okay, okay...I got the picture."

"It could be leaking, Simon—but probably not. Or, it could be pressing a nerve. Or both. In either case, not good. We'll know for sure after I talk with Dr. Cutter. He's not only my boss; he's the best thoracic surgeon in the area. He knows how to slap dacron patches on aneurysms like nobody's business."

"Boy, you are worried."

"Huh? Me? I don't want to lose you."

"Now that you found me, huh?"

Will thinks about that. "Well, yeah."

Even later, Will and Cutter stand near the Nurse's Station, studying x-rays.

"William, this thing could blow like yesterday. You saw it on the MRI. I got a bypass to do tomorrow, but it can wait. You want an angiogram to make sure?"

"No, I know you're right. Why the added risk? I'll tell him what we're going to do."

"Great. And you're our guest at the Opera next Friday, right?"

Will nods, exits. Cutter is impressed with Will. *Finally, someone who trusts his gut...and respects experience.*

Simon's in bed, thinking. Will sits backward in a chair, facing Simon, waiting patiently.

"You gotta learn to trust your gut, Doc, and not rely on so many statistics."

"How else can we make up our mind? Nine times out of ten, the stats tell the story."

"You think *those* are stories? I got news for you. I'll...think about it."

"What do you mean you'll think about it? There's not much choice here, Simon. If you want a third opinion, I can get it, but—"

"No, I'm sure you know what you know."

"Okay, then what don't I know?"

"Well, now, that's another question." He thinks for a moment. "What made you become a doctor?"

"Aw, Simon, what does that have—?" He stops himself. "Okay. Okay. When I was 16, I saw my grandmother eaten up by cancer. I suppose that's when I decided. I know, it sounds corny, but I couldn't do anything for my grandma—." As Simon leans forward in interest, he focuses: "But I can help you get through this crisis...alive."

Simon smiles. "I see. You know, there's all kinds of 'crisis.' What kind do you think this is?"

Will's eyes narrow. "Is this a tricky...or just a hard question?"

Both men look at each other, nodding, taking in what was just said.

Simon breaks into a big smile. "Where did you learn to doctor?"

Will looks around and takes a deep breath. "Well, I went to Columbia in New York and then to Harvard Med. I did my internship at Tufts, then Mount Sinai for my residency in Internal Medicine. I also have a Master's in Epidemiology and Public Health."

"Very impressive, but do you know how to dance?"

Taken by whimsy, Will, laughs, stands, snaps, and dances an Afro-American dance step while singing falsetto, a la C & C Music Company's, 'Everybody dance now, uh-uh-uh-uh....'

Simon slips out on the other side of his bed and begins a slow, earthy movement which Will imitates...until, "Are you out of your mind?! Get back in bed! That's enough!"

Simon complies. "You must be able to dance if you are to heal people."

"It's not a Med school class. Maybe you can teach me your steps."

"I could do that, but it's better if you hear your own music."

Will goes interior for a moment, then rises, walks in a circle, lost in thought. He looks to Simon, who smiles back peacefully...

Will lights up. "I know what you're saying."

"You do?"

"It has to do with the difference between doctoring and healing."

"Maybe."

"And maybe it's your father...or your grandfather. It's in your blood. Are you a...a medicine man?"

Simon's eyes are closed. Will rises again, takes a step back.

"Well, you get a good night's rest. You won't be able to eat anything after sundown. But I'll be right there in the O.R. with you tomorrow, okay?"

As Will reaches the door, Simon asks, "In my shirt pocket...a bag."

Will takes a leather medicine bag out of the pocket of a shirt on a hook. As he approaches Simon's bed, he starts to untie the bag. Simon releases a choppy, hissing sound, holds up a cautionary finger, and shakes his head. Will understands and hands him the bag gingerly. Simon clasps it, closes his eyes, and Will leaves.

33

THE BOY WANTS TO FLY

An hour later, Simon is sleeping. Suddenly his eyes open and he lifts his head to look at the leather bag in his hand. He sees the little bag pulse. He feels it with his hand. He smiles and lets himself back to sleep again.

His eyes twitching in REM sleep, Simon may not be aware that the bag is moving stronger now. The walls of the hospital room turn red and the mournful sound of a cold wind seeps through the windows and the head of a bear fetish pokes his head out of the leather bag on Simon's chest.

Simon's dreaming eyes open. He looks directly down at the fetish moving slowly across his chest. He sees the fetish morph into a man wearing the traditional dress: the head and skin of a bear. As the bear approaches Simon's face, it becomes so large so fast that now it looms over Simon in his bed.

He sits up, looks around. The hospital has become a wooded glassy glade at dawn and his bed has become a burial blanket on a large, flat boulder. The Bear's-head dancer beckons, Simon follows…to a ceremonial fire not far from the base of an Indian funeral bier. He hears drumbeats and looks and sees other biers, all with people lying in traditional attire.

While Simon dreams, at his cornfield at the Pueblo, there is high-decibel heavy-metal blaring its anger from a careening car that churns up dust and skids to a halt next to Simon's field. A door flies open and Danny, a tall awkward boy, staggers out, bends over, and pukes. Moments later, Dayone in only an arm cast, Jesse, and Armand, beer bottles in hand, clamber out, laughing at Danny. Dayone totters into the field, unzips, and, while he is peeing, Jesse playfully shoves him. Dayone pitches face-first into the corn stalks; one of his ever-present drumsticks falling out of a pocket. Having now pissed himself, Dayone gets up, zips, and angrily gives chase. In moments, the others have taken uprooted stalks and are thrusting and dodging as they charge about in swordplay, destroying much of Simon's corn. Dayone, attacked from all sides, finally pulls up his own stalk and joins the mêlée.

Simon's still dreaming. He's in a funeral glade. Suddenly, as if it were choreographed with the beating drums, a high-standing bier flies apart and collapses all around Simon. He turns and sees Dayone, in a heavy metal T-shirt and jeans, rhythmically swinging a shining stainless steel baseball bat at the biers. The Bear's-head dancer stands under one, oblivious to or hypnotized by Dayone. With his next swing, Dayone causes one of the biers to fall on the Bear's-head dancer, crushing him. But the dancer emerges unscathed from the rubble and pulls off the bear's-head. It is Frank, his face made-up half war-paint, half pink-face, as in his Albuquerque show. He beckons. The activity in Simon's face disappears...and he sinks into a deep dreamless sleep.

An hour later he is sitting on the edge of his hospital bed. The red-tinged sky behind him, Simon almost smiles. For a split second he flashes on an image from his dream—that of Frank beckoning. As if answering Frank's call, Simon heads for his clothes.

Outside, Simon exits a side door, fully dressed, unnoticed.

An hour and a half later Simon thanks the pickup driver for the ride and starts walking slowly up the dirt road, the Pueblo's tall water tower in the distance.

Now further down the road, the water tower above him, his eye catches something...high up on the tower.

Three figures on the high platform—Jesse and Armand, and even higher, Dayone is walking the rim, his arm bandaged but now not in the sling.

Suddenly, they see each other at the same moment. Dayone is looking down, defiant, sad—a martyr.

Simon is comfortable allowing a soft subtle smile slowly to enter his face. "The boy wants to fly," he says to himself out loud. He waves sweetly to his grandson and turns and heads up a little-used dirt road towards his summer house, fields, and corral.

As he heads for his horse, he sees beyond the corral his destroyed cornfield.

Simon walks without emotion through the scene of mayhem. Half the stalks are pulled up or broken down. He bends down and picks up Dayone's drumstick. His blank face now fills with peace and commitment. He reaches into his shirt and pulls out his fetish bag.

"I understand." He takes a step and stops. "What do I understand? That I am no longer a farmer." Another step and stop. "But I must feed my horse."

Will paces in front of his desk, every few seconds stopping to record something on a little device in his hand, "Causative agent...and cure. Psycho-neuro-immunology: more than the germ causes the disease. Pasteur said seed. Claude Bernard said soil. On deathbed Pasteur agreed with Bernard. Indian sees soil as sustenance. Need to know more about the Navajos and the hantavirus cycle. May be essentially analogous to Tularemia and the Native Rabbit Hunt around here before early summer Corn Dance—."

He is startled upon seeing Wynema and Lola leading pregnant Tessie Vigil past his open door. Wynema beckons.

As Lola leads Tessie into an exam room, Wynema draws Will aside.

"Mirriamma thought it best she come here," Wynema says softly.

"I'm grateful for a second chance. I, uh—"

"You don't have to explain."

"I was going to call you this evening."

"We don't have a phone. And I keep my cellphone off. Try smoke signals."

"Can you read smoke signals? Nah-h-h."

Louisa appears as Lola leads Tessie into an exam room. She quite upset. "Doctor, the hospital just called. My father is missing. He left without—"

"Missing!? I was headed to the hospital in another half hour. Simon and I—we talked. I explained everything to him. Dr. Cutter, who's going to do the operation, made it perfectly clear that—." To Lola, "Please start the work-up on Mrs. Vigil."

Louisa leaves.

As he steps away from the door, "Wynema, do I—? Am I missing something here? What else could I have said?"

"It is his choice."

"Technically, yes, but practically, no. You understand?"

"Not really."

"Well, we have to find him. He's in danger."

"I'll show you where he lives."

"Can you wait a sec. Let me see Mrs. Vigil first. Louisa, will you come with me?"

Wynema nods. Will steps away and enters the exam room. As Louisa closes the door behind them, she hears him talking to Tessie, "I'm glad you came back, Mrs. Vigil. I will be more understanding from now on."

In her car, Wynema drives Will to Simon's room off the plaza. Neither notice in the shadows between two close adobes, Frank's Harley. Wynema and Will jump out and go to Simon's door. They hear sounds of a scuffle within. Wynema hesitates, then slowly opens the door. Frank is stomping and jerking around the little room coupled with a half-naked very young Pueblo woman whose arms are around his neck, legs around his waist, head thrown back and flailing. Frank is chanting, panting, having a helluva time. Will is quick to close the door, just as Frank turns in their direction. Will and Wynema look at each other, their reactions mixed.

Finally Will yells through the door, "We're looking for your father!"

"Go 'way!"

"Simon is in medical danger. Do you know where he is?!"

Frank flings opens the door, zipping his pants, stoned and angry. "Who the hell are you?"

"We met backstage in Albuquerque. I'm Will Kornfeld, your dad's doc—"

Frank finally recognizes Wynema...and now Will. "Oh, it's you." Looking at Wynema and thumbing Will, "You're still with Mr. Mashed Potatoes here?" He turns to Will, "Yeah, you're the new white bones, bleaching in the Pueblo sands." Back to Wynema, "What about my father?"

"Your father walked out of the hospital early this morning. Do you know where he is?"

"What's wrong with him?"

Will steps in, "He's got an aortic aneurysm that could fulminate at any moment. But it's correctable—if we catch it in time."

"Even if that old drugstore Indian thought he really was sick, what makes you think he'd belly back to some honky doctor?" To Wynema, mock-sensitive, "Am I too rough here? Too nasty-poo?"

"You're drunk, as usual...and mean. We came to find your dad and you want to play these bad-boy games."

"You, who are stealing the soul of our grandmother, and our old secrets, for some doctoral *feces*...you shouldn't talk about playing games."

He thumbs Will again, "And now you're going to dilute our blood—with him!?"

Will takes an involuntary, aggressive step, but Frank holds Will off with an index finger pointing like a pistol. To Wynema, "You don't know where my father is? If he's sick, then he'd wanna get healed by a real healer. Where else would he be?"

"Mirriamma!" She shakes her head, angry or disappointed—at Will, or at herself.

Frank takes a step back into the room, stumbles as he pulls on his boots. The young woman with him hides under the covers.

Will is focused, "C'mon, let's go, if you two think you know where he is."

Jacket in hand, Frank exits on the fly.

Will isn't sure what they're doing, "We're following you!"

Frank heads for his bike. To Wynema, indicating Will, "Who's he think he is?" Wheeling on Will and putting on an East Indian accent, "Is my father your Indian guru? He's from a very high caste, you know." Then back into a straight and hostile voice, "Yeah, that's it. Well, you just back off, Jake. Cuz I'm Esau, the oldest son! Don't be snatchin' his blessings out from under my nose." He turns to Wynema, rubbing it in, "I'm really surprised. You of all people should have known where he would be."

Frank roars away on his motorcycle. Wynema's expression slowly changes from concern to committed calm. "Simon's not in danger."

Will is dumbfounded, hurt. "I may not know a lot about your ways, but I know aneurysms. He is in grave danger."

"He's in good hands," she whispers, "...yours...and Mir-riamma's."

34

Open Yourself and Go!

Simon's horse is tied to a post next to Mirriamma's backyard ramada. Inside, in a setback niche, up against an adobe wall, Simon sits on a stool while Mirriamma smudges him with smoke.

Then she fans herself with the wing, remembering. "I think it was winter of 1939, and you and me were just kids, and my father took you, me, and your grandfather all the way back from Albuquerque, in that Model-A Ford, 'member? There was only four Indians with cars here then."

She steps inside a back door, into the kitchen, and brings a steaming pot outside, smells it, then pours a dark tea into a glass. She hands it to Simon, who takes a hot sip. She encourages him with a finger to drink more.

"Then, when we got home, and it was snowing, 'member? Your grandfather told everyone what he said in that meeting with all the Pueblo Governors. The doctors had told him he would die—"

Simon interrupts, "But he told the Governors he would not die." He's flooded with swirling memories, until a transcendent thought enters his eyes. "You think I can do the same, uh?"

She urges him to drink more tea. He does. She squats. "That's something only you and your medicine know. Your grandfather lived for another year and...and he brought unity into that Council. Unity. Life, death—they're both sacred."

"Maybe I used to know what is sacred." Simon looks at his fingers and rubs them together. "I can't feel it anymore."

"The fingers you use to feel the sacred are just frozen. Put them in a bowl of hot water and they'll come back."

Simon shrugs. "Unity isn't talked about much these days, ain't it?" He sways on his stool and stares into the fire. The herbal decoction is having the intended effect. He looks to Mirriamma, takes another sip, and nods. She rises, beckons. He follows her inside. "I'm ready," he says.

Mirriamma sits at a formica kitchen table facing Simon. On the table between them is a three-legged *metate* in which smolders some charcoal she took from the living room fireplace. The smoke rises through a hole in the ceiling. In the ceiling a vent, controlled by a long stick attached to a damper. On the table between them, Mirriamma places various religious objects. Simon sits quietly, intensely focused, tears flooding his eyes.

Now Mirriamma and Simon's eyes are closed, and she speaks softly, intermittently in old language, almost chanting. Her lips quiver. So does his. They breathe...until they slowly become aware of the sound of a motorcycle.

Outside, Frank parks and takes a drink from a pint in his saddlebags.

Their work interrupted, Simon and Mirriamma now stand in front of the open, dark doorway—as if they had been waiting.

After verifying the facts told by Wynema and the doctor, Frank paces in front of Simon and Mirriamma. He turns to his father, "You make no sense, old man! You believe those doctors, but you won't let them operate. It's a white-man's disease you got. Use white-man's medicine to fix it."

"With the white-man's way, maybe I live 80 percent chance, maybe I die 20 percent. But with our way...I know I won't die 100 percent before our Feast Day. Then—."

"Sounds like stubborn to me."

"I need the time and a clear head. There's some things I must do— for me, for the tribe, for—"

"Go ahead and kill yourself. Whose fault will *that* one be?"

Frank leaps on his Harley and over the roar crosses himself cynically and yells, "Be sure and dispense absolution on all my sins before you split, old man!" Fishtailing, he's gone.

Unseen behind a clump of chokecherry bushes, Wynema and Will sit in the car and watch.

Mirriamma and Simon slowly walk next to the creek that separates the Pueblo into two significant halves. She stops and steadies herself with Simon's arm. Then she points to one side of the village and holds up four fingers. Then slowly turns to the other side and holds up four fingers again.

"What's she doing?" Will whispers to Wynema.

"I may be wrong, but I think she's going back to the basics with him." She whispers dramatically, more out of astonishment than not wanting to be heard. "She's reminding him of how our village is structured. There are two halves. There are many names for these halves, but here they call them Summer and Winter...."

They see how Mirriamma's arms weigh something huge and abstract and then come to a balance.

"Yes, yes, she's reminding him that there are these two forces that dance through everything. They hold us like the Sun holds the planets in right relationship—"

"What the Chinese call the Yin and the Yang of it?"

"Sure. We have it right here structurally embodied in the way the two moieties, as the anthropologists call them, divide the village into two parts—each with four clans—that balance each other through both competition and cooperation."

Mirriamma quickly points to a raven that like a kingfisher drinks from the creek on the fly. She bends over and whispers in Simon's ear: "If you jump on a whirlwind, you go where the whirlwind goes."

Simon groans wryly, "I'm too old for this."

Mirriamma laughs, "No, you're finally old enough."

As they disappear behind some drying racks, Wynema turns to Will. "Let's go. You'll talk to him later."

"Later?! Are you out of—? Are you sure? Cutter's going to cut me to shreds."

"Your first duty is to Simon's vital force, not to some A.M.A protocol."

"I'm where I am because I follow those protocols, and follow them well."

"Then let me take you somewhere else, where—where the 'protocols' have a very different ontology."

He softens. "Okay. I'd like to get to know all your ontologies."

＊

Simon and Mirriamma pass a friendly woman taking a few chiles from a hanging string. One chili falls from her string. Mirriamma picks it up and asks with a gesture if she can have it. The woman smiles and happily blinks yes.

Mirriamma bites the tiniest piece from the tip. "Heat," she exclaims. "A sweat would be good but there is too much static around here, okay. You know what I'm thinking?"

"That spring up on Two Hawk?"

"Good place to talk to your ancestors. You told me once your great-grandfather is buried halfway up there. He'll show you the rest of the way."

"I haven't been up there in thirty or forty years. There's ten creeks coming down that watershed. I'd never find it. I could pack you up there though on a mule?"

"Let's go back to my place. I got a map."

"You got a map?! I don't think so."

"It's in the smoke."

＊

The next day damned if Simon didn't find himself on his horse, plodding up the northern slope out of the Pueblo, chuckling to himself that he let her talk him into this. When they went back to her place and sat before the fire pit she sprinkled Mugwort leaf onto the coals. The smoke made his head swim. "You must come home, Simon," she said. "First you'll return to the Earth, then to your tribe, your family, and finally to yourself."

"Who will guide me? You?" he asked.

"Your own homesickness," she replied.

Simon's thoughts are interrupted by the sight of a large aspen tree, not tall and straight like the others, but thick and twisted. He guides his horse around the back of the tree and stretches up in the saddle.

There it is! By God there it is! A large agate rock he placed into the trunk of the tree almost forty years ago, the bark having almost completely engulfed it since then. He smiles and settles with more confidence into his saddle, then looks up and to the east. He smiles again and nods and checks to make sure no one is there, then disappears up the first draw on the left.

He moves slowly now between other aspens, the leaves from last year softening the sounds of his passing. *If I could change into a tree,* he thinks, *and grow quietly and wait for birds and squirrels to visit me and not hurt anyone...ah, that would be good.*

Then something else Mirriamma said pops into his head. He was sitting on a low bench and Mirriamma was walking around him, sprinkling cornmeal in four lines to match the four directions. Before them on the table were a number of sacred objects. He remembers reaching out tentatively and picking up a decorated stick. "You see," she said, "you don't need anyone to show you where your grandfather is buried. Open yourself...open yourself and go!"

She had placed four pieces of colored cloth before him as well—black, yellow, red, white. He remembers gently placing the stick down on the red cloth with conviction and then Mirriamma chuckling, "Yes, yes, yes!"

Holding the reins of his horse, Simon stands before a gravemarker. He places the decorated stick next to it.

An hour later he is still sitting on a rock not far away. Quiet, opening, more comfortable now, he cocks his head. *Do I hear the water here? No, I am still too far away.* He gets up slowly and goes to his horse. He uses the rock to help himself up into the saddle. As he does he steps on a twig and it snaps loudly, spooking for a moment both horse and rider.

35

Not until the Wolves Become a Pack

At that very moment Teo, sitting on his couch his arm around Tessie, jumps with a start.

"Teo, what is it? You just nearly caused me a heart attack."

Teo stands. "I'm sorry. I don't know. I must have dozed off or something."

"Teo, what is it? You don't doze off and jump like that." She offers him her hands and he pulls her up, both of them involuntarily grunting. "You got something going. What is it?"

He looks to the window, then touches her gently on the shoulders. "Woman, mirror of all my sides, I pass through you to the window." He crosses, looks out to the mountains.

She is suspicious. "Come on now. You're talking strange."

"He's up there. I know it!"

She knows he's talking about Simon. "Where?"

"I think I know where."

"How do you know?"

"Because it's what I would do if I—"

"If you what?"

"If I was lost and there wasn't much time and—and if I didn't have you."

She smiles and bobs.

"He's up there, Tessie, and he's traveling light and I'm gonna take him some food and salt...and that old drum of his." He wheels and heads for the kitchen. She doesn't doubt him for a second.

On foothills rising to a high mesa, Teo drives a rutted, curvy road. He looks confident, almost happy. At a fork, about to turn right on one of the few dirt roads that will take him up the north side of the mountain, he notices something to the left. Just a little dust rising above the trees down and to the west. He stops, backs, turns, goes slowly to investigate.

He had passed this little used overgrown road that takes off to the west. He gets out of his truck, looks down at the ground carefully and the plants growing there. *Something's just passed this way. Oh, yes.*

As before, the road turns sharply downhill and breaks out into the open towards the west, Teo stops and gets out. He looks down through the trees and rock outcroppings. Another small cloud of dust is just settling. He steps back to his truck and quickly exchanges his boots for high-top Pueblo moccasins. He takes off his red shirt, exposing a faded camou T-shirt.

Teo moves skillfully and silently through the trees, bringing a mesa just below into view. About a thousand yards ahead, through scattered piñon and juniper—no aspen at this level—a vehicle equipped with two or three radio antennae. There's an insignia on the door but Teo can't make it out from this distance and angle. He moves carefully closer, unseen by what appears to be three men. Now he sees the survey gear and, yes, the vehicle belongs to the U.S. Dept. of Energy. The three Feds have a good view of the reservation land that sweeps away to the west and north. One has binoculars, one a clipboard, and one a radio or satellite cellphone. Out past the Rio Grande, Teo can see the helicopter that cruises slowly along the river somewhat below the altitude of the three men.

The men move further away from the vehicle to an even better vantage point. Teo stalks, approaching rapidly, carrying a young juniper bough in one hand and a thick, piñon branch in the other. When the men turn his way, he freezes, using these for camouflage.

The survey team's voices are now audible but unintelligible, as Teo moves, still unseen, towards the D.O.E. vehicle. A few moments later, he is squatting beside an open window. When he is able he peers into the window and glances at some papers on the seat. Struck by one, he reaches in and pulls it out and reads. Soon he puts the documents back on the seat and leaves as invisibly as he came.

Teo knows exactly where the steaming, bubbling, geo-thermal pool is. His kiva leaders took him here with three other young men upon graduating from kiva instruction. Teo approaches carrying Simon's drum. He looks around...no one. He scans the ground, smiles, then sits down...and waits.

The hot-water bubbles up from below; the cool water falls four feet from a creek above.

It doesn't take long. Maybe two minutes. Simon appears from behind the falling waters, his head dripping with green weeds and moss that drape across his sneaky smile.

Teo laughs softly, "I knew you were here."

The Ancient Green Man speaks: "I'd say you did if you're here."

"I didn't know you could get behind that there waterfall."

"Now you do."

They laugh. Dunking himself, washing away the moss, Simon invites Teo into the warm water. Teo, anxious to tell Simon something, checks himself, agrees, and takes off his clothes.

Later, only their heads above water, the men continue talking.

Teo is seriously concerned. "They had a copy of some kind of order and it was signed, Victor Moquino, Governor." Teo snorts. "Basically it gave them permission to inspect or survey certain places on the rez. For what? The Council hasn't voted for the storage facility yet."

Simon nods, with less distance than usual.

"Victor has signed an executive order...to get the ball rolling. He committed us without—"

Simon raises a finger as if to speak, "—without the Council's approval. Done all the time."

Simon dunks himself one more time. "The business of government is business."

"Yes, but here's another example of Victor writing checks his ass can't cover. The business of business is controlling government."

Simon speaks calmly but his tone is strategic. "Do nothing now. No need to tell anyone yet...not until the wolves become a pack."

"Who're the wolves? Us or them?"

Simon smiles, raising his finger, 'Ah-ha!' "I saw a coyote chasing a rabbit through the sage. I knew the coyote didn't have a chance. Unless—"

"Unless the pack was lying in wait."

"Ah-ha."

Teo slowly sinks down in the water to his nose, feeling empowered, not only by the strategy but by Simon's calm confidence.

36

Two Women in Mu-mus

Not far to the southwest is a well-know, historic, unique ancient ruins called Bandelier Monument. Glorious, mysterious, inviting—these crumbling walls and footprints of rooms and walkways and buildings of indeterminate function—they nestle among the hills and meadows now. Stones and adobe structures fallen centuries ago. Will and Wynema wander in awe, feeling the spirit of the place.

Wynema leans against a crumbled wall. Will is enthralled.

"Thanks for bringing me here."

"I thought you'd like it."

"In one of my grandfather's letters from Israel, he explains what it feels like to walk through some of the ancient Jewish or Hebrew places. I feel like that here...in your place. I don't know why."

"A feeling's a feeling. No explanation needed."

Wynema moves away but she extends her hand back to Will as she goes. He follows after.

"Our people lived and loved and sang and danced in these places continuously for eight centuries. And then—"

"Do we know what really happened to them?"

"There are stories, differing stories."

In another place, a few minutes later, his curiosity gets the better of him. "What about privacy? I mean, there seems to be just this one big room. I don't know, maybe privacy is a cultural value?"

Wynema smiles and perhaps blushes. "Well, for the more intimate things, they found their privacy...somewhere."

Will takes her shoulders in his hands. She slips gracefully away. She directs him to a corner ledge in what once was a room.

"Just sit down here and close your eyes and try not to think of anything. Just be open...to whatever comes."

Will becomes a little nervous. "What do you mean?"

Wynema smiles, eases his shoulders back, and, taking a pendant from around her neck, she places it in Will's hand. "Hold this. It's my oldest possession. It was my great-great-grandmother's."

Will closes his eyes, takes a deep breath and tilts back his head against the wall. A tremulous smile creeps into his face. His fingers trace the shapes of the pendant in his hand. Suddenly, he opens his eyes with a gasp and looks down at the pendant in his hand: The ancient Indian image of the swaztika stares up at him.

Will regains his composure, but he is embarrassed. Wynema looks from the pendant to Will.

"Oh, I'm sorry, this is our ancient symbol—backwards from the German swaztika. I didn't mean to—."

"No, I—it was like a dream or—. When I was maybe seven or eight, I was taking a bath and my grandfather came in to wash me. He rolled up his sleeve and I—I guess I was at that age when you start to notice things and I saw there were some numbers on his forearm. I asked him what they were and he said a tattoo, from his youth, a silly mistake. But when I asked, out of love and innocence, when I would get to have a tattoo like that he—he grabbed me up out of the water and held me and squeezed me so hard I could barely breathe and kept saying over and over, 'never, never, never, my boy, never, never....' He never mentioned it again, and neither did I. But I remember at school, I used to secretly write numbers on my arm."

Will looks to Wynema. Her eyes are filled with tears.

With Bandelier behind them, they walk towards the car, holding hands. Will suddenly stops, choked with emotion, and turns to her.

"There are so many who don't know—they just don't realize that the Native Americans have had their Holocaust, too."

Wynema is deeply moved. Will continues, "I hope I can do a good job here. But I feel like I'm stumbling into a world that's—well, that's fascinating but forbidden."

"Every kiss is like that."

Will freezes. Melts. Immobile as he watches her face draw closer and closer to his. It takes them forever to kiss for the first time.

It's evening in Santa Fe at La Posada Bar and Dr. Steven Cutter and Will sit at a table sipping margaritas.

"Opera doesn't start till eight, Will. Relax. I think you'll like Jessica's friend."

"But Steve, I think I'm interested in someone else."

Cutter earnestly taken aback, "Really? You just got here. Fast worker."

"Nah, It's just that, well, I just want to focus on my work. Is your wife's friend really named Starla, Starla Rain?"

"You'll like her. Trust me. Listen, I want to talk to you about the aneurysm. We can't wait for this one. Why'd he walk out?"

"At first, I thought it was me, but—"

"Isn't his daughter your Clinic Director, fercrissakes?"

"Yes, but he's got a troubled past, and, well, his grandfather was a famous tribal leader who—. I don't know. But I know he's not afraid of dying. There's something else. He wants to work through something personal, maybe something traditional, before he—" Will is exasperated. "I don't know. I don't know why he left. He said he'd do it after his village's Feast Day. Whazzup with that?"

"Doctor, get this one in and prepped. I can do him in three hours. He'll be back out picking corn in two weeks. Tell you what. I'll fly up tomorrow. And bring your patient with you and I'll talk to him. And don't worry I'll be sensitive to his cultural needs. Meet me up behind the old drive-in movie. You'll find it. Around 10 o'clock tomorrow and I'll talk to him."

"The drive-in movie?"

"Yeah. There's an little dirt strip out there that's kinda tricky. I mean, if the wind's from the east, you take-off directly into a mountain. But it's fun to land on. He'll show you where it is."

A woman's voice turns the heads of the doctors. "Hi, Will, I want to introduce you to Starla, Starla Rain...."

The next day Will and Simon are standing next to the BMW talking about what it was like to go to the drive-in back in the day—

"What are we talking about?" says Will abruptly. "I never went to a drive-in theater."

"You didn't."

"Hell no. I'm too young. You had me thinking I really did."

The sound of an approaching Cessna turns their heads. The plane floats ten feet above the runway until it seems it will never land with enough runway to stop. But it does, barely. The aircraft taxies over and shuts down. Cutter gets out wearing a Hawaiian shirt, followed by Jessica Cutter and Starla Rain—both of them in mu-mus. Will and Simon looked at each other with mutual incredulity.

Simon leans over, "Is he fixing us up with dates?"

"He's trying. I went to the opera with the one on the right."

Simon asks with a subtle look if Will's interested.

Will shakes his head no with the slightest of movements.

⚓

The women stand on the far side of Will's car. Simon, Will and Cutter on the far side of the Cessna.

Will is now pure physician. "We've gone over your scans and X-rays and, well, you really have no choice, Simon."

Simon smiles at this remark.

"There are risks," adds Cutter, "but they're minimal. The operation is straightforward. You could have years in which to enjoy your life, your family, your people. Do you want another opinion?"

"Yes. My father's, and my grandfather's, my grandmother's, on my mother's side."

Will loosens his collar. "Simon, what are you saying? I thought we had an understanding."

"It's not you I am saying no to. It is only to the operation." Then to Cutter, indicating Will, "He got the makings of a good healer, don't you think?"

Cutter isn't charmed. "He's a doctor. I'm a doctor. We do what doctors do. We're pretty good at it. Look, Mr. Zamora, nobody can force you to do anything. But the reality is, the wall of your aorta has weakened and won't hold much longer."

"It'll hold until my village's Feast Day. I won't die before then. I've got time."

"Feast Day?"

Will turns to Cutter. "It's in mid-October, Doctor." Then to Simon, "No one knows when he's going to die."

"Some things we can know."

Cutter and Will stand next to the open door of Cutter's Cessna 185.

"Get that aneurysm on my table, or your good Indian is gonna be a dead Indian."

Perturbed but resigned, Will nods solemnly.

Starla leans over and whispers in Will's ear, "Come on down to Santa Fe next weekend. Please. I want to show you my etchings."

"Say what? Did you just—"

"I'm serious, silly, I just pulled some new ones off the plates. It's what I do. I want to show you something that I think you'll appreciate. They have, well, a Judaic flavor to them."

Cutter helps the women climb up into the aircraft.

37

The Snake Woman Saw Me

Days later, Victor and Dayone are about to get out of their car into the parking lot of McDonald's in Española, a nearby town.

Dayone is clearly upset. "This is really a bad idea. I'm tellin' ya."

Victor holds up his hand for silence. They get out of the car. An Hispanic man approaches.

"Here's the manager. Show some respect."

"Aww, shit."

The manager, a friend of Victor's, wears a uniform shirt and hat. He ia clearly the boss of his small domain and greets Victor with a formal handshake. And he is clearly not comfortable with what he is about to say.

"Thanks for driving out here, Governor. Here's the story. Your boy here, he—he may be a good kid and all that, but it just isn't working out. I run a sharp, hard operation that serves my customers with quality and service...and cleanliness."

Victor is impatient, but coolly courteous. Dayone is mortified.

"So what's the problem?"

"Your boy is just too slow. He doesn't want to work."

"He's only been on the job two days. Is that enough time? Maybe he needs—"

"Well, Victor, one of the other workers saw him spit into the Special Sauce."

"That's a lie!" Dayone shouts.

Victor grabs Dayone and pulls him back toward the car.

"Thank you, Raul."

"I tried to do you a favor, Governor, but I got a business to run."

Victor is angry, swallows hard, and tries to speak calmly. "You did and I'm grateful."

The manager walks away.

Victor is beside himself. "You leave us no choice but to send you away to Group Home? I wanted you to give me some help."

"Yeah, what? Help you do what?"

"By making San Lucas a better place to live. We could have organized the teenagers, maybe clean up the place."

Victor, however, turns away from Dayone's searching eyes at just the wrong moment, losing Dayone, and Dayone loses it.

"What's that mean!? Pick up garbage, or rat on my friends."

Victor hides his hurt with anger. "NO, that's not what I mean! Your friends got a responsibility to our village just like you do. Just like I do."

Dayone backs away. "Stop preaching to me!"

"Don't you go now!"

"You're not the cops."

Victor rubs his face, regains composure, tries again. "I'm talking to you like a man. You tell your friends it's time they gave something back. Like get an education and use it to help their people."

"Their people!? Their people don't show my friends no respect. Their people don't understand what's happening in this world. Their people trash our music, our fun, our ways. We have ways, too. Their people don't know how our brothers and sisters on other reservations all over are dying like flies...or wandering off alone, out there, so they can get a job, have some money, buy a car. Where do you think Ruben was going!? Why do you think he had to go!? Do you think he wanted to stay here?"

"You talk like you belong to some other tribe out there. This is the tribe you belong to."

The boy turns and wanders away. "I belong to nobody." Then he runs and disappears.

Victor's face fills with frustration, anger, anguish. He wants to reach out...but doesn't know how.

⁂

A few blocks away there's a video arcade. Jesse, Armand, and Denise, a 14-year-old waif with hardened, suspicious eyes, watch

Danny masterfully load points at a large-screened arcade game called "Dance Dance Revolution". The place is filled with sounds—electronic, grotesque, incessant.

Jesse looks around, pulls out a half-pint bottle and swigs. He looks at the label. "Cin-na-mon S-chi-naps. What is this?"

Armand grabs the bottle. "It's goo-ood!"

Dayone stalks in, angry. Everyone just looks at him. Focused amidst the noise. Dayone looks to the half-empty half-pint. Armand hands it to him instantly. Dayone chugs it...until Danny turns and grabs it and hands it gallantly to Denise, who titters and takes it.

The friends lean forward and listen to Dayone's story.

Jesse is incredulous, You did? Shit, man, I'm never eatin' a Big Mac again!

Dayone steps over and places his hand on the video game. Danny steps aside, happy to hand it over. Dayone stands there preparing to play, his eyes are half-dead, half-lethal. After playing for a few seconds he stops and turns. "It's the end. I'm outta of here."

Danny, at another game, "Yeah, me too. I'm outta quarters."

"No, I mean I'm leavin' this shithole. I'm going to California, where Ruben was going."

Jesse gets excited. "On the beach, man!"

"Bikinis and big tits!" adds Danny as he slides his arm around Denise.

As Dayone turns back to the game, "Nobody yelling, telling me what to do."

Danny puts his hand on Dayone's shoulder. "You should go, man. Hell, you should all go. Nothin' keeping you here."

"What about you? Ain't coming with us?"

"I would, man, but me and Denise we're gonna have a kid."

Dayone doesn't care who's coming. He motions to Armand to take over the game. "There's a Trailways out of Santa Fe, comes around 2 AM every day. I called once and asked."

Jesse's steps up. "I'm goin' with you." Then to his younger brother, "But not you, Armand...too young. But I'll send for you, and you'll come next year. I promise."

"That's cold, man," says Armand fully disgusted. "I can do arithmetic better than both you guys and you're going need someone like that."

Dayone is grim but determined. "I'll get us some money. Meet you back here at midnight. We're doing it, okay, Jesse? Be here, okay? We're dust."

It's 9 PM at the Moquino house and Louisa is asleep in a chair, the TV still on. Dayone slips into the kitchen through the back door, takes a set of keys from her purse, then sets about stuffing his backpack with a flashlight, food, and a few other things. He winces as he flings the backpack over his wounded shoulder.

Dayone and Jesse move quickly and quietly along the narrow dirt road leaving the Pueblo. Jesse looks back, fear filling his face. Dayone is implacable.

As they approach the Clinic buildings, they spook some horses in a nearby field which in turn spooks them. "Jesus!" whispers Jesse, his adrenaline rushing. When they reach the back of the Clinic, Dayone points to Will's house indicating silence. But then seeing Will's car is gone, he says, "There's nobody home...or anywheres."

With Louisa's keys, Dayone lets them in through the back door. It's dark. He moves to the reception desk, withdraws a flashlight.

Jesse stands guard while Dayone looks for and finds the petty cash box. He pockets the currency, hesitates, then puts the keys in the box. He hears something, hisses to Jesse who flicks his head in a look of question.

Dayone motions for silence. "Did you hear something?"

"No, man, except me—I farted."

"Let's get out of here."

They move quietly towards the hallway that leads to the back door.

Outside, in between the back door and Will's house, Will and Wynema, arm-in-arm, are just returning from a nighttime walk. As they kiss, Will sees a light flash inside a window. She sees it, too. Will motions for her to wait for him there.

Will steps up quietly and sees the back door is ajar. As he reaches for the door, he knocks over a broom.

In the hallway in front of Louisa's office, Dayone freezes, whispers, "Shit!" Then on quick tiptoes they make for the backdoor.

As they approach they see the door slowly opening. Dayone rushes against it with his good shoulder.

Will doesn't see it coming and the door flies opens and smacks hard into his head, sending him flying back against the post supporting the porch roof. Will falls, seriously stunned. The boys jump over him. Jesse disappears around the corner of the building. Dayone looks back at Will, hesitating. He steps back, looks down—until he hears Wynema call.

"Will!"

Dayone flees but looks back as Wynema approaches. Her expression says she recognizes Dayone as he disappears into the night.

Jesse makes a beeline for his uncle's house, where his uncle, a Gulf War I vet, sleeps heavily under a thick blanket of anger and alcohol.

Dayone runs wildly, scared, without direction. The loud sound of an accelerating vehicle makes him veer away. The door of a nearby house slams shut somewhere and forces him back in the other direction. A porch light from a house allows him to see a crumbling adobe wall over which he leaps. He's in a pasture now, surrounded by scattered, dark trees. He is winded and almost crying as he runs.

Dayone suddenly notices where he is—near the corral next to his grandfather's summer house. His mind races. He hurts. A few moments later, Dayone has Simon's horse bridled.

Standing a few yards away, however, Simon looks quietly at the boy. In Pueblo, Simon says, "Grandson."

Startled, deflated, Dayone doesn't run. He sinks to the ground. Simon now squats in front of his grandson—and the boy doesn't care anymore, about anything. In a soft mumbling confused disheartened voice he recounts it all, in bits and pieces what he has done.

Simon is nodding, integrating what he's hearing. Now he searches his heart as he speaks. "You knew the risks. You took them. You... you should go back."

Dayone turns away and Simon sees a tear roll down the boy's cheek.

There is silence between them now. Nothing more. Though neither knows it, the two of them now go to the same place inside themselves: to emptiness, to a mountain-top from which they each embrace their pasts, one long, one short, but equally painful, alone, and lost.

A dog barks. The night expands and contracts in an instant and brings a chill to them both. Simon starts to repeat, like an echo, what he had just said. "You knew the risks. You took them. You—" But he stops himself abruptly. His eyes flash wide for a moment. He takes a deep breath. He reaches out to touch Dayone.

"I did that once before—"

Dayone looks into his grandfather's face but doesn't understand.

Simon continues, "—to Frank, a year after his mother died. He was with his grandparents in Arizona. He came back to be with me, but he was only 11. And I wasn't fit to take care of him."

Dayone is trying hard to understand.

Their eyes meet and look deep as Simon speaks. "But I won't do that again. I won't."

Simon stands, takes a step, stops, turns, and now with purpose in his eyes, "Did anybody see you?"

Dayone looks at him for a few long seconds—a profound sadness becomes the mortar that holds him together, every cell in his body—and then nods. "Yeah, the doctor, and that *mestiza*...the Snake Women."

Simon's energy sinks back down. *The doctor. And some woman. Doesn't matter who. Someone. What was I thinking?*

Suddenly, there are light flashing off the tack room shed. The Tribal Police have arrived. Dayone sadly hands the reins back to Simon.

A few moments later, the police have Dayone in custody. As the car drives away, Dayone, in the back seat, his anciently sad eyes on Simon.

38

More than One Holocaust

Somewhere else far away, in a nightclub that is unknown to any-one who lives more than a mile away from it, our performance poet and hysterical historian Frank Zamora is about to scathe and scourge his audience once again joyously. It could be the south-side of Chi-cago, or maybe just off East 14th in Oakland, or what's the name of that barrio on the port side of Houston? It doesn't matter. Frank goes where his hip hate resistance iridesces: on the carbuncles of our body politic. He is ghostly now in the flat light of the spot. With a look and a gesture, his audience settles into their seats.

Chumba is powerful yet invisible at the controls, like a Noh thea-ter puppet master. Behind Frank, the screens fade up slowly. Frank steps to the side. He points to the screen: a stop-action still of the White House, the President and his entourage exiting towards a wait-ing limousine. Frank pulls a cellular phone like a samurai short sword from a holster behind his head and dials.

The next photo, the President of the United States is seated at his desk in the Oval Office. His assistant is speaking on his cellphone.

Frank speaks either for himself on his cell or as the President's As-sistant, changing character simply by shifting his body from left to right.

Frank slowly eases the cell against his ear and becomes the Assis-tant. "Hello."

Then mellow, as himself, "May I speak to the President?"

The image up behind him, of the Assistant handing the phone to the President. Successive stills reflect the "imaginary conversation."

As President, "Yes, what is it?"

Then as himself, at first calm and lethal, but gradually gathering mania, "I almost voted for you, sir. But then, I remembered...and I didn't vote at all."

As President, "Voting is a franchise, a responsibility."

As himself, with more energy, "Yes, sir, I agree. But you owe me too much already. So, I was thinking I'd just settle for royalties on everything you took from me. Just a couple of percent on each Pontiac station wagon, a surcharge for each Cleveland Indians home run, a toll bridge over the Potomac, the entire town of Seattle!"

"I don't know what you mean, sir."

As himself, "Auschwitz, Meidanek, Babi-Yar—".

With each name mentioned, the stills of the President grow larger, grainier, until the President's scandalized open mouth fills the screen.

"—Treblinka, Wounded Knee, the Trail of Tears, seven-hundred and fifty-thousand Palestinians, a million Armenians—you put a bounty on the heads of California Natives. Lots of holocausts, Chief. More than six million Natives have been final-solutioned."

"Stop! Stop! What do you want me to do?"

"Nothing. Except admit it. On the six o'clock news. Say you're sorry. Build a Native American Holocaust Memorial. No, fuck the Memorial. How 'bout just a good education and a guarantee of a job."

"Okay, okay...."

"But if you do the Memorial, build it on the lawn of the White House."

Frank puts away his cellular. The screen goes black. He paces slowly giving his audience time to reflect.

"Justice?" asks Frank. He turns to leave, then turns back again. "Well, at least no more denial. The journey of a thousand tears begins to end with the end of denial."

Act III

We're All Connected

Sell a country! Why not sell the air,
as well as the earth? Did not the
Great Spirit make them all for the use
of his children?

~Tecumseh, Shawnee

～

39

COLUMBUS PLAN B

There are all kinds of heroes, martyrs, saviors, messiahs, saints. They're necessary for two reasons: they show us someone who is unafraid of death; and they give us the ultimate protagonists for our stories. We're herd animals and need our stories to quiet us at night.

⁂

Just before Frank's performance begins, Chumba does something to heighten the experience. As the audience enters, mills, chats, drinks—as the waiters do their thing and chairs shift and the traffic outside comes and goes—as all these noises mix, merge, and become the unnoticed ambient background—Chumba records it all. Then he mixes them all back into the mix and slowly, imperceptibly, increases the volume. The ambience is thus amplified on itself, so that when he cuts the mix, the silence is louder—

—which he displaces with the reverberated sounds of something dripping in a cavernous urban sewer system. These are the sounds that emanate from the empty stage of Frank's performance.

It's dark, only faint fugitive indeterminate light. All the audience can see is a tall, wet-looking, concrete wall with metal ladder rungs disappearing somewhere above. A cold, thin crescent of light shines on the floor. Now the sound of a heavy manhole cover scraping open, widening the crescent on the floor to a circle. The police sirens growl louder, as do the grunts of men and their labored footsteps. Coming down those rungs is Frank dressed in ragged jeans, layered old shirts, frayed, sleeveless Levi jacket with a thunderbird design, and a bandana. At the bottom, he is startled to find that he's not alone. He peers nervously, aggressively, at the rapt audience.

"Who the hell are you?"

Then no matter what the audience says—and they are often quite uncontainable—Frank says, "Yeah, well, I discovered this place!"

He listens to them, then, "Look, I dogged my way through the Grease Pit and the Barricades to get here. Landed yesterday. Figured because I found this place, you know, I'd have it all to myself. Kinda like Columbus."

The audience chitters and he struts and his breathing becomes easier.

"Hey, is this all Columbus' fault? I mean, he got the okay from the King and Queen, right? Hell, he was just doing his Christian duty, bringing us religion, saving our pagan, heathen, ethnic souls. Thank God for that! We probably couldn't've lasted another thousand years. He was just bein' European, bringing back gold for the big guys and to strengthen our immune system givin' us measles and smallpox. Hey, but what about this!? What if there'd been a Columbus Plan B, and he'd gone back and said: 'There's people there already and they got something goin'. They have more because they need less. Harmony not dominion is their religion. They respect women. They have almost no cavities'? I mean, can you imagine!? Might be an America today so different we don't know how to even dream about it."

He dances around a bit as he heads back towards the ladder. But his eyes catch something in the audience, on a table—a glass.

"Yo, is that clean water? Can I have a taste? Just a taste?"

40

MY GRANDFATHER THE WARDEN

Will's BMW is among many vehicles parked in front of the Tribal Courthouse across from the Governor's office. Outside, Simon is pacing slowly, hesitantly, between two open windows. He can hear Will's voice within.

"Your Honor, is there any way—I mean, I'm still new here and I don't know, but is there any way that I *wouldn't* have to press charges?—"

Simon hears the rustle and the murmurs this causes. It disquiets him.

"—I mean, Your Honor, so that you all could find perhaps another solution that, well, that would be less disruptive to everyone."

Simon steels himself and enters the building.

Dayone and Victor sit before Tribal Judge Augustino Reyna, a soft-spoken Council Member. Dayone stares numbly. Victor's face is frozen and sere, in spite of the tears he wipes away.

Will, forehead bandaged, sits nearby, looking at Louisa who breaks into quiet sobbing. In other seats, Wynema, Teo, Clarence, and two Tribal Police officers.

Judge Reyna ponders. He scratches an ear. "It's a caring thought, Doctor, but many have tried, and they failed to make him one with his tribe."

Simon enters quietly and moves to the furthest corner. But the judge and others notice. Though they try to cover their reactions, they are surprised to see Simon here.

Victor stands. "I do not want to lose my boy, but I see I have already lost him. He has become a danger even to himself. Maybe by going to Group Home he can come back when he is ready...and help his tribe."

Judge Reyna tests the suggestion with his own version of it. "It may be time for the boy to go to Omaha to work things out. They can control him there and teach him how to...well, yes, behave."

Will surprises everyone by standing again. "But aren't there counseling services—I mean, maybe through the hospital or Youth Services in Santa Fe?" Will nods his respect to the Judge and sits slowly.

Breathing deeply, Simon stands and takes one step forward and speaks humbly. "What would our grandfathers have done? What would *their* grandfathers have done?"

Expectancy floods all the faces. Victor stands, trying to negate Simon's meddling. He wants Reyna to recognize him and to ask Simon with a subtle gesture to sit back down. *Why all of a sudden are you butting in? Everyone knows your place. And we know your pain, but so what? They chose you, and you chose them. You can't see what's really happening in the world, or here in your own village. You got something up your sleeve. Don't fuck with me. Your time is past.*

Simon raises his hand, palm facing himself. "We should not send away one who needs us most. We haven't remained a tribe because we sent away our problems. My mother's grandfather, Delbert Gurule, when he was a boy, he was wild like that with no home in his heart. So the elders gave him a choice: either his family would lose all irrigation rights, or he would stay one year, always at the side of the clan chief, who was Delfino Naranjo. Delbert grew up to be much respected."

Judge Reyna raises a finger and muses, "Under house arrest...hmmm."

Simon continues. "A boy needs his people to tell him that now he is a man. They took me away from my family, *my* tribe—and the ways of my clan. They gave me an education—from which I have never recovered."

With that, Reyna, Clarence, and the police officers cannot contain their quiet laughter.

But Simon continues: "When the parents are lost, the temptation to send away our lost children is...powerful. But we can't do this anymore. That is my thinking."

On most faces, an ancient knowing and a sympathy for Simon's words. Victor's breathing is short and shallow. He starts to shake his head, but stops as Louisa turns to him and holds him with a look.

Reaching deep, knowing this is an important decision, Judge Reyna looks back and forth from Victor to Dayone.

"There would be details to work out. Governor?"

Victor stands slowly, reluctantly, but Simon speaks first."

"Let the boy be placed on my summer land. Let him show you that he can police himself. Let him stay six months at my side and have work to do. Let him make and keep his promise to you, or else you will keep your promise to him—and send him away. But let it be his choice.

When Will stands to speak again, Clarence and the officer next to him express visible disapproval at the presumptuousness and lack of manners of the outsider.

"I haven't reported anything to the Bureau. Give the boy a chance."

Wynema motions for Will to say no more.

Judge Reyna looks to Victor, but Victor's face reveals nothing. "Dayone, do you understand what is being proposed?

Dayone, pressured but trying to be cool, looks around at everyone. "It's either Group Home jail in Omaha or I'm a prisoner on my grandfather's place and he's the warden."

"That's right. If you stay, you must be on your grandfather's place, or with him at his side, at all times. Even he cannot permit you to go anywhere else. This is for six months. Then we will talk again. If you break the rules, even once, you will be sent away, without further discussion. None. If your grandfather indicates you are belligerent or uncooperative, you will be sent away immediately. What do you say? What do you choose?

Dayone slowly points at Simon. "I choose him.

41

HIS MOUTH AGAINST THE HORSE'S CHEEK

A few days later, at Simon's summer house, the place is neater, even sparer than before. There is an extra cot, made of a piece of foam on a piece of plywood on top of four plastic milk crates. Simon is kneeling in the center of the room. Before him, on a piece of cloth, the rattle and his fetish. He lights a sprig of sage, stands and wafts the smoke along the length of Dayone's bed. He sinks down on the bed, closes his eyes for a moment, and prays, chanting softly.

After hearing what he believes is Mirriamma whispering somehow inside his head—*Your deepest fears are the demons that guard your deepest treasure*—his eyes snap open suddenly.

In front of his house, Louisa drives up with Dayone.

She does most of the work unloading Dayone's stuff: a suitcase, two cardboard boxes, and a backpack. Dayone is sullen and ill-tempered.

Simon exits the house as Louisa gets back into her car. She looks out her open window and says nothing as Simon slowly draws near. She, on the verge of tears, looks up into his face. Simon touches her cheek as she pulls away.

Inside, Dayone is unpacking his very teenage stuff, measuring a rock poster against a wall.

Simon watches for a moment, then speaks gently. "You won't be unpacking those things just yet. This is a place now for new ways."

At the Clinic, in Will's office, Victor and Manley are seated. Will paces behind his desk. Tension in the air. Louisa knocks, sticks her head in, and everyone turns.

"Uh, Doctor, on Lupi Churino: Ampicillin, 250, Q.I.D.?"

It takes a moment to register. "Huh? Oh, yeah, that's fine. Oh, Louisa, can you stay for just a moment?"

Louisa speaks to someone outside in the hallway. "Go ahead with that Ampicillin."

Then, stepping in and closing the door, "Doctor?"

"Please sit down." Then to Victor, "Louisa and I have been discussing the health survey, Governor. The analysis software we can get from Washington, but the clinic just doesn't have the manpower to generate the data. Do we, Louisa?"

Louisa is uncomfortable in her official role in front of Victor.

Will smiles. He understands. "We'd be months going through the medical records; even then it'd be incomplete. The only way would be a field survey."

Manley brightens. "If you do that, I've got a cadre of college grads working out of our Albuquerque office—and some in Denver. I could bring them into the picture."

Something troubles Will. "Interviewers should be familiar with the people they're interviewing. Asking a question the wrong way is worse than not asking it at all. In public health, we call it "GAGA": garbage asked, garbage answered. We need professionals. And they should be Native Americans."

Louisa ventures tentatively, "He's right."

Manley has manifold solutions. "Okay. I'll bring in the Mescaleros we trained to run the same sort of thing up there."

Will asks, "Wouldn't it be best to have Pueblos?"

Victor nods. There is a pause while everyone thinks.

Suddenly, Will: "Okay. Here's what we do. If you give me ten smart San Lucans, including two who can handle team leadership spots, I'll train them all in one eight-hour session. You do that, and then I'll take responsibility for the survey."

Victor is quick. "Good." He stands, shakes, exits. Manley hurries after him.

Will and Louisa are somewhat stunned by the abrupt conclusion. "Louisa, you should head one team. I mean, would you? You know how to deal with people."

"I think Wynema would make a good team leader. She has a lot of education."

Will's body language changes at the mention of her name.

～

At dawn on a day that is bright and crisp, Simon enters his summer house, zipping up his pants. He sees that Dayone is still asleep. He goes to the foot of the bed and grabs the plywood, lifting Dayone's legs higher and higher. Dayone, in his sleeping bag, starts slipping towards his head. When his body curls his head hard against the wall, Dayone grinds himself awake.

"Hunh!? Wha--?... are you crazy or something, old man?"

"I'm out of the crapper now."

Dayone tries to stand but his feet get tangled in the blanket. "Yeah, well, that's good to know."

At the corral, Simon finishes throwing hay to his horse. Dayone holds onto the head of the horse, pushing his mouth against the horse's cheek, not letting the animal go to his feed. Finally, he does let go.

Simon steps back. "You ever been responsible for anything?"

Dayone's look of hostility is replaced by a blank stare. Simon nods his head as if to say 'I thought so'. Then shakes his head as if to say 'That's pathetic'.

A few hours later, on the porch, Simon rubs his sore back as he sits on the bench. The boy paces back and forth on the dirt before him.

"Whaddya mean I can't take care of the horse?! I can polish your jewelry, huh, and I can fix the roof. I can shovel shit, pull weeds, and tend to the goddamn irrigation ditches—but I can't ride the horse?"

"No, I said you can't take care of him."

"What you mean is I can't ride him! I know more about horses than about dirt farming."

"When we take something out of the wild and make it depend on us for survival, it puts its trust in us. So—I have a responsibility to that horse. Not you. I do."

"But I wanna do it!"

"But I *have* to do it."

"Yeah, like when Frank was a kid and you sent him back for others to take care of. Like that's real responsibility, man."

This hits Simon hard. Dayone picks up a rock and just throws.

42

MEN WITH NO WOMEN

Morning at Will's house behind the Clinic. He exits carrying his white lab coat and eating the last of a dripping burrito. But when he sees Simon hefting a huge rock slab, he wolfs his food and rushes to him. "Are you out of your mind?!"

"No, I'm fixing a walkway."

Will immediately takes the heavy slab from Simon. He notices Dayone sitting stolid and distant on the ground against a propane tank. "No heavy labor, remember. No more work at the clinic for you. Or get Dayone to help you. Go home! No, go to the hospital. Have the operation."

Simon doesn't say anything. He just smiles politely and nods. Will is suddenly stopped in his tracks. He looks back and forth from Simon to just about anything else. Inside, something collapses. He closes the distance between by half. Then softly, "You won't, will you? Ah, Simon, why not?"

Will, still holding the heavy rock, asks Simon with a look what to do with it. Simon points to the prepared place. Will lays in the rock. When he stands up again, Simon and Dayone are gone. Exasperated, he runs to his car.

They're walking down the long road away from the Clinic. Will drives up, opens the passenger door.

Dayone jumps into the back seat and hunkers.

Simon gets in the front. "I thought you was going to work."

"I am," says Will annoyed. "I mean, I will. I'm working right this minute."

They drive in silence.

Simon looks out the front window and to the right, then points towards some foothills.

"When I was a young boy, we would race our ponies from that rock...to that rock."

They drive on a ways, each turning inward, each in his own reverie.

Will's turn. "When I was boy, my grandfather would pull me out of school and we'd play hooky together all day. Just the two of us."

Simon looks at him and smiles and grunts and bounces up and down just a bit. "I had one friend I could never beat, though, no matter what horse he rode. Santiago."

Will smiles and offers his counterpoint. "We'd go to baseball and hockey games, to the circus. Once we went to the Brooklyn docks just to watch some huge freighter unload zoo animals."

Simon grunts again and slaps Will's shoulder, then points from one rock to another.

Will now smiles and grunts, then pulls an old photograph from behind the sun-visor and hands it to Simon.

"My favorite was going to Coney Island and eating Nathan's hot dogs. That's my *zeyda*."

"Zeyda?"

"Means grandfather in Jewish."

"Good word. Zeyda."

"His name is Abraham. That's me, and that's the Coney Island Ferris Wheel. So cool."

Simon takes the photograph—is drawn into it. "Wow! The colors! You know, Dahyanee, my wife, she could ride, too. Long, colored ribbons tied to her shirt." He outlines swirling circles in the air with his hand.

They arrive. Will turns off the engine. Dayone gets out and stands sullen a few feet away. Simon hands back the photo.

"My grandfather tells me," says Will wistfully, "that my mother—you know, she was younger than I am now when she died—she used to dance a lot before she met my father. The next step for her would have been professional. Some days she couldn't move from one room to the next without dancing. It was in her. If it weren't for a few photographs, I wouldn't even remember my mother's face."

Simon settles back, sighs, closes his eyes.

After a while, Will asks softly and awkwardly, "How did your wife die?"

After an even longer while, Simon answers flatly, "Dahyanee has been dead a long time. I miss her. You miss your mother. Even though she died when you were very small, you still miss here." He pats Will affectionately once on the shoulder, then steps out of the car.

But Will doesn't miss a beat, "As your doctor, Simon, I can't accept your decision not to have the operation."

"No, but as my friend, you must." And he walks off. Dayone follows.

Will is unaware that he is digging his clenched fist into his cheek. His grandfather—how this old Indian man makes him think of Abraham. *Sure,* he thinks, *it's an obvious connection. But why do I feel cold and ashamed? What am I guilty of? Nothing. It's just ye-olde non-descript Jewish guilt again. Comes with the turf of me. Bullshit! I'm going to dissolve that one away in this lifetime, by God.*

When dawn comes the next day, atop the tallest pueblo building, a silhouetted man wrapped in a blanket turns from the west's darkness to face the sun rising over the eastern mountains. There is a wooden rail on that roof on the side next to the mountain in the east. There are marks carved in that wood. Ancient marks. Reminders. Place-keepers of the Mountain. And the places on the Mountain where the Sun and the Moon will be twice every year. Once going. Once coming. It's remarkable. The precision of it. Their calendar.

An hour later, at one of the central Pueblo crossroads, a number of San Lucans, late teens to early 60s, all wearing green armbands, are moving to or from the front doors of nearby houses. Will, Wynema and Louisa stand in the middle of the road. Louisa nods, turns, and heads toward a house. Will points to his clipboard.

Wynema looks, nods, politely exasperated.

"I just want to remind everyone about the 're-Q's', says Will a little awkwardly.

"If they can't get an answer," Wynema wearily replies, "Louisa or I come in later to *re-question*...yes, I think we've got it, Doctor." She looks to see that no one is watching, then quickly straightens the collar of his shirt and is instantly self-conscious. As she turns away, Will takes her arm. She smiles warmly, but communicates this is not the time or place. He releases her and begins speaking softly in gibberish to her—literally gobbledeegook with a Russian accent—expressing nothing but the pure emotion of longing.

Confused, but polite, she listens intently, seeking to understand his meaning. After 10 seconds, which is an extremely long time under these circumstances, she "gets" it and blushes. She puts up a hand. He stops. As she slips away, in her Pueblo tongue she says, "*Thank you,*" then in English, "for sharing your heart." And with that she snaps her fingers.

Instantly, Will closes his eyes. For five seconds. With a grin slowly overtaking his face. When he opens his eyes, of course, she is gone. He thinks, *Was she ever really here? Am I?* And he laughs out loud, until a data-survey-taker steps up and asks him a question about one of the questions on the questionnaire.

Not far away, at Teo and Tessie's house, Tessie stands at her door, watching an interviewer walk away. She can see Wynema out in the street. They wave to each other, then Tessie closes the door and turns to Teo who is about to sit down in a big soft chair to resume his reading.

"Why were you so uncooperative?" she asks him.

Teo is rubbing hard the underside of his nose. "Don't like the whole thing."

"Is there anything bad about health questions? The doctor is trying to help."

Teo shrugs. But Tessie pursues it. "Is it because it's really Victor's idea?"

Teo is slowly raising his lowered head, as if he were struck by an idea. "Maybe. No. Yes. I'll be right back. He steps out to the street."

Out on the street, one of the volunteer interviewers, Ramon, is talking to Wynema. "Wynema, does it count even if they're stepchildren from two marriages before?"

"Yes, absolutely, even if they're from ten marriages before, we count them."

She sees Teo in the distance talking to Will.

"Okay, Ramon, I'll re-Q Mr. Padilla. You get Mrs. Mirabal and the Correo family."

Ramon leaves. Will approaches her.

"How's it going?"

"Good."

Will looks back at Teo, who's carrying a new drum from the back of his truck into the house. "Mr. Vigil, Teo, is he a good man? I mean, was he a good governor? He was the previous governor, right?"

"He's very smart. Very pueblo. Not as good some say with the administrative stuff as Governor Moquino, but very dedicated, compassionate. Why do you ask?"

"He wants to see the survey results."

Wynema is impressed. "Good citizen, too. What did you say?"

An interviewer trots up, hands in some forms, takes some blanks from Wynema, then leaves.

"I said okay. He also asked me about Simon, but I told him I can't talk about my patients."

"That can't be a hard and fast rule. I mean, some things you can talk about and some you can't. Right?"

"It's much easier and safer not to talk about your patients at all. For their sakes."

"You two are a lot alike...you and Simon."

Will looks at her questioningly. Ramon calls from across the plaza.

Over her shoulder as she walks off, "Two men with no women in their lives."

She is shocked at herself for speaking these words.

43

THERE'S ALWAYS A WAR GOING ON

Dayone leans heavily on his hoe next to a series of small irrigation ditches. Sighting along a ditch, he plumb-bobs the hoe between thumb and index finger. "This is cool," he says to himself. "The way it works. Hmpf...." *In just that way, like gravity. Like the way it's everywhere the same. Treats everyone and every thing like they're the same. No big assholes and little frightened children. So the water is made to deal with the land, rising and falling, but so what? The water stays its way and always finds its own level, like that....*

Then a wave of anger hits him. He tries to think what he's angry at. But he can't put his finger on it. It's as if he wants to be bored and angry.

From the bean-field, Dayone can see his grandfather at the corral cleaning out his horse's hooves. Dayone's attention snaps around towards a clump of juniper stubs bordering the field. Jesse, Armand, and Danny surreptitiously beckon. Dayone shakes his head, indicating Simon, motioning them away. Not to be put off, the boys move on all-fours, almost on their bellies, along the dry ditch to get closer to Dayone. Dayone looks down at Jesse who mimes smoking a joint.

Then Jesse whispers, "C'mon over into the trees. We got something for you."

"I can't leave this place."

"Pretend you're going to take a piss."

"I can't do shit unless he's with me."

Jesse taunts him. "Hey, man, we were going to rock out in California, man. At least sneak out tonight when the old man goes to sleep."

Jesse "smokes a joint" again, but then, as he spots Simon approaching, he and the others flatten down in the empty canal behind the bean stalks. Dayone rolls his eyes, then heads towards Simon who, aching a little under the ribs, inspects the ditches and points.

"This is good...'cept for over there where the water'll back up."

Dayone is somewhat defensive. "It'll flow. What do you bet? A beer?"

Simon just shrugs, starts to leave, then, taking Dayone's hoe, he opens the main feeder canal. Water rushes in, which forces the three boys to stand up, revealing themselves...dripping wet.

Jesse tries to wipe off the mud caking on his sleeve. "This is bullshit, man." And to Simon as he leaves, "And it's cold, man, low and mean for a grandfather to be a jailer to his grandson."

Simon isn't fazed. A faint smile plays. He turns and points. "See, over there, how the water slows up. If the ditch is a lot wider, it looks a lot lower. Tricky, eh?"

Dayone is seriously interested. "Where?"

Simon's eyes lock onto Dayone, and go deep—their first simple two-way connection.

Jesse, 20 yards away, turns and spits. "Grandfathers suck!"

Simon wheels on him. "I know your great-grandfather."

Jesse ain't afraid. "Bullshit you do! He died a million years ago." The boy turns away.

"He's still alive in my heart. I was with him, holding him...when he died."

Intrigued, Jesse slowly returns—along with the others. Throughout the following, Dayone looks from Jesse to Simon.

"He was your mother's grandfather, and his name was Santiago. He was the best horseman I ever seen in my life."

Jesse isn't going to be taken in by this old fart. "Neah-h-h-h."

"Oh yes he was. We were in the war together—far away on the other side of the world, on an island called Iwo Jima. If you can listen, I can tell you who he was."

"It's better than working," intones Dayone.

Jesse doffs his wet shirt, squats, crosses his arms. All five hunker down. A dust-devil plows into them and dissipates.

"Santiago was a straight sergeant. Took over our platoon when our master sergeant got shot. I didn't know nobody in the Corps until he showed up—"

"What do you mean, "corps?"

Dayone quickly, "The Marines, man."

Simon takes a deep breath. So do the boys. "Like a miracle, for me. He saved my life...in more ways than one.'

Armand innocently enough, "Is the war still on?"

Danny has to have a say, "There's always a war on, stupid."

Simon looks off into the distance, and then turns to Jesse. "Do you miss Ruben as much as Dayone does?"

Jesse looks down, bobs a tight, silent "yes", then looks at Dayone for acknowledgement.

Simon grunts. "Well, that's how much I miss Santiago. Even years don't make it less."

After a moment of silence, "We'd been fighting the Japanese for two days. Half our platoon was gone. Santiago and I promised each other that if only one of us made it back, he'd—." His voice sticks. He looks away briefly, just as the boys quickly, quietly look at each other. "—he'd bury some corn, and sing a song—"

Now Simon turns to the boys and, making no attempt now to hide the emotion, softly but firmly looks at each of them in the eyes. "—you know, for the other, at the bottom of the Puye Cliffs. That way the spirit of the one who died would find a way home again."

Jesse has to ask. "Did you do it?"

Dayone quickly answers for his grandfather. "Of course he did!"

With a little difficulty, Simon stands and looks off again. The three boys follow his gaze. Dayone, however, looks carefully from Simon to Jesse and back again...impressed.

Armand simply asks, "How did he die? Did he get shot or blowed up or what? What're you guys looking at me for!?"

"On the third day, we knew we were going to die on that island. You don't say that, of course, but in our hearts, we knew. We might have made it if it hadn't been for the Sun. You see, that morning it had rained and the sky was dark, and the Japanese had....

At the main Indian Health Service office in Santa Fe, Cutter pores over a thin, newly-bound report in a green cover. On the desk is a thick computer printout. Will waits, admiring Cutter's shelved collection of Indian pottery and kachina dolls.

Finally, Cutter, "Looks good. Do you have cross-tabs by parentage for the subjects who aren't full Pueblos?" Off Will's nod, "Good. This goes in my quarterly report on you to Washington. This'll look good."

"Thanks."

Then Cutter in a softer voice, "Some advice. Some things look good in your 'cume' file—and some things don't. This looks good. Getting involved with a native girl—that's a lot trickier." Off Will's look of question, "What's going down gets aroun', m'man."

44

IT'S CALLED LEADERSHIP

Inside Victor's office, the sun streaks in hard with a garish glare. Victor and Manley stand next to a table, looking down at the print-out, a couple of optical disks, and the green-bound survey report that Will now opens and points to. He is troubled.

"I can go over it in more detail later, but this is the summary overview. These graphs show that the tribe's health is currently ac-ceptable—according to national health standards—but look at this. Diabetes, TB, and heart disease are worse now than they were 15 years ago. There are trends that could indicate the immune systems are under attack—."

Manley arches his eyebrows matter-of-factly. "Polio's down."

Will screws his mouth around. "Nobody gets polio anymore if they're vaccinated."

"Aha!" grins Manley, "If they're vaccinated! Take credit where due, doctor. This is good work. The tribe's medical Dow Jones may be off a bit right now, but then—everything's cyclical."

Manley worked for the Feds as the last Nuclear Waste Negotiator, disappeared for a year and then was hired as the Executive Director of a consortium representing 16 corporations. Private companies, Man-ley believes, are far better equipped to develop new opportunities.

Victor breaks the reveries as he turns to Will, "You have to get back to the clinic?" Then, off Will's troubled nod, "If we're no worse off than anyone else, this ought to help us get the grant. I appreciate your work and your opinion, Doctor. I'll let you know if we need anything else. May I?" he asks, reaching for the report.

"Of course," says Will as he leaves respectfully and closes the door.

Victor almost whispers, "This downtrend in our health. I'm concerned about it, Manley."

But Manley misunderstands. "It won't be a problem. My proposal prep team can massage the data and omit the irrelevant items. The Feds will see this report as positive. They'll see the Indians are getting sicker at a slower rate than whites, even blacks. Which is good if you look at it from the right angle."

Victor thinks about it a long time. Then nods.

Will is driving fast down a dusty, bumpy village road. He hits a deep pot hole, bounces high, hits his head hard, stops, rubs his head, gets out. He looks at his little car and the road he travels. He shakes his head and rubs the soreness...again.

Will is standing next to a Toyota Tundra salesman in between two trucks on the line. Will is obviously talking about the various options. It's boring so we won't go into the details here.

Now, down one San Lucas dirt road after another, villagers look up at the passing pickup, sparkling in its newness, daring the dust to cling. Their expressions show they are variously surprised, impressed, pleased. It's Will, wearing a new but unassuming Western straw hat, behind the wheel of his spanking new, dark green, all-wheel-drive, Tundra pickup. He's as happy as a street slider with new blades.

In Victor's office, Teo looms over Victor's desk. Angry.

Victor is more controlled. "What do you mean?"

Teo is incredulous. "What do you mean, 'What do I mean?'? I'm talking about the tribe's health! I read that survey."

Victor is smooth. "I would have shown you a copy. All council members. But it was the weekend and one of them was on vacation, so—"

Teo sweeps back again, glowering.

Victor, unperturbed, "We both have the same goals. The MRS money will be used to upgrade tribal health. You can see that."

Teo hisses the Pueblo equivalent of —"*Bullshit!*"

Victor rises like the Devil who's just taken his due. "You probably have to go—and I have some business to take care of."

"I saw the D.O.E. crew out there on the overlook, surveying, armed with your letter. You already signed it. You had no right!"

Victor checks, turns, smiles. "As a former governor, Teo, you know I have the right to sign executive orders—especially if we're going to keep up with—" and then, in Pueblo, "—*the whites*".

"I piss on your Executive Right. You don't have the moral right— not the ancient right! The council, Victor—the Old Council, the True Council!

"I have the right, Teo."

Teo stares. Then, as he exits, he hears Victor's last words: "It's called leadership."

Will awakens abruptly in his bed and looks out the window at the glorious dawn. "This is going to be a great day!"

Half an hour later he's pulling up at Mirriamma's place. Where to park? There's a large, dusty station wagon. Inside the vehicle, a woman sits patiently while three kids play tag outside around the vehicle. Phipp's "Wind River Trading Co." pickup sits next to it. As Will gets out of his new truck, he glides his hand lovingly over the hood.

Phipps strides from around back carrying a small clay pot. When he sees Will, he unloads, "Hey, Doc, look at this. One pot. That's all she'd sell me. One lousy pot. The old lady's poor as sheepherder's dog. It don't make sense."

He points all around him at everything. "Look at this place. She's got a coupla dozen sittin' out back. I'll tell you what, if you wanna make some extra money, seriously, I'll buy anything you can get her to sell to ya."

"Just how poor is a sheepherder's dog?" swipes Will as he passes.

Phipps notices Will's new ride. "Woody wheels, Doc."

Will heads for the front door, but then changes his mind.

45

She's Entering His World

Under the ramada-cum-workshop in Mirriamma's backyard, an older man is burnishing a satin polish into the black glaze of a new batch of Mirriamma's pottery.

"Is Wynema...Mondragon here?" Will asks tentatively.

The man says nothing. He just lowers his head humbly. Will, undaunted, continues around back. Chickens scoot. A girl, 14, feeds hay from under an army tarp to a tied-up goat. Three women, all around 70, are squatting down behind a large plank, wedging a new batch of clay; they are covered with clay stains, wet and dry. Undistinguishable, Mirriamma is one of them.

Wynema approaches, holding a infant. Will looks around, as if to create a space in which only the two of them exist.

"Cute little papoose," he says sheepishly, pointing the baby.

"'Papoose' is a derogatory word, Will. No Indian will use it."

"Right. Sorry. I didn't know that. I thought—wait! That Israeli cabdriver was wrong! Papoose is the name of Tonto's horse. Little Beaver is Red Ryder's sidekick!" He voice becomes softer. "Trivia. Nevermind. What I wanted to tell you was that—what I need to tell you is—" He's melting now, "what I'm dyin' to tell you that I'm thinking about you almost all the time, and I—"

Wynema immediately becomes embarrassed and lowers her head. Out of the corner of her eyes, she glances at Mirriamma.

"I...I don't know what to say," she says uneasily.

Will twitches and fidgets, "And I wanted to show you my new truck."

"Do you want me to look at it right now?"

"Not if you're busy. It's just that it's Saturday, and I thought we could—"

All he can do is pantomime driving.

"I guess so."

"I'd like to meet your Mirriamma one of these days."

As the infant she holds starts crying, "Now?"

Will looks around. "Well, no, as I'd rather go someplace with you right now."

Wynema stands taller, more in possession of herself. She starts to nod, yes, but sees a man and a woman coming. She quickly but carefully hands Will the infant. "Stay right here."

Will looks to the infant and smiles, then slowly looks around at everyone. He stops, looks around, then turns directly to Mirriamma, who sits eyes lowered, steadily working. A moment passes, then she looks up at Will. Their eyes connect, until Will lowers his eyes and smiles childlike. Gladys Bernal steps up next to him, offering to take the infant. He hears Wynema from around the corner.

"*Gia*, they've come!" comes Wynema's voice from around the corner. "Yes, over here—watch your step."

She appears, accompanying a man and a woman in their 40s. She passes the man on to Mirriamma, who rises and takes him by the elbow and walks him, back and forth in the yard.

Wynema leads the woman to the workbenches under the ramada.

Finally she steps back to Will. They watch Mirriamma and the man.

Mirriamma bends down and scoops up a dung beetle, shows it to the man, and laughs. The man speaks, but what he says is a jumble of strange sounds and a few English words, nothing intelligible.

Will is fascinated. "But that's not Pueblo."

"No. Just sounds. No sense. Flapping tongues. Just like you the other day."

He smiles, but he's curious about what Mirriamma is doing. "Why?"

"She's dancing with him."

"Dancing? Now what do you mean by dancing?"

"She's entering his world."

"By speaking gibberish with him?"

Wynema, highly focused, "He was wasting away. He's gained 25 pounds in the last two months. Every time they get together, she finds just the right way to connect with him."

"When you dance with someone, you mirror them, right?" Suddenly, he grabs her hand and tries to dance.

She quickly demurs. "C'mon. Not here. Show me your truck."

Back in front of the adobe, they move slowly around the vehicle. He opens a door for her inspection. She sees a blue velvet bag on the seat. She's drawn to it. Reaches out. Pauses. Then carefully picks it up. A smile creeps in.

"It's a *talis*," says Will, "a prayer shawl my father left for me. I got bar-mitzvahed in it. I'd forgotten it. It was in the glove-compartment of my old BMW."

She quickly hands it back to him, someone else's medicine bag, sorry she's touched it.

He pushes it back into her hands. "No, it's okay. Really. Tell me why didn't you go with the Fellowship at Cambridge? Those offers don't come by often."

She's intrigued with the bag. She hefts it, timidly smells it, then puts it back gently on the seat.

"Just before I was supposed to return to New York, you know, to finish packing for Europe, for Cambridge—about two months before you arrived—well, Mirriamma took me way up to the mountains, to a hot springs that even you would think is sacred—oops, no offense, you know what I mean."

She leans back against the truck and lets the sun flood her face fully. "She put me in the water, all the way up to my neck, and then went away. I lay back—I closed my eyes—and that's when I smelled him. I slowly opened my eyes and there was this huge male coyote slowly moving towards me. I didn't jump, I didn't move. I didn't breathe. He came right up to me and smelled me and then licked my eye."

She pauses and turns into Will, only a breath away. "But now here's the thing—just a couple hours *before* we went up to those springs, on the way up there, Mirriamma asked me if I had ever felt the Earth's heartbeat. I told her no but that I'd like to—." Wynema pauses and looks directly at him: "Well, when that coyote licked my eye, I felt it—the heartbeat. And I still feel it." She reaches out her hand towards Will as if to say 'If you touch my hand now, you, too, can feel it'."

He doesn't hesitate. He slowly takes her hand. They look into each other's eyes.

"I'm not sure," he says innocently, "if I feel anything, you know, like that."

Wynema gives an elfin laugh and shakes her head. "Well, okay, I'm beginning to think it was a dream or an hallucination. I've never doubted myself like that before, Will. But, I mean, the next day, after a coyote licks my eye, I call the Fellowship, and I—well, they say okay to my putting it on hold for a year. What I did was strange, but their allowing me to do so was strange, too."

"It is strange. I admit," says he, "but it's probably just a coincidence. I mean, it's great, but—what else could it be?"

She turns away as if to ponder something.

He wonders whether he said something that offended.

"You're Jewish, right? And I'm Indian. We come to things differently. We—."

"Somehow I sense you just answered my question, but I really don't get it. I'd like to say I got it. I'd like you to *think* I got it—."

She wheels and strides up the hill, beckoning him to follow.

He moves after her. "What about Cambridge?"

"It's been there a long, long time. It isn't going anywhere."

"Wow, that's sort of the kind of answer I gave my grandfather when he asked me why I didn't take the job at U.C. Med in San Francisco, I mean, instead of coming here. He thought I was nuts. What's with us? Why do we do these things?"

There are more trees here. She pockets herself in the middle of three closely growing piñon pines. "I don't know if I've ever done anything like this before. What do you think?"

Will scratches his ear. "You mean why you didn't go to Cambridge, or why I didn't go to California?"

She points at herself.

"Okay," he ventures, "maybe you don't have much respect for the way whites study Native peoples, and you—so maybe you don't want to be an academic in a white-man's university. Maybe you just want to do your thing."

Wynema has to think about that one. "Maybe. And maybe *you* didn't suffer like your grandfather, and therefore don't deserve any special privilege."

Will is shaken. "Wow. That's a shift. Okay, so we're back on me. So, if that's why I didn't do U.C. Med, why'd I come here?"

"You came to fight the survival fight that your grandfather fought against the Nazis—but for another tribe. The Jews are a tribal people, too."

He is overwhelmed; he can't answer. He moves to embrace her, but she slips away. He follows.

By some isolated goat pens, on a rise, they sit on a broken fence rail. Behind them to the west, the Rio Grande Gorge and the endless high desert of desire.

Will isn't aware that his hand is hovering above hers about three inches away. "I am going to fall in love with you."

"Tomorrow or the day after?"

"Yesterday."

"You're heading backwards."

"To the garden of eden."

"Hah! Is that how you see our village here?"

"No, I—I was thinking about what it would be like to—to see the world through your eyes."

"My eyes?"

For a moment, Will cannot speak. A shiver runs through his body. "Your eyes have been licked by a wild creature. Therefore, they are young and ancient at the same time. They got me."

Wynema just stares ahead reflectively for the longest time.

He, too...until his cellphone, with a text message. "Somebody needs stitches. Looks like I gotta be git to gitten. I'll call you tonight."

He heads back to his "woody wheels".

"Okay," she says out loud, but she's thinking *From a New York accent to an Okie accent. That's weird.*

A few hours later, Simon is sitting on a bench in the shade of his ramada. He's polishing a piece of jewelry and watching old re-runs of

Star Trek Next Generation on a portable DVD player that Louisa got him for his birthday. He hears a vehicle approaching.

Will jumps out of his new truck with an elated face. Dayone is fixing a broken rake with bailing wire and duct-tape.

Will is ecstatic. "Do you only dance when you're healing, or can you dance when you're in love?" Somehow Will becomes self-conscious that Dayone might overhear. He tries to draw Simon away. But Simon doesn't move.

Simon thinks for a moment, and then flatly, "They're both the same thing."

Will hears, steps back, understands, yips, and starts dancing around.

"I feel like dancing now!"

He spins and spins—then suddenly stops, and lowers his voice again.

"My boss, in Santa Fe, says that becoming involved with a Indian is a no-no. I have a feeling that Wynema's people wouldn't think too much of it either."

Simon seems to be pondering it. "Well, it's only natural. If there were no forces to keep peoples separate, there wouldn't be no different peoples." As he starts for the house, "But I figure if two people dance the same dances together, they should stay together." Then turns back, "Find the rhythm. Reach for it—it's right down there." He points to the Earth.

Dayone, closer now, stands transfixed, mouth open. Simon raises his hands, palms facing out, and disappears into his house.

46

Go by Way of Two Hawk Mesa

On another day, in the high desert rolling hills, a horned toad scoots, stops, cranes up. Cresting the rise just beyond are Mirriamma and Wynema, on foot, gathering herbs. Wynema's thoughts are elsewhere. She stumbles. Mirriamma assesses the moment, then motions that she wants to look into Wynema's basket.

"Your head and your heart are looking for your feet in different rooms."

Wynema smiles at herself. "More like two different worlds."

"He's a good man, the doctor, and he's smart—in a way. But he won't stay here. Two, maybe four years. Understands some things about us, though. You go with him—probably travel a lot. Bein' part Sioux, you probably like that. Sioux are great travelers, you know. You're gonna know who you are very soon."

"Can't you just tell me what the right thing to do is? I'll pretend it was all my idea."

"No, but there may come a time when I must tell you what you cannot do. Ha, ha, ha! Then again, *sometimes you just have to explore the canyon.*"

Explore the canyon—she's heard that before somewhere.

When she looks up, Mirriamma is off gathering herbs again. *Who's she talking to?*

"*You little devil, I found you. You been hiding. Off visiting the Shoshone? Some of you coming home with me. The rest of you, go grow and be happy.*"

Wynema questions silently, *How is she able to talk to everyone—and everything? More than talks. She interacts—she intermixes her life and theirs. How she do that—?*

293

﹏

Days later, in front of Will's house, Wynema sits in one of Mir-riamma's three old vehicles—the one that started this morning—engine running. She turns it off. Sits. Puts her face, as if covering some embarrassment, into her hands.

Will, in jogging clothes, runs by, stops, surprising her. "Hi!" He's so happy to see her.

Wynema takes a big breath, then blurts, soft and nervous, "Next Saturday, a week, we're going, at dawn—you'll need some camping stuff. I'll come for you. Six a.m. You want to go?"

"We? You and I? Like somewhere together? Well, yeah, I mean, sounds great, but—no 'buts'—Yeah!"

"And shoes you can set a horse in and wade a creek or boulder-hop in."

Wynema starts the old car and drives away, leaving Will stunned and circumspect, standing just outside his front door, feeling his happiness well up and over-flow. With an explosive yell, he jumps, spins, and dances his way back into his house.

﹏

The next day at sunrise, Simon is peering into his horse's ear. He casts a glance from his little house to the sun, gauging the time. He is pensive. He steps under the shed-roof and heaves a broken bale of hay into the back of his truck. As he looks to the house, that pain in his back again.

Now, he's on the other side of the house, at his chicken coop, putting the last gathered egg into an old egg carton.

A few moments later, he enters the house and finds Dayone, still in bed, his head buried in his pillow.

"I'm going away for a couple of days. You can come with me—or stay here—on your honor, stay here."

Dayone is groggy and, of course, grumpy. "I'll stay."

"Can't leave this place."

"I know, goddamnit. I'll take care of your horse."

"Nope. Taking him to Teo's."

Dayone uncovers his head, gives Simon a dirty look for the insult. "Where're y'going?"

"To the mountains...."

Dayone sits up abruptly. "For how long?"

As Simon exits, "For as long as it takes."

"Why are you going?"

"I don't know exactly. I'll go. I'll find out. I'll let you know."

"That's it?"

"I'm supposed to have an operation. But I don't want to. So I'm going up to find out why I don't."

Dayone jams out of bed, grabbing for his clothes.

"Sounds like bullshit to me, but, hey, if you think you can do it, I'd like to see you try. Worth a laugh."

Driving very slowly down some dusty Pueblo roads, Dayone sits on the tailgate, holding the rope leading the horse. The pickup is loaded with a bale of hay, two bedrolls and a duffle-bag. Simon stops outside an adobe house where a woman is sweeping. Simon gets out carrying his carton of eggs.

He returns waving two cookies at Dayone. Behind, the woman waves and thanks them in Pueblo.

As Simon approaches his horse, "Can you beat me to Teo's from here?

Disgusted with the idea, "I ain't running nowhere. I didn't get a whole lot of sleep last night."

Simon snorts. "Ridin' the horse?"

Dayone springs up. "You sayin' I—?" In one fluid motion, he unties the horse, twists the rope into a hackamore, leaps on bareback, and gallops away. Simon smiles slyly, gets in, drives off.

Dayone, hair flying, gallops the horse down a shortcut.

As he approaches the plaza, there's Jesse and Danny, sitting on a thick and glowing adobe wall, well-armed with brightly colored water-cannons, squirting screaming little kids down below. They hear Dayone yelling to them, but when they look up, they see him disappear behind a building. They quickly scramble to the other side of the building where they can "shoot" Dayone off his horse.

But when the horse emerges, there is no Dayone. Yes, there is! He's swung off on the far-side flank, clinging to the horse's mane: unshootable. Then, he bounces his feet off the ground once and swings back aboard—triumphant! Jesse and Danny are impressed.

"Shit! I didn't know he could do that," harumpfs Danny.

Jesse shouts after him. "Where're ya goin'?!"

Dayone just howls with joy!

Simon arrives at Teo's, gets out, looks around, then back down the road. No Dayone. His face falls. Did he misjudge the boy? Did he trust too soon? He turns, hefts a half-full gunny sack of oats, and heads dejectedly around the side of the house.

In the backyard, Simon comes around a corner and stops. There is Dayone, quietly rubbing down the horse. Teo watches.

Grinning, Simon heads for an unused corral. As he passes by Dayone, "He's a pretty good horse, ain't he? In his time, he was a helluva fine damn good horse."

Is he talking about the horse, himself, or Dayone? He looks at his grandson and a gentle, easy smile slowly emerges. Dayone can't look away—until he must look away, and then he steels up again. But not so much as before.

Simon sets the sack down and turns to Teo. "Going up to the mountains for a few days."

Teo brightens. "If you're going up to the Puye cliffs, go by way of Two Hawk Mesa."

"I was thinking along those lines. Here's some oats for the horse. And a bale of hay out there."

As Simon leaves, Teo gestures the need for further talk.

"I lost my temper with Victor," sighs Teo. "Told him I knew he'd signed that order without the council's approval. I didn't think it out. I just attacked. Dumb."

Simon grins with just one side of his face. "Flushed you from the tall grass, eh?"

But Simon absolves the mistake with a touch to Teo's shoulder and a fatalistic shrug. He makes to leave again. "These things take time, and my vision isn't clear. This is why I am going up...with the boy."

Teo understands. "Umm, yeah, good, good to open yourself again."

"Like a hollow bone...if I can."

Dayone, curious about the conversation, moves to a workbench and begins to play upon a large ceremonial drum.

Teo brightens, "And you will dance again!"

Simon goes dark. "Be patient, dammit! I'm just one old man."

Simon is retreating again within himself. Dayone is getting into his drumbeat.

Suddenly, Teo turns on Dayone, flaring. "Stop! Until you understand what that drum is, and what it means to make one, you may not touch our clan's ceremonial drum. It is our way."

Dayone is instantly hostile. But a beat later, his expression changes: he becomes thoughtful. He looks self-consciously from Simon to Teo. Then, with a nod of his head, shows acceptance, perhaps respect, and backs away—to the horse. Simon and Teo look to each other, sharing the significance of the moment.

47

I Don't Want to Play These Games

Simon's truck grinds uphill, mountains to one side, the mesa and the horizon to the other. Dayone sits shotgun, pointing out the window at sundry things with his drumsticks. He names each thing in Pueblo, as far as he knows them. If he doesn't, he names it in English, whereupon Simon says the word in Pueblo. Then Dayone whispers the Pueblo word to himself. This goes on, without any acknowledgement from either of them, until they reach the top of Two Hawk Mesa.

What a view! Literally takes your breath away. Even from Dayone, who is affected by his own emotion. He tries to hide it, but the view grabs him and make him blink his eyes. He feels it's stupid to feel this way. He even gets a little angry at himself for being so wimpy. "Fuck," he says to himself as he finally yanks himself away from the view.

Simon doesn't understand, but he likes the feel of what's happening.

Backed up now almost to the edge, sitting on the tailgate, looking out over the expanse, Simon and Dayone eat apples and fry-bread and chili out of plastic containers.

Simon points out over the mesa. "What do you see out there?"

"Desert...big...nothing much."

Simon points to the north. "See there where those mountains there hit the floor? That's where I used to start out my best hunting trips. Well, right down there is where the government wants us to store that radioactive crap."

Off Dayone's bored nod, Simon continues: "Yeah, wait a minute. I'm talking big concrete buildings, fences, guards with guns, and research facilities—they say they wanna build on unused land, way out of the way, they say. They say it's only for 40, 50 years maybe. You know, temporary. Then they'll move it to somebody else's backyard. And we should do it as part of giving back for, you know, for what they call "the shared infrastructure". Pretty good, uh? You know what 'infrastructure' is?"

"Roads."

"And you know what they want to store there."

"Nuke shit."

"The Feds want to give us money only just to consider the idea."

"I know. My dad's all crazy to do it. Well, nobody uses this place out here anymore, do they? If my dad's honest, the village will get a lot of money. If he's not, they'll get less. Who gives a shit? You and I won't get anything."

Simon thinks about his own question. "Out there I see the life of our tribe, all the way back to the beginning. Remember what I said about my responsibility, my agreement, with my horse?"

"Yeah."

"Well, when the first people built something here, they had an agreement with the land. They would protect it, honor it, and the land would take care of them—"

"Yeah, well, my dad says we oughta take the money, man, because if we don't, the government will get the land anyway and at least this way the tribe gets something back. Same same, only better, he says."

Simon thinks hard about what Dayone just said. He starts nodding earnestly. "But, can we care for the land *and* give it away—at the same time? And can we care for it, if we forget that it is sacred?"

"It's just a bunch of desert."

"I swear to you, it is much more than that. There was a great chief once, of a tribe called Duwamish—"

"Duwamish? Never heard of them."

"Hmpf. His name was *Sealth*. The whites call him Seattle."

"Like Supersonic, man."

"He spoke well. He said, 'the earth does not belong to us. We belong to the earth.' He was right like that there, don't you think?"

"You could look at it that way. I mean, how can people who die and get *buried* in the earth *own* the earth? Dude. Get real. Gotta be the *other* way round.

As Simon gets into the truck, "Hmpf. You're not so dumb. Let's go, grandson."

A few moments later, however, they're still just sitting in the truck. Simon behind the wheel thinking. Dayone getting impatient. Simon turns, looks back out across the desert."

"So what do we mean when we say something is sacred?"

Dayone snaps a look back at the desert, then to Simon. As self-consciousness sets in, he sneers, starts bouncing. "Where the hell we goin', anyway?"

Simon harumpfs one more time through a faint smile and drives off.

An hour later, at the foot of an almost disappeared, overgrown road or path that heads up a tall and narrow twisting canyon, Simon pulls over, stops the pickup, and gets out.

Reaching over the tailgate, Simon takes a frayed, rolled-up WWII army mummy bag and throws it to Dayone. For himself: a couple of tattered army blankets. He walks ahead.

Dayone catches up. "How come we didn't keep driving? The road goes on."

"I like to walk to where we're going. On my own two feet. Shouldn't take no cars in there, anyway."

"Where?"

But Simon only points ahead with his lips and chin. Dayone slowly look around.

The Puye Cliffs are a magical place, ancient, hallowed, preternaturally beautiful.

Dayone is taken by the sight. "Where the fuck are we?!"

"Heh."

"What is this place? I ever been here? As a kid or something?"

"Maybe. I dunno."

Simon and Dayone walk deeper into the canyon, looking up at the cliffs as they become steeper, higher—.

"'Member I was asking you about sacred?

"Yeah-h-hhhh." Dayone's voice says it all. The Cliffs rise up around them, engulfing them. Whoa, this place is cool."

"That's one thing I like about you," says Simon matter-of-factly. "When you finally get something, you really get it."

Simon wanders this way and that. Dayone does so, too. They're drawn to all the various angles from which to see this place. They have to explore it. They have to actively see this place in order to see the relationships between things. The way horsetails grow stark up out of boggy soil next to a creek. They have to go over there and look, and then look back. They have to look at places from different vantage points. They have to put their hand into the shaft of light that breaks from the canyon rim and just touches the moss growing under a little waterfall. This place makes them do this.

You walk and look. You take it in. Then you move ahead a bit and sit down. This place *wants* you to see it. They give themselves to it.

Sometime later—it is dusk and Simon sits quietly by himself.

Dayone returns from exploration. "I'm hungry. Whatcha got?"

Simon hands him a canteen.

"Whatcha bring to eat?"

The two slowly face each other, saying nothing. Dayone starts bobbing and snorting as it dawns on him what's happening.

"Gonna starve my ass, aren't ya!?"

"You and I are at the edge, Grandson, carrying a lot of weight, and we're gonna fall off unless we—"

Dayone, with grim irony, "Clean up our act?"

"You got that right. See what I mean?"

Dayone grabs the canteen and bedroll and starts walking away. "I'm outta here. You tricked me. I can walk back."

Simon stares at the dirt, gloom entering his face, listening to Dayone walk away, turning once to watch him go.

On a ledge forty feet up the less steep side of the cliffs, Simon piles pine needles onto a blanket, then dumps them into a sheltered area beneath a looming rock. He spreads the blanket over them. A coyote's howl tests the changing light. A twig snaps. His eyes dart.

Half an hour later, it's dark. Simon still sits there, alone, wrapped in a blanket. A skunk waddles by. He looks from the skunk to a ledge even higher up, back and forth. After a long while, Simon speaks, "My grandfather brought me here, a few months before he died."

There is silence. Then, from that ledge higher up, Dayone's voice breaks the silence. "I suppose you think I'll be out here with my own grandson, someday. I fuckin' doubt it."

Without changing expression, Simon turns to the voice, "Yeah, maybe, if you live that long. If we still have the land."

Holding his mummy-bag, Dayone slides off the side of the ledge and as if he's snowboarding, lets gravity glide him down the scree-gravel slope. He stops just above Simon. "Dj'you know I was there, all the time?"

Simon shakes his head. "You're good. Damn good."

Dayone approaches, offering Simon the canteen. Simon demurs.

"Keep it. Got me a secret spring up there."

"You know, old man, you're crazy, you know that? Dj'you bring me out here to have some kind of warrior vision Indian crap like that?"

"I dunno. Depends on if the Old Ones have anything they want to tell you."

They sleep soundly. Dawn finds them up an adjoining narrow defile. Weathered cliffs soar up on both sides of them. Simon washes at a small spring. Dayone hangs motionless from a tree's limb, feeling himself growing longer.

Simon remembers what they were just talking about. "I slept in a big room with 50 other boys from tribes all over the country. Lotsa different languages. None of us were happy—and I became angrier than almost anyone. Most of them were scared. Hell, I was scared. — But mostly angry."

Dayone considers it and, for the last time in his life, calls his grandfather 'dude'. "Heavy scene, dude."

Back at their bedrolls, Simon sits on a rock, trying hard to remember something. Dayone rolls up his bag.

Simon unconsciously massages his shins. "My father had a song of power he used to sing when he wanted to clear his mind. What's wrong with me? I just had it and now it's gone."

Dayone struts to where the sunlight has moved. He taunts, "Oh, maybe I know the song." And with that he breaks into an imitation of an elder intoning a song. Simon listens...until the kid bursts out laughing.

"Ha-ha-ha! I just made that up! Pure fuckin' bullshit. Noamsayin'?" Then dead-serious: "Now *that's* funny."

But Simon, lost within himself, holds up a shaking finger announcing he's just about got it. "No, you almost had it. I heard it in all what you did. You *fuckin'* almost got it!"

He is trying hard to remember and Dayone is laughing at him.

"*Yai, ya, ya-nai, he-na yaaaa....* I almost got it." Simon keeps singing, reaching for that old, elusive song.

Dayone takes his drumsticks and, using a rock as snare and gravel as brush, he joins in...and after a while with his voice.

This goes on for a long time.

From that upper ledge, where Dayone had hidden himself, a mountain lion looks down on the two small figures making strange sounds. These sounds fill this place. The big cat just lies down, unseen, and listens.

An hour later, where the canyon opens up into a wider glade, Simon and Dayone, dark against a bright sky, crouch behind cover, surreptitiously watching something.

Two deer are grazing. They look up. They do not see Simon and Dayone, their eyes quietly watching from behind a thicket.

Dayone is alert, exhilarated. He moves very slowly, as he pantomimes taking an imaginary arrow from an equally imaginary quiver, nocking it in an invisible bow—he aims.

Simon whispers, "Here. Try this arrow." He, too, pantomimes handing Dayone an arrow. "I made it. It will fly true."

Dayone chuckles, but takes the imaginary arrow, nocks it, aims....

Simon scrunches back around on the ground. He offers his leather pouch. "Wait. Before you shoot, let us offer cornmeal to the great spirit to show our respect to the deer who would give himself to us so that we might survive."

Dayone whispers, "Oh, man, I don't wanna play these games."

Simon whispers in choppy bursts, "No. Killing for the sake of killing, or for sport—without gratitude—those are the games."

Dayone thinks, then takes the pouch. He narrows his eyes at Simon.

48

CONDENSING TO A POINT

In the afternoon of their second day, on an exposed outcropping, halfway up one of the cliffs, Dayone sits silently as if in an eagle's eerie, surveying the area below.

Simon appears behind him. "This is a good spot," he says approvingly. "You will see and hear a lot from here—if you are quiet. I'm gonna go find places I haven't been to since I was—well, probably your age."

"When you be back? Couple hours?"

"Couple of days."

Dayone stands, stretches—sits back down, apparently undaunted. He doesn't fuckin' believe the old man.

At the bottom of a narrow path rising up along a cliff, Simon begins a slow, difficult climb, the two share some parting words. Simon looks down, out of breath, hurting but happy.

Dayone listens to the old man struggling. "I know what you're trying to do. Go on. I ain't afraid."

"I know you're not. If I thought you were, I wouldn't've even brought you here."

A crevice in the cliff appears next to Simon. He sticks his head in. He looks around...there! A petroglyph, old and weathered. He takes off his medicine bag, wedges it into a crack near the petroglyph. "Here, you guys can chat while I rest." He sits and looks silently out at the view. Dayone is still within earshot.

"Nervousness, restlessness, fear—they will come," says Simon. "Don't know how to tell you to fight them, so ignore them, just like you ignore advice from adults."

Below, Dayone sits calmly. "That's easy, old man."

＊

Tucking his medicine bag back into shirt, Simon plods on, his breathing mixed with the whispered sounds of an old prayer that comes to him. His spot awaits him further up.

＊

Far out to the west, the sun sets. The last sunlight disappears off the top of Dayone's head. The chill hits instantly. He wraps himself with his bag, Pueblo style, then to himself, "This is stupid. Didn't even bring my music. ...Goddammit, even talkin' to myself!"

As he hugs his knees, a honeybee lands on his hands. He doesn't move. He just stares at it. "What do you want? I ain't afraid. Go ahead, bite. Sting me—I don' care." The bee just walks around his hand, smelling, looking, sensing.... "I told ya I wouldn't move. You better get home—you'll freeze your ass off." But the bee keeps searching—down the index finger, across to the thumb, out the thumb, then back again. Dayone doesn't move.

The bee finally stops on the thick fleshy muscle and web between finger and thumb. She turns around and around slowly, as if orienting herself. Dayone watches, barely breathing, a smug smile playing in his face. The bee's abdomen throbs as she positions herself with the tiniest of movements.

With his free hand, Dayone slowly moves and cocks his middle finger and his thumb for an easy flick—but then watches in astonishment as the bee injects her stinger. Dayone doesn't move. The bee doesn't move. They just watch each other.

"I ain't gonna move, bee. I just gonna watch you die. You move and you'll pull out your guts. Stupid bee...."

＊

About a mile away, where the path is forced out onto a promontory overlooking the canyon, last sunshine, Simon lies face down in the dirt, arms and legs spread, his ear against the Earth. His eyes closed, a softness on his face, he is whispering something we cannot get a fix on. Only the Earth hears.

＊

The next morning, waiting for the Sun, Dayone is seated, leaning up against the cliff. He knows this is where the Sun will appear first.

He rubs his stomach with both hands because he has never in his life experienced this sensation—of being this hungry. He reaches for his canteen: empty. "Fuck." Then that spot on his hand where the bee stung him—it itches like hell. He scratches and sucks at it and scratches some more.

Over the course of the next few hours, he will begin to seethe inside and to talk awkwardly to himself with huge anger rising—all to cover the fear of being so hungry. The hunger will call to him, taunt him, rise up and loom over him. But by and by it will change its tune, its message of worry, and the fear will dissolve away like some mist over a pond. He will start to breath deeper and longer and with a gathering elation. He will stop himself abruptly and look at the joy suspiciously. He will mock himself. His boisterous side will taunt his conscientious side and win him over for a while. But within an hour, unwittingly, he will have switched his point of view to his conscientious side. He will put down his boisterous side for being unable to recognize his own fears.

"You will not be able to grow or step up out of the shithole you've dug for yourself," he says now in a cranky, hoarse voice. He sinks back slowly, endlessly, into the solid rock behind him.

He begins to doze. Does he hear the gradually rising sound of many horses' hoofs? Does he hear them in his sleep? He looks off down the canyon.

There are mists everywhere about him now. They are blue. They are yellow. He cannot keep his eyes open. He starts. Through his drowsiness, through the mists, he sees a small herd of mustangs racing up the canyon, approaching. Then he sees two Pueblo youths, long hair flying—they are riding and driving the village's herd of horses. One at the lead. One at the rear. He sees himself and Ruben!

The mists become dust from a bolting herd of Mule Deer. They, too, slowly disappear.

Dayone, drifting in and out of the dream, dreams of himself falling deeply asleep.

But at the clack-chattering sound of a huge raven harried by a smaller crow, Dayone starts awake. He looks around. Nothing. No horses, no deer, no dust, no sounds. Except above. Dayone looks up.

There, the raven again, on the wing. The bird flies so slowly—*th-wap, thwap, thwap*—and then dives and sails right by him, no more than six feet away—*thwap...thwap....*

His face fills with delight, peaking at the sounds, "*caw-caw-caaaw...*". Then as the cawing dissolves, he falls into a fretting sleep again.

A few moments later, the raven flies in, dark, translucent as a ghost, and lands a few feet from the sleeping boy, on a log that turns into a ceremonial drum.

Dayone's eyes slowly open. He sees the raven fly up to a nearby ledge and start to bob and click.

Moments later, the boy is climbing up the cliff to the ledge. Gaining it, he finds a crow's-nest, with two eggs. The raven on-high throws down a raucous invitation. Dayone looks up.

He nods at the raven. "For me?"

He looks at the eggs, picks one up, and with a poke from a twig, opens one ends of it and sucks it empty. The energy of that one egg instantly engulfs him. Gratitude now rewrites itself into his DNA.

⁂

There are places, there are spaces, there are moments that are magic. They are magic because they rule over our rough and hurried lives. They dissolve away our fears and force us to connect with a deeper reality. We are made vulnerable *and* powerful at once in those moments.

⁂

The dreamy day passes. Cycles within cycles. Little wheels. Big wheels. Spinning.

Far out to the west, past the Rio Grande, a wall of lightning runs the ridges of the black mountains. For a moments, over the course of a few hours, they glow bright the mountains.

The summer rain runs down a flat rock and fills the canteen. Dayone watches, for at least an hour, the tiny stream of water fill his canteen....

⁂

Simon feels the rain on his hands, arms, face. *There are many different kinds of rain. Some are light as a whisper and merely tickle. Some fall like stones, with hours in between each bucket drop. Some*

call on the wind for help or sneak up under the window just to take a
peek. Some wait for you to think it's over then hit you when you step
outside. Some make rhythms like your mother's heartbeat and melo-
dies that run like horses in a canyon. When I reach for them, they are
gone. Some will let you work or dream and lift you up on a pillow of
spray. Others will call your name over and over from every direction
and never give you a moment's peace. Some of them will breathe life
and purpose into your blood and will feed your root-ends there. Some
of them, warm or cold, will suck away all your air and laugh in the
face of your disaster. Some rains are sent to wash you away to the
center of the Earth. Down, down your mountain just to begin again.
Some rains are gentle, some are rough—like my Dahyanee's words
they fall and do me good.

Grandfather and grandson—each man condensing to a point.

49

LIKE A HERMIT SINCE SHE DIED

The next day. Simon pushes against the rock cliff and stretches his calf muscles. But he moves quickly back into partial shade. The rock is bare here and glares harshly in the sun. He is weak and dehydrated. He sits on his bedroll and leans back against the rock.

Softly, as if he were talking to the boy standing right besides him, he says, "Dayone, my grandson—am I pushing you too hard, too fast? Good horses train slowly, learn quickly. Have I abandoned you too long?"

He hears a woman's voice—Dahyanee, his wife. "You love the boy, Simon. He knows it. Are you worried for him?

Simon looks to his other side, as if she were there. "He may not trust me yet."

"Do you trust me?"

"I was a jealous man. Sorry 'bout that. I trust you now though."

She answers him. "'Ts'okay. Better get back to our grandson, what you think?"

"Yeah. Talk to you later?"

"Yes, later...not now, later. Let me give you a kiss."

As he struggles to turn around on that narrow path, a wind almost knocks him off balance. He takes a deep breath and slowly heads down.

Simon lets the mass of the mountain carry him gently downhill. As he approaches the place he left Dayone, he thinks, *I'm feeling pretty good. Yeah, this is where I left him. I'll just sit here and wait for him for a while. It's only fair.* An hour passes. *Maybe he went down to sleep in the truck. No, I don't think so.* Another hour passes.

Then he hears an ungodly sound, high-pitched and curdling coming from below.

"Yep. That's my grandson," he says out-loud. "He likes to mess with your head."

He starts walking down out of the canyons, knowing he's being played with. He's light-headed, but he feels the Earth.

Down the arroyo, converging with other arroyos coming down. Leveling out.

Sure enough. There's his grandson sitting in the driver's seat, revving the engine and somehow causing that terrible noise. As Simon approaches, Dayone races the engine one last time. Simon sees how Dayone has jammed a discarded ram's horn into the truck's exhaust and, with a piece of leather, created a reed over the pipe to trigger the sound.

꘎

Dayone's driving. He also seems to be keeping his thoughts to himself.

On the dusty road down, they sit quietly, their heads slowly drifting from side to side, taking it in.

When they bounce up out of a bad pothole, Dayone breaks the silence.

"Did you have a fucking vision, grandfather?"

"Talked to myself a lot. What about you?"

"Nah, saw some deer, they weren't horses, they were deer, and just watched a lot of birds...until I thought I could fly, ha-ha-hah!"

"Did you fly?"

"I thought I did, but, you know, I didn't.

"Sounds like a vision to me."

"Who did you talk to when you talked to yourself?"

"To myself—and to your grandmother. Hmpf—she wasn't as angry with me as I thought she'd be."

"Oh, okay, so you talked to her then. Has she forgiven you?"

Simon is taken off guard. "For what?"

"For hiding all the time away from everybody, like a hermit since she died—is what m'mom says. And for killing her."

Simon turns his head slowly to Dayone. "She said that?"

Dayone lowers his eyes. A moment later, he puts his arm around Simon. "Don't worry, Grandpa. Anyone who cares knows what really happened."

50

Who Can an Indian Trust?

Simon is waiting for the clinic to close. He's leaning against Louisa's car. People leave. The sun goes down. The staff leave. Louisa locks up and heads for her car.

He's looking at the ground.

"Hi, Papa. You going home, too?"

He doesn't answer. She unlocks her car.

Finally, he looks up. "I'm leaving."

"Leaving where?"

"The pueblo. San Lucas. Alex Olguin, the deputy, said I could borrow his camper. Going on the road. Have me some fun. I know, sounds silly I guess. I should take Dayone with me, if it's okay with you and the judge."

"This is crazy. You're not well, Papa. Have the operation and then you can do whatever you want."

"No. It's not worth it. Frank is right. He's the only one who has it right." He louder now. "The smart Indian should know by now not to trust anyone." A long pause. "Not himself. And not his daughter."

"What are you talking about?"

"Dayone. He blames me. For the death of Dahyanee. Is he living with this all the time? Am I? Are you? Is Frank? Why do I stick around? He said it!"

"I don't care what he said. It doesn't matter what he said. It's what you heard that matters. What you've programmed yourself to hear. Let it be. *Father, you loved her. That's all that matters.* As for Dayone—have you looked at him in the past few days? Don't you see the changes, Papa? You've done a miracle with him. A miracle."

"I thought you—."

"You let the demons lose again, for just a moment. No biggy, Papa.

"After all these years, after all we've been through. I'm still a jerk."

"No, Papa. You're a healer."

Simon kicks a clod, looks up into the sky, then to his daughter. "I know what I have to do."

51

Boulder Hopping Blind

A few hours earlier, before the Sun came up, Will is fast asleep. Strewn about his bed, his packed camping gear that he put together the night before.

Outside his window, a magpie calls to his gang. Will bolts awake, automatically reaching to turn off the alarm clock. He jumps out of bed and trips over his gear.

A few minutes later, fully dressed, he jams out his front door, looking down the driveway in anticipation, then hurries back in.

Between the kitchen and living-room, he paces—until the tea kettle whistles. As he turns the gas off, he hears a horse whinnying. He spins, runs, opens the door.

As he steps out, his mouth falls agape. Wynema, in a well-worn, dark-brown canvas coat and an old straw hat, sits her horse with power and assurance, holding leads to two other horses, one saddled, the other with a lightly-loaded pack rig. She pats the saddled mare.

A couple hours later, sun-up on a little-used, dusty road that tracks off until it disappears over the horizon, they ride side-by-side. Will wears a fleece-lined levi jacket and his new straw hat. He slides around sensuously in the saddle, barely containing his excitement.

Wynema sits deep in her saddle; yet she keeps her horse collected. "You look good. You like it, huh?"

Chest swelling, Will feels just great. He wants to arch an eyebrow and incline his head and say, "Why thank ya, ma'am," but he doesn't. He just bobs his head in rhythm with the pace of his horse.

Small juniper and cedar trees, chamisa and sage, scatter away on both sides of the riders. The Sun at their backs, they move slowly towards the Gorge.

Halfway between them and the Gorge, on a huge solitary rock that juts 200 feet above the high plains desert, two Golden Eagles sit on a gray fallen tree. On the tallest upright limb, their nest. They see the riders approaching. They see the Gorge beyond, cutting across the vast plateau like a deep wandering gouge from the Creator's finger. One of them, the female, flies off towards the Gorge.

She flies over the rim of the chasm, dives down towards the river and the animals she will feed on below.

A few minutes later, a fish grasped tightly in her talons, she rises up, up, and as she passes the rim again sees the riders, dismounted now, standing as close to the edge as they dare.

Will and Wynema hear the eagle's *screeeeeeeh* and watch it heading back to the rock.

Will is mesmerized into silence.

Wynema slowly looks to him. "Beautiful, eh?"

Will lets roll a soft growl from his chest. "Water. Wind. Sun. A lot of water did this."

"A long time ago," she replies.

"From the point of view of the Earth, not such a long time ago."

Wynema steps up easily into the saddle. *Like an angel,* muses Will, *climbing into God's lap to whisper a simple but important secret.*

A few minutes later she eases her horse down into a huge, dry, well-worn gully that runs towards the rim of the canyon. Unconsciously, he holds his horse back. He isn't aware his breathing has become fast and shallow. It's a big decision for him, but finally, just as she looks back, he allows his horse to follow hers. They begin their descent along a steep and narrow ledge that runs down one side of the gully.

The switchbacks end. Now it's become more than a mere gully: it's a many-times flash-flooded canyon of its own.

Still the path stays narrow. The light caroms and crackles off every wall, every rock. And the shadows. *Oh, Creator, how many colors in the shades of crevices, contours, corners, edges can you name?*

Will is incredulous. "This is really the way down? My god! Horses don't fall?"

"Not if you feel her between your legs all the way down to the center of the earth. Your center is her center at the center of the Earth."

Will tries to relax. Inside his head he can hear himself say, *Trust the horse. I mean, my God, the horse must trust itself. Gotta be! One slip and I'll ride the flank of this beast 150 feet right down onto those!* He looks at the well-defined sharp edges of basalt boulders gaping up at him.

Every few minutes, Wynema turns about and looks at him. Her horse doesn't care, as she turns on her center. *The horse can smell the water of the river ahead,* she thinks, *It's good to see such a competent man and surgeon utterly at a loss for a sense of security.* She is a student of ironies.

Suddenly, the eagle—the male this time—comes fast on a wave of compressed air. He will be down flying a foot over the river in a few moments. The pressure-wave almost knocks Will off his horse. Wynema, nor the horses, seem to register the passage.

Will tries forced relaxed breathing.

Wynema and her horse are one motion. She points to the widening view of the Gorge, then without changing the undulate motion, slowly turns around in her seat, a soft but wicked smile on her face. When Will sees her, he slowly inhales, his eyes goes wide, and finally a little smile. "Ah," she says, and turns back ahead. She's a little annoyed with herself that she enjoys seeing a big man suffer like this. But only a little annoyed.

All this time, the horses plod on, slowly, confidently, their unshod hard hooves somehow gripping the hard hot smooth rock.

An hour after the eagle has come and gone, they make the river. She remembers coming here with some cousins when she was young. He is amazed that such a place exists. The steep vertical sides to the canyon walls—such an array of colors. And he's never seen such huge cottonwoods. He's already grateful for the shade he knows they'll soon provide. There's tamarisk and willow brush near the river's edge—at least he thinks it's tamarisk. And a trail along the river where huge, white boulders washed and smoothed by a thousand years of river wait patiently for the next supernova. Some sandy shores, but mostly walnut gravel and fist-sized rocks. Moss on the rocks or swirling slowly in little backwater eddies. Echoes. Falling rocks. Birds darting. Ducks passing by. Mounds of ants. Dragonflies flying ecstatically coupled—or maybe just ungainly and necessarily coupled.

Then he sees something gliding through some shallows, propelled by its tail. "What's that," he says in a hushed whisper, "a beaver?"

She glances once, then lets her eyes dart elsewhere. Finally, "Muskrat."

They walk their horses slowly along a trail not far from the water. At a bend in the river, near some cottonwoods, at the foot of another arroyo, they stand, holding their horses and each other's hand. Spontaneously, Will unleashes a sound, not loud but unique. It immediately echoes back from the mouth of the arroyo. Then Wynema with a tone of her own—longer, an octave higher. Will takes a breath and rejoins the choir. For a few minutes they intone together. Ravens, bluejays, magpies, squirrels–all manner of resident singers here join in. On a ledge above them, a bobcat sticks her head out of her lair, then immediately disappears.

Wynema hobbles the horses and lets them graze. Water, grasses, no predators, they're happy. Saddles off. Stuff unloaded. Will changes his boots and she her mocs—for water-friendly running shoes.

Now they're running, in shorts, t-shirts, along the wide gravel banks and beaches that border the water. Without even looking, their feet miss the rocks and vegetation and land safely on the soft, crunching gravel. Their strides are long and unhurried. But now the rocks thicken, they get bigger and closer together. Still they run, Wynema leading. Now they must run *on* the rocks and slabs, leaping from one to the next. And yet they maintain their speed. *Incredible*, feels Will! He's aware that he's not looking at where to place his feet. He trusts them. He looks way ahead. Somehow his finds the flat surfaces or the soft rounded tops, the ledges where his feet are sure and solid. Faster and faster it seems. Bigger and bigger the boulders and rocks. Wynema still ahead, squeals, whoas, and laughs. Will the same. He follows, amazed at how certain she is of every step, every foothold. What footholds? There is no path. There is only joyous headlong pursuit, trust, power, and glee.

As they run, the river approaches on the right. So she veers right. She doesn't slow. He's right behind her. She leaps—out onto the boulders in the shallows. Without faltering, he follows. The boulders are bigger here—six feet, eight feet—it's ten feet down to the water now! *Yai!* She leaps out—into the river. He follows. It's cold! It's smiling! It's alive! The river engulfs them.

Up they come thrashing out of the water, yelling, swimming for all they're worth, to the farther shore. Then crawling, two primordial creatures, dripping with algae and slime-weed. A glop of snails and a crawdad fall from her shoulder. A spray of moss covers his right eye. They make sounds like "yai-yai-ya-yaiii..." until they collapse, roll over and look at the Gorge rim so high above them.

It's hot. Will takes off his shirt. But she's up and darts over the water, boulder-hopping again. Will follows agilely, almost out of control. Laughing and squealing.

She makes it to the far shore and disappears into an outcropping of tall rocks at the foot of a huge talus of fallen cliff debris. Will reaches the other side, out of breath, and scrambles quickly after her.

He reaches the back upper end of the outcropping. He negotiates the rocks and terrain adroitly now. He's feeling his power. His confidence. And more.

He looks. No Wynema. As he starts down on the other side, he looks across an eight-foot chasm to a grassy ledge that cannot be reached by any other way. Something moved! Back out of sight behind those bushes there!

Yes, tucked into a vertical crevice, she hides, breathing rapidly and deeply.

He, respectful of the distance, leaps, lands, almost silently, into a crouched position. He scuttles like an ape on all fours, his ass higher than his head. Should he go this way...or that? Slowly, on fours, always keeping three of his four feet connected to the Earth.

She, hearing something coming, sees there is only one way out, knows she must move now or never, looks up, only the sky. She listens. Nothing untoward. She's got to move, sticks her head out, left, right—where is he? She presses back against the cliff and releases her held breath. Now her own breathing, her heartbeat, the wind in the cracks and through the crevices—fill her head. Suddenly, she stops. Slowly, she turns and looks up again. Will has climbed up the out-cropping and come around and is now slowly descending. He slides down next to her, his arms like the rain, or first sunlight, or chocolate over ice-cream—embracing her. She melts in his arms. And they kiss, slowly, totally, letting it build. They whisper.

He, "I'm lost."

She, "Me, too."

She pulls him out and around and down onto the ledge with grass. Holding one hand of hers, he goes down on the grass on his back and pulls her down on top of him. And she sits astride and smiles mischievously as she pulls off her t-shirt, her common everyday faded wet t-shirt, to reveal herself, her whole body naked in the Sun.

The light. From behind. Refracted by the red rocks tinges her flanks and breasts and sets them on fire. Slowly infinitely she lowers herself, allowing first one, then the other breast to brush his mouth. Then again, and again, never lingering too long, but moving, like thick sweet sugar water, flowing over his lips, his cheek, his eyes. Nothing lingers. Too alive. He inhales, forever, and knows this feeling for the first time.

*

Both Golden Eagles are back from hunting now. But when they flew over the humans a moment ago, they recognized the sounds—the preternatural sounds of coupling—and it had a calming effect on the eagles.

It had a similar effect on the bobcats snuggled deeper into their dark burrow no more than fifty feet from where Will and Wynema slow-fucked their way into a new relationship.

The sounds of their ecstasy melt into the sounds of the canyon, the breezes that blow for a moment and die away, the sun pinging off the rocks, the merging of all the colors and sounds and movements—it all just trails away into an afternoon far, far way.

*

A little later the ravens come in high doing slow barrel-rolls down the length of the canyon. They see the river below and two tiny figures stretched out naked on huge, smooth white boulders far below.

Their hands reach out and touch.

He, "What are we doing?"

She, "Colliding in mid-air."

They hear the cawing. They look up. They point.

The ravens see them pointing and show-off with another series of barrel-rolls.

He rolls on top of her. It's his turn.

It is evening and thirty degrees cooler. Dressed warmer, they sit on a driftwood log next to a fire, their backs against the side of a big rock.

He, "Do you think you could love me? Hey, I'm just asking."

She, "My body talks and it says it wants you...."

"Somethings come first. Yes, I understand that."

"You understand a lot. But what do you know?"

Will runs towards the fire, leaps it, and wheels like a specter, and grins.

"I don't know about you, Will, but there are many voices that call to me."

Will runs back around the fire—kneels before her. "What do they ask of you?"

"To answer the call of my spirit."

"Is there a purpose greater than love? Is there?"

"Perhaps not."

After eating and tidying up the campsite, they make love again.

Now they're on their backs, spent, looking up at the river of stars that flow down the gorge. From this perspective, the upper rim of the gorge is the shore of that river.

Breathing heavily, Will whispers, "Come over here."

Wynema, dreamily, "I'm too tired."

"Can you sleep?"

"No. I'm too excited."

"Let's count the stars."

"Okay. One—"

"Two—"

"Three—"

"Four—"

Wynema, "You missed one."

Will, "Where?"

"Over here."

Will rolls over to her. "Mmmm, I think I should start my count all over again. One...."

52

EVERY MAGPIE A LEADER OF A GANG

The next morning early at Simon's summer house, Dayone, holding two bowls of oatmeal, sets one down next to Simon, who wakes at the approach.

"Here's some food, grandfather..."

Simon looks at him, acknowledging the respect, and sits on the edge of his bed, looking very old.

"...and I wanna make a drum."

Moved, yet childlike, Simon nods, "Me, too."

Teo looks up from his workbench. Simon and Dayone are waiting patiently for an answer. Teo sets down his gouge. "Well, I was planning to go up above Taos next week to find some good logs. I got some friends there who take me way back into the forest where no one goes."

"Where no one *can* go," interjects Dayone. "I know, I tried. Me and my friends wanted to see their private lake up there, and they just popped out of nowhere and they told us to get our asses gone. How'd they know we were there, anyway?"

Teo looks from Simon to Dayone. "I guess you can come, too—t'look for your own. Would it be okay with you if we offered some prayers when we get to where we're going up there?"

Dayone is incredulous that the ex-Governor is asking him for permission to pray. Nodding his head thoughtfully, "Well, I guess so, sure.

When Teo picks up his lathe-gouge again, Dayone steps over to Simon and smiles a bit too proudly. Simon raises a finger—and the boy immediately adjusts his pride. A worker calls out in Pueblo to

Dayone, "*Hey, you wanna see something really* cool?" Dayone leaves
and Teo turns to Simon, gesturing approval.

Simon acknowledges this. "I have things to do. I see that now. But
I am too weak."

"So what you gonna do?"

"I am going to ask Mirriamma to do the *Pahos* Hands-in-the-Dirt
with me."

Teo is surprised, but "It's up to you," is all he can say.

Adds Simon, "I will stand with you in Council after that."

Greatly moved, Teo puts his hands on Simon's shoulders.

Mirriamma's place is above the level of the village, a good view
for a protector. All night her oven filled with pottery has slowly
cooled. This morning, in the workshop area, they are taking pots out
of the oven, inspecting them. The two women look up simultaneously
in the direction of the hills. A lone rider on horseback approaches.

Mirriamma, in Pueblo, "You better make us some mugwort and
lemon grass tea."

Wynema only guesses. "Simon?"

Mirriamma grunts a yes. "I love men. They're so soft and vulnerable, like little rabbits coming back to their burrow."

A few minutes later, in Mirriamma's prayer room, newly swept
and all things sacred carefully set on their shelves, she and Simon quietly sit on stools, rolling ritual cigarettes, medicine for entering prayer.
He wears a wide, red headband—she a black shawl with white piping.
Their eyes follow Wynema as she enters with two cups of hot tea,
then leaves.

Mirriamma leans toward Simon, her eyes referring to Wynema.
"She's gonna choose the path of medicine, not just because she comes
from Bear clan, but because she's gonna have to give up the way she
knows things to find out another way of knowing. Eh?" Simon leans
closer to hear her whispered voice. "That's part of the road. Never
easy. *Ai-yai-hu.* I see in both of them something of the gift." Off Simon's look of question, she answers in Pueblo, "*You know, the doctor.*"

Simon nods. "*He's got a lot of honor from his people, lot of respect, but his grandfather's pain, it chases him from shadow to*

shadow." He continues in English, "Unless he knows his grandfather's pain, he cannot know his grandfather. And maybe if he doesn't know this, he cannot know himself. What you think?"

"Ah, that's why you like him. So what are you going to do?"

Simon laughs, nervously shaking his head. "Well, I'm not going to die too soon—but soon."

She makes the sound a she-bear might make upon settling down to nurse her young. Then they light their corn husk cigarettes and sit and pray.

After another while, Simon shifts, "When they took me to the hospital I was—I was unconscious. I was—"

"Between the two worlds."

Simon grins, "I was, wasn't I?"

"Yes, but—you chose to come back. Why?"

Simon sweeps his hand from his head to his toe. "To clean out the old tube."

"You can do it."

Without a thought, Simon shifts to Pueblo, "*Yes, but not without your help.*"

She is taken off guard.

"I want to do the *Pahos Hands-in-the-Dirt*—with you."

Mirriamma's eyes flash, then narrow.

"It's been too many years. I don't remember."

What she does remember is this: At the base of a sheer cliff halfway up the biggest mountain behind the pueblo—and it's that magic hour of light just before sunset, seventy-five years ago—two old women, wearing gray shawls, and a 13-year-old Mirriamma, wearing a similar black shawl with white piping, cling close to a small fire. The girl is kneeling, grabbing the Earth, anguish in her face. The old women sing. One spreads cornmeal on the ground.

Mirriamma gives herself to the memory. Simon, however, stays connected with his voice: "You remember okay," he intones. "You were very sick, hard hit by the fever and the infection. You nearly died. Hah, I know you—maybe you did die, you never told me. But *you* know. *You* remember. There are many roads here right now, trying to cross, trying to find the place where they meet. They are here, they are there—but you don't forget. I know you."

Mirriamma opens her eyes. Uncertainty weighs on her.

Simon continues, his arms slowly gesticulating like skewed lines that don't meet. "They are everywhere, moving about, but they are not connected. Don't know if they ever were. Between two worlds. Yes, I need the heavy-duty version, sister."

He crosses one forearm definitively onto the other, forming a bond, a commitment, a decision. He stares for a while at the hole in the floor before them. The smoldering coals suddenly burst into flame. He reaches and throws a few small sticks on top. Then, "But they want to connect. If you—if *we* cannot do Hands-in-the-Dirt, I will have the doctor's operation, and I will die whenever, who knows when, okay, without a road to bring me back to the old ones, and that is *not* okay."

When Mirriamma raises her hands, palms facing Simon, his face drops in dismay. But then Mirriamma turns her hands palms up—and Simon's face brightens. He sighs with relief and gratitude.

As he rides off into the darkness over paths he knows, like the voices of grandparents talking in the living-room, Mirriamma stands at the fence looking at him ride away. Wynema comes up next to her, looks out, then lays the left side of her head on her hands on the fence and sighs, deep in thought.

Wyema, in a voice she uses when praying, *I experience the night. I experience the unique relationship between the night and me. Two unique beings, the Night and I, interpenetrating each other.*

Mirriamma smiles and smooths the young woman's hair. "What's that from?"

Wynema raises her head. "You asked what I was feeling. That's what I was feeling."

Mirriamma makes a sing-song sound from her chest. "That's a healing song your great-grandfather used to sing. You said it in the modern language. Listen how it goes in the old language."

Hardly anyone speaks the older dialect. Mirriamma sings her father's song for Wynema, who is surprised and rocked by the similarity.

"I never knew your father. I don't remember that as a song. It was just what I was feeling when you asked."

First the night, then the day, then everything else, says Mirriamma in response. *"That's how the song ends."*

&

Dawn fights to get into the darkened room. Will is soundly asleep in his bed and Wynema lies next to him, her face hidden in the covers. Of a sudden, he opens his eyes and pulls back the covers: Wynema has become Mirriamma! He closes his eyes tightly and becomes still and small and begs for sleep to return. He knows it was a momentary hallucination.

Later. Wynema awakens, senses, sits up and—no Will.

Wrapped in only a blanket, she opens the front door quietly. Soon the Sun will rise—there at the reddening—and shine in her face. She looks left and right. She thinks she hears something coming from the roof.

On the rooftop, a figure stands in silhouette against the glow, also wrapped in a blanket, looking out across the village.

She watches him for a couple of minutes from the top of the log-ladder, then steps off onto the roof. Track with her as she walks quietly toward him, never before has she wanted to understand…a man, like this.

He stares off directly into the rosy glow now threatening to explode like a volcano from the top of the mountain. Tall, thin, wavering at the edge. Tears in his eyes, suddenly he becomes aware of her. He starts to say one thing, then clearly takes another tack:

"There are things that are happening, things that are making me question what the hell it is I do. Did you know that health survey we did was for some nuclear waste thing? Victor never told me! Are you in favor of it?"

She shakes her head slowly. "No, of course not."

"I got the finest education a doctor can get. But it's not enough. Not enough to help Simon."

"Yours is a medicine developed in a white society for a white culture."

Will sighs for the whole world. "We're all just people."

"We're more than that—every person, every culture, has a purpose. Be patient."

327

"No! Simon—he doesn't have time. I don't want him to die. He doesn't have to die. Why does he refuse?"

She lets him be. She looks at the first fierce yellow piece of the sun showing.

Will takes a deep breath and sighs. "How many dead bodies have I touched? Thirty? That's all. Med school, hospitals. Maybe thirty. Well, my grandfather, when he was only fifteen, he had carried countless hundreds of dead bodies to the crematoria. He never told me this, but I know. I know that's what it was. When his son, his Isaac, my father, and my mother, Rosa—when they died in that burning car, all the dead bodies came back to haunt him. I think they followed him to Israel. That's why when I took him to Israel all those months ago, I didn't stay. I couldn't stay. The truth is I was afraid of all those dead Jews."

Will starts to fragment emotionally, to crumble. "This morning, I turned over and it wasn't you I saw. It was Mirriamma."

Wynema is surprised, but unafraid. "It wasn't Mirriamma, and it wasn't me. I don't know how to explain it to you—it was something old, something Pueblo, coming through both of us. And you saw it, Will. You saw it."

"Mirriamma is a healer. I'm not a healer—I didn't learn healing in medical school. I'm a mechanic."

"How do you know you're not a healer if you don't know what a healer is?"

He slowly draws her shoulder towards him. "Is it possible for me to be there, you know, with you, when she does a healing, a curing, a—?"

"They're not the same thing—a healing and a curing."

"Okay, okay. I hear you and I don't understand. But I want to. I want to learn the difference. Is that possible for me?" He softens. He pleads. "Do you think I could? Would you ask, for me? I mean, maybe it'll help me understand and, you know, reach Simon."

Wynema takes a deep breath. "Okay. I'll ask."

She leans into him, opening her blanket to him. He does the same....

In a supermarket on another day, Mirriamma pushes her cart slowly down an aisle. She selects a meat thermometer, studies it. Wynema approaches with a ten-pound bag of rice, puts it in the cart. She reflects for a moment, then a little nervously. "So, would it be dangerous? Or a distraction to you? Or Simon? If he came?"

Mirriamma ponders and puts the meat thermometer back. "Never used one of these."

"Because if it is, if it's inappropriate, I'll tell him that he can't come and he'll understand."

"Our doings aren't dangerous. They only remind us of our relationships. They make our commitment clear, allow us to see what our responsibility is to this or that. So, I guess, if you feel strong on this, you bring him. Maybe, if we're lucky, he can feel it. Most can't, you know."

"My heart is really reaching out to him."

"How much?"

"I guess a lot."

Mirriamma picks up the meat thermometer again, shows it her, then bursts out laughing.

"Ya know, in white society, they measure everything. In Indian society, we don't measure anything. What makes sense to us, they call magic. But what they call science, we call magic. Heh-heh. Funny that way."

53

Los Burros se Buscan para Rascarse

There are back roads in and out of the village. Only the villagers know them or use them. And besides they're on Indian land. No trespassing. There's one place, next mountain to the south, that has a great view of San Lucas. At night, if there's a moon, and there is tonight, the Pueblo looks like a painting. Not real. Unreal. Surreal. More than real. Like tonight.

Sliding now into your view, up close, Frank Zamora, at the vista point, sitting on his Harley, looking out, seeing the Pueblo below in that way.

A heavy-set woman, late 30s, drives by in a rattling pickup loaded with firewood. Recognizing Frank beside her, she backs up and lowers her window. "Hey, Frank, is that you? Goddamn!"

He turns his head slowly and stares at the woman. Then he turns back to the view. He's plenty drunk.

The woman, as if they'd been chewing the fat for hours, sighs and says, "So you just get in, uh? You come back to go the Arts Fair at the Pueblo, uh?"

Frank shakes his head with a look of disgust. "Not with a ten-foot pole. Hey, is my father dead yet?"

This pulls the woman snap-back right out of her romance. "Of course not! What a thing to say! Frank, you drink too much!" Put off by his disrespect, she waves him away and drives off.

He settles back, unperturbed, looks off and starts his engine. It throbs. He closes his eyes and feels it. The Harley throb. The women can do with it what they want, but for a man, it's the mufflers—a Harley is tuned to resonate with a man's testicles. Tested and made that way right from the factory.

Slowly he drops his right wrist and the throb rises up through him. Eases him. Calms him. Sends a short shot of juice into his circuitry. Every real rider knows this is how and why a Harley riding drinking man stays alive as long as he does.

&

At the Pueblo, hundreds of tourists and other spectators crowd around an open area at one end of the plaza where fifty dancers, in two opposing lines, move in a processional to the singing and drumming of blanketed, older men. Feathers and colors and sound-making adornments bedeck the dancers. Their steps are simple and soft and declarative of tradition. Nothing more—as far as the guests are concerned.

When the dance is done, they move slowly to another niche among the buildings and do it again. The crowd follows and observes politely. Three or four times this happens until, finally, the men and dancers disappear up a narrow path between some buildings. When the spectators attempt to follow merely out of herd instinct, they run into Sotero who's smiling shyly. He raises his eyebrows impishly and points across the plaza where some food stalls are now opening for business. He makes the simple gesture for eating. The herd turns and retreats.

Colonialists, says Frank to himself as he watches from his bike at one corner of the plaza.

He cruises through the gawkers slowly, low-slung on his chopper, nodding to friends and fans and others who are quite taken by the sight of the perfect Mad Max Indian Warrior.

One of the hip and muscled Latino locals, accompanied by a few associates, raises a finger. Frank stops. They greet each other with grunts and the latest hand and fist greetings.

"Yo, homey, lookin' good, eh."

Frank just nods and looks around. "What you doin' here, Chucho?"

"Lookin' at tourists lookin' at you. Amazing how they stick together wherever they go. Like ducks in a pond."

Frank flicks his wrist and the Harley spits and roars for a second, sending people scurrying. "More like donkeys, *coño*."

"*¿Como e'?*"

Frank hits it in Spanish, "*Los burros se buscan para rascarse.*" This sends Chucho spinning in laughter. Frank moves on.

Chucho's girl is Anglo and asks with her eyes what the fuck's so funny. He points to the tourists. "He said, 'Donkeys come together in order to scratch each other'." Everyone laughs again.

In fact, the tourists do stick together, mainly on one side, near the trees. It's hot. So shade is at a premium. "The dancers will return in half an hour," someone says.

Many side streets are set up with booths selling something fine and beautiful and expensive, or something cheap and imitative, or something just to eat. White artisans in New Age cowboy mufti sell well-crafted Indian jewelry they made themselves. Ironies abound.

Frank parks his bike. The young but big-bellied Arts Festival co-ordinator spots him.

"Hey, Frank, good to see ya. Are you still on that college tour? Any new albums out yet? Hey, listen, I'm in a jam. Lost my emcee. Stiff as a skunk. Would you—" He looks around nervously. "—be willing to announce the awards? Lots of teenagers here, so be cool, you know, make all this important to teenagers. But you know, I mean, people know you and—"

Frank shrugs, nods okay, "What the hell!" He waves to some fans walking by. Back to the coordinator, mock serious, "Twice as many tourists this year, Rodney. Really starting to pay off bein' an injun."

But Rodney really isn't listening. Too many details on his mind. He looks at his watch. "Meet me at the podium in fifteen minutes. It'll only take ten minutes. I got it all written down." He shakes Frank's hand then hurries away. Frank needs another drink.

⁂

Not far away, Victor is talking with the new governor from neighboring Santa Carmina and glad-handing a few important locals.

"Governor," says Victor, "if you can get your people one-hundred-percent behind the MRS like my pueblo is, we'll have more than consensus. We'll have a local lock, and we'll win that grant and share the benefits through joint land use. I'm sure of it."

The new governor of Santa Carmina, Hector Too-Tall Atyas, is bold and younger and wants to impress from the get-go. "But Victor, if you do that you get only half, not all, of the grant. Doesn't sound like you. Why do you really need us?"

Victor leans in. "There's strength in numbers. We'll each get more than half. Trust me." Victor knows Hector won't go for it. Too conservative, too cautious. But when San Lucas wins the grant, Victor will have more clout regionally. He's looking forward.

As they pass by, Wynema and Will dip their heads in respect and greeting to the governors.

Wynema is imagining what the two governors might be talking about. *Whatever the conversation, it wouldn't be the same if one of them were a woman.*

Had Will been just a visitor, a spectator, he would have watched detached, respectful, observant. But now his perceptive faculties have been altered, realigned, and he has no sense of orientation. He doesn't know who he, as observer, is, no point of reference. He's watching a science fiction movie, with aliens doing everything they can to assimilate, but just not succeeding. He's neither fish nor fowl—neither an insider nor an outsider now.

Wynema suddenly becomes aware of Will. "Hey, if you like this, wait till New Years, you'll really see something. I'll take you to the Deer Dance."

This brings Will back. "I'll see what?"

"People on the rooftops, and down by the cottonwoods, colorful clothes, everybody, everywhere, watching these two lines of men, the hunters, facing one another. And then two young women, in black shawls and white boots, slow dancing with their gourd rattles, come leading the animals in. Each man a different animal, little boys as foxes, all moving slow, following the women. They're all just playing a part in what they see life is all about." And then more to herself, "Or what we used to see."

They pass but don't see Simon and Teo on stools in the shade of a nearby adobe. Dayone stands quietly behind the men, listening to the sounds coming from the plaza—until he hears his uncle Frank doing a P.A. system sound check.

"...More monitor...good...we're set. All right then there." Then louder and cocked to gather all ears, "Let us bow our heads. Our great white father, who art in Washington, horror be thy game—."

Surprised, Simon looks over his shoulder at the stage, where Frank, wearing a wireless headset-mic, has just thrown himself into putting on an impromptu show.

The visitors, like browsing drifting shark, converge immediately towards the stage. The over-the-edge tenor of Frank's amplified voice is the blood they sense.

He lowers his rasping voice, "Yeah, could I have just a little more in the monitors?" Then projecting strong again, "Our kingdom won, our lives are done, our earth has become your victim. Give us this day our daily dread and make us lie down with your television and other crunchy addictions."

There're all there: Simon, Dayone, Teo, Louisa, Victor, Gov. Hector Too-Tall Atyas, Will and Wynema. No one is uninterested.

Rodney, the event's producer, hears this and comes running. But he trips off the side of the plank bridge over the creek and falls into the water, his knee hurt and bleeding.

The tourist-crowd's reactions run the gamut: giggling, appalled, saddened, curious, oblivious, angry.... They oscillate rapidly between fear and fascination.

One big Texan wearing his Texan finest is there with his family, standing mere feet away from Frank on stage. And his wife is right off the cereal carton—big-haired and seriously called Queenie. Their almost as big-haired daughter—call her Teen-Queen—resembles her mother's protege. But Teen-Queen looks positively aghast as her mother hands her a local tamale to eat.

"Iiiiikh, Mommy, how gross! What is it?"

"Oh, Shoogie, it's a tamale, Indian-style."

Frank turns his head to clear his throat, but forgets that he's wearing a headset-mic. "Hail money, mother of greed, blessed art thou among wisdoms and blessed is the fruit of thy loom—disease us."

Teen-Queen looks around and lets the tamale drop to the ground. With her booted foot, she surreptitiously tries to cover it with dirt.

Frank, acknowledging scattered applause, sees the squooshing of the tamale and leaps out with a whoop, calling maximum attention to himself. Drunk or stoned, he's agile and strong. He flies through the air and lands, wireless microphone still working, right next to Teen Queen.

"Oh, thank you, sweet princess. Thank you for plop-dropping on this, our sacred ground—" He scoops up the tamale, "—the fruit of thy tube, possibly even making it more sacred. Just as if you were standing in St. Peters Square in the Vatican, with your panties down around your ankles, plopping a turd." His voice booms across the plaza.

Frank slowly crushes the tamale and the dirt in his hand, the juices running out through his fingers and down his arms. Christ-like, he extends his messy stigmata'd hands and moves menacingly towards, then capriciously away from, Teen-Queen, who is mortified and scared.

Raising his arms, Frank plays to the crowd, "Thank you for blessing us the way the whites have blessed us for years, by leaving this hallowed little log on our holy ground."

Frank moves again to Teen-Queen, as if to embrace her. "Come, let me anoint you with the blood of the land, the holy mother of us all, and make you a priestess in the sacred order of summer-fall-winter-*scheiss*...."

Frank's gooey hand snakes out to her face, but her father intercepts. Frank dodges Big Tex, but splats a hand onto Big Tex's white shirt. Thus, the big Texan comes unglued. A mêlée breaks out. Like hockey players, Indians and whites, and Hispanics just for the hell of it, converge and rumble.... Are there rules as to who is your enemy?

A few moments later, Frank, bloodied, is being dragged away by two tribal policemen, still spouting venom as he goes. "You tourists are dopes! Dupes! Duds! These dances are staged for your silly benefit, don't ya know. The real shit happens somewhere else! Le'go a me!"

All that took was a moment: a congealed social exclamation point. Life, in the tourist lane, goes on.

Hauled away, Frank loses it completely. He splits into two different people arguing with each other. "Go ahead, take my picture! Red alert! My shields are up. They'll never take me alive. Who me? Yes you! I'm good—I love the Indian. No, you killed your mother, the sacred Earth—"

As the tribal police are about to put him unceremoniously into their squad-car, Frank sees Simon approaching, his one and only father.

"...and you'll never be forgiven!" he rants on aiming now at Simon, unaware that the wireless mic, though signal weakening, is still on, piping his pain, in static bursts, across the plaza. "No, I'm just a child of the earth—how could I kill my own mother? Screw your the Earth and take her for all she's worth. Yeah, and your old man wears his pants on backwards—"

One of the uniformed tribal policemen, Alex Olguin, takes the wireless off and disconnects it, then opens the backdoor of the SUV for Frank.

Simon steps forward, "Officer—"

"Grandfather."

"He's had too much to drink. Happy to be here, but impolite to the visitors. A bad combination."

Officer Olguin agrees.

"Let me take him home, Alex."

Frank explodes, "I am home, dammit! I just can't live here anymore!"

As the officer sizes up the situation, Frank blurts again. "He'll send me back to Grandma again. To steal him a fifth. Watch out for him, he's sneaky!"

"Sorry Simon, but I have to book him. You can come along, though."

They are driven to the Tribal Police Office. In the back, Frank's head lolls to one side for a moment, then snaps back, looking back and forth from Simon to Officer Olguin.

"This is a ruse, a set-up. I can tell. Why do I have that feeling that I ain't gonna see you again?" His expression changes sharply. He pumps himself up. "Ya know what I should have told 'em? I should have told them that you're all one-way people. There's no circle in your lives. You're the homeless ones. Not me." And with that lets loose a ghoulish peal of laughter.

Frank is booked. The Tribal Police Chief, Ron Tatum, stares at Frank while talking to someone quietly on the phone. Olguin stands near by. Simon and Frank sit at a bench.

Frank stands. "I dance, Simon—I dance all the time. That's my poetry, my performance. It's a pulse, to and from the Earth, from the water in the Earth, from her quakes to her red-earth quickening. It sometimes just throbs, throbs in my blood, *Grandfather....*"

Half an hour later, they're in the back of Officer Olguin's vehicle again.

Frank slouches back into the seat. "It's the only thing that keeps me alive, you know–is the dance. I think I'm gonna dance myself dead. That's how I'm gonna go. How you gonna go, Simon? I can see it. You're gonna be sittin' down, sitting down on the job when you die. What d'you think?"

Simon simply says, "Your nephew is coming home."

"Comin' home? Ah, coming home coming home. My nephew? Dayone. How sweet. Dayone is a war casualty. Bastard child of rock 'n roll. Pickled in gutter juices. You'd think he'd like to dance, you know, the way he likes his drummin' 'n all."

"They tried to send him away, but I—"

Olguin pulls up in front of Simon's place just off the plaza. He opens the door for Simon.

Frank jumps out the other side, off now on another tack. "Us Indians are the ones's got to spread out across the land. Dissolve into the cracks. Colonialize *them* bastards! Invisibly! And then, when we're just disembodied spirits, visiting the lonely nights of white women wannabes, then...then we'll rise again, and everyone will become Indian. The once-and-future holy people! Hey, I'm ready to go out knowin' I was right."

Olguin has listened patiently, with great interest actually. But his radio clatters and he gets back into his vehicle and leaves.

Simon holds the old weathered door open for Frank. "I should never have sent you back. I admit it. Should have kept you with me. Been tough, but together we might have worked it out. Who knows? I apologize to you for that."

Frank jumps away, into the deep recess of the doorway next door, "We could have licked our wounds...."

337

He peers out, steps out, and slaps himself in the face, a performer forcing himself ready. "Are you fixin...fixin' t'die. Ya ain't afraid of dyin', ya just don' wanna leave the chillun a-cryin'? Is that it, Simon? Where're we goin'?"

"Right here. Nowhere. My town house."

Frank wobbles in.

A neighbor watches from a window, until Simon closes the door behind them.

Simon helps Frank get into bed. "I made a remembering-stick fetish. I only saw my grandfather's once or twice."

He pulls off Frank's boots and looks at his hands. "But I never forgot it. I will use it in the *Pahos* ceremony. And I will pray to *Gnatum-si* for you. Then we will talk. I don't know what else to say."

Twisting in the blanket, Frank refuses to relax. He fights it. He wants to fight. But he's tired. He reaches up and tenderly touches his father on the cheek.

"You do that, Dad. You do that then." And passes out.

Simon turns, sits on a bench next to a window, and stares into space.

54

The Flavor of Names

Is there a way to unite the two? Is there a way for the two dances to come together? The two cultures? The two ways of seeing? Can they work together, harmoniously, creating something greater than—? Could it be like a jazz fusion? Two cultures, two rhythms, two identities making music. Appreciative of each other. Not threatened by each other. Cooperative rather than competitive. It may have started in be-bob music but now there's jazz fusion in many art forms. Painting, dancing, even making community together. *I'm not here to make you love me. Love whom you will. But I am here to help you. What goes around comes around. It's all good.*

❧

Outside the wind is keening, howling, sighing, crying. The moon's an aspirin.

❧

"What are we doing?" she says snuggling up closer.

"In medical terms?" he yawns.

"Sure, Doc. Go ahead. Go for it."

We're...*In bedum matinum. Postcoitum magnum opium. Delirium tremendum. Ecstasis dulcis...* . We're juxtaposed," says he.

"To what?" says she.

"To each other. We're tumbling, spinning, turning, burning, melting, kvelting—"

He proffers a joint and offers to light it.

"No thanks. I told you I quit."

"Oh, right." He lights the joint for himself and takes a toke.

"Smells nice, though. You got the makings of a good dancer, Will."

"What about the makings of great dancer?" he ventures.

"Be here now," she inclines.

"You're not always being here now."

"I know," she sighs. After a pause, "I'm bisexual, Will."

"Wow."

"That's it, 'Wow'?"

"I never slept with a bisexual before."

Long thoughtful pause on both sides of the bed, then he, "I'm trisexual."

"Trisexual?"

"Yeah, I *try* whenever I can." She doesn't laugh at his joke.

And with that he's on top of her lusty again, and he pins her arms back and looks at her with "trimordial" longing. She tries to move her arms but he's holding her. His sweet longing turns lascivious. As he descends salivating towards her left breast's nipple, she cocks her body and lifts one leg into his groin and keeps lifting from his balls—which causes him to immediately rise up off her. Like a snake she's coiled and sitting on her haunches.

"Whoa," says Will, "I get the point."

"Sorry, it's just a reflex when someone—. I'll lie back down if you want."

Not quite sure how he feels, Will lies on his back, inviting her to snuggle again and rest her head in the crook of his arm. Wynema does so.

"Your name is William, right? Doesn't sound very Jewish."

"No it doesn't. You're absolutely right. Some names just sound more Jewish than others. Not that they actually sound Jewish in and of themselves—it's just that some sound less Jewish than others. It's an important distinction. I'm talking about American first names."

"How so?"

"Well—John doesn't sound Jewish. What Jews would name their sons John, the fourth gospel?"

"That's funny," she says, "because I actually knew a guy in college whose name was John and he was Jewish."

"Probably he was Jonathan, a very Jewish name. John with an H, no irony. Gotta have irony. Stephen works. He's the patron saint of stonemasons. Ever see a Jewish stonemason. Irony. Douglas is okay, but marginal. Melvin, very Jewish, but it's not used much anymore. Alan's good, one L or two, so long as it has two A's. Allen with an E, not good. Think about Allen wrenches. Of course, all the Old Testament names are good. But some are too good, over-the-top, you know, like Jedediah or Uriah. Jeremiah on the other hand—lots of Jeremiahs out there.

"I know lots of Irish Jeremiahs, she interjects.

"Not my fault. Ezekiel, no way. And Amos," he laughs, "no, he made cookies"

"How about Richard?"

"Passable, occasional, doesn't stick out and say No, not Jewish. It's okay. Rick if fine. Ricky, for some reason, the nickname, is way better. Lot of Jews named Ricky. Jerry is good. Jerome is very good. Much better than Gerald. But Jerry is good, like Jerry Lewis, Jerry Seinfeld. Lawrence is good, too. Larry works even better. Myron used to be superb but like Melvin is avoided like the plague."

"And James?"

"Way too New Testament. Jim is very goyish. But strange enough, Luke, not Lucas, is pushing up in the numbers. Lot of Lukes coming in."

"Then how about Matthew?"

"Even more! Huge. I don't understand it. One of the main Gospels. And Mark, too. Also very good. Matthew and Matt are huge. Matthew and Jacob and Isaac are very popular. Gregory asserted itself in the Jewish community for a while, especially in the 60s and 70s, but now is definitely in decline. Daniel, always a winner."

"If Larry is good, how about Harry?"

"Oops there. Wrong turn. Used to be a contender. But Harry or Harold has joined Melvin and Myron and Herbert and Albert. Gone with the eastern seaboard immigrant winds. Oh and I should stick in Sidney, too. Whoosht, gone."

"Wait a minute. You said John didn't work at all. Then what about Jack which is a nickname for John?"

"Ah-ha, Jack. Before John it came from Jacob. Jacob is very good, like I said, so Jack is happening all over the place."

"Dennis?"

"Forget about it. Completely Irish."

"Simon?"

"Simon, Simon, Simon. Right. From Shimon. Big in the New Testament but look at Shimon Peres, Labour Leader in Israel. That tells you it's an Old Testament name too. So that accounts for its recent upsurge."

"Sam?"

"Big. It was big, then it died down. Now it's big again. As is Max. Max is very popular now, even with non-Jews. Go figure."

"Maybe because of Mad Max. How about Andrew?"

"Getting bigger. I don't know why. It could be huge in a year or two. Sort of like Anthony. SUV-driving Jews—and there's more of them than you can imagine—have fallen in love with Tony. So Anthony is a comer."

"Michael?"

"Oh, Michael. It sounds as Christian as you can get and yet it's incredibly popular. Mostly rich Jews though. The poorer ones don't go in for Michael as much. They go for Peter. St. Peter. Weird, uh? Alvin and Alfred used to be good but now they gone the way of Melvin and—"

"Myron!"

"Correct. Very good."

Wynema's out of breath. "Okay, so tell me, because I'm sure you could go on for hours. How does a nice Jewish boy like you get to be named William which sounds so arch and white and British?"

"I'm glad you asked. My father named me after his grandfather Velvel—"

Wynema explodes in stoned-out fiendish glee. "Velvel!? Your real name is Velvel! Wasn't it the name of a mouse—"

"It was the name of a mouse in a cartoon movie or something about coming to America after the Eastern European pogroms. I'd rather not talk about that. Velvel is the Jewish name closest to Wilhelm, the Kaiser, which some German Jews felt obligated to name their sons in the 19th century. But they preferred Velvel and...and all its diminutives. I'm not sure but I think Velvel is the 19th century version of the 18th century eastern European Jewish name of Faivel which we usually use in its diminutive form of Faiveleh."

"Faiveleh?"

"That's right. That's why my grandfather calls me Faiveleh. That's his name for me. If you ever get the urge to call me that, restrain yourself and use the even more diminutive form of Fav. Fav I can go with. But only when we're alone. Deal?"

"Deal."

"What do you want to eat?"

"Lox and bagel?"

"Deal."

Two days later, back in bed.

"You said you were bisexual. Therefore you sleep with women."

"I have sex with whomever I'm attracted to and trust. I've had sex with the Sun."

"You what?"

"It's wonderful. You ought to try it. Wanna see if the Sun will have sex with you?"

"You're talking about masturbation on a hot and sunny day?"

"No. I'm talking about having sexual relations with the Sun."

"What do you mean then by having 'sexual relations'?"

"You're asking me this? What have we been having?"

He becomes a little embarrassed, fumfers, and growls out of frustration.

"Okay, then," she says, "tomorrow is appropriately Sunday. Supposedly we both have the day off. Let's go see if we can have sex with the Sun—together."

55

GET IT OUT OF YOUR SYSTEM

The next day at 11 o'clock, Will drives in his balls-out truck to Mirriamma's to pick up Wynema. He's nervous, thrilled, expectant, dubious, and can't keep from sniggering to himself every few seconds. She startles him upon opening the pickup's door.

"Whah! You startled me." He laughs. "I'm feeling goofy."

She replies, "Good, get it out of your system now."

They drive. In and out and over twisting, crossing, half-invisible dirt tracks that snake off over the *llanos*. A small antelope herd darts out of nowhere in front of them.

"That's a good sign," she says, touching his hand."

"A good sign of what? Is every natural unexpected event a sign for you?"

"Sure."

"How do you figure out what they mean? Who taught you?"

"It's not a 'figuring-out' kind of thing."

"Right. Feeling. I forgot."

"And no one teaches you. It's just something you give yourself over to."

"Someone had to teach you how to do that."

"Everyone, everything teaches you how to do that. It becomes a habit, a yearning, a value, a new way of seeing."

"I don't understand."

"That's right. Now you're getting it."

"Huh?"

"Turn left, turn left, then up that road on the right."

"What road?!"

They climb up out of the high desert into the hills gathering now with taller trees. "There," she whispers, pointing to a jutting escarpment of huge bare rocks glaring in the sun. "That's where we're going."

The invisible road becomes rougher. The power to all wheels digs in. Rocks thrown up by the tires thump loudly against the underside. Will starts with each hit. She doesn't. Dust is kicked up. At one point the truck ruts and slides. "Turn into it," she cries. "Ah, there, that's better."

"I love the power and grab of this truck," he says, then growls softly himself.

"Enjoy it while you can. Over there," she points, "and park. We walk the rest of the way to our...hallowed ground. But don't park it under the trees. They'll weep pitch on it and you'll play hell taking it off."

She tosses him the canteen. He follows her out of the trees onto a natural ledge that rises sharply towards a promontory. He sees there have been campfires here before. A petroglyph of the Sun and Moon passes by his head as he follows her, his excitement rising. He doesn't stop to look. He follows. The tall rocks thin out. They walk out onto a flat place of pale golden sandstone that looks out over the mesa to the right and the mountains to the left. There are only two little clouds in the sky to the south. And, of course—the Sun.

She takes the canteen from him and sets it down carefully under the edge of a jutting flat rock.

She walks out to the edge. The rocks and scree fall away beneath her. He steps up next to her. Vertigo catches him for a second and he steps back quickly. She smiles and reaches a hand to him behind her. He tries again. "Look at that crotch there in the mountains," she says. "That's Blue Dog Pass and there's a road down there that climbs up onto the other side—goes to our sacred lakes. No one goes there without the permission of the War Chief. You'll remember that, won't you? Anyway, that's south and there, riding right above, you see, voilá, the Sun. Close your eyes and feel it."

"I'm not closing my eyes this close to the edge."

"Just hold my hand and close your eyes. For just a second." When he does, she says, "Now just breathe in and say to yourself a few times, 'Beloved Sun, I have come to you with love and respect and gratitude.'"

He does this, or tries to. But after a few seconds he squeezes her hand, gasps, opens his eyes and jumps back, clearly dizzy.

"That's okay," she coos. "Come with me." She leads him back but only a few feet to the flat place in front of the canteen.

She points. "That's the south. Put your feet to the south. You're going to lie here. Push away the rocks and little things you don't want to lie on." She does the same three feet away. "Put the highest point under where your knees are going to go. That's right, about there. Now without looking at me if you can help it, take off your clothes and lie down feet pointing south. Oh, but before you do that let me offer something to the Sun."

She takes a leather pouch from her pocket and takes a pinch of corn meal from the pouch and let it fall away into the wind and over the edge and says something in the old language.... "There. Okay," she says, "now a little water to cool the rocks and connect us to the Earth." She takes the canteen from the flat rock and pours thick lines along where his body and hers will go. "Now take off your clothes and lie down along the wetness and try not to look at me."

She does the same.

Not eagles, but two hawks, mates for life, 500 feet above them, can see them perfectly. They circle, swoop, and come close to colliding. They have already mated so no dalliance for them, only curiosity. Pale and rosy brown and pink the two naked human bodies beneath them. The hawks know this spot. They have eaten a rabbit they caught right there where those humans are now. The female hawk screams once.

Wynema sees the hawks, but she says nothing to Will. She closes her eyes and listens to him breathing. She listens to everything. She must go slowly. She has never taken anyone here before.

After a long time. "Okay, so you just breathe and feel the sun. The warmth of the sun in the rocks and the warmth of the sun in the air."

And then after another long time, "Now reach down and slowly pull up your scrotum gently exposing your perineum to the sun. Rest your hand on the rock again and breathe. Feel the sun. Feel it right there at your perineum. That's the Gate. That's the Gate to the Earth which you're now giving up to the Sun."

It isn't easy for her to talk and give herself over to it at the same time. *I will do this,* she thinks. *I will try not to think of his body. I hope he will not think of mine.*

I will breathe and feel the energy, he says to himself. Suddenly, he involuntarily squeezes and feels a rush of energy entering his penis. "Ahh," he breathes and reaches for her hand. It's only inches away. He takes it and squeezes it. His penis swells. The heat. The Sun. Yes.

As he relaxes his hand, she pushes his hand away and gently lets it slides off onto the warm rock again. "Let the Sun do the work."

Think of the sun, he says to himself, *not her, not her body, not her smooth golden body. The Sun!* he yells inside his head to himself. *Listen to her.*

"Now feel the warmth," she continues, "entering your body. At first the skin all over takes it up. The nerve endings stir and dance. But you can feel it, you can almost see it, sinking deeper through the muscles. You will be tempted to watch the fiery colors dance under your eyelids. But that comes later," she whispers. "The heat of the Sun is seeking out our bones where it will want to store itself for a while. Feel it sinking in. Feel it getting closer. Feel yourself opening again at the Gate. Feel the heat there. Let it in. Let it be joined by the heat rising from the soles of your feet. Feel that heat and the heat entering at your perineum -- feel them join and mix now in your hips. That's the energy we want. Energy follows thought. So just imagine that heat in your hips now migrating towards your penis and testicles."

She says nothing else for a long while. A lizard takes this opportunity to scoot a little closer and stop. As if it were doing pushups with all four legs, the animal rises up and down, up and down.

"Oh God, I do feel it." *And I'm not masturbating,* he laughs quietly silently to himself. *Oh yeah, I feel it. Whoa...mmm...steady...relax the body around my beautiful swelling dick—.*

She hears him now. "Mmmm." She breathes heavier and deeper herself. "Mmmm—" the sound of her sound escapes from her, too.

Every fifth or sixth breath of his he vocalizes softly with a "Mmmm".

Now the heat is theirs. It's all one. The rocks. The air. The sunlight. The hips. Filling them. His hips want to move, just a little. He lets them. She, too. "Mmmm."

Groans softly. Slight movement. Deeper breaths. The Sun takes them, fills them, invests them with power, with light, with color, with sweetness, with intensity. Filling them. Flooding them.

Involuntarily he reaches with his hand to touch himself. His fingers cup his scrotum, his thumb slides underneath is swollen penis. But he doesn't take hold. *I'm not going to masturbate*, he says to himself. *I'm going to let this happen.*

His hand doesn't move. But the energy from his hand kicks in, it feeds the roots, focuses the energy at the roots. *It's okay. Let it happen.* He opens himself. He feel the energy, the sexual energy rise up from his feet, up the inside of his legs, towards his penis, fill his penis and reservoir of energy under his penis. He doesn't think these things now. He just feels it. He hears her, too.

The Sun possesses them both. Now they are more connected to the Sun than to each other. They open themselves to the power of the energy, direct from the Sun to them. Direct! From the seed to the bloom. *From the infinite source to that place in me of regeneration. The Sun loves me!*

Beyond the joyous sexual energy rising in him now, he can hear her moaning softly. He tries to ride with it, in sync with it. But he can't. He can't control himself. The feelings now are too strong. Her sounds become his sounds. They become part of everything entering him now. He gives himself over to it now. He isn't thinking anymore. Thoughts come but they are exploded away just as soon as they would speak. They disappear in a kaleidoscope of colors inside his head, inside his heart, inside his very feet.

She is more in control, which isn't good. *Isn't optimum,* she notes to herself. *I can give myself to the Sun. It is so easy. So powerful. Listening to him, feeling him work it, gets in the way. Can I sort this out? I can sort this out. I can't let go of having to sort this out.*

She feels the Sun enter her womb. She watches it rush in entering her from below. She watches it bifurcate as the sunlight hits her cervix, half veering this way half running off that way. Spinning now in opposite directions the sunlight whips up and spirals away into her fallopian tubes. "Ahhhh," warming herself there, feeding her, nourishing her where she keeps her eggs in her ovaries. "Ahhh..." and a moan escapes her though she doesn't hear it or know it.

He doesn't hear her either. But he feels it. It's part of him now. His hand has fallen again to his side onto the hot rocks. His penis is part of the rock. His penis is the rock on which he lies. The Sun that has entered and filled the rock and now fills him. Waves of the heat from the rocks convect and flood up into him. He thinks of her body. He thinks of the Sun. Her body. The Sun. Back and forth until he isn't thinking of these things anymore one by one. Just beyond the Gate he can hear the wind, the wind that always announces orgasm. He feels it. He wants it. But he needs more stimulation. He stops himself from taking his penis in hand. His hips move. Only his hips and everything else inside him. *Ay-yainnng...ayyaing...ayaain....* His feet reach, his fingers reach...the heat, the overwhelming flooding warmth, the Gate, the light, the buzz, buzzing...the roar...*Ay-yaingg....* His head flails slowly back and forth. His eyes tightly closed. The colors bursting, colors he's never seen before. Beyond bright, past incandescent. A fiery shimmering green and gold he's never seen before—.

And Wynema is rising with him. *He's going, no worries—he did it.* Now she gives herself over to it, to the power she's known, learned to join with...she's happy for him, He's going over, he's doing it... mmm...mmmm...*hunta-yeh, hunta-yeh, hunta-eyeh...* the heat comes—the heat comes—but then she hears him. She hears him coming. Without touching himself. With only the Sun! Only the Sun, whose consciousness includes us.

He gush-cums. Strong deep pulses of his nectar stream out of him back up into the Sky to the Sun.

"AHHHH..." and she feels a few drops of semen like ice hit her shoulder and cheek and lips.

She smiles—she gloats—*he's coming—he comes.* She cools, just enough—the flooding waves of heat pass her by. She got close. He came. She's thrilled. He's gone, gone, gone. He gave himself to the Sun.

They lie there, not yet knowing how happy they are. There is truly no hurry to return. They are gone and they stay gone for a long while. She floating in a wave of otherness, of compassion, for him, for all

things. Blissful. He in a state of amazement, of power, like a speck of
the most intense fire in the far reaches of the coldest space shooting
somewhere at an incredible pace, faster than light itself, as fast as consciousness.

When his breathing changes, she covers his hand with hers.

"I want to make love to you," he says.

"No," says she.

"Okay."

"But you can lick me," she adds, "anywhere, any way, for as long
as you like."

"Okay," he whispers, as he remembers the fires that slowly crept
up the inside of his own thighs and tries to soothe those places on her
now with his tongue.

But he doesn't soothe her. He excites her again. Just so. And she
gives herself to it, to the sunlight now in his tongue. Her wetness
meets and merges with the wetness of his tongue. His tongue pure
sunlight splits her, opens her, reaches for it slowly and finds her lower
heart. Her hands on his shoulders slows him down, gentles him, tunes
him, entrains him. His buttocks rise and fall. His hardness finds the
hardness of the warm rock beneath him. She feels the energy run
through them both. A wind comes up rippling the waves of pleasure
about them. It teaches him her rhythm, the pulse she needs to reconnect to the Sun. Then down from head to the soles of her feet, then up
again through him, into his tongue almost still now, both of them
moaning and crying— "*Hunta-yeh, hunda...hunda, ay-ai-ai*—" and
she comes and gives herself to the Sun. Waves of gratitude to the Sun
course through her, across her, over her, under her—and she whim-
pers softly now—and she sees falling away into the distance a con-
vulsing ball of fire, blue fire, blue fire, receding until suddenly like a
UFO rise quickly towards the Sun, then into the Sun, then return to
the Sun, then become the Sun. Gone.

Her breathing changes. His breathing changes. He lies there, the
side of his face on the inside of her thigh. His thoughts swirl, try to
focus, but swirl away in a jerking motion in sync with a heartbeat
somewhere, someone's, not his, not hers, but pulsing life, gently softening, receding, merging. He relaxes. She relaxes. She puts her hand
on his head. It feels cool to him.

As they drift off into a kind of sleep, the last thing he thinks of is the coolness of her hand.

She stirs. He awakens. It's ever thus.

He looks up to see her touch her lips with her middle finger and wipe off a drop of his semen. She smiles as she licks her finger with her tongue. "Liquid sunlight," she says. He smiles but cannot hold his head up and settles it back onto her golden place and inhales her. The sunlight warms them again. But this time so gently, just to comfort them. To soothe them and release them back into the Earth.

After a while he rolls off and finds a place next to her, their eyes only a few inches apart. He moves to kiss her as her hand moves away reaching for something. As he is about to kiss her, she pours water from the canteen all over him. He screams. He laughs. He yells out loudly as he wrestles with her to grab the canteen. But she is too quick for him, too clever with her knees and elbows. She knows how to keep him away.

"I want you."

"Not today. Today you belong to the Sun. His heat is feminine, too. You gave yourself to it. You will anger him if you take me now. But you did do me good. You got me. I was finally able to let myself go."

"You mean, you didn't come with the Sun?"

"Nope. Only with your tongue. Thank you."

An hour later, the hawks watch how slowly the truck winds its way down the hill. They fly off, hungry again for food. On the hunt.

Inside the truck, he is not driving. She is. He is looking out the passenger window, smiling. *This is a magic place*, he thinks. Then softly, "Boy, you and this place. What a pair. I don't believe it.

"Heh-heh," she chippers.

"I believe it, but I don't believe it."

"H-h-heh."

"I thought we were just going to fuck. I'll never doubt you again."

"Good." She wants to floor it and bounce across the mesa and make him hold on tight for dear life. But she doesn't. She just settles into the seat. She could get to like this truck. But then she thinks of

Peak Oil, and the environment, and looks at her watch. She catches herself and snorts and he asks her, "Huh? Where you at?"

"Running my stock scripts. It's just amazing how human we are after all."

"After all what?"

"Never-mind. I think you're ready."

"Ready for what?"

"For whatever comes next."

And they drive off across the mesa heading to the Pueblo. They pass a dusty sedan parked among some scattered junipers and piñons. The hispanic woman in the back seat rises and falls slow-fucking her man beneath her. She turns her head smiling and watches them pass.

The colors darken slightly. The shadows lengthen. The winds die down. The Earth turns under them.

56

The Silly Nits that Go for His Okey-Doke

A few days later. Sundown. Mirriamma's place. Four people are converging from different directions: two men, Will, and Wynema. The sounds of the night are replaced by soft singing and drumming now coming from within.

Wynema touches Will's elbow, to make sure he lets the villagers enter first.

Trying to hide her apprehension, talking softly, "There's nothing you need to know or think about. In fact, don't think at all."

She laughs nervously at herself. Will nods and otherwise acts slightly more relaxed than he feels.

"So, sit quietly," she whispers. "Otherwise just relax and take it in. You don't have to do anything. Okay? But really, don't say anything, either."

She starts toward the door, but he grasps her hand, gently bringing her back into him. Slowly, with gratitude and serious appreciation, he moves to kiss her. Before their lips touch, she pulls away. Will collects himself. They go in.

Inside the prayer room, there is little light. Mirriamma, chanting with a soft, high, and far-away voice, is shampooing Simon's hair. He sits on a stool, bending forward over a tub. A tall, thin Pueblo woman kneels on the floor, preparing more shampoo prepared from Yucca root.

On a long bench along one wall—a man is drumming. Next to him another man, fingering a fetish;. And further, a woman in a shawl holding three owl's feathers under a black cloth. One of the men who just entered crosses and sits next to the drummer. Carrying a padded drumstick, he joins in the soft, throbbing beat.

Wynema and Will enter the room quietly, respectfully. They see Teo lost in shadow and prayer on the other side.

Now Mirriamma and Simon are sitting on the floor before a ten-inch hole in the ground, praying in ancient words.

Outside, some villagers have gathered. They sit on some garden chairs around a fire. They listen actively. They're part of it. But this is as close as they'll come tonight. Every now and then, when the drumming stops for a moment, or changes its beat, one of them will stand up or stomp a leg or raise an arm and exclaim something, a word or two only, and then resume listening to the drumming.

About an hour later, Simon is slowly dancing with a bird-like, yet heavy and plunging step. There is more smoke in the room now. Cedar smoke and sage.

Will watches enthralled, inhaling long and slow. For a moment, he sees his grandfather dancing, Abraham, not Simon—a 58-year-old Abraham holding a 6-year-old Will in his arms, dancing a Hasidic dance-step. But Teo, Mirriamma, and the others are there in his mind, as well. They pray or simply sit and watch Simon dancing without judgement. But Will sees Abraham—!

Will's head reels as he tries to ground himself. He tries to turn to Wynema, but cannot. A soft agony rises in his face. Until he sees Simon again. Ah, there, he can relax again.

Simon suddenly falls to one knee, grabbing his head, his ear, twisting around, searching, as if struck blind. Widen. Will stiffens. Wynema quickly places her hand on his thigh, calming him. Simon continues to crumble. He collapses prone in front of Will, his arm extending, almost touching Will's foot. Will, instantly the doctor, looks to Wynema. She seems oblivious. Will reaches out and comforts Simon's hand, his fingers moving subtly into pulse-feeling position. Will's face registers concern, as his fingers search with more purpose, more panic. Will looks around. No one else is concerned. Cautiously, he starts to rise. He looks to Mirriamma. She is serene. She smiles slightly with soft assurance, holding up her palm to Will to indicate do nothing.

But Will looks at Simon. He sees his patient unable to breathe, turning blue, veins bulging—

Everyone seems to be slowed down into a dangerous state.

But not Will. There's panic gnarling into his face. He lurches toward Simon, his arms outreached. Mirriamma purses and points her lips fiercely, then raises her hand, palm-out, towards Will. Wynema, quickly, instinctively, does the same. Mirriamma expels a big breath of air. In that moment, Will loses all control of his body. He falls, almost gracefully, to the ground. Neither Mirriamma nor Wynema moves—until a subtle reaction betrays Wynema's realization of the power she's just participated in. Mirriamma is immobile, unconcerned, focused. No one speaks. Zoom out slowly...freeze frame.

That night late 60 miles away in Santa Fe, in an old warehouse that used to belong to the railroad, Frank is performing. He is costumed as a 50-year-old Indian woman scrubbing clothes in a big galvanized tub. He and the tub are on a small carousel controlled by a computer that matches a 360° rotation with—on the video screens behind him—a 360° camera-pan within a dirty, dilapidated house on an eastern Montana reservation. Go Chumba!

As the carousel and pan begin, Frank invests his character: "I'm a half-breed. Been that way for half a century. So am I a white girl with dirty blood, or an Indian with only half a chance to make it to somebody's happy hunting grounds? I grew up in South Dakota. Yankton Sioux on one side, Chicago plumber on the other. Raised Indian. Raised white. Same thing. Pickup trucks, gun racks, cowboy boots, flannel shirts...squatting in the badlands. Bone-tired, dirt-poor, hairpulling...just trying to survive. A lot of rage on the reservation, telling me to get out because I'm too white. But now it's heaven-on-earth to be native...like being from some space planet and people want you to be big medicine and do sweats and dance and drum. And they'll pay. It's racist, though. It's racist. My grandfathers killed my grandfathers...and they all killed the medicine men. The hoop was broken. It was not passed on. Hell, we were too ashamed in the 40s and 50s to learn from the old ones. We wanted brand new pickup trucks, TV, a house with a picture window. We wanted to pee indoors. Back then, guys my age, old enough now to be elders, they didn't learn the old ways of rattle, drum, and secret words. I drank beer with them and bumped up and down in the back-seats of their raked-out Chevies, out in the snow-covered prairies of Big Sky country. Those guys didn't know jack shit about none of that stuff. Didn't care neither. Why should they? What would it get you? Wave an eagle feather, pay your car payment? Look what it got the grandfathers. Dead is what. So if you hear differently from some shaman guy, you can bet there's an angle to it. An easy way to make a buck. He may know plenty about Indian stories and the old ways...so do I. Read it in a book.

Frank steps into the tub. "My Indian grandparents died before I knew them. Don't even know what they were called. Never bothered to find out."

He sighs. "Still, I guess your shaman earns his keep, putting up with the silly nits that go for his okey-doke."

Black out.

Act IV

It's All Sacred

But in reality we are accompanied
by the whole universe.
~Ruth St. Denis

57

SHUT-UP AND DANCE

"The Tayelet"

Did caravans from Egypt
and the Negev once bring honey?
The bee that alights on his knee,
an oasis from flight, seems
to confirm this. A bee
can take a long time to die,
a hive, longer. Connections alive
between the hives
even longer. The death of a bee,
death of a blink of the Eye of Man.
Every atom in a hammer
has just been struck.

From the moment they enter the Club—stoned, drunk, or straight—the audience tonight is hearing the sounds that Chumba want them to hear. They are low and work subliminally at first. But they are digitally enhanced and, as there are small, deep-presence speakers everywhere, wall-to-wall. Their purpose: to set up the scene subconsciously, to align the molecules, to redirect and reframe the doors of perception and otherwise charge up and engorge certain limbic reflexes and resources. Chumba Ito is nothing if not a four-dimensional psycho-engineer.

So what does Chumba have in store tonight? If I said imagine the sounds of a Las Vegas casino gaming room, you'd be more than half-way there. But the sounds of a casino on an Indian reservation are not quite the same. The ambient volume here is lower by 20 percent, and there is more chit-chat and telling of jokes, in Spanish, English, and the native tongue. Add peradventure a sprig of amazed Danish traveler, the mewlings of a devoted local who believes she should be rewarded with more wins for her loyalty in losing, and the distant screeching of an irate macaw that belongs to the floor manager—well, that's the audio track that Chumba has prepared for Frank's performance tonight at Gingowey's Powwow Club just outside Denver on County Road 416.

Chumba Ito does a superb job of sound editing, and he has no doubts that Frank appreciates his work. Though Frank doesn't say so often, once or twice a year he breaks down into complete if drunken honesty and cries and swears he'd be nothing without Chumba's sounds, lights, and multimedia video. "Nothing. I don't exist without your sounds."

Listen now to how Chumba's even included the sounds of tourist buses arriving and unloading in front of casinos. It's a packed house at Gingowey's. The regular customers have learned how to participate in and add to these preliminary mood-sets. The newbies behave like polite visitors in a celebrated exotic zoo. The remotely-articulated stage lights move slowly as if hunting for something. They mimic the garish primary colors of the electronic slot machines. Moods are being adjusted. Chumba is God and Frank his Prophet Excelsiah.

Chumba pushes a button and eases a slider and the multi-screen monitors they've set up in the Powwow Club flicker alive to captivate the travelers. Now we see visuals to match the sounds: the buses and cars arriving into the parking lot of some Casino and unload. Gamblers coming and going—some obviously amateurs, some (not so obviously) pros. Incessant neon flashing, digital signage exploding. Chumba runs a rapid montage of a casino in action, inside and out.

Anglos, Hispanics, Afro-American. A few high-style Natives in business suits talk with other suits. But mostly poor working stiffs, slammed high-speed into slow-motion, with a purpose. Extreme close-ups of slot-addicts snarling-wincing at the evil machines that com-

pulse them on and on and suck them dry. Where the hell did Chumba get all this footage? Casinos don't allow video-takers; with their own surveillance cameras watching, they're onto the videolopers in a trice. How does he get them—unscathed?

Some say that Chumba has two hidden cameras on his person running at all times—one in the corner of the sunglasses he wears and one in the device he uses to tie up his hair at the back of his head. He is a video-ninja: in and out, getting what he needs quickly.

He finds a rhythm in the flashing lights and repetitive sounds, and softly fades up Indian trance-music. Frank stalks on—the stage lights hit him. The monitors dim fifty-percent. The show is engaged and Frank lays it on.

"Hey, wake up! Open your TV-glued eyes. I am the last of your Mohican-do-anythings, left here as the final ritual flashing reminder that you have salvation at your technology-tortured fingertips...."

The image on the screens shifts to a wide, high-angle view of a busy casino gaming floor. When Frank points incriminatingly at the screen, the image smashes to a close-up of the three spinning wheels of an old-time slot machine slowing down.

Frank is whispering, but with Chumba's help at the controls his wireless mic gives his whisper presence and a spectral nuance. Chumba now tortures a little hip-hop into the space music.

"Look to me! I am Injun Joe, Crazy Horse, Christ on a stick, Tonto, old Iron Eyes crying, doomed to die for your pass-the-buck/ make-a-buck quick-winning sins. Snake-eyes and bones, genuine Injun mega-memes—you lose! By this time, next time, sometime, there will be but splat left of us. Crapped-out. Thin winnings. Oh, yes, weep, weep for the coal miner's canary, the last of his tribe, the Indian, a spotted owl, chewed up and spit out by sacred progress. Revered and almost loved by the power-paradigm the American Indian is. Finally, all-l-l-l gone, reservations cancelled, we become your heritage, proudly sported by baseball teams so bravely named, coin collected, hood ornamented, ultimately selected for the U.S. Hall of Shame."

He points at his listeners one by one. "And the last among us will be the first to forgive, as even I bless you, children, for you have fuck-ing sinned." For one blinding second, Chumba's lights flash like light-ning and the sounds of bolts cracking and thunder and a synthesized

Wagnerian arpeggio compressed into that one brief second! Frank wheels, stops, "Oh. You've also never apologized."

The multi-media screens behind him dissolve to a peaceful view of Santa Lucîa Pueblo at sunrise. Smoke rising from the adobe houses. Quiet. Snug. Archetypal.

"And now let's begin today's lesson in permaculture—"

Outside Mirriamma's house, Teo's grandson, Rio, is standing at a window peering in as inconspicuously as he can.

Inside Mirriamma's prayer room, on a buffalo hide covered day-bed, under a blanket, Will sleeps, his head almost off one end, his feet over the other. Sitting next to him, her aged hands holding a preserved raptor's wing and an abalone shell full of smoldering herbs, Mirriamma flicks smoke along his entire length. Will opens his eyes abruptly and sees Ethel Goodmorning, an associate of Mirriamma's, holding his hand and smiling at him with more than a couple of teeth missing. Ethel turns to Jerry, Teo's son-in-law, who stands grinning nearby.

These are the first things Will sees upon regaining consciousness. He sits bolt upright but is immediately dizzy. He grabs what he can sitting on the edge of the bed.

"They've gone t'our house, Doctor" says Jerry enthusiastically. "Tessie's baby's come! Teo and Wynema—they sent me to get you. And Jolene says our baby's gonna come real soon, too!"

Will shifts around and looks to the center of the room. He recoils when a bright shaft of early morning sun dazzles him through the whiffs rising from last night's fire-pit. He tries to rise, but cannot.

Mirriamma bends over and looks him very closely in his eyes, then, "You'll be all right," she says with simple professional confidence and disappears into another room.

Will tries very hard to put it all together. He stands, reels. Jerry steps in under him.

"Hey, you know she said you'd be like drunk, so, ha!—I guess you'll be okay then."

"Tessie said that?"

"No, Mirriamma. Tessie had the baby."

"The baby. Is it all right?"

"A boy! Popped out like a buttered egg."

Outside, at Jerry's pickup, Will grabs the doorjamb as vertigo hits again. Rio regards Will's height with all the more awe and curiosity as it wavers and threatens to fall.

Jerry gets into the driver's seat, but Will just sits there, his door still opened.

"Rio," is all Jerry says. The boy jumps out of the back, carefully closing Will's door, then quickly jumping back in.

Jerry hands Will a watch. "Here ya go. Guess you broke the crystal on your watch last night. Oh, and Louisa says if you come now you can scour the baby yourself, whatever that is, but I can take you home, if you want."

Will, absently pocketing his watch, "Scour the baby? Oh, the Apgar score. No, yeah, I'm coming—I guess. The hospital?"

"No way! At home!"

⁂

Teo's living room has become a birthing room. A few grandmothers sit softly singing a prayer. Tessie lies beautifully postpartum, propped up, looking at Wynema, who holds the new baby for Will as he examines him. Still off-balance, he steps back, his job done, and becomes self-conscious. Tessie, Teo, Louisa, and now Mirriamma and Wynema, are clearly avoiding his eyes. It's too soon for personal connection.

Teo, awkward but happy beyond words, relieves the moment. "C'mon, ever'one, let's have some food and drink! I hope Jolene waits a day or two to have her baby. I'm wiped out."

"You?!" someone asks. "What'd you do? Something?"

Laughter. Louisa follows Mirriamma into a side room. Wynema looks at Will, then follows the other women out. Teo leads folks to the food. Dayone and Simon enter. Simon, a spring in his step, is surprisingly happy, social, and enthusiastic.

Tall Will takes this opportunity to become very small. He sits on a low stool next to the singing women and disappears inside himself as he considers everything. He looks at his watch and takes his own pulse—until he realizes his watch has stopped. Broken. He head swims.

Simon and Teo just stand next to the dining room table, stare and squirm, bursting with joy and tears, and can't say a word, except bite their lips and nod. A few relatives and close neighbors step in for congratulations. Teo waves to them and points to the food. He turns to Simon.

"You looking strong."

"I'm very strong. And the baby?"

"Strong. I'm 56 and I have another baby! Twenty-four years later. Bam! A son."

"This is good. This can only be good."

Simon sees Will subtly gesturing to gain his attention. When a neighbor talks to Teo, Simon sidles away towards Will.

They exit the house and walk towards the workshop area. Simon takes a deep, glad-to-be-alive breath, and smiles. For a moment, Will cannot find the words— "What happened to me last night?"

Simon turns, steps, stops, nods, gathers his thoughts. "Do you feel good or bad? I feel real good myself."

"I'm not sure. I collapsed, right?"

"Took four of us to put you in a bed."

Will rubs himself, feels himself, ponders, "The last thing I remember...I thought you were in trouble. I—"

"I guess I went with the helpers."

"You went where?"

Simon searches his mind. "I was journeying, and you, you moved into Grandmother's fog at the wrong time."

"Fog? What are you talking about? I got up, went to you, and more like walked into a wall or—or someone hit me. I don't know."

"You don't remember nothing else? Hmmm. How can I explain something I don't understand in a way you, a doctor, understand things?"

"Well, you've got to."

"The Hands-in-the-Dirt *Pahos* business was very good for me."

"Was something in the smoke? Did I—did I drink something? Or did I somehow pass out and hit my head?"

"When I was a boy I saw my grandfather do the same thing like that to Hector Mirabal the day Hector went crazy and killed all his horses with a bowie knife."

"Do what!? What same thing!?"

"Stopped him from getting hurt."

"What stopped him!?"

"Yes—that is an important question. Yes. I see that now."

Simon extends his hand and checks it for steadiness, then feels own pulse. He starts to breathe deeply and quickly.

"What the hell are you doing?"

"Hyperventilating myself a little bit."

"Why?"

"'Cause I feel like treating myself to a little extra oxygen, I guess. I'm trusting myself more these days. Can you tell?"

"How come you didn't send for an ambulance?"

"For you or me?"

"Me! I mean, people don't just collapse like that." Off Simon's simple shrug, "Geez, Simon, I thought your aneurysm blew right there in that—that ritual."

Simon smiles big. "Well, that was a healing more than a ritual, I think. You'll get it, don't worry. If you check me now, you won't find any weakness here anymore, least not for a while."

Simon places Will's hand on his solar plexus. Will's eyes shoot open wide as he jerks back.

"What you got?" Simon asks innocently.

Will sits down on a bench. "I felt something."

"Yeah, me, I hope. Did it feel good or bad?"

"How do I know? I never felt it before."

"My God, man, that's the most basic thing about being alive. Feel good, feel bad, I mean—you oughta know what you felt felt was good or not."

"I don't know! Something moved and something—buzzed or tingled. Never felt that before! —It didn't feel bad."

Simon steps left, steps right, faces Will. "Good! Ya see, it takes faith." He slaps Will on the shoulder, surprising him. "That's it! Last night—you got hit by somebody else's act of faith. You can feel it, eh? Can't say it happens all the time. Happens in the moment. Not everybody can do it, I suppose. That prayer, all last night, what we gave ourselves to, kinda turned us into tubes that take in power, maybe you call it energy—you know, MC squared 'n all that. Came to me one way, hit you in another. Mirriamma has a clean tube. Lot of power. Helped me to find my faith again—for my family, for my tribe—before I go to the other side. I had help. Now I'm fine. You were on your own. Sorry 'bout that."

Will stands, steps back, and looks Simon up and down. "You look all right, I admit that. Maybe better than I've seen you in weeks, but—but I feel like a fool, like I just slobbered all over myself. God! If you're healed, I want to know how."

Simon nods, smiles. "Healed is one thing. Helped is another. I'd be grateful for either."

Will, exasperated, turns unsteadily and heads around the side of the house towards the front. Simon follows.

"Where's my truck? Did I bring my truck?"

"I drove it here. Nice truck. Did I tell you you got a real nice truck?"

"I want an explanation."

"Forget explanations. Just let yourself dance."

Wynema is talking on her cell with her father in Montana.

"...So, that's what I've been up to, Dad."

"I don't understand everything you do. Never have. But I have confidence in you. You know what you're doing. I trust your instincts."

"Thanks."

"If you're not going to Cambridge this year, what're the chances of you giving us a visit up here some time?"

"Pretty good, first chance I get to visit anybody."

"I believe in you."

"I know."

"When your mother was dying, she told me those words. She meant them. And I mean them."

"I know. But I'm not sure of anything, really. I'm not as confident as you."

"That's okay. You doing any sweats?"

"That's what's holding me together, I think. Mirriamma loves sweats. So I do one for us quite often. I picked a river rock, though, and it exploded."

He laughs.

"If you find that little yellow dream pillow of mine, would you send it?"

"No problem."

"The center of the picture is shifting for me, Papa."

He thinks about it. "That right? What do you make of it?"

"Could change the future history of your grandchildren."

"What will be will be. As long as you're doing sweats, you'll make the right choice."

"You just saying that?"

"I'm serious."

"I didn't call too early?"

"What you think?"

"I gotta go."

"Talk to you later, my daughter."

"Love you, Dad."

Above the village, on one of the jutting ledges on one of the flanks of the big mountain, Wynema sits looking at her cellphone. *Should I take the red pill...or the blue?* She pushes the green button.

"Hey, you," answers Alána's sweet voice.

"Hi."

"Hi."

Wynema takes a deep breath. "I know I haven't called. I'm sorry."

"You bad. What am I to think?"

"That I'm confused. That there's a lot happening that I don't understand."

"Maybe I could have helped. *C'est pour ça les amis, alors.*"

Wynema twists and turns. "I know. I'm sorry. But I wanted to confront the changes by myself. Now I don't know if that was a good idea."

"Do you love him?"

"Of course." After a long pause, she continues. "Everyone thinks love is a simple concept. *L'amour est tellement simple.* It's not. I love you. I love my father. And Will—his name is Will—a few others. And—and I love Mirriamma. I understand my connection to all of them, and you—but not Mirriamma."

"I don't follow you."

"I know what each of you means to me. How you fit inside me." Another pause. "She's my great-auntie and all that, but that's not my relationship to her."

"Somehow I think it's going to be a lot longer before I see you."

"The way I think and see things—they're changing. The way I re-act to—to everything, I—"

"I could have told you that. You should have called."

"I know."

"Hm. I forgive you. Forget it. Actually, there's nothing to forgive you for. Something else is going on. Something important. When you want me to come out?"

Wynema sighs. "I don't know."

"Let's look at our calendars. I'll call you."

Wynema brightens. "Okay. I love you,"

"You're full of it."

Wynema is taken off-guard. "Huh?"

"Love. You're full of love. I feel ya."

"You love me, too?" asks Wynema shyly.

"Yeah. I love you, too."

"I'll call you soon."

"Bye."

"Bye."

Will is on the roof of his house, moving mindlessly along the edge, from one corner to the other. He's talking on his cell to Jahbig.

"I dunno. It's been weird."

"You haven't returned email or answered my messages in days or weeks or months!"

"C'mon, Jah, it's been a few days."

"More than a week."

"Okay, okay, relax. I almost died."

"You what?!"

"Can't talk about it. Confidential. Well, not confidential—but re-ligious. Can't talk about religious practices here."

"You doing the ganja, mon."

"Hardly at all. This place is trippy all on its own."

"Welcome to the real world, bruddah. You be jammin', mon."

"Shut-up. Listen. Any chance of you coming out here, if only for the week-end?"

"I don't think so. Not until next month. Whazzup with you?"

"Nothing. I don't know. I just want to talk."

"You in trouble? Talk."

"Nevermind. I'll be okay."

"Now you really got me worrying."

"Can you come out? I'm in love."

"Then you don't want me coming out there, you fool. You dig it, mon. Just don't tell me it's an Indian woman."

"I am seriously in love. I am so seriously in love. I thought love was supposed to make you feel like you're in heaven. But I feel like I'm at the center of the Big Bang of Creation—"

"Hold on. Hold on! Did you say 'The Big Bang of Creation'? Ha! I just had to repeat that."

"No, it's just that everything—I mean, her smell drives me crazy. I mean, you talk about altered states of consciousness. Okay, okay—you call them pheromones, Doctor—but I'm telling you direct into my brain. Slam! It's immediate. I've got to research that. Nah, forget about research. More powerful than LSD. Her energy and my energy—and even her knowledge and my knowledge, her skills and talents and mine—dude, I'm telling you, the—the whole thing is cosmic. See, ya never thought I'd ever use the word "cosmic", did ya?"

"No, you got that right."

"I mean, our destinies, hers and mine, so clearly come together and form something bigger than both of us!" Then softer, "I'm serious, Jah-mon, I can see the future and I want it!"

"Lighten up, mon, you're scarin' me. Hm. On the other hand—sounds pretty good." There is a long pause. Jahbig shifts. "Like I said, are we talking Indian princess here?"

"She's half Pueblo, half Sioux."

"You're in trouble, mon! Maybe you should come out *here* for a while."

"If this can work, we'll be bringing together the Alpha and Omega of medical and healing sciences. We'll sleep it and eat it and live it and love it—and out of it something different from any of them will be born. The next species of human beings, Jah! Do you hear what I'm saying?! E-vo-lu-tion!"

"I'm hearing the biggest fucking romantic that I ever hope to see. I don't know whether you found the love of your life—or just a good life of lovin'. But, hey, mon, I'm glad you're happy."

"Happy? Yeah, I'm happy, but I'm more than happy, I'm beyond happy. I'm weirded out, haven't a clue what I'm doing here as a doctor, but I've found the love of a lifetime and—"

"Can I give you some advice?"

"No. Definitely not. But thanks for offering—"

"Will! Watch the river. You hear me? Just do your work and watch the river. How's the old man, your friend with the aneurysm?"

"Simon. Well, yes, something happened—I mean, no, we haven't done it yet, the aneurism, but—"

"Whazzup wi' dat?"

"There's no way I can explain it to you. None. I wouldn't know where to—. Do you know how the Chinese can take out a thyroid without any anesthesia? Just with acupuncture? Or how a hundred-and-fifty pound Chi Kung master can drop a 250 pound man with the flick of a few fingers? Well, I think something like that happened to me."

"You learning Chi Kung, mon? That's good."

"No! I just got dropped, knocked-out, you know, rendered unconscious, from across the room, by an 88-year-old woman."

"You fell in love with an 88-year-old woman?!"

"No! Nevermind. Thanks, I feel better already. Go back to work. I hear a 'code blue' behind you."

"They got it covered. They got everything covered over here. You need anything? I bet I could get you a new SynTech Defibrillator for cost. I know the rep."

"Jah."

"Yeah, mon?"

"I can't get Simon to go to the hospital for that patch on his aorta. I can't get him into the OR."

"Is he afraid?"

"He's not afraid. He doesn't care if he dies. He just says he wants to do something for his tribe—I don't know what—before he dies.

and he trusts this medicine woman here to keep him alive until after their Feast Day, their Saint's Day. My boss, Steve Cutter—I told you about him, great cardio-man—he wants to do him like yesterday and is getting plenty pissed at me for not getting him on the table. But with Simon, it's not money, insurance, bad experiences, or religion—he just won't do it unless I tell him it's 100 percent certain."

"Well, you can't. It isn't. It's 80 percent, maybe 90—maybe only 70 percent out there. What's his problem—besides the aneurysm?"

"He says the medicine woman, the *curandera* here, is 100 percent."

"I don't understand a damn thing you're sayin', Will, but it sounds plenty strange. Is any of this complicated by your falling in love?"

"I don't think so. Other other hand, everything is complicated by that."

"Oops, now they *are* calling me, certain. Gotta go. So, are you coming out here or am I coming back there? You sound pathetic. Check your calendar. I could maybe get four or five day break the weekend of October 17ᵗʰ."

Will thinks for a moment, then, "That's great! Because I think there's some special doings going on here that weekend. Might be a great day to be here, show you around. I'll check it out."

Will hangs up with a big smile—which instantly disappears.

Wynema, in front of the Clinic, a few days later, is guiding an older couple into the clinic.

As she exits, Will rushes out to catch her. "Hey."

"Hey. Just brought the Romeros in, Juan and Lucy. They have a weird rash and Mirriamma wants you to look at it."

"Sure. I'm feeling better. You?"

"I'm feeling great."

"I still have a lot of questions."

"Of course, you do. Want to go dancing tonight?"

"What kind of dancing?"

"Any kind. Just all-out shake-it-loose dancing."

"Okay. Let's get the kinks out."

"Good. Oh, my friend, Alána, is coming for a visit."

"When?"

"I dunno. Sometime in the next couple of months. Soon, I hope. We haven't decided."

"Could you ask her to come on October 17?"

"Why October 17th?"

"Because that's the day my best friend may coming for a visit. You know, Jahbig. The Jamaican, OB/GYN."

"Ahhh, I see."

"You do?"

"October 18th is also our Feast Day. Good day to show our friends where we live."

"Yeah, that's what I thought. Cool."

⁓

Wynema and Alána are skyping, just hooked up.

Alána leans closer to her computer. "Do me a favor."

"What?"

"Move that light behind you to your right, a little bit, and aim it up a bit."

Wynema is embarrassed. "Come on, gal! Forget the staging."

"No. When you're lit right it's like food to me. Candy. Drugs."

"So, I have a date for you, if you can make it. How's October 17th?"

"And why that date?"

"Because the 18th is Feast Day here. It's a good day for first-timers to see our pueblo. And Will is having his best friend visit that weekend, and I want to give them time together, and Will, he's a little clingy—in a *good* way—so when they're together, I'll have you. Would it work?"

"Yeah, but—give me more. Give me something to think about before I get there. I don't want to give you cheap and easy answers all on the quick."

"I don't want any answers. I just want to be with you."

"Give me more—for my sake, not yours. It's Mirriamma, isn't it?"

"Yes." She pauses. "I know she's an old Indian woman who's very smart and caring. And she has a very special place here among her community—I told you, the medicine woman here."

"And everybody loves her."

"No, actually, not everyone loves her. Some haven't a clue who or what she is. And there are some who are afraid of her."

"So she interests you. Maybe more than your sign language project and Cambridge and—?"

"No. That's not it. Well, maybe it is, in a way. My connection to my work—I've become very conscious of my connection to my work. It's taking me over, sorta—kinda like maternity takes over a new mother. Hard to describe."

"Those are the best kinds."

"Huh?"

"Of connections—the ones that are hard to describe."

"Oh. Yeah. Right. Thanks."

"So October 17th, then?"

"We'll pick you both up. In Albuquerque. See if you can get the United flight that arrives around 11 P.M. I miss you."

"Yum."

Wynema lowers the phone and shakes her head a little, and smiles. But the smile disappears within seconds. *She knows. That's why she's not jealous. She knows. She knows Will isn't a threat. Now she knows...that Mirriamma is.*

She reaches out, spins the wheel of her iPod, searching for the right song. Then it hits her. She finds the song and pushes a button: Buffy Sainte-Marie.

"*Little wheel spin and spin, big wheel turn around around. Hearts they shrink, pockets swell, everybody know, and nobody tell. Blame the angels, blame the fates, blame the Jews or your sister Kate. Teach your children who to hate, and the big wheel turn around around. Little wheel spin and spin, big wheel turn around around.*"

Will's in his office, his door open. Lot of clinic action in the hallway. He's eating a huge, colorful, fresh salad for lunch. He's on the cell with Jahbig. "...So, You're coming in, October 17, on United 2324, arriving 10:30 P.M. We'll pick you up at Albuquerque International. Then we be cruisin' across the high desert, just the four of us, into the night—."

"The four of us?"

"Yeah, you'll get to meet Wynema's best friend, Alána. She arrives an hour later, also on United. I can't wait to see you, man."

In autumn, high up on the flanks of the tallest mountains, the aspens indulge themselves in a frenzied display of harvest colors. Fire on the mountain. Like moths, people are drawn to look and behold, to visit, walk, and play.

A few villagers still plant a few relatively large fields, with grasses for their cattle. This is the time of year for harvesting. Some pueblos—not San Lucas—maintain small herds of buffalo, for meat, but mostly for love, as a reminder.

In the smaller gardens, too. Some villagers have built or bought small greenhouses, for extending their growing seasons. Some are homemade, out of plastic over hoops of PVC or old windows. Very few have ventilation windows that open and close automatically according to the temperature and humidity.

Time to bring in the apples.

A harvest time for Will, too. He has to incorporate what's happened to him. The *Pahos* healing. Falling in love. Feeling more comfortable at work. How to get Simon to have his operation. So much. Too much? How to make sense of it all.

The lovers get some time by themselves. Wynema takes him up into the aspens. She asks that they not speak today. A silent day. All Will wants to do is express his love.

"I'm bursting. I gotta tell you how much—."

She covers his mouth with her fragrant hand. "Transmute it," she says as she bends down and gives him a leaf that looks like a spider's web on fire.

Will sits in a comfortable chair next to the corner fireplace, reading a book by a doctor called *Theft of the Spirit*. Wynema bought it for him. It will take a second reading before he lets himself understand its simple message.

He runs up the mountain with stronger legs and lungs.

❧

He's more at ease with his patients. Louisa tells him so.

❧

Wynema is up on the mountain overlooking the village where she was born. In a meadow—a shelf, a shoulder off the mountain, backed by canyon walls. Above her is that cleft in the cliff where a dozen years ago she engineered the wind to bring water to the high-lying, sacred cornfield. That field's been fallow for a long time.

She listens as deeply as she can to the sounds here. She wants to hear the grass and all the plants grow. And she is studying these plants every day, from a traditional as well as a scientific perspective.

For the moment she is at peace. There is a gentle, constant wind. There are smells that connect everything. She pushes doubt aside and affirms everything. She knows how afraid she's been, and how angry—but those are not even memories right now.

She watches magpies come and go, strutting, pecking, strutting, pecking. She laughs when it strikes her that the magpie is a West Point cadet always on parade. She dated a cadet three years ago whose name was Coster. The innocent irony of the sound of that name never left her alone.

Today, she looks out over her village...and feels it.

"I could use some help," comes Mirriamma's voice from not far away.

Mirriamma uses a walking stick. With its aid, she can bend over and pick the plants and flowers she's looking for. "Here's one you'll know."

Wynema looks at it until it hits. "Oh, yeah, this is hops."

"*Ta-khwe-ta-tani.* We use it with rose petals and mugwort to make 'dream pillows'."

"I used to have a cousin here, Gloria, who ran away with a crazy Kiowa just before I left. She gave me a dream pillow. I still have it at my dad's house. I asked him to send it to me."

Mirriamma beckons Wynema to come closer, and whispers, "Did you know it's related to ma-ri-juana?"

"Hops? As a matter-of-fact, I did."

❧

A few minutes later and further into the meadow, "Ah-ha!" announces Mirriamma. "I found it! This one with gray sometimes white leaves and its wooly flower we used to let our sheep eat all the time. But if you take it and boil it down and mix it with fat or lard, it's good for burns. Spread it on the forehead for fever, too."

"I'll bet that's called Winterfat," says Wynema remembering. "I heard Jerry Ortiz talking about it, I think."

"He's Navajo."

"I know that."

"Sometimes it's good to know that."

❧

"See that pink flower, nodding off that tough, little stalk? We call it *honka-di-no*, the fart flower, because we use it to relieve too much bad gas. But we also use it for fat ankles."

"Edema? Swollen ankles?" Off Mirriamma's nod, "Ah, a diuretic." Wynema plucks a little flower and crushes between her fingers. "It smells like an onion."

"Yeah, lotsa people like the flowers in salads and soups."

❧

"Is this Lizard Tail?" asks Wynema as she steps over some seepage from a spring. "It has little white flowers and yellow sun-cones, crawling along the ground next to the water."

"The root of that plant is powerful. We brew it up to treat ulcers, indigestion, and even lung complaints. And you can dry it, too, all of it, and powder it and use it against infection."

Wynema is impressed. "A disinfectant?"

"Yeah, that, too, I guess."

"I like its smell."

❧

"I think this one is called Prairie Clover, but it's more like a pea than clover. Look, it has a pea-pod with two little seeds in it."

"Some people make a tea and drink it, but I use it on the chest."

"As a poultice? For what?"

"For better breathing."

❧

Wynema stands on the precipitous edge looking out.

Mirriamma points to Wynema's feet. "That's Ricegrass you're standing on, and over there, dancing in the wind. We used to harvest this in the spring, cooked it and ate it like mush. It's no good this time of year."

&

"See those tall hot-pink flowers? That's Mosquito Plant. Use the leaves to make insect repellent."

&

Some hours later, back home, Wynema helps Mirriamma out of the car and into the house. The wind is blowing fiercely. The older woman holds her scarf one. "Where'd that wind come from? Glad it didn't bother us this afternoon. We did good."

"We did. Let's sort them at the table. I'm going to look them up in this book I just got."

Inside, Mirriamma settles into her kitchen chair on one side of the table. "You do that. You do that."

Wynema starts to unpack the cardboard boxes. Carefully, she tries to order then across the table. Her new, big book of botany within reach.

&

"Here's one I recognize. Pussytoes."

"We call that *Ateh-nat-t'ka*, or Little Leaf. I make a tea of it for people with sour blood."

"What's that?"

"I don't know, but I know it when I see it."

"That's helpful."

"We got another one like this, but it has pink flowers, not white. That one we use as an eyewash."

"For what kind of things?"

"For when the eyes look like they need to be washed out."

Wynema thinks for a moment, then taps her forehead and says "Duh."

&

"That one is like the *Ka-ni-gonkta*, but we call it *Kta-bo-sati*, because it's waxy and the color of butter. If you chew the long-root that grows between each plant, you can cure the lung irritation."

"Like pleurisy?"

"Yeah, I think that's what it is."

"This little daisy-like flower smells like chocolate."
"*You can eat the leaves. Lot a people used to plant them around their gardens. My father did, because he thought the deer were afraid of it. I dunno 'bout that. Butterflies like it, though.*"

"And this daisy?"
"Uhn. See it has the bigger leaves. I forget what we call it, but chew it up and put it on snake bites. It'll keep fleas off your dogs, too."

"This one looks kinda like that Knotweed we saw yesterday."
"Use it as a heart medicine for a weak heart. Simon's father told me he finds it out where he goes hunting the pronghorn. I like that meat, pronghorn. Simon's father wasn't all that bad, you know. We think he has Navajo blood back there somewheres."

"My God, this has to be another Knotweed."
"Yup. We call it *ti-ni-fta-mo*."
"Blood-stop?"
"Yup. Can you guess why?"
"Probably has a lot of vitamin K and stops bleeding and excessive menstruation."
"Bingo!"

Mirriamma yawns. "That crazy trader, you know, Phipps, he brought me some of this and said it was rare and was used by the Comanches and Apaches for shampoo. I know that. What's he think, anyway?! He called it Buckbrush. We call it *Sa-la-amato* because if you make a tea it will shrink—what do you call them—?" She points under her jaw and to her armpit.
"Oh, you mean lymph glands?"
"Yeah, maybe. People who bleed too fast can use it, too. This is another one that Phipps keeps bringing me."
"He creeps me out."

"He just wants another of my pots. He thinks I make pots for money. I don't have time to make money. Anyway, he called it Monkeyflower. Why don't he bring me a monkey? I'd like that! Anyway, we used to use it some way, but I forget. But I like to put the flowers in my salads when I find them myself. Fresh and spicy."

Wynema pulls out her laptop and plugs it in on the opposite side of the table.

Mirriamma picks up another cutting. "Everyone calls this Milkweed. We call it *Ka-ni-gonkta*."

"Star-fire?"

"Yeah, that's right. Always five points to the pink flower. My grandfather Juan G. used to use the milky sap like a chewing gum. We used to use it in cooking all the time. But if you feed it to cows and horses they'll get sick. Won't die, though."

"This blue-gray agave, like the yucca," Wynema says looking at her big book, "grows one flower every 25 years."

"My cousins, on my husband's side, they knew how to make it to get drunk. Not very pretty"

Wynema puts another under her nose and sighs.

"Oh, that's the famous Locoweed."

"Yeah, I think the Chinese call it Astragalus. I love the heavy, sweet odor."

"We use it in some healings. Clean out the tubes. Can make you puke."

"Here's one looks like an Evening Primrose."

"Don't know about that. We call it Drops of the Sun, *Pa-ahto-kumsi*."

"What's it good for?"

"Nothing."

"You mean, you don't know, or forgot?"

"Of course, I know, *silly girl*. You put the flower in a bowl and put the bowl on your table—."

"For what?"

"For beauty."

Wynema looks at her quizzically, then bursts out laughing.

        ~

"This plant is called *Gan-o-hing-pa*."

"I know that. I know that! It means 'belongs-to-spider'?"

"Very good."

"That's interesting, because I think the whites call it Spiderwort. Funny, huh?"

"The whites, huh?"

        ~

"Oooh, here's the dreaded Datura or 'visioning plant'. Don Juan talks about it a lot."

"Better know what you're doing with that. We call it *gi-hon-pata-po*, or Night Hawk. But it has nothing to do with hawks. It means the moth that comes at night to get drunk."

"I could get drunk just smelling them."

"You be careful."

        ~

"Here's a kind of Larkspur, I'm sure. Says here it's poisonous. Called the Geranium-leaf Larkspur."

"Navajos know how to use it. But I don't. That's why I'm mad at the Navajos. They won't tell me."

        ~

"You know the Chamisa?"

"*Ta-fo-honk-tio*."

"Says here that's the Rubber Rabbitbrush."

"Navajos use that for yellow dye in their wool. Just yellow. We do, too. But we go deeper. The inner bark will give you a nice green dye. Hah!"

        ~

"This one has those five-petaled flowers, too. I love the way the purple-red petals fold back and lie so open."

"We use those for woman-healing. It brings things together. After a baby is born—you know."

"I do now."

"Children used to play with the seed pods all the time."

        ~

"Says here this one is Barberry and that the Blackfeet use it as a bitter tonic, for gall bladders and liver congestion. Is that right?"

"I suppose so. We use for hangovers. I can't find enough of that one for San Lucas Pueblo."

*

"Here's another Bluebell-like thing. I can't find it, but I'll bet it's another Borage cousin."

"You need a porcupine for quills for all your doings? Where this grows you'll find porcupines. They love it."

*

Next day. Outside. Sunny. Now Mirriamma sits at a long table outside under the ramada. She's taking her sorted plants and stringing them with a needle on a white string. Wynema is stringing up the lines full of herbs. Here they will dry.

"Here's the Clematis!"

"Oh, that's another one they say is poisonous. But I use it for sore throat by chewing the leaves and stalks. The flowers are good for bad headaches that come only to one side of your head. From a little poison comes lotsa healing."

*

"I've noticed these before, I think."

"Yeah, around this time of year, when the leaves turn yellow, they have a blue-black berry."

"Spikenard!"

"Yeah, *wey-ko-deka*. Delia Armijo makes the best jam out of them."

*

"This one with the star-shaped flower—my husband ground up the root once and dried it and used it to make his grandfather sneeze"

"Why?"

"To blow out the boogers, of course."

*

"Wow, look at these giant trumpet flowers! From the color and shape, I'll bet it's related to Borage."

"Don't know about that. But the Hopi use it in their religion, so I never step on it. I like the Hopi, no matter what anyone says."

Mirriamma stands and stretches a little. "I'm tired. I'm gonna go take a nap." She stops and thinks for a moment. "You know, if I help cure someone and make him stronger, this is good. But if I cure someone and make him stronger and *also* help him connect to the Old Ones, then I am very happy."

≈

Another day, Will is back on the phone. This time with Cutter. "...I can't, Steve, I have to respect their ways. If I don't, I risk losing their trust."

"Trust is good, kid, I told you that. But authority and confidence in our best practices—you've heard of them: standard operating procedures—they come first!" His voice changes to flat and final. "They have to. Unless you have concrete evidence that contravenes what the tests we've already done show, then you stand to lose big time if you don't get the job done. Have I made myself clear on this?"

"Yes, sir."

"I don't care if we're dealing with Captain Picard of the Starship Enterprise—when it's a true medical emergency, the Bones calls the shots. Clear, Number One?"

"Clear."

"So, I'll give you two days to work things out there, but I better see your aneurysm on the OR's schedule by Wednesday morning. Fair enough?"

"But—there's something happening here that may have now mitigated the urgency."

"Oh, and just what that might have been? A psychic-healing by Mother Teresa?"

"Uh, right, well—let me get back to you on this, real soon, and, uh, we'll figure out what the right thing to do is."

"Have you been drinking?"

"No. Absolutely not."

"Well, the right thing to do is the aneurysm stat."

There is a long pause.

"Okay. Okay. I'll call you."

"Don't call me. Call the OR."

≈

On Tenth Street in the southwest corner of Berkeley, a few blocks from the Bay, there is a warehouse, now a large, open-space studio where Chumba Ito stays when he's not on the road. This is his home-base. This is where he creates and tests his equipment, where he writes the software that drives the hardware that.... The big truck that takes to the road his considerable equipment he keeps here, in his living-room. He takes very good care of his equipment.

The floor is concrete. The building steel. But Chumba has softened the sounds of this place with over 150 carpets and remnants gathered from rug stores all over the Bay Area and plastered on every wall and ceiling and floor. Out from the wall and below the ceiling, a lot of inch-and-a-half pipe scaffolding and grids to hang screens, speakers, wires, lights.

It's almost midnight and Chumba is sitting on a board high up on a scaffold, looking down on a lot of technical equipment he's set up. He's wearing his usual faded-black well-worn coveralls. In one hand, his cell. With his other, he takes a thick, black "pen" from a pocket. As he waves this device slowly left and right, a camcorder mounted down below on a jib arm tracks with precision the pen's movements.

He speed-dials his cell. "Yo, Frank."

"Chumba!"

"What you doing, Injun?"

"Going down on the cutest girl you ever did see." And he is. He's in his camper with curtains drawn, parked under the bright lights in the middle of one of the biggest, newest casinos west of Albuquerque, standing up between the flying legs of a woman who might over 18. She's lying on her back at the edge of the bed that's cantilevered over the cab. His pants are down and another woman, not as young, is giv-ing him a rapid hand and blow job from the front seat of his pick-up—through the back window of the cab.

"Then why'd you answer the phone, Frank?"

"T'see how many things I can do at once, just like you, Chumb. But if it ain't crucial," says Frank trying to steady himself against the redoubled efforts of the woman in the cab, "I'll call you tomorrow."

"I think I'm going hunting, Frank."

"What's that mean?"

"For new ideas."

Frank is becoming a little impatient. "Like I said, man, I'll be there next week."

"No. I'm going to take some time off. To think things out."

"What's going on?"

"Nothing."

"No, there's something else. What is it?"

"There's nothing," insists Chumba scratching his balls.

"You're lying."

There's a good long pause in which Frank licks his middle finger and twirls gently the proffered clit.

"You're right."

Frank steps away from the women, pulls up his sweat pants. "Then give."

"I'm getting bored, I guess is what is."

Chumba waits patiently for Frank to speak.

Frank, picking his nose with his thumb, "Hey, we work together. We jam. An idea hits. We jam. Until we find something new that works."

"You're stuck, Frank, at wherever you're at. You're moving but you ain't going nowhere. That's my truth, Frank. I want new sounds, new screens, new emotions. Got to take off for a year maybe. I'm really hungry, Frank, for something else."

Frank flashes on how they met. *At an electronics trade show in Las Vegas. Frank had said casually while looking at an array of the newest flat-screens: "You think there's a device I can put on me while performing that will make a video camera track my movements, automatically, across the stage?"*

Chumba was standing next to Frank. His eyes narrowed and he turned his head slowly to the Indian and smiled. "I can show you that and more. Much more."

Chumba had flown to Vegas from Oakland. Now Frank was driving him back to Berkeley in his camper, towing his Harley. It was non-stop performance-enhancement all the way to the Bay. By the time they reached Chumba's warehouse-studio, they knew they were going to work together.

"You share this with anybody?" Frank asked.

"Share it? Nope. Gig it out here and there? Yeah. Why?"

"Do you earn enough to pay for all this shit?"

Chumba looked around. "Probably not," he said deadpan, "but my mom and pop, they have a good business in Hawaii. They believe in my work."

Frank looked around. "What kind of business?"

"Ice cream. They make it from macadamia nuts."

Frank breaks the silence. "So you're bored, eh?"

"Basically, Frank."

"Yeah, well, I been there."

"I know you have, Frank."

"Shit."

Chumba stands up on the scaffolding and switches the cell to his other ear. "I gotta stretch out 'n go deep for a while, ol' dawg. We'll get together in a year or so and compare notes. Who knows?"

"Well, you never know. How come you didn't tell me you wanted to do this?"

"I told you as soon as I was sure. I'm sure."

"I ain't boring, Chumba. I'm a lotta things, but I ain't boring."

"Yeah, that's right. You ain't boring. But I'm bored, Frank. It's me, I s'pose."

"Maybe it is you. Maybe you are bored. Maybe you're depressed. Have you gone clinical on me? Maybe you need the right meds. I can get you anything you want, ya know."

"No offense, Frank."

"None taken—you sonuvabitch! What about goddamn common-courtesy, man?! I mean, okay, but gimme a year lead time! Fuckin' careers at stake! Or at least six months! Okay, how 'bout fuckin' three months?! I mean, we're fuckin' friends ain't we?! What about about our commitments, our friends, our fuckin' customers!? Not to mention our fans! Goddamn it, you have fuckin' people out there who love you, man. Who are fuckin' addicted to you, *coyo*."

Chumba starts to slowly climb down from the scaffolding, like a monkey in slow motion. "I know it's cold, man."

"What the fuck are you talkin' about...pardner?! Cold ain't even close enough! It's fuckin' unholy!"

"Okay, then. I'll give ya three months." As Frank slowly, hugely inhales to respond, Chumba adds quickly, "But, you really should take a year to write a book, Frank. New raps. New rips. New explosions."

After another long pause, Frank with resignation, "Fine. Maybe it's time to go underground. Or go on a fuckin' speaking tour." He raps for the young woman in the truck cab to get with it and points to his penis. "Or go to Bolivia. There's a lot of good shit happening in Bolivia with the natives, man." Frank laughs once to himself. "It looks like it's Jiminy Cricket telling Pinocchio he's going on a fuckin' leave-o'-absence. Well, we'll see who takes a leave of absence."

"Sounds good. Go back to your pussy. And good road to you."

"See ya later." Frank lets the cellphone flip slowly snap against his fingers.

From the cab, "Frank, I'll give you a blow job every day if you'll take me to Bolivia with you."

From the cab-over-bed, "Me, too."

Frank sniggers once and takes a pull from a pint. Then he puts a 20 dollar bill as a bookmark in each of two copies of his book and gives them to the women. "Go find your folks, girls."

Half an hour later, Frank is high on heroin.

58

We'll See Who's the Better Injun

Another couple of weeks, and it's Wednesday morning, October 17th. The San Lucas Tribal Courtroom is a five-minute walk from the central plaza. It isn't built in any special way to show itself off. But there are two floors and colorful if modest tribal insignia indicating its authority. On the second floor there are a couple offices and a balcony or shaded walkway that opens off the Courtroom. The judge, for example, might walk and talk with lawyers there.

On the street out front, two young boys careen out of sight around a corner of the building, just as the sound of a Harley motorcycle rips the peace. The boys of course come bouncing back quickly, gawking at Frank who cruises in and stops in front. A cocky, very young Pueblo woman, wearing torn and stressed goth clothes and too much makeup, is riding up behind him. She slides off, looks at the boys, kisses Frank hard.

Frank slaps her gently on the rump. "Run along home, Rita. Don't tell anyone who paid for your tattoo. Our secret. Maybe I'll see ya later."

Frank is road weary. He sighs, looks to the Courtroom balcony, to the boys, to his watch. He enters the building.

⌀

Upstairs, just inside the Courtroom's double-doors, Teo is handing a gift to a friend who works as clerk to the judge. Both men are beaming.

Teo holds up his finger as if what he's about to say is of crucial importance. "I must be married to a saint and I didn't know it. I mean, I never saw a birth happen so easy. One minute she smiles, then she makes a strange face, and the next minute she makes the sweetest sound, "*ooooyaiii-ii*", and out comes my new son!"

They both see Frank entering the big room through the other door on the far side. Alex Olguin, the uniformed policeman who cited Frank at Santa Camina's Feast Day, follows him. They're heading for Tribal Judge Donald Reyna's office.

Inside Judge Reyna's office, Frank stands contraposto, glancing at things on Reyna's desk. Reyna is looking back and forth between Frank and a report. Reyna's very old mother, Reymunda, is sitting on a chair in the shadows wearing a scarf and quietly embroidering a powwow shirt. She is almost invisible.

Inside his head, Frank is giving himself instructions, *So just chill, Paco, and be respectful and remember that Reyna's mother saved your sorry ass twenty years ago by not telling the police that it was you who let the air out of all four tires of Governor Lujan's car. And now you had your fun at the Arts Festival, so just say you're sorry and let it go.*

"Frank, I appreciate you're coming." The Judge looks at his watch. "And on time. So what we got here is—I'm all for freedom of expression, but not at the expense of the tribe and its religious events."

"Religious? Sacred?" Frank can't help himself. "Let's not go there. I mean, some things are religious and sacred, yeah, sure, they are. But tourists? No way? Some things are sacred, some things are cancerous. So look, Judge, I don't know why I came today, either. If you want me to pay a fine, I'll pay it. You want me to spend some time under key, shit, I'm used to it. But these damn tourists are pigs—I'm tellin' ya, Don, and somebody's got to show 'em how toxic they are. You can't do it, bein' who you are 'n all, I understand that. I do, I understand that. So I took it on. Got a little messy, I'll admit—."

The judge sets the papers down and scratches his head with both hands. He turns to the deputy Sheriff. "Alex, I guess you don't need to stay. I'll work something out with Frank here. Thanks for coming in, yeah? Oh, and remind your uncle that the Council meets in two days, kind of a little earlier than we expected. So his hunting trip— maybe he ought to postpone it, yeah? And our own Feast Day is the day after, okay?"

"Yeah, I'll remind him, Judge. Thanks." Alex leaves and closes the door.

Frank is a mixture of soured, bored, and guilty child.

The judge takes a fancy, reusable toothpick from his desk and picks between two particular teeth, then puts the pick away. "Show them how toxic they are? You don't show them, Frank. You gut 'em and leave 'em for roadkill." Reyna waves his fingers a few inches in front of his face. "Why'd you come back, and on time at that? I mean, hell, you being one of our more famous Indians, 'n all?"

Frank doesn't say anything at first, but then ventures, "Well, I wanna go to that Council meeting in two days. Don't worry, I'm not going to say anything. I just need to sit and listen."

"You sit and listen?! That'll be the day. But Victor runs a tight meeting. You fuck up and he'll throw you in jail for month. And I'll back him."

"Yeah, well, I also got a proposition for the Council. It's about an arts center for our Pueb—"

Gracie, the Judge's secretary opens the door. "Judge Reyna, Simon Zamora and his grandson are here."

"Ah-hah!" blurts Frank.

Gracie makes a gesture that says she doesn't have a clue why they're here.

As Simon and Dayone enter, Frank lets loose. "Did you call in my daddy, Judge?"

Reyna ignores this and greets Simon, *Good day, Grandfather.*

Frank taunts his father, "Were you worried about your little boy gettin' justice under the Law?"

Judge to Simon, "I think we're going to work this out okay, Simon. Maybe wait for us out there for just a few—"

"Sorry, Judge," says Simon, "I—"

But Frank is tweaked. He gets down on one knee before his father. "Oh, please don't send me down the river, Massa! Don't send me away again."

Reyna signals to Gracie, who leaves, closing the door behind her.

Simon's equanimity almost breaks. To Reyna, "I thought I'd come, you know, out of concern."

"Is that it?!" hisses Frank, "Out of plain ol' concern? How 'bout a lot of concern? How 'bout some get-down-on-*your*-knees-and-ask-for-some-fuckin'-forgiveness concern!?"

Dayone wants to push Frank into the wall. As he lunges, Simon's hand darts out and grabs the boy's arm.

"Frank!" commands Reyna flatly.

"I could do that, Frank," says Simon softly, "if that's what you want."

"I don't gotta want it, Simon. You do!"

"Good or bad, I'm your father, maybe mostly bad, I guess, but I thought I'd, you know, like that, before I die, try to be there, if you —"

"I'm 33 years old. I've been a grown-up since I was nine and *both* my parents died on me." As he says "both", he smashes a fist into a palm.

Reyna stands. "That's enough, Frank. When your father came here a few months ago and offered to help Dayone find out what he wanted, he—"

"Oh, so that's it! Now he's offering to help me and I'm a little boy again! Yo, if you want to arrest me for trashing the tourists, then let's talk about that. But this?!" He points to Simon, "Well, fuck no. I'll be outside, Judge. If you want to lock me up, send ol' Alex out after me and we'll just see who's the better Injun."

Frank storms out the door. The others stare in silence.

Simon breaks it. "I thought I'd try to—wanted to say something he could hear—so we could meet each other in a different way."

"It's his problem, Grandfather," says Dayone.

Simon shrugs and, with a gesture, asks, "Anything else?"

Reyna shrugs, "No, sorry, but—."

Teo sticks his head in the door. "Hey, Judge. I thought I saw Simon go in, so I—is this business or pleasure, because I'm definitely in the business of pleasure today!"

"You here gift-giving for your new baby?" Simon is relieved and happy to see his friend.

Teo nods and places a brown paper bag on Reyna's desk. "Here, Judge. Got one for you in my truck, Simon."

Simon turns and with only a look asks Reyna if he may continue speaking. Reyna nods yes.

Simon turns back to Teo. "'Bout that Council meeting in two days, I'll go because you—"

Teo, too, looks to the Judge for permission. "Just come and support us with your presence. Victor's got the votes. But, you may have found your power too late, my friend."

Simon puts his hand on Dayone's shoulder and says, "We won't lose. The Old Ones will not let this happen."

Dayone stares at the two men, who are staring at each other.

"I may not agree with you entirely on this, Teo," says Reyna, "but I understand your position. If we want to be a sovereign nation, we have to act like a sovereign nation. Taking money to do a feasibility study makes a lot of sense." He turns to Simon. "Why now you into the doings after so many years?"

Simon thinks for a moment. "A man should not die without healing the wounds of his life, and I have been too long apart from my people."

Teo takes a step closer to Simon. "And Frank?"

Out of politeness, the judge turns to some papers on his desk. Simon takes his leave and indicates to Teo that they can talk about this outside. Dayone holds open the door. Simon puts a hand on Teo's shoulder, and Dayone closes the door behind them.

The Judge turns to the old woman in the corner in the shadows. "It could be a long day, Mama."

59

WE ALL SAW IT IN THE SMOKE

Thursday morning early. Will is running down a dirt road in the foothills above the Pueblo. He's wearing lightweight hiking boots, shirtless, his sweatshirt tied around his waist. He's sweating and breathing hard, sometimes grunting, especially when his foot rolls over a rock putting great stress on his ankles. In his head—flashbacks:

He's in Mirriamma's prayer room again. The *Pahos* ritual is in progress again. Semi-dark. Mirriamma sings something in Pueblo. If only he could understand:

"I ask the Creator G'na-tum-si to help me heal this man, Simon, so he can get ready for his journey."

Will stumbles as he leaps over an old fallen fence. But he's up and running, hearing, searching, not understanding:

"I ask Grandmother Earth to help me heal this man."

He sees Mirriamma bent over, almost to the ground, holding a fetish made of feathers, carved wood, and bird skins. Gracefully, she turns 90° three times as she speaks:

"I appeal to the Directions, to the Day and the Night and the Seasons, to send their individual powers to help me heal Simon, a good man."

He sees Simon, dancing like a ghost, passing his body completely through Mirriamma's:

"To all you Spirits, to these Ones respected by our Ancestors, my wish is for this man to walk straight and strong, be healthy, have a good heart, and have love for other people."

Will crests the rise and flies onto a flat, open meadow full of flowers. But he doesn't see the flowers at all. He sees what his mind wants to remember. He sees Wynema, sitting on her heels before the fire-pit, eyes open, seeing nothing, seeing all, lost to him, listening to Mirriamma:

"This man, Simon Zamora, is an old friend. His father and grandfather, his grandmothers, all loved him and he loved them. He has been a good friend to me. I ask the Higher Powers in everything to help this man by giving him the strength to do what his heart tells him to do before he rejoins the Old Ones. And I give thanks now for these good things to come. Whoo-oh!"

Will's legs now act as powerful hydraulic pistons slowing his rate of descent as he flies down a long steep slope, eventually coming to a stop a few hundred yards up hill and behind Mirriamma's house. Ribcage heaving, he walks down towards it.

On the other side of the house, Mirriamma is working her pottery under the ramada while beyond Wynema sings and leads the man who speaks in tongue in a simple dance step. Both are laughing. Stepping around a corner, Will stops, takes it all in. He's nervous. As he takes a breath to speak, Mirriamma preempts, "I know how you feel. 'N your father, too."

Will is taken aback, but before he can respond, Mirriamma asks, "You believe that?"

He takes a deep, realigning breath. "Believe what, Grandmother?"

"That I know how you feel. And your father."

Will lets out a breath he didn't realize he'd been holding so long. "Uhhhh, you mean my grandfather? I never really knew my father. Well, I did, but I was nine and, uh—."

"Yes, but in your case it's the same thing."

"Well, yeah, I guess so. Sure. But, uh, I was wondering—."

Mirriamma has a very loving, motherly smile on her face. "I know. Look, you and Wynema are both gift-givers to your people. But you have different people."

Will looks around and then sits down cross-legged in front of Mirriamma. "I can be a doctor to your people, too—a good doctor."

She nods slowly, then very gently, "Not until you speak our language."

Will again starts to react defensively, but stops, sighs, and instead, "I know you're not going to answer my questions, so I'm not going to ask them."

Mirriamma nods, grunts, and smiles. She spits something from her lip, walks to Wynema, says something to her, then leads the other man away who by now is pointing feverishly at all the flies bouncing around like sparks in the dusty sunlight. Wynema comes to him, sits at the nearby pottery table, and motions for him to sit opposite her.

He sits. "It's been days since we talked."

She hands him a ball of clay. A flick of her head tells him to work it. His clay-work mirrors his emotions.

She is at once sad, animated, and earnest. "You are very important to Simon. You are part of his life's road now. He dreamed you before you came here."

"I know." He ponders the moment. "Wait a sec. How do you know? Did he tell you?" Off her negative, "Did Mirriamma tell you?"

She softens. "No. We all saw it," pointing inside the house, "...in the smoke." She feels his exasperation. "There are different kinds of knowledge, Will, and some of it comes in its own time, when we open ourselves and—"

"Weren't you worried about me? I mean, to lose consciousness like that."

"No, Mirriamma said you'd be okay." Off his look of incredulity "Will, I trust her in her domain as much as I trust you in yours."

"'Domain'. Such a cold word. What are we talking about? No, wait! I'm sorry. There is so much I want to learn, so much that you can teach me. I—"

"What is it that I can teach you, Will?"

"Magic."

"Whoa, that's serious business for a top medical scholar to say."

"What happened to me at Mirriamma's?"

"I don't know how to explain it. I don't even know how to begin."

Will's heart is breaking. "Wynema...I...I've fallen in love with you...in a way I don't even understand."

"I know. For you love is a joining, a wanting to join, a mixing of two people, for a long time, maybe even making a third or fourth, a family."

He looks into her eyes for many seconds.

Her eyes are soft. They soften even more. "I've loved you, Will, we've loved each other, and I care very much for you, but I cannot join with you. That is not for us right now."

He grabs a hold of whatever he can. "For now? You mean, bad timing? Maybe some other time? But we only live, we only love, really, in the moment. That's when it happens. That's when we feel it. *Im lo achshav, eh-matai?*"

"What's that, Will?"

"Another ancient language. It's Hebrew, and it means 'If not now, when?' It's a calling to the moment, I guess. Am I pushing too fast? Is that it? Am I just wanting too much too soon? I mean, is that even possible?"

"No, Will. You want exactly what you want whenever you want it. That's what wants are all about. For you, life is wanting everything now, everything good, filling up your life, each thing making room for every other thing, and all of it working together towards some fulfillment only you can imagine."

"Yeah, that's right, I guess. Isn't that what everyone wants, each in their own way?"

"You're discovering a new world. I'm trying to hold an old one together. A year ago, I'd have joined you. But I've changed. My life has changed. My life has changed me."

"Me, too."

"Will, I care for you. Very much. I told Mirriamma that, and—"

Will interrupts, "What does she have to do with you and me?"

"Shhhh-h-h. Listen. She also knows that you and I are searching for ways in our life that have nothing to do with us—you know, as man and woman. I'm beginning to see—" As Will tries to interrupt, "Please listen! The healing was very powerful, for both of us. I can only imagine what Simon went through. But there are forces—"

"Are you telling me that this—this voodoo is stronger than my love—than our love? Wynema, that doesn't make—"

"Voodoo?"

"I'm sorry. I didn't mean that."

"Something's changing, Will. It's larger than us. It's the picture that contains the picture that contains us. It really is. I'm not being melodramatic here. I'm not being—I'm not exaggerating. These are the times, Will—they finally arrived—when the forces of what's out there finally come crashing in or everyone's lives, not just one or two, here or there, but everywhere. It's happening locally, but it's a global thing. The planet is about to take one giant leap—or it's not. And if it doesn't, it's catastrophe for all of us. The Earth will survive—oh, She may have to start over in so many areas, but She definitely has a life, too, and will abide and mature and someday pass away. And if this is where we're at, right now, one and all, globally, existentially, then that's where we're at. But we still have to ask what do we do? Each of us. Do we just go on as if it weren't happening, falling in love, willy-nilly, even wonderfully? Will, this is the time for all the locals with a will to live to act local and find coherence within and cohesion with-out, with the place they call home. Oh, this sounds so cold. I'd love to fall in love! Dreamt about it all my life. You, too, uh?"

Will's eyes are filling. "What I feel can hold us together for a life-time. I know it. My feelings go beyond anything I ever even thought of before. It's right. I know it is. Think about the tribe, the concept and viability of the tribe. Not your tribe of old or mine of old. But tribalism today. What is needed from it! We each come from that. The experience of tribalism in your life was interrupted. In mine, too. We can bring together the best of that connection and—and—and form it into what's needed in the future for our one single shared world to survive! Do you know what I'm saying?" When she doesn't respond, all he can do is ask, "What do you feel?"

"Your feelings are good, Will, and they're strong. And my feelings for you are strong, too. You've probably already figured out that around here the concept of strength is very important. But I don't know enough to represent my tribe—and in my case I have two tribes—Pueblo and Sioux. The tribe of my mother, however, is asking me to stay—well, some of them are. Some would definitely like me to leave. But I look at the whole, Will, and try to see where I can serve the best. That's it. But you and I—"

He crushes the ball of clay with a fist, "I don't understand any-thing!" He stands, starts to storm away—then stops himself, breathes, sits again. "I don't understand anything! Life is a combination of many factors. It's up to us to put them together. And make them work."

"The American Dream."

"What's that suppose to mean?"

"That we can have it all, always more, never less. If technology can't find a way, then the upward mobility of our careers will make it all work out."

"I don't understand. I don't understand anything. I mean it. I thought I did. But I don't. This world is a lot more unloving and dangerous and self-destructive than I ever thought."

"Is it the world, Will, or is it me?"

Will's eyes lock onto hers. He tries to go in. To fall into her eyes. To reach her, finally, through her eyes. She is looking at him, right here right now, silently saying "This is who I am."

After a silence, Will relaxes. "I'm not the pure scientist you may think I am. There's a part of me that believes in magic. Yes. I was all set to go to U.C. Med in San Francisco. What a set-up they wanted to give me. I had made up my mind. But then—it's really strange—I was just about to see some performance, totally by accident, and it turned out to be Frank, you know, in the Village, and I sat down and turned over this coaster and I saw *my name* and *the name of this Pueblo*— and I must have taken it as a sign, and something clicked and I must have decided to come here. Just like that." He reaches into his shirt pocket and lays down the coaster in her hand. About to break, he rises suddenly and goes.

Wynema turns the coaster over. "WM - San Lucas - 87526." Her eyes widen in disbelief.

◆

Will comes wild-eyed around the corner, desolated utterly, imploding—his hands caking white with clay.

60

WORKING WHILE YOU SLEEP

Dawn of a new day for Dayone, in the cornfield next to his grandfather's summer house. He's pulling up cornstalks and putting them in
piles. They're headed for the compost pile next to the corral. As he
carries a big, awkward bundle towards the corral, suddenly, he
freezes, then lowers himself very slowly—until he is squatting. He sets
the basket to one side and moves onto his knees. Cautiously, he
crawls forward a step, freezes again. He moves his head slightly to the
right, past the weeds and the thick cornstalks: a rattlesnake stares
him, face to face, only a few feet away. The snake's tongue flicks.
Dayone holds the stare and appears to relax. The snake rattles once,
then flattens, turns, and starts to move off. Instantly, Dayone dives,
his hand flashing out grabbing the snake behind the head, immobiliz-
ing it. The tail thrashes violently but Dayone quickly takes it in a gentle hand and cradles the frightened creature.

Softly he says, "Aw-sus...sus...suss. Be calm, Grandfather Snake. I
am not going to hurt you. You know that. Simon told me you would
come for the harvest."

He stands and heads for the house. "Let's show him you are
here."

Dayone approaches the little house. Simon, standing bare-chested
in profile in the window, is holding up a shirt to the morning light.
Seemingly talking to someone, he doesn't see Dayone.

"This is a fine shirt, don't you think? My daughter made it for
me."

He puts a hand on his belly just below the sternum. "I apologize.
It is my fault you were ready to burst. But our agreement is a good
one. I will use no force to fight you, and you will rest now and give

me the time I need. This is a good shirt for a meeting, but I want to wear a different one when I die."

Dayone stands in the doorway listening, fascinated and troubled. He starts to turn away, then realizes that he still holds the snake. As Simon starts to don the shirt, "Grandfather, look who's come back."

Simon is overjoyed. "It is good. It is a good thing. Yes."

He nods, smiles, but with his hand, he indicates Dayone to carefully put the snake back. Dayone bobs his head okay, but flicks his tongue to the snake once before he exits.

Dayone and Simon, both clean and well-dressed, reach the Clinic door just as Sotero does. Dayone, carrying a paper bag and a small, rolled-up rug, respectfully holds the door open for the old man.

"Good morning, Grandfather."

Sotero's eyes sparkle. "Good morning, Dayone." Then to Simon, "You here for sickness, Simon? I was hearin—"

"Nope, just a friendly visit. No sickness today."

Sotero is not the oldest member of the village, but damn near. "Just a visit? Now that's a good thing. My granddaughter says I got to see the doctor here so that he can tell me about his medicines, no doubt. The Old Ways are good sometimes. Are we living in the Sometimes Times? Does one forest push out another? Summer and Winter don't come at the same time. I used to know the answers. *Pahos*—been good medicine for you, eh?"

Simon lets the older man, now laughing to himself, enter first. "Yes, Grandfather."

Dayone follows the two elders inside.

It's busy. Lola and Rebeca are trying to get preliminary information from patients who are speaking too fast.

On the phone and clearly upset, Louisa is talking to a friend and superior at IHS in Santa Fe. "No, he's still sick I guess. Didn't come in today, either. But it's okay and it's Friday, thank God! ...I'm sure everything is okay. Some food poisoning maybe. ...Nah, don't say anything to Dr. Cutter or anyone there. Okay?... Yeah and I'll give that new ointment to your cousin. I know her daughter's worried.... Okay, bye."

Louisa hangs up and bends to Sotero's ear, who looks around with a "Who me?" look. She whispers apologetically, "Doctor Kornfeld is not feeling well today."

Sotero brightens, "Good, good, then I'll just pick it up some other day. They don't spoil, do they?"

"What are you talking about, Grandfather?"

Sotero pats Louisa warmly on the hand, then turns and leaves, a happy man.

Louisa shakes her head and smiles, "Is Sotero losing it, Papa?"

"Nope. I was talking to a few of his friends and they was saying he's finally finding it." Simon chuckles once.

Dayone steps away to talk to Lola's daughter who's just come in to "borrow" some money. She's only 13, and her top and bottom are designed to show maximum cleavage and crack.

Louisa bends towards her father. "Papa, I think Doctor Kornfeld he's in love and—and it's not going so well." She nods knowingly, sadly.

Simon shrugs and points towards the back as if to ask "Is he at his house?" Louisa nods glumly. Simon steps away towards Will's office just as Dayone returns.

Louisa is pleased with his appearance. "You look kinda handsome today."

"Can I talk to you, Mother?"

Louisa becomes a little anxious.

Dayone pulls out the paper bag. "This is for you. The first corn. Simon's—and my—first corn."

She starts to speak, but he continues awkwardly and takes a cloth bag of cornmeal out of the paper bag. "And this cornmeal from Mirriamma. When you are ready, I will pray with you for the first corn."

Louisa is stunned, and speechless.

"When you are ready, Mother."

He exits. She breaks down crying silently in released joy.

Simon reappears, carrying Will's little tree. "We'll talk later, okay? Right now I gotta see a man about a tree. I see now it takes a while after a Holocaust to reconnect with the Grandfathers. One or two generations may not be enough. Maybe that's why it hit him so hard."

Louisa asks with a look what he means.

"The Fog. By God it knocked him flat. That's what Mirriamma meant when she said that he didn't have his Grandfathers behind him. I made it through because we do. But it is not his way."

In his house, in his bedroom, in his bed, unshaven and still wearing sweat clothes, Will lies curled up on his side. Staring at the wall.

Simon enters and sets the tree on his dresser. "I am giving this tree back to you."

"Why? I'll just kill it."

"You won't kill it. You ever read the Bible? In there, it's like a promise in there, like that."

Will closes his eyes, then turns over, facing away.

But Simon continues, "You know, the first book, that's Genesis—it's all about fathers and sons—and brothers, like that, ya know. I got two kids—Frank and Louisa. I had another, Joseph, but he died real young.

Simon pauses, and Will doesn't move.

"Just before you came here, my father told me about your tree."

"Your father?"

"In my dream. This is a father-and-son tree."

"My father died when I was nine. Now my grandfather is dying. That was his tree. He gave it to me. Now I'm giving it to you."

"You can't give away a promise."

"I didn't promise anything."

"Some things you promise just by being a son. Or a grandson." Simon shifts his weight slowly from foot to foot. He looks intently at the tree.

Will sits up, wrapping himself with the blanket. "Doesn't it go both ways? Don't fathers and grandfathers have promises to their kids?"

Simon pauses, then nods slowly.

Will hisses through a lowered voice. "Well, my grandfather-father demanded things from me. He didn't ask, he just demanded. Like some kind of destiny that had control over me, and I owed it allegiance! ... I bet you demanded things from Frank."

This throws Simon instantly into troubled thought.

401

Will doesn't hide how primal his emotions. "And what about mothers? The Bible's full of mothers. You never mention your mother. Or my mother. Or Frank's."

Long pause. Simon crumbles a clod of soil from the tree's pot. "You're right. There are promises made to mothers, too. Very complicated. Anyway, you still want to ask your grandfather something? But maybe you can't. But you want to, before he dies. Well, maybe, through this tree, you can still ask him."

He takes another deep breath, then starts to exit, but stops and turns at the door. "When we refer to our Grandfathers, you know what we mean?"

"I think so," says Will without looking up.

"You have a sense of how we see them, how we hold them, how they help us."

"Yeah, I think I understand."

"Do you have Grandfathers?"

"No. Not like that. Just my one and only grandfather, and he—."

Will lifts his head and gives a most piteous look of not-understanding. His head falls back into the pillow.

"Are your Grandfathers a source of guilt and pain for you? Are you grieving for their suffering? Maybe."

"My Grandfather Abraham suffered. We're Jews. We suffer. I don't know why. His brothers and sisters and parents and grandparents they all suffered. I can feel their pain. Sure. But what do I—what should I—feel guilty about? That's what I don't understand about being who I am."

"Maybe pain is easier to talk about than guilt." Simon is earnest. "Pain is what one suffers. But guilt is a form of punishment."

"Punishment for what, though?"

"That's what I can't figure out, either. Your Grandfathers, nomadic tribes out of the deserts, and then not too happy in eastern Europe—what promises did they fail to keep to their God? That kind of guilt could be tribal. You know what I'm sayin'?"

"Look, Simon, I don't know why we're talking about God and Grandparents right now. You know I've fallen in love with Wynema. And I thought she loved me. I don't expect you to understand that.

I'm sorry, I—I just don't want to talk to you or anyone right now. Okay?"

"Okay."

Will curls up as tight as he can and wraps the blankets and pillows around his ears.

Simon doesn't move.

Will has techniques for forcing himself to sleep. As a med student he had to learn those techniques. And soon he sleeps. Twenty minutes later, his eyes flutter open. Consciousness returns. And then an awareness. Suddenly, he jumps up and faces the door. There's Simon, still sitting on that stool. A blank expression on his face.

"What the—?! Simon, have you been here all along?" Will snaps a look at his watch. "How long have I been out?"

"I don't know. Maybe one walk to Garcia's market. I'm sorry about your love life."

"What do you know—? Never-mind. I think it's over. Different directions. I don't know. I really don't want to lose her. Can you go away, please?"

"I know the feeling. Maybe worse. This life can be very melodramatic if we let it."

"If we let it? You mean, there's something I can do so that I don't lose her?

Simon thinks about it, then points. "I think it was the tree."

"Why's this damn tree become so damn important?!"

"Yeah, it has kinda taken over, hasn't it? That's why I think right now this tree is going to teach you how to connect with your Grand-fathers in a good way." Another pause. "Your people are long people, aren't they? You know, they been around a long time?"

"Hebrew is one of the oldest living languages."

"But you don't speak it?"

"No. Not really."

"Right now, you're worried about your love life and your grand-father. You're in trouble. Deep trouble. From north to south, from east to west. You've been hit in every direction."

"Simon, please go away." But then, quickly, "If you were a high priestess in the Ancient Order of Aphrodite, what would you advise me at this time?"

"Don't take offense, but I didn't understand a word you just said"

"I'm sorry."

"Actually, I probably did understand, but—" He pauses, "but I'm a disaster in that area."

"I understand."

"Then why did you ask me?"

"No, I meant—never-mind."

"You and me, we live inside of Time. But the Grandfathers and Grandmothers, they live in a place outside Time." He taps his chest. "They talk to us through here. Maybe not in a voice, you know. What they communicate becomes a part of us. The best part. Like that."

They both just sit there for a long while.

Simon rises, goes to the potted tree, smells it. "This tree, so small so young, has caught the breath of the Old Ones and every day it breathes and you breathe and the cycle is—." Simon snaps his fingers loudly. "In your language—Oxygen. Carbon-dioxide. Oxygen. Carbon-dioxide.... You know, like that. There are many ways the Grandfathers talk to us. This is one of them." He pushes the potted plant a little closer to Will. "Why you think the Creator put so many different smells into all the plants?"

"To attract different insects?"

"That's pretty good."

"Huh? Was that what you were thinking?"

"No. But I want to think about that one for a while." He hands the tree to Will, then turns to the door. "This tree is yours, William. It has much to give you. Smell it." As he exits, "then go back to work. Oh, and give it some time. Boy meets girl. Boy loses girl. What happens next depends on you."

"I thought you said you were a disaster in this area."

"I used to be. I'm better now."

Dayone appears in the doorway and stands there respectfully until Will looks up. "What?"

"Well, I just wanted to say I'm sorry—y'know, for breakin' in 'n knockin' you down, and ya know—.

Will waves a grumpy "No problem."

Dayone lingers, feeling awkward. "My grandfather—how soon will he die?"

Without even looking up, "Unlike anyone else in the world, your grandfather seems to know the answer to that question. But he won't let me operate—"

"He talks to it, Doc, to that bad spot under his heart. And at night, late, I hear him praying. He didn't used to pray. Me neither. Anyway, keep him alive, okay? He talked about you in his prayers, like you was his son."

Dayone leaves. Will heaves a big sigh and gets out of bed.

Half an hour later, Will appears next to Louisa at the Nurses' Station. He's a tad on the rumpled, unshaven side of life. He wears a faded sweatshirt with a picture of Geronimo and three fellow warriors and the words "Homeland Security Since 1492".

"What's going on?" he asks in as normal, as straight a voice as he can muster.

Louisa is pleasantly surprised. "You okay?"

He shrugs and asks again with a look, "What you got?"

"Mr. Sanchez is in Two."

Scanning the proffered chart, "Delbert Sanchez? Which one is he?"

"Bobby's father, Lucy's brother—and she's Council Member Churino's favorite daughter-in-law."

"Oh, and, uh, will you collate the Tribal Health Survey Reports and my notes. I've got less than an hour-and-a-half before I'm due at the Council Meeting.

Will starts to enter the exam room, but Louisa touches his arm.

"I love my Victor, Doctor, but this report. It's a bad report."

Will stops. "Do you mean it's inaccurate or it'll have a bad effect if I submit it?"

Louisa is sorry she said that. "I mean maybe the data is accurate, and our village may be less healthy than it was. But think of the tribe having enough money to do something about it. Victor knows I want more funds for health services here. Preventative health services. This report could kill our efforts to fund the very things your report says we need."

"And your father talks about something that he says is even more valuable. But I haven't lived here, I know, long enough to know about these things. And I'm only twenty-nine—what do I know?"

"My husband believes one thing on this MRS, and my father believes another. I don't know if you can understand, but I can't tell you, or anyone, what I really think."

Will's face falls. He understands her predicament.

After a moment, shyly, she adds, "You should shave. Oh, and wear a tie and your lab coat. Rebeca was nice enough to iron it."

Will sighs and he reaches for his lab coat on a hanger on the wall. He walks into Exam Room Three. A moment later, he exits and enters Exam Room Two.

Half an hour later, inside Exam Room One, Sotero sits on the table, shirt off. Will, stethoscope dangling, is writing in Sotero's chart and nodding as Sotero speaks.

"I almost made it home. I was gonna go fishing. But my daughter caught me. Made me come back."

Will taps the chart he's writing in, as if to say, "Back to the question I just asked you."

Sotero nods, shakes his head, nods again. "Wouldn't be so bad if I didn't have to get up to pee so much at night. I do my best work when I'm asleep."

Will glances up, "When you're asleep?"

"I'm paid to dream a lot."

Will sighs. "Are you taking your medication regularly?"

"Regular with the feelings, or regular with the clock?"

"With the clock. With the calendar. You know, on the schedule I gave you.

Sotero understands clearly now. "Yes, some ways I do. Sometimes...when I do."

Will glances nervously for his watch. But he's not wearing it. He slaps his wrist as inspiration strikes. "All right, here's what you do."

Will moves quickly, taking three empty bottles from a shelf, and yellow and pink hi-liters from his pocket. He circles one label with yellow and a second with pink, and third remains white.

"In the morning, when the sun rises bright and yellow, you take a pill I'll give you from the bottle with a yellow sun on it. At noon, when the sun is in the south, white with heat, take one from the plain, white bottle. And then, in the evening, when the sun settles pink in the west, take a pill from this pink bottle. Then the night will be good, and you'll sleep better."

Sotero is listening raptly. He nods, slides off the table, and puts on his shirt, smiling.

"I can do that, Doctor! I forget pills, but I always remember the sun. That's my job, too! You know, you're the first doctor come here who speaks my language."

The words catch Will's ear.

Stretching high, Sotero places his hand on Will's shoulder. Will instantly stands straighter, inhales. The two men just stand there for a moment, faintly smiling. Then Sotero exits. Will hangs back, emotionally moved.

Sotero sticks his head back in the door. "Hey, Doc. You give me a ride on your way to the Meeting?"

"How did you know that I was going?"

"Where d'you think the saying 'A little birdie told me' come from?"

Once again, Will is stumped. "Old Indian proverb—or legend?"

Sotero shakes his as he leaves. "Indian birds."

61

FOREST DESERT OR MARKETPLACE

At the central plaza, there is more than the usual movement of people. There are tourists, but only a few, walking among the half-dozen stalls and tables. It's sunny, but the wind is blowing. It's a clear, crisp day.

Outside the Tribal Government Offices, a dozen men mill about. A few women stand by their men or talk quietly amongst themselves. Clarence, on a mission, exits, looks around, gestures to a friend. They both quickly disappear into the building. Some old men smoke and chat.

Phipps arrives in his one-ton flatbed. People make way as he locks his vehicle, sets the alarm, and heads towards the Governor's office. His beard, his handlebars, his well-bent but greasy hat, his jewelry, clothes, gait—every inch a modern Indian trader. He wipes his nose just to make sure—an old habit.

In a dark passageway that runs around to the back of Governor Moquino's Office, Jesse, Armand, and Danny peer out. They are impressed with Phipps' mountain man "plumage" and charisma. For years.

Especially Danny. "Don't he wear rad clothes? An' I bet he's tough, too, 'n fights to kill, man."

Armand is viscerally moved by the white trader, afraid. "I bet he'd eat human beings if he got lost with them in the mountains and snow—and got hungry enough."

"He could take even the doctor."

"No way! The doctor'd kill him. He's quick an' works out. Check him out, man, I mean it. They have knives, they even call them "scalps", man, fuckin' sharp! Plus he knows all the important places on the body.

"Fuck, *coyo*, he ain't Superman, an' mos' important is he ain't even a dirty fighter. He'd lose 'n die."

Jesse sticks in his two cents. "He'd get eaten."

"My guy ain't fat like your guy, man."

Two teenage girls trot by on a horse. The boys' attention shifts.

In Victor's office, Phipps stands in front of the Governor's desk pondering....

"You're making a mistake, Governor. With all due respect. You and me been in lots of business deals over the years. We made a few bucks, 'n I b'lieve we're gonna make a pile more, if we're smart, and don't kill the goose what lays the eggs. Ya know?"

Victor looks at Phipps as he looks at most whites that come to deal. *It doesn't matter,* he thinks as he watches the trader glance over all the Indian art work in the room, *what the deal is. The important thing is to show them that they are dealing with an equal, or a better. Adaptability. The terrain may have changed, but we're all still hunters. Instead of the forest or the desert, it's the marketplace that rules. So I will listen to every dealmaker. You never know when you can learn something you can use against your enemies.*

For Victor, you're either family—or clan or tribe—or you're enemy, potential enemy, on the battlefield. And today the battlefield is global and it's called the Marketplace.

Then Phipps adds, "To keep this Pueblo pure 'n workin' 'n earnin', ya gotta stay on the fact that tourism is only gonna grow. Whites are cryin' fer things Indian. You watch! Tourists expect you to be yourselves, year after year, and the fact is that if they get any whiff of *nukular* taints and a drift away from tradition—which is why they come here—why, yer business, and let's face it, tourism is yer big business, will dry up and blow away sure. Forget that MRS. However much money they're gonna give, it'll have an end to it, and it ain't gonna be more than what tourism is gonna give you over the years."

"Martin, it's time my people took possession of their own lives. Tourism is a service business, made up of servants. I want more for my people."

"Victor, just hear me out. You know I got yer best interests at heart. Been a friend of the Indian all my life. Hell, I know what makes 'em special, what makes them Indian. Bring on that MRS and all the other crap what'll come with it, and you can kiss this land goodbye. Yer kid won't have a reservation to grow his kids up on. Tourism—them bein' them and you bein' you—will be dead. S'don't try and convince the Council too hard. Let 'em be Indians and—"

Victor stands and speaks softly. "I got the votes. Don't have to convince anybody."

Phipps doesn't like it, but he nods, knows when to retreat. *Something's up his asshole. The only reason he's not interested in my money is because he's making more money somewhere else. Or he's figuring on it.*

Will stops his truck outside the tallest adobe complex where Sotero lives. In through the open window, the old man says, " "Big meeting. Guess I should change my clothes, huh? Maybe I'll go. They might need me."

Will smiles at the cute old coot and drives off slowly.

At the Tribal Council Hall, the council members, dressed for the meeting, begin to arrive. Some in traditional blankets.

Victor, clearly energized by impending success, enters the building. Jesse and Armand, riding double, come galloping by, then turn into a side-road just before two girls round a corner, looking for the boys who've "borrowed" their horse. The girls head off in the wrong direction.

Teo, Simon, and Dayone arrive. The men go inside; Dayone remains outside, moving to the side of the building out of the sun.

Armand, on the panting horse, sees him. "Yo, Dayone. What's going on?"

"Waiting for my grandfather."

Jesse still hasn't come to accept Dayone's new life. "We got Peggy's horse. Come on!"

"We're going up to the creek," sniggers Armand. "Le's have some fun. We'll be back before the meetin's over. Get on!"

Without even smiling, "No thanks."

Jesse knows his friend well. "You can ride in front."

Dayone looks the horse up and down. "The horse having fun? He needs water."

Jesse is suddenly embarrassed. "Yeah, well—that's why we're going to the creek. Shit, man, whaddya think?"

"Bullshit." Dayone waves them off.

The boys ride away slowly.

Dayone leans on the adobe wall, observing things around him with the keen interest of a sentinel.

Inside the Council Hall, it's already two-thirds full. Victor's Sgt.-at-Arms is closing the shades. Simon sits not far from Teo, who sits at the Council table.

Victor raps his cane three times on the floor. Within seconds all are seated and quiet. He nods to Manley who in turn nods to one of his aides who dims the lights.

With a remote in one hand and a laser-pointer in the other, Manley is authoritative and smooth, as he speaks to the Council and begins his multimedia Powerpoint presentation on the screen set up for the Council Members. Superimposed on a magnificent aerial image of the Pueblo: "SAN LUCAS PUEBLO—THE PATH TO A RICHER FUTURE."

"You've already discussed what the MRS is. Let me tell you what merely doing the study, *just the study*, of the MRS could potentially mean to you."

Back outside, Dayone is still sitting against the same wall, observing everything. Will, in his white coat and carrying his green-bound health survey report, parks his truck and enters the building, nodding to Dayone. Dayone looks into the eyes of the Doc to see if there is respect there. There is.

A young white couple, one carrying a clipboard, the other a camera, attempts to follow Will as unobtrusively as possible into the building. But they are stopped at the door by a villager who appears out of nowhere. They are quietly but definitively turned away.

Peering around the corner, Dayone sees this and smiles grimly. He cracks his knuckles.

Inside, Manley moves confidently from chart to slick chart. On the screen, a computer animation of the MRS's storage areas shows automated equipment ferrying nuclear waste safely into chambers created for just this purpose.

"...a marvel of safe, efficient automation. But machines have to be serviced, and that's just another of the opportunities open to the people of this tribe. Employment, jobs, prosperity—those are the keywords in this context. The guidelines are few but very, very strict—and you control them. We specify the safety precautions, you control everything else. It's perfect."

"It's the perfect target." Teo doesn't care if he's interrupting, not if it's Manley.

Manley is used to this. "What are you saying?"

"There's no risk *now*," says Teo enigmatically.

"I've already told you, there'll be three layers of security. Three layers of insulation and isolation. Three layers of protection."

"Let me ask you, Is terrorism increasing in the world?"

"Yes, but—what does that have to do—?"

"If I were a terrorist, I'd see an MRS as a great target. Seems to be that's adding a grave risk to where there is none today. How you get out from under that?"

Victor raps his cane. Teo settles back into his big leather chair.

Will enters and sits down behind Victor in a seat pointed out to him by Clarence. Will nods to Teo and Simon across the room.

Manley continues, "As for the health issue, before proceeding with San Lucas's application for Federal funding, we had to establish a health baseline for the tribe. In that way, when the money is used to improve the welfare of the tribe, you will be able to prove it, justify it, and again, control it. If we can use that piece of land way far out on the back end of the Pueblo—think of the possibilities to both of you."

Outside, Dayone is at this moment considering what the warrior-guard of his Pueblo should be aware of, the direction from which any potential threat to his tribe, or even this meeting, could come—. That's when he sees Frank at the back end of the alley, receiving three pints of whiskey from a man in the passenger seat of a pickup.

Frank motions for the man to keep the change, then stashes a bottle in each back pocket, palming the third as he walks, and strolls towards the plaza, towards Dayone.

"Dayone, Dayone, child of the child of my father. What the hell you doing, you little shit?"

"Council Meeting inside."

"Supporting the tribe. Holding up the wall, are ya? Good thing, little brother. I gotta talk to your father this afternoon about something that will put this tribe on the map in a good way, not none of this toxic waste shit."

Frank leans against the wall.

"Okay," says Dayone dryly, "Tell me about your plans for world fame".

Inside, Manley uses a red laser pointer to indicate certain data on the screen's changing graphs, charts, and tables. "Now we just commissioned a survey of current health right here in San Lucas, thanks to the doctor and staff of your own local Health Clinic. Our company helped pay for that survey which benefits the entire Pueblo. But it's just a taste of the possibilities. Look at what we found—."

Will listens intently to Manley's interpretation of the survey.

It's clear by his body language that Manley believes he is masterfully negotiating some otherwise potentially difficult terrain. "And here, while it appears that tuberculosis has begun a resurgence, that is no different, as you can see, from what is happening in the U.S. at large."

Will shakes his head.

Manley continues, "And here, note that infant mortality has improved significantly relative to the tribal-versus-national correlative. The grant monies from an MRS feasibility study can lock in those trends for a long time to come.'

Will bends forward and whispers to Victor. "I don't think he understands the report I gave him, Governor."

But Victor waves him off.

Manley, "There's no question, is there, that this, in itself, is a clear demonstration of the value of available and responsible medical care?

My hats off to this survey and hopeful that the monies you *deserve* will only make this kind of health care more available."

Will starts to stand. Victor sits him down and whispers.

"No. You must wait."

"But this is the crucial part of the survey, sir."

"It is not our way. You must learn this, Doctor."

Will sits and listen, very uncomfortable. He sees Teo, very distraught, bending over to whisper something in Simon's ear. Simon holds up his finger, urging patience.

Everybody's urging patience, but there doesn't seem to be a lot of patience in the room.

"Suicide and alcoholism, shown here, are well above national levels. Proof, I suggest, that the American Dream is not being made available to Native Americans in general, and to San Lucas Pueblo in particular. But that can change, like that, when you capitalize on what you own." He snaps a finger.

Will's agitation grows as the projected image changes.

"The building of a Monitored Retrieval Site, an MRS, on otherwise marginal tribal lands, would surely turn the tide for those whose despair at ever finding financial success, or even financial subsistence, has driven them to self-destructive behavior. Go with your strength. Go with what you own and control. Make these things work for you!"

Finally, Will can hold it in no longer. He stands and passionately states his professional objections. "Excuse me, Mr. Manley. I apologize for interrupting you, but you are grossly misrepresenting the data that I was asked to gather for this Pueblo."

Most of the various Council members look at each other, all variously alarmed at Will's interruption and his disregard of tribal protocol. Victor is angry. Teo is torn.

Will ventures, "Look, TB on the reservation began its resurgence years before the rest of the country. Second, infant mortality, while it is *growing* more slowly than the national average, was already so far above it that the difference in growth rates is irrelevant."

Manley shows nothing. Teo starts to rise, but Simon reaches out and again gently restrains him and whispers, "Let the Romans do to the Romans as—."

Will continues, "And third, any student of psychology can tell you that lack of money is only one of dozens of reasons for suicide or alcoholism. The health survey that I conducted was done not to show how health would get better with an MRS." He looks around, nervous but committed. "I now see it's to help the government protect itself against lawsuits based on future MRS-related health claims. I'm sorry for the interruption, Mr. Manley, but your interpretations are simply, and significantly, wrong—and worse, misleading."

Will sits down. The crowd murmurs and shifts. Manley's expression betrays nothing. Teo looks around expectantly, agitated, uncertain what this means. Victor stands. The Sgt.-at-Arms turns on the lights.

Victor waits—commanding a silence. "I agree with Doctor Kornfeld. The health survey is valuable to our tribe, but of no real importance to the funding-for-study proposal. But it will be of enormous help in the future. Thank you, Doctor. And thank you, Mr. Manley. We can proceed without the rest of your presentation because I think your points have been made very well. We will finish our discussion and then we will vote. Council Member Churino, it is your time to speak, and then we will break for lunch."

Manley walks away to his seat, not quite understanding what's happening.

Churino stands. "To all of you I say this. My two sons are good men, but they have no work. We are not hunter-gatherers, we are not farmers. Those days are past. We are workers And your Council are business-men, representing the best interests of what all of us owns— our land."

62

ONE-EYED ANGER

As the discussion continues, it becomes clearer to Will that this is a place only for the Governor and the Council—all others are here at the pleasure of the Governor. While the decisions made here are formal and official, almost everyone knows that the decisions have already been made.

And Teo—he's been a governor. None of this should surprise him. And yet it does. Unobtrusively, he scans the room. He studies each Council member. And then something Frank once said pops into his mind. Frank had just come home after the publication of his first book. He was drunk, of course; but he stood there in front of Teo's house and recounted how he happened to attend a fairly high up Mafia meeting to discuss who had commanding control over the profits of a dance hall that was being set up on the border between two families' turf. He said the meeting reminded him very much of his own tribe's council meetings.

In the vestibule just outside the two large doors to the Council Hall, Manley and his two aides are already packing up their gear when Victor comes into view with Will and Clarence. When he sees Manley, he separates from the two, indicating privacy.

In the background, confident and enthused, Churino is talking to some other elders. He is pointing, as is their way, with his chin to Will.

Victor approaches Manley alone. "I had to do that, to keep from losing control of the—"

Manley is corporate-smooth, "No explanation is necessary, Governor. Your job is to keep your eye on the ball. My job is to be G.

Gordon Liddy at the target waiting with you for the arrow to arrive. I know what our goals are, and I will do whatever it takes to achieve them. As long as we're moving forward, we'll get there."

Manley doesn't really believe that. But Victor does.

Impressed by the steel in Manley's voice, Victor gestures acknowledgment, then waves for Clarence and Will to follow .

They exit through the backdoor to the Council Hall.

"Our ways are different, Doctor. Don't make any other assumption. What you did, your interruption, was...was—"

"You're right, Governor. I wouldn't have done it if he were a council member. Sorry if that showed you disrespect. I didn't mean it."

Victor's train of thought wanders as he looks off: he sees Frank and Dayone, still leaning against the wall near the front. Frank is stashing one of his pint bottles in his jacket pocket. Dayone stares into space, uninterested in Frank, waiting for his grandfather.

But Victor is concerned. "Clarence, see if those two are drinking. If they are, get Tribal to lock them up. If not, bring my son to me. But first, find Reyna. Check his office or the Court Room. We need his vote."

Clarence heads towards the Plaza.

As Victor reenters the Council Hall, to Will, "Doctor, I trust you implicitly to do what you were trained to do. I will not interfere in your work with my people. You bring the latest medical practices—as far as the budgets allow—to your job here. Please trust me to do the same for my people in the job they have chosen me to do" Their eyes connect. They shake. Victor smiles warmly and leaves.

Clarence crosses the narrow dirt road and disappears into the Tribal Court House.

Will takes a few steps into the shade of a portico, not sure if he's upset more with himself or the way things are done here. He can see Frank and Dayone, but with the sun at his back they don't see him. Will pulls a banana from his pocket, leans against a pillar, and watches.

Frank is motioning for Dayone to follow him back into the alley between the Court House and the adjacent building. Dayone takes a few steps into the alley, but then stops just below the second-floor windows to Judge Reyna's office. His eyes dart quickly to the plaza, then up the alley, just as the sun flares off the chrome air-filter cover to Frank's Harley parked at the end of the alley.

"Ya see, little brother," Frank says with squinty eyes, "it ain't ol' alcohol that sucks your tit after all. It's one-eyed anger. It's youth betrayed by a dying social order. And that just pisses the shit out of me."

"I know what you're saying, but who the fuck are you talking to?"

"I'm talking to you."

"No, you're talking *from* you, yeah, always you, but you're not talking *to* me. Not to me! Knowm'sayin', Uncle?

"Well, well, well. Growing some hair on your balls, nephew."

Frank opens one of his pints and takes a swig. "But you're still a minor. This here is bad for minors. Okay for adults. Does damage to kids. Kids still have a future. Adults do not. You'll respect me if I don't give you a sip. But you'll like me if I do. Life is full of knives that cut both ways. Screw it, little brother, have a honk."

Dayone doesn't take bottle, doesn't even look at it. "You love to hear yourself talk."

"Look, *coyo*, maybe I sold my soul to the bottle and the thin white line, but I sing stomping songs of glory and the women just keep on comin'...heh-heh-heh."

He raises the pint to some deity. "Flood your gullet with the sweat of Her thigh. Long live Red Cloud's anger!"

Frank takes a long pull, then extends the pint to Dayone again.

Neither is aware that Judge Reyna, in his office above is listening to the interchange below.

As Dayone slowly takes it, his eyes narrow and he looks from the bottle to Frank. He starts to bounce from one foot to the other, nervous, taunting, hostility rising.

"I thought you were cool, Frank, but you're a dumb shit. Every chance you get to wise up, you blow it. You don't even know what's going on. Not with your tribe. Not with me. And not with your father. He's dying, Frank."

"Take your drink, asshole, and give it back. No, goddammit, just give it here."

Reyna steps up closer to the window as he puts on his vest. He looks down with interest, unseen.

Dayone regresses to teenage taunting, but the bite is man-to-man. "You want me to take a drink or you don't, Frank. You gotta tell me what you want. You're my elder, aren't you?"

"Are you deaf, Manolete? Give it back."

"Fucking Indian-giver. All my life I looked up to you." He toys with the precious little bottle. "You want this back?"

He extends it, then jerks it away. "I always thought Simon was the asshole, because of the way you treated him, but it was you who was fucked up all along. Here's your dose, man—"

Dayone tosses the pint. Frank lunges, fumbles. It falls and breaks.

"You little dip-shit! I'm gonna kick your fuckin' ass!?"

Frank goes for Dayone, but stops and recovers his cool.

"No victory for Dayo. That's why I buy 'em small and portable—dip-shit slut-sucker."

Frank turns and pulls another pint. But when he turns around, cap untwisted, Dayone is in his face and, with lightning speed, slaps the bottle away from Frank's lips, sending it down to join the other, in pieces.

Frank comes unglued. "Godfuckin'dammit!!"

Dayone runs off a few feet, ready to flee. On the verge of tears, he's breathing fast and shallow.

Once again, Frank holds his temper. "I'm not going to forget this. And I am going to whip your little red ass. And I'm going to cut off about an inch of your ear. But not today. I have to make a proposal to the Council today. But I promise. And I got another. Gonna do me just one."

As he takes out his last pint, Dayone collapses inside and sinks slowly down to the ground, against the building, under Reyna's window.

Reyna is staring out the window when Clarence enters.

"Victor wants you to—"

Reyna holds up his hand, intent on Frank and Dayone. Clarence comes to the window, looks out.

"Oh, yeah. The boy's AWOL from his grandfather, and they're drinking. Victor wants 'em locked up while the meeting's—"

Judge Reyna turns away from the window, then softly, "I don't see a boy disobeying an order, or drinking. I see two men discussing a family problem. One that must be faced."

Reyna heads out his door. Clarence, confused, follows.

Outside, Dayone holds his head in his hands. Frank, fire in his eyes, his face contorting, towers over the boy, chugs on his pint.

Dayone looks up at his uncle, unafraid. "I don't give a shit what you do to me, asshole."

Frank caps his pint, pockets it, then reaches down, grabs Dayone, jerks him up and slams him against the wall. Dayone grunts in pain, but doesn't defend himself. As Frank starts to push him into the wall again, Dayone reaches around, grabs the pint from Frank's hip pocket and dashes it. Frank yells, throws Dayone down, and is on him, knee on his chest. As Frank cocks to strike, two hands lift Frank up and press him into the wall face first.

"What the fu--!"

It's Will, holding Frank immobile. Dayone is up quickly and disappears around the corner. Slowly, cautiously, Will lets Frank's feet touch the ground.

Frank is livid. "You sonuvabitch! You stick your big nose in here—yeah, you prance in here like some Peace Corps hero, dropping your doctor gifts on us like we're some backward country."

"That's simply unfair. That's not why I'm—"

"Unfair? Hey, I'm a third-world loudmouth in a first-world country. I know how to manipulate white guilt. Oh, shame on me."

"You're not on stage now, Frank."

"Hey, racism killed the Indians. It's tryin' t'save us. Not all racists are equal." He pokes Will in the ribs. "Some are slow...some real fascist."

"You don't have a clue who I am, or why I'm here."

Real sweet and sarcastic, "Sure I do. You're a self-hating, Injun-lovin' Jew who wants to be my friend."

"You don't have friends. Not your style."

"Bingo. Indians aren't friends with whites. They're curiosities. You think I could be anything but a curiosity to you?"

"You're so full of yourself. And you're a racist yourself!"

Will turns and heads away towards his truck.

"Answer my question, Doctor White Bread."

Will stops, turns, steps back a step, "If the Nazis came for me, would you hide me in your home?"

"Hai-yai! How long you been carrying that one around?"

"Both are peoples who've been holocausted."

Frank sneers and laughs and points—. Will covers his self-consciousness by wiping his mouth and walking away.

Frank follows a few steps. "Is this a Holocaust thing? Guilt driving the big Jew to help his little brown brothers? To me you're not one of 'the chosen'. You're just another white boy who was brought in to profit, gawk, and rule."

Will turns again, towering over Frank, He leans in face-to-face, hot. "The last time you and I talked, you called me Jake. You remember that...Esau?"

Frank is undaunted by Will's tone or imposing physical presence.

"Oh, shit, here it comes. The ghost of Simon-Isaac flying down to bless the good son and bugger the bad one."

"You hear what you're saying? To you, Simon's already a ghost!"

"Good medical diagnosis, Doc."

"He's not dead, Frank. Not yet! You still got time to get his blessing. Or give him yours."

"Listen, Jake, the old man don't have a thing I want."

"Bullshit! Then what are you doing here?"

"I live here! What are you doing here, Jew boy? Sniffin' out Injun snatch?"

Frank underscores the "snatch" with another finger poke to Will's chest. Will's arm flashes out, grabbing Frank's wrist, bending it back.

"You don't live here," hisses Will. "Not really. You just come here to take a dump and leave the tribe to clean up your oh-so-poetical shit."

Frank kicks for the groin. Will reflexively deflects, stiff-arming Frank against a wall, perilously close to a large cactus growing nearby. Frank regains balance, tucks, and instinctively returns with a switch-blade out. Will beats him to the punch and goes in without hesitation, this time deflecting Frank's knife arm across Frank's own chest, and grabs him in a bear-hug and squeezes hard. Frank tenses, goes wide-eyed for a moment and cannot move. Their noses are almost touching. Will is fiery-eyed. Frank goes interior, as Will whispers lethally.

"My grandfather survived Nazi death camps so that I could be here helping you and your tribe. He walked into rooms stacked with dead bodies and he pulled gold teeth out of dead mouths and took jewelry off of dead fingers so that real racists could turn his people into soap. You don't know who I am."

Will, shaking with emotion, shoves Frank away and is stunned to see that the knife has stuck into Frank's arm. Frank shows no pain, but when he removes it, blood spurts pulsing everywhere.

Will takes a step back, "Artery!"

When Will gets Frank to the Clinic he finds it in an uproar. "What the hell's going on, Rebeca?!"

"Oh, the police picked up Daniel Paisano, that crazy guy who's always spouting gibberish and dancing around in a weird way. He dropped a kerosene lantern and some old women got burned so Lola went—and Jaime's mother was one of the women and—"

"I'm taking Frank to the ER. Can you assist me?"

"I'm not qualified, Doctor. Amalia should be here any minute."

"You're now qualified. Battlefield promotion. Follow me."

In the ER, Will scrubs. While Rebeca holds a compress against his wound, Frank opens a glass cabinet and grabs a bottle labeled 'ethyl alcohol.' He opens it and drinks.

Rebeca tries to stop him. "Frank, don't!"

Frank pays no attention. "Antiseptic against *wasichu* cooties."

Rebeca is incensed. "Frank, you shouldn't talk that way."

Will pulls on his rubber gloves. There is a long tense silence while he prepares a syringe of anesthetic. "I'm sure needles don't bother you."

Frank pulls away his hand from the compress abruptly. The liquor-thinned artery spurts across Will's white coat. Will clamps a hand on it.

"With so much alcohol in your system," says Will with narrowed eyes, "you probably don't need this. But what the hell—." With that, he jams the needle into Frank's arm—with gusto.

Frank is the stoic Indian as he receives the injection.

As Will pulls the syringe out, Frank leans forward, "Ya know, Doc, I got this friend in Denver, a prostitute, a beautiful soul really, who's into a little S and M for the upper-classes. I think you two would hit it off."

Will turns to Rebeca. "Where's Louisa?"

"She's doing a house call, I think, to check on Tessie and her new baby."

The two men stare at each other while the anesthetic takes over.

Now Will is holding Frank's arm, cleaning, examining the wound. "Gotta take the skin back, suture the artery first."

Will picks up a scalpel, looks at Frank, and cuts. There is one more thin spurt of blood before it is controlled.

While Will, head lowered, sutures, Frank stealthily reaches over and picks up the scalpel.

"Hold still, dammit!"

But Frank positions the scalpel on Will's forearm, ready to cut. The two men lock eyes. Then Frank looks to the blade and slowly, gently, glides it across Will's skin. The cut is shallow and bleeds only a little. Will is shocked, but before he can react, Frank takes his half-open wound and crosses it over and against Will's cut. Frank looks at Will with a thin and malevolent "gotcha!" smile.

Rebeca cannot stifle a little scream.

"Now Jacob, you and your Esau are blood brothers at last. And you'll be intrigued to know that I am HIV..." He draws it waaaay out, "...negative!" then laughs maniacally.

"I'm going to call the police," says Rebeca sliding away towards the door.

"Rebeca, please bring me a compress." As she does so, "And, Rebeca nothing you've heard or seen in this room leaves this room. Patient-Medical Staff privilege."

She nods without saying a word.

"To no one," Will adds.

"I'm a professional, Doctor."

"Thanks. I appreciate it."

In his office, bandages now on both their arms, Will, breathing heavily, takes a clean white coat out of a closet, while Frank snoops furtively into Will's cabinets and drawers. Will, barely in control, pushes Frank away from his desk, then wheels around, pointing at the potted plant.

"That little tree, it's mine, my grandfather's actually, but your father dreamed it. I brought it from New York. Make any sense to you?"

Frank inspects the tree. "Simon's a spooky shit, ain't he? I never used to think he was. But now I think he is. Maybe it's an improvement. Back to you, Jake."

"Whatever Simon's got, you've got, too, Frank." Off Frank's flipped finger, "He's your father, Frank!"

"He abused my mother! He abandoned me! He's nobody's father! And your fuckin' little tree—means shit all!"

Will hurries to leave and get back to the meeting. "Your father told me this tree is about me and my grandfather. But it's not. It's about all of us and all our grandfathers. It's about you and Simon. And me and Simon. And—"

"Wow, talk about giving new meaning to going native. You're hanging onto the living dead, man."

"Did you even know he was going to speak at the Council meeting today? It's an important meeting."

"No, and I couldn't care. This nuclear waste site shit is old story, same story. Casinos, mining, pollution, dissolution—he doesn't understand those things. He's getting ready to leave this life. 'Bout time. Hey, you wanna buy a new lease in the after-life?"

"Bullshit. I'm going back there. And as for this Jacob and Esau crap, I'm not stealing your father's blessing. You're giving it to me!"

"What a yahoo. Tallest fuckwit I've ever seen. In one ear an—"

But Frank is too drunk. He moves erratically, flailing at demons, then bolts. "Ya can't get anything from him, Doc! Ya just don't know! He's a treacherous bastard." He lurches into the hallway. "He'll le'go the rope when he's s'posed to hang on. Don't be at the other end of it. You let him in, you blink, and he's gone!"

As Will pulls out of the Clinic parking lot, he passes Frank stumbling away. At the last second, Frank leaps and jumps into the back of the pickup. He sits against the cab, holding his knees and scowling. Will glances back, his face grim, he shakes his head and drives on.

Frank pulls out the bottle he took from the Clinic. With one inch of pure alcohol remaining, he chugs it.

At the Tribal Council Hall, Will pulls up and gets out and notices Frank is gone.

He heads into the Meeting. At the door, the Sgt.-at-Arms acknowledges and lets him pass without a word.

He enters the Council Meeting Hall, drawing eyes.

Teo is speaking. "Yes, they did this at Mescalero. Well, you can talk to some of them, but it depends on who you talk to. It's been a real shakeup. Some were helped, some were hurt. Some are enthused. Some are devastated. How can I say? The effect is not always...physical. It can be psychological, generational, it can affect us at the deepest levels." He balances his thoughts with his hands, "How can you weigh the physical against the spiritual?"

Will sees Wynema and beckons. He leads her back into the foyer where they can talk.

"I'm not giving up on you," says Will, "on us." Shushing her interruption, "What I actually mean is that I'm not giving up the feeling. I know you've got your road. Take it. Do it. I've got my road, too, like you said. But I may speak your language yet."

Off her look of question, "Sotero told me so."

She whispers, "Sotero? I don't understand. You've been talking to our—"

"That crazy old coot. Yeah, one of my clients. I'll tell you later. I almost killed Frank today. Then I doctored him. But I didn't heal him, that's for sure. What a piece of work. I'll tell you about that later. Simon speak yet?"

She shakes her head, then leads him back inside.

63

WALKING ON THE FACE OF UNBORN CHILDREN

Victor notices them. They notice Victor. Will wants to be incon-spicuous.

Teo is still speaking. "Why do they target low-income and minor-ity communities with facilities and wastes that are dangerous? Our brothers and sisters from the Chickasaw, Sac and Fox, Shawnee, and Caddo tribes—they applied for these funds, but they pulled back. They withdrew their application. We should find out why. Let us at least wait a few years. This is a momentous decision with some seri-ous implications that may not be reversible. You don't want to think about seven generations? How about six? Do I hear five? That is all I have to say."

There is silence. Victor waits. Everyone waits. Teo looks to Simon.

Dayone's friend, Danny, raises his hand and stands, and waits for the Governor to recognize him. Victor takes a deep breath and shakes his head no.

When he doesn't call on Danny, the boy begins anyway. "I know why the Sac and Fox tribe said no."

There is a long pause, but this time Victor takes deep breath and forces patience.

The boy is hesitant and mumbles. "My name is Danny Ortiz and I'm a friend of Dayone's and I haven't been a good person here or anywhere really. But Dayone kinda got me thinking. So I went to a friend's computer and looked it up on the Internet and it's because the daughter of Jim Thorpe who won a gold-medal in the 1912 Olympic Decath-o-lon and who's a member of the Sac and Fox tribe in Okla-homa told her Council—she said," as he reads from a piece of paper, "'I knew diddly squat about radioactivity. So I went to the library right away. When I read that you can't see it, can't smell it, and can't hear it, but that it is the most lethal poison in the history of man, I knew our sacred land shouldn't even be associated with it.' She said that in 1992." And with that stumbling reading Danny sits and looks down and is embarrassed.

Victor uses his silver cane of office to rise slowly, thoughtfully. "It is late and all of us have spoken many times. And questions have been asked and answers given. And we have thought long and hard about the opportunity before us. We can vote our hearts, and feel good about our decision. This is okay. And we will go on with our ideas and with our lives, in a tribe of strong and healthy clans."

Victor taps his silver-capped cane on the floor. Once...twice.... It quickly becomes the only sound heard...until Simon rises.

"I would speak." He bows his head.

Suddenly the eyes of the Council members betray their interest.

Simon slowly lifts his head and makes a graceful, curving motion with his hand.

"Shall we turn this way on the Road, and say yes to this money? First the money, then the study, then this very safe building to protect us from the nuclear poison on the land we have known forever. Looking back, forever is a good feeling. Our grandmothers and grandfathers are there. But if we look forward, 'forever' doesn't look as good. Everything we do must carry our grandmothers and grandfathers into the future, for the sake of our grandchildren and great-grandchildren. You know what I mean. I know you do."

Now the Council members move more than their eyes, and glance slowly, inconspicuously, at each other.

Simon takes a deep breath and continues. "Everybody knows you gotta have reverence for the Earth. Even people who fly to the Moon and look back know this. When what you hold sacred grows small, your wars grow big. Very big. I fought in two of their wars. Men will fight wars when they forget that they come from one Mother Earth. Amazing, when you think about it."

An old woman sitting next to Reymunda Reyna begins to cry. Wynema is looking inside herself to the center of the Universe. Will is looking at her. A man sitting on the other side of Wynema touches his son's knee.

There is a long pause and no one cuts it short.

"How do ancient, gentle values stand up against these new and exciting ways? Tell me, do our old ways stand a chance?"

Another long pause.

Victor is stone, a fiercely thinking stone. Simon has thrown him backward and forward in time. He is not here right now. Victor is thinking about all the many times as a young man he reached out to the Old Ways and offered himself in their service. He is also thinking about how all his ideas were rejected. How ashamed he felt, or was made to feel—inadequate. But thinking forward, has he not become Pueblo Governor? And he will consider running for State Senator in a few years. Being the first Native Governor of the State is not out of the question.

"I say yes," Simon answers his own question. "Years ago, I met a man of the Onondaga. He said: 'Every time we walk on the face of the Earth, we are walking on the face of unborn children. We must care for these children,' he said, 'and walk lightly'."

In this pause, Simon turns his head slowly, but his eyes see only Victor.

"We must not walk with those who do not respect the land."

Victor is an unblinking statue of attention, right here right now.

"Because if we hold to our ways, like that, they will walk with us someday."

A faint smile of pride plays at the corners of Teo's mouth. The man sitting next to Teo taps him on the leg and makes a motion with his cell that he's going to text someone. Teo nods approvingly.

Wynema suddenly inhales, then closes her eyes.

A quarter mile away, Mirriamma, at her house at that moment and holding a black fetish with bright red feathers, sends two younger women hurrying off in different directions.

Simon points to his navel. "This belly button reminds us where we come from, that we are connected to our Mother, the Earth. This land is the only land we've ever had as a people. Only land we ever will have—as a people. Without this land, there is no people."

Clarence, eyebrows pinched, nods slightly in serious rumination.

"This land is our Mother in a way few people left in this world can know. Maybe this is only an idea, but it's a good idea, that we should hold onto—maybe forever."

Will's face can't hide his welling emotion. Wynema's face is less open.

Council member Churino glances towards the seated villagers. He sees an old woman nodding affirmatively to what Simon is saying. Churino shakes his head subtly in stubborn denial of Simon. He simply does not see the connection. Gilbert Reyna, the Judge's brother, followed by three others, enters the Council Hall. The four move slowly to stand next to a window.

Two women attempt to enter through the big doors. The Sgt.-at-Arms looks around at all the people, seated and standing. "Go tell your father that he should come, because we have enough women in here now."

The women are incensed, but turn away and leave.

"My son says the Indian must die for our values to live. Same kind of thinking as we had to destroy the village in order to save it. It's poetic, I guess, but silly. No, the Indian must live. To die is easy. To live is harder. Mother Earth *is everything*. And we are part of that. She needs us and not just for color."

That makes a few people chuckle.

Frank is standing on a chair against the wall in the back of the room. The alcohol comes to the service of his biased inner mantras—all he hears are platitudes. He doesn't really hear what Simon is saying. The fact that Simon is saying these things here, however, is having a profound effect. It is heating him up inside. Competition.

Simon's voice grows soft, yet all hear him clearly.

"The Great Spirit, *G'na-tum-si*, gave me a mind to think about many things. I have thought, like that, about this thing, this MRS. If it came to us in reverence for our Mother, I would think maybe—."

Frank's eyes grow wilder. Inside, he slides from gnawing sadness to seething anger.

"—maybe yes, let us study about this temporary toxic storage thing. But, right now, no, I don't feel the sacred in any of it. Do you?"

Wynema and Will squeeze each other's fingers fiercely, unseen by anyone. Will looks up and sees Dayone peering in the highest open window. Dayone is standing on an ancient log-pole ladder he's moved into place.

The silence in the room is palpable, almost making Simon's soft voice reverberate.

"Our people have lived and died with the seasons of our Mother for you know how long. It is a cycle and everything that goes in must go out. Like breath or food or knowledge. To do this MRS is to take in something called uranium—that cannot go back out for a million years. They call it half-life. It can kill a people. It usually lives way under the ground. Mother Earth protects us this way."

For the last half hour villagers have been steadily, quietly filling the room. It takes but a few minutes for word to get out. Cell phones help. The two women turned away return with their father. As they follow him into the room, one of them sticks her tongue out at the Sgt.-at-Arms.

Frank almost falls from his chair and must push aside some stand-ees to get a little closer.

Simon continues: "Teo has spoken to you about money. There is much to say for money. Much to say. But come on now. Let us be a lot more clever, a lot more wise, than we have been. Money and new ways will come in—but what makes us different, what makes us our-selves, will disappear. We're few enough as it is. Maybe that's what will happen, but is this something we *want* to help happen? To see ourselves disappear? I don't want us to disappear. I don't care about myself, I guess—but, the clan, the tribe, the connection to the Old Ones—you all know about that better than I do. It must be possible to stay who we are and live comfortably. I believe that. To live com-fortably, after so many are now gone, all across this land. To live comfortably—that would be enough if we could stay a people and remember the Old Ones. The Earth made us into who we are. She must have had a reason. No, I don't want to become like the Great Salt Lake or the Dead Sea. I cannot say to you to kill our Mother in this way for then we will surely disappear."

Frank careens past all those standing to a place where all the Council can see him. He is dark, keen, and mad. "Oh, are you wor-ried at last that you may have done something to our Mother?!" The irony is thick and vengeful and perhaps there are a few there who do not understand it—but the older ones do. Frank stumbles over a seated person's leg in the aisle. He struggles to pick himself up.

People, the Council, look to Victor for what to do. Victor rises. He tries to keep his eyes down as he gathers his thoughts to take control—he must do something—but somehow he is drawn to look up and to the left. The Cacique, the spiritual leader of his tribe, gestures to him, which makes Victor sit back down.

Frank moves erratically towards Simon, his eyes, rabid, hallucinated, wildly casting around the room. There is barely any room to move now, and there are still other villagers trying to enter.

Victor is motionless, mesmerized. Grudgingly he remembers something his uncle Paul Benitez used to say: "Anyone who can command the attention of the public with simple words has something to teach you." Victor has always been jealous of Frank's freedom.

"And how 'bout all of you," Frank roars, "who pretended not to know?! Where are you when they take him away? For killing his mother...or in order to give him a little extra, you know, tender-loving care? Which do you suppose?"

Then snapping back to Simon, "Why didn't you fight them harder? Wasn't he worth it?! Why was he so easy to let go of? Get rid of the little killer?"

Rocked inside, rigid without, Simon's eyes unfold the direct hit.

"'Go live with your in-laws,' you said. 'Your mother's parents will take care of you now. This is good. This is better for the boy'."

Frank is being crushed in the dark painful unstoppable moment.

Will looks to Wynema. He clearly isn't understanding what's happening. She whispers, "He's talking about himself." Will winces, digs deeper to understand.

Simon unconsciously backs into someone who backs into someone—until a young man about thirty reflexively steadies him.

Everyone there is now here, in the moment. It almost seems like pockets of people are swaying imperceptibly back and forth together, dancing with father and son. There's an undulation here.

Victor looks off again. The Cacique is gone. But another old man is sitting there, and he's looking directly at Victor. He raises his hand for a moment, palm facing out, and smiles. The Cacique's proxy, telling him basically to let things continue, to do nothing....

Victor reacts against being controlled. He wants to stand and do something about this. Frank is way off topic. But he cannot budge.

Frank moves into a shaft of light coming from the highest window, the one through which Dayone is watching. He continues: "His good looks buy him friends. It makes a man of him. Oh, yeah, they made a man of him."

There is a clarity now to his soft insanity. The listeners are not as tense as they usually are when Frank 'talks to them'.

"Say, when is the next Corn Sprouting Dance?" He stops and just stands there. A woman sitting next to him offers him a plastic bottle of water. He takes it, drinks quickly, leans against a big log pillar. Nobody moves.

Except Simon. He steps forward—his voice sounding more like chant than answer.

"This thing, this money, this 'opportunity'—will make us angry. Anger. Can anyone imagine why the Indian is always angry? How could that be? Look around you. Read the history books, even *their* history books. It's been a massacre. But you know what? I think it's almost over. They're in trouble. Their system is crashing down around them."

This brings a slight stirring to the people there. Simon turns slowly and faces Frank. "That's why it's better to hold on a bit longer, without taking money from someone who doesn't know us, who doesn't care about us and really looks at us as idiots for holding onto land that could be turned into something productive...profitable."

Frank erupts with an almost ghoulish laugh, but abruptly stops and looks blankly at his father. "Profitable!?"

Simon checks a lancing pain in his chest and continues. "You see, their ways are falling apart, because they lost their friends. When you lose your principles, you lose your friends. That's the way it goes. They outfoxed themselves. Newspapers, television, big money—talked them into electing to power people who kept taking more and more power, more and more money, and then stood there as example of what it means to be American. They lost their old stories."

Frank blurts, "Major readjustment coming." And then drops his head onto his chest.

Simon continues in sad rhythm. "Their economy is going to collapse. Sorry 'bout that. That collapse will definitely trickle down to us. And their environment, the Earth where they walk, it can't take the abuse anymore. Their connection to everything is broken and they know it. That is why—that is why—they will come to us soon, not to take our land, but to learn how to relate to it."

Frank snaps up, "Hee-hee! I tol' you that! I tol' you that!"

"When that happens, I don't think it will serve anybody's interests to have toxic waste here. Bad move. Go to jail. Do not collect two-hundred dollars."

The villager sitting next to where Simon stands is taking a Rolaids from its pack. Simon gently leans over and takes the antacid and puts it in his own mouth.

"Tell 'em, Pop." Frank turns to his people. "Don't be stupid! Why are we always so stupid?"

Simon takes a few steps and looks at a neighbor. The neighbor nods in encouragement.

Simon continues. "Maybe finding something profitable can be done without hurting our Mother, I don't know. What I do know is putting toxic waste on land we consider sacred is not the way to find out. There are other ways, and you and Victor can find them together. But you gotta look. And then you gotta speak your words, your truth, what the Grandfathers are telling you."

He walks towards the exit a few steps, then turns and walks back. "You know that land being talked about out there for this thing—you know right in the middle of it is Two Dog Rock."

This animates the man with the Rolaids, who grunts and bobs up and down.

"Just a big stone next to two withered trees. Nothing much." He puts his hand on the rolaids-man's shoulder. "Juan's grandfather here was born in the shade of that rock. Why do we remember that? Because *his* grandfather, Popo, later went to Washington and got the government to give back Bear Lake and now nobody goes up there but our people—as is proper. He helped save a holy place. From that rock up to the lake—I know the way. *Hi-na-ney na-way-o*. It's all part of it."

Simon takes a huge breath and turns again back to Frank. "When you and I lost Dahyanee, everybody here lost Dahyanee." He looks around the room. Almost everyone in the room is connected to him now. He turns until he sees Frank. "You, my son, are angry—always angry. But you had words to give your anger—shape and form. Horrible beautiful words. But I twisted up inside and ran to the cliffs and cried in silence. I lost my words. You found the words. Big difference some ways. Kind of proud of you there."

The doors to the room open slowly, revealing many villagers who found out that this is where they needed to be.

With a serenity past pain, Simon looks deeper, "And Jealousy. That's the other big Indian sin. Anger and Jealousy. Anger got you, Frank. Jealousy got me. But I never doubted that you were my son. My jealousy was a disease, aimed at any man who looked at my wife. People and cultures are crazy today that think they protect their women this way."

There is a momentary shuffling in the room, then stillness again.

Victor looks up. *Ah, the Cacique hasn't returned. Maybe now is the time to move. How can I let the likes of Simon and Frank control the meeting this way?!*

"Oh, everybody loves their mothers," intones Simon. "But do we love the Mother of us all? What is the quality of this love? How much strength does it give us? This is the strength we will need in the days ahead. That's why I say we're no longer a dying breed. We know how to teach this love of the Earth. It's in our blood. *That* they never killed out of us."

Frank is back standing on his chair, looking out over the heads of everyone, steadying himself by a protruding ceiling viga above his head. "It's not nice to kill your mother!" Like some gargoyle come alive, he taunts it down over everyone. He searches every eye that suddenly is upturned to him. Simon relaxes, becomes still, releasing the moment again to his son.

"Oh, Father, you come talking like this after twenty-plus years and expect to flow back into her arms?" Frank leaps off the chair, one knee buckles, but he stands quickly. "Even if the tribe welcomes you back, will She take you back, our mother, the Earth, in spite of the fact that we rape her away every day!? She should react to you like our white-blood-cells react to foreign toxic invaders." He turns on some villagers to his right: "Why do you keep those old dead cars around, rusting—a sculptural monument to how you feel about your-selves and your lives and the Land? And the washing machines! Oh, and now I see we're starting to pile up old computers and TVs and stereo equipment at the back ends of our property. How very modern of us."

Will doesn't understand everything, but he watches in anguishing empathy. Wynema's eyes are filled with tears of knowing. She lets her eyes drift and takes in a long slow breath. She feels the breathing of others around her. Everyone's breathing has slowed down together.

Frank wails: "All her mountains, and rivers of gentle red blood, so full of life, good to her children. Killed...died...dead." His madness returning to sadness, "Where were all of you?"

Simon's eyes do not focus as he roams the inside of the outside of everything that is happening.

Frank looks at everyone and sees no one. "We forget that the truly good stuff we get, we get from our Mother? But go on about your life. Don't worry. Buy into their money. Keep up with the Gomezes. Play the capitalist, materialist game. Forget the boy—he'll make out—maybe come back and save us someday!"

He holds everyone in thrall, spittle collecting around his mouth. His words are spat out and slurred.

Will whispers, "How can someone so drunk be so eloquent?"

Wynema whispers back, "Think of Winston Churchill."

"Yeah. Or Dylan Thomas."

Slowly, softly, they touch fists.

Gone from the window, Dayone pushes his way in, through the press of people, towards his grandfather. He wants to be closer.

Frank notices him and bursts out loudly again. "That's what you told Dayone! Go to Omaha, you'll return a savior! Now my father is talking about becoming the saviors of the flamingos, the pink skins, because they've done *so* much for us that we now owe it to them to save their sorry asses! Didn't I write a poem about that?"

Frank staggers toward Simon, he on the inside of the U-shaped Council tables, his father on the outside standing in back of Teo. He twists out his secret question and releases it: "You won't be able to answer them unless you've already answered the question for yourself. Did I kill my Mother?!"

Will slowly turns to Wynema with a look of question. She looks at him, then looks away.

"You will all ask with me—come on now, all together, 'Did I kill my Mother?'" Frank actually gets four or five people to respond to his cadenced call.

Council Member Churino whispers under his breath, "May my totems protect me."

Almost everyone there knows what Frank's explosive question means. It's on their faces, the implosive memories, the empathy, the shame, the sadness, the guilt—the common, unspoken, shared knowledge. Individually and collectively they see a candle-lit adobe room twenty-five years ago, not very far from this very place.

They see Simon, forty years ago, forty-nine years old, and raging with drunken jealousy. They see him grabbing Dahyanee's shoulders, shaking her fiercely. She is angry, fearful, and disgusted with his behavior. From a doorway, the cries of Frank, 9, and Louisa, 15, as they plead for their parents to stop yelling at each other.

They hear Simon shouting, "How can you treat me this way!? I am your man, you know my heart, and yet you go with another man—"

They feel Dahyanee, at her wit's end, "I've done nothing, Simon! There is no one else. Please, for our children, believe me!! Please, Simon—!!"

They see Frank only nine years of age stepping into the room. They hear over and over, his small rising voice grappling up through the yelling of his parents, "You leave my mother alone. You leave my mother alone...."

They see Simon, Dahyanee, and Louisa go silent looking at little Frank, standing a few feet away, aiming Simon's pistol at his father.

"You leave my mother alone."

Dahyanee screams. Simon lets out a grotesque, grunting cry of anger—and lunges, reaching for Frank and the gun. They see him grab the barrel, twisting it away. But as he yanks, the boy's finger pulls against the trigger. The pistol discharges. They hear Dahyanee sigh and buckle—shot in the throat. They see the blood—they cannot see anything else but the blood. They see how the blood and air mix now and fight each other, not knowing which way to go. They see her last movement jerking her hand to her throat, a hand that carries a handkerchief that now covers the fatal wound. They see it changing from white to red.

They see the horror exploding into father and son, how both of them reach with loving hands to her throat, to stop what has happened, as if to simply touch the wound away. They hear Simon say, "Go, run for help."

This is what most of them see, the death of Dahyanee. They see the life-spirit leaving her face. They see this reflected now in his eyes.

All return to the present upon hearing Simon shuffling towards the two big doors and the reddish light of a sun not far above the horizon. They know: this is when magic happens—when they get to relive one of their stories.

People make way for Simon. He stands in the doorway looking out. Those close-by hear him say, "Soon I will go help them carry her body." As Simon walks slowly back to his chair, a spontaneous silence descends upon the room. For a few more minutes this story will continue. No one asked for it, but for a while longer everyone, even Victor and the other Council members, will stay with it—*Ta'ani wawakho: "remembering together"*—with father and son. Dayone follows quietly, respectfully, a few feet away behind his grandfather.

The story they remember of years ago will contain the sounds of the villagers as they bear the body of Dahyanee, on a ladder and blankets, twice around the plaza. Are they praying, singing, chanting? Call it what you will, the villagers are each in their own way vocalizing their connection. They will stop and place her bier before the corn-drying rack that she always used. She was renown for her splendid braids of corn. They will spread some corn pollen by the beehive oven she baked her bread in.

And they will all remember there were no visitors, no spectators, no tourists—all those who were not from this place, not members of these clans in this tribe—they were nowhere to be seen. This is what happens when the Pueblo is shut down, all visitors are guided away and an ancient stillness returns. The mounds which seemed like piles of rock and old wood to the tourists—but which are the all-important *kivas*—now thrum with the drumming from deep inside. All the *kivas* in the village—they are now the living hearts of the Pueblo, singing, praying....

Old men stood closest. Women slightly back, some quietly wailing, red clay on their faces and arms. All watched in chiseled grief. Louisa then, only a frightened teenager, was crying. Simon and Frank standing in shock and horror. Simon with silent tears streaming, feelings held in, steeling himself for the rest of his life. Frank's emotions shuddering before the specter of never holding his mother again. The Abyss—remembered in a story that will never be written down.

Victor "returns" first and raps once softly with his cane. Then again slightly louder. Those trained to listen turn and look. But almost everyone else stays with Simon. With their eyes, with their heart.

It will take a few moments, thinks Victor, *for the meeting to resume. I will be patient. We will wait. I am not insensitive. I know how important these memories are to my people, to my wife. While Simon was talking, everyone was thinking about what happened to him and his wife. Everyone running the same story at the same time. Powerful. I have to remember that.*

Everyone who cares knows what happened. Everyone but Simon and Frank. Louisa knows. Dayone knows. Victor knows. The Council, the villagers, the police know. Simon and Frank, however, are about to unburden themselves and know it as if for the first time. [omit?]

Wynema whispers into Will's ear what everyone else know. It takes less than a minute. Will moans involuntarily in sympathetic grief.

Unnoticed by anyone, a woman from the Governor's staff enters and whispers something in Victor's ear. His expression changes dramatically. He turns slowly in his seat and looks at the woman fiercely. She nods in confirmation. He whispers harshly: "He just left, and this is what he did?!" Victor is outraged. The woman nods again. "Why would the old man do that without consulting with me!?"

The clerk cringes and hunches her shoulders. "Can he do that? Can the Cacique shut down the Pueblo without your permission?"

Victor steels himself quickly, and with gesture lets the woman go.

He thinks, *In the middle of the meeting? No! We had an understanding! He is not so foolish to challenge me in this way. If he wants my help to rebuild the kivas—. Well, let him wait a year! Sonuvabitch!*

He looks over to where the Cacique had sat; the other old man, the Cacique's associate, sits with the faintest smile.

Simon reaches his chair and looks at Frank with fatherly compassion. Then he looks at everyone and says, "No...no...no..." over and over as if to each person there in the room, and then to Frank, "No, my son, you must understand, you did not kill your mother."

Frank collapses inside. Villagers move aside as he weaves unsteadily towards the side door. Frank wheels and looms, "Why didn't you ever tell me that? Just that. Nothing more."

As he reaches the door, he turns, his accusing glare asking everyone the same question. No answer. "I was just a kid." He exits.

Simon trembles violently from the crumbling of his emotional armor.

"I killed her. Not you. I killed her with my jealousy. Long before you became angry."

Simon lowers his head humbly and crosses slowly towards the front doors.

Faces of people—they're not smiling, but there is a warm, confident knowing just under the surface. They are experiencing what is happening here, participating in it.

Victor tries to refocus—on his responsibilities. He cannot let them go. He has discipline. *At the right moment*, he thinks, *I will step in and take charge again.*

Simon falters as he crosses the threshold. A neurological reaction to the release of something inside? There, he almost stumbles. Will is instinctively alerted and leans forward to move. But Wynema grips his fingers tighter. He leans back and forces himself to relax. She takes a deep breath and nods to herself.

As Simon exits the building into the slanting light and heads for the plaza, he says, to no one, to everyone, "How many more days to our Feast Day? I can make it. You hear that, Dahyanee? Our son knows for sure now. You hear me tell him? I was always afraid—that he would not be my son anymore—if I told him some other man was his father. That's why I always tried to leave him alone." As he shakes his head, "Boy, I wouldn't do it that way again."

Many villagers follow him out. Though he greets everyone he passes as he moves slowly into the Plaza, he sees no one really. Everyone he passes sees him, and greets him, but they do not take him out of himself. It is unspoken. They do not touch him. Not now.

They know he is with the Grandfathers. *He will see our grandmothers and grandfathers, too. And they will see him and know that we are not far away, thinking of them. It is good.* And so they pass by with love and respect and let it go at that.

They watch him walking unevenly towards shade trees and a bench on the other side of the plaza. They see him shaking his head—then glancing off, averting his head. Is he breaking down or jumping back and forth in time?

"Not afraid now," he says, as if to someone sitting at the other end of the bench. "I don't want to be angry anymore." And then, "I can see you, Dahyanee, sitting right there. Ha-hah!"

Older villagers close by can see her, too.

Will now watches from the doorway, concerned. Wynema steps up next to him.

"Do nothing, Will. You're here as family. Not as doctor. This is not happening just to Simon."

"To you and me."

"It's not about you and me."

"It's about all of us."

"All of us."

Simon sits on the bench, shyly, next to 'Dahyanee'. Almost wailing in a high thin voice, he says, "I always never could not see you, Dahyanee. I think I was crazy in love with you all the time."

"Let's stay with Simon," Wynema says leading him outside into the sunlight. "The Council will do what it does."

64

Unless You Know Your Time

Inside the Council room, with merely a simple movement of his silver-tipped cane, Victor holds all Council members in their seats. Then he turns to all non-Council Members: "Let those who want to leave now, go home, it is okay, go home now if you want. Five-minute break and then the Council has important, timely business to take care of here."

Teo looks across the room at Jolene. He knows she is here on behalf of her mother, his wife, Tessie, who is home with their new child. With only his eyes and hands, he tells his daughter: "Go tell your mother that these have become some doings. That there is healing here. That we are in the hands of the Grandmothers and Grandfathers...." Jolene supports her belly with both hands and slowly nods and rises.

Again, with simple gestures, Victor asks the Council to focus back on the matters-at-hand. "It's all there, in the papers before you."

Bringing order and decorum back into the room, Victor commands silence and then says: "We will take a vote now." He glances around the room. Only the Council Members and their staff and a handful of people remain.

Reymunda Reyna somehow appears behind her son, Judge and Council-member Reyna. She whispers something in his ear and disappears silently.

Reyna stands. "I have it from a reliable source that you have somehow just shut down the Pueblo—without consultation with us, Victor."

Victor is taken off guard. But only for a moment. Without looking up, composed, in control again, he says, "The Cacique and I didn't want to interrupt your thoughts or the doings here and so we thought it best we exercise our sovereignty by unilaterally closing the Pueblo to all non-villagers. It's as simple as that. As to the specific reasons and for how long it will last—it won't be long. But in the interests of sovereignty, let's not tip our hand too early. We should conclude the business of the day."

All the council members nod their heads and absently sort through the papers before them. They've been here before. They know what to do. They've made their views known. They've taken a position. They've declared their intention to move forward, to be strong, to understand the outside world and bring that connection safely and soundly to their people. That is their responsibility, as given to them by the clans. Did they not just a few years ago vote to bring a modest money-making casino to this village? Yes, they did. A major change.

Victor raps his cane on the floor twice, definitively. With his other hand, he indicates to his assistant on his left to take the tally. Victor points with his mouth at council members, asking for their vote. "All those in favor of the motion—"

Simon, on the bench is still with Dahyanee, "You were too nice. How could I mistrust your heart? Maybe I just wanted to hear you say you loved me. Hah! So foolish me. Very insecure of me."

As if Dahyanee got up and walked away, Simon stands, stumbles, and chases after her.

Dayone doesn't hide the fact that he is there to protect his grandfather and so follows at a close distance.

Nearing the trees at the bottom of the Plaza, in the south, Simon stops, reflects, "Like a child wants to hear how much his mama and papa love him. We never grow up."

Some curious but younger children scurry after him, but not too close when they see how imposing Dayone is.

Some villagers simply stand and watch with deep caring, while others choose to walk around the Plaza and, as they pass Simon, incline their heads once or twice out of respect. But they do not enter Simon's world. They simply support it by their presence. A child asks a mother to take him home and feed him. The mother shakes her head then silently asks the older sister to pick him up.

Some people choose to walk, as is their way, clockwise around the Plaza. Doesn't the Sun move clockwise around the Earth? And the Moon and the Stars? They walk around their fire-pits clockwise as the Old Ones have done for thousands of years.

Whether it is to see all these things as they approach, or to turn back time, or to show a simple sign finally of strength—today Simon is walking counterclockwise. The villagers can see him and greet him as they pass. It is good.

After a slow and halting circuit of the Plaza, Simon returns to the bench. With both hands to steady himself, he sits. Dahyanee is still there for him. The woman sitting on that tree-round-stool not far away, nods, points to the bench then closes her eyes and continues her soft song.

As Simon settles, "You know, even when I went to war before I even knew you, I dreamed of your hair and the smell of your shoulders and behind your ears—." He looks to the other end of the Plaza, points, tries to stand, but cannot. "You can dance, Dahyanee—always could. Ai-yai, so slow, so powerful, like *Chi'iiná*, the mountain lion. Why was I so afraid you'd leave?"

Wynema and Will have merged with the villagers walking around the Plaza. More people come. They pass by an alleyway next to the biggest adobe structure. Up the alleyway, they see Sotero saying something animatedly to Danny, Jesse, and another boy. He makes a decisive gesture, then hands each boy an eagle feather with colored wool wrapped around its base. The boys run off feather in hand in three different directions.

The couple silently pass by another crooked little road running off from the plaza. A few doors up, Martin Phipps sits smoking a long, very thin cigar, in a chair just outside the gallery-livingroom of a San Lucas potter. Jesse runs out of the gallery, followed by the potter.

"They say the Pueblo is closing," says the potter to Phipps. "All visitors have to leave now."

Phipps is put-off and insulted. "I ain't no a visitor. I lived here with you people over fifteen years."

"Well, maybe you can go inside and stay out of sight."

Jesse tugs at the potter's arm and scowls.

"Sorry, Martin—but you gotta go. Now. An emergency. Come back tomorrow, yeah okay."

Phipps stomps out. "I've put more time and money into this pueblo than any other white man."

Hunting for his brother, Armand runs by, hiding his head from Will and Wynema. He is quickly followed by two women speaking Pueblo in hushed, intense tones. Wynema is now surprised by what she understands.

"The Cacique is closing the Pueblo. Only members of our village may stay."

"What do you mean? Just like that? Who's the Cacique?"

"The leader of our tribe."

"I thought Victor—" He points back to the Council Meeting Hall.

"Victor's just the Governor, the Outside Chief. The Cacique is the religious, the spiritual head of all the Clans and he—"

Sotero and two elders, blankets round their bellies, approach. One of the elders turns to Will. "I'm afraid you'll have to go back to your house now, Doctor."

Sotero speaks softly in Pueblo as he points to Will with pursed lips.

The elders nod in solemn greeting and pass. Wynema is impressed.

"What is it?"

"The Cacique just said you can stay—because you've been taken as a son by Simon.

"The Cacique?"

"Sotero."

"Sotero's the Cacique?!" Will is dumbfounded. "I've been walking around not knowing who the Cacique is."

When Simon's singing becomes a little louder, Wynema looks up into the gathering dusk—and then all around. "You sense the difference?"

"No visitors?"

"Yes."

"The vibes?"

"Yes."

Will takes a deep breath. "Yeah, it's something."

"Something's happening."

"A religious thing, a ritual?"

"Not exactly, but—." She glances at him and stops, takes a step back and puts her hands on her hips.

"What?"

"The last of the sundown light is on your head, because you're so tall." She watches it—until it is gone. "That's it. Now it is night." And she starts walking again.

"Just like that?"

"Just like that."

As they pass Simon's bench and see Dayone standing not far away, he whispers, "Have you noticed the boy?"

Wynema now takes a deep breath and releases it slowly. "Day-one? I have."

In a lean-to carport, in an alley not far from the Plaza, Frank sits like a gargoyle, immobile on his Harley. Suddenly he wakens and with a liquid flair, arches his body upward, then comes down with a stiff right leg onto the starter lever, bringing the hog to life. Slowly he drives away, disappearing into the gathering darkness.

Not too far from Simon, near a the largest tree in the plaza, is another bench. Wynema gently pulls Will's sleeve, urging him to sit.

"Can we just sit here? I mean, shouldn't we give Simon his space?"

"It'll be all right. But don't say anything. And don't touch him. Without moving very much, look around. You can see that the villagers are not leaving. In fact, Mirriamma has come. Don't look, but she's watching from Estelle Sanchez' window on our right. And I see my cousins, who rarely come here and never talk to me because my father is of another blood—you know, from a far-away tribe. These cousins live almost an hour away and they've come—and they don't even have a phone or a cellphone. Do you know how old this plaza is? How many feet have tamped the Earth here? If you sit still and listen, you can hear them singing."

Suddenly, Will looks at his watch. "You and I were going to pick up Jahbig and Alána in an hour! We can't leave."

"You're right."

"I'm going to call Jah. He's probably at the airport right now, and tell him to call ahead to Albuquerque and have a rental car standing by. Half an hour later he can meet Alána and together they can drive up here and call us. Don't worry. He'll understand. It'll be all right."

Wynema nods deep in thought.

⁂

Under a shade arbor at one corner of the Plaza, three men have begun to drum on a single large ceremonial drum. How do they play it so that it sounds so soft, so far away, and yet so enveloping all at once? The villagers—milling about, talking softly, only a few words, to their friends and family—when they hear the drumming, they become instantly aligned and connected.

There are some four or five people standing next to the drummers. Slowly, rhythmically, they dip down their bodies towards the Earth or lift themselves up just a little towards the Sky, and then again, over and over with the drumming—as if to bring the Earth and the Sky together, to remind them they are One. The men and women nearby spontaneously, very subtly at first, start to dance.

⁂

Jerry suddenly appears beside Will and Wynema. "Teo sent me to tell you that Victor and the MRS thing just won the vote."

Wynema sighs and nods as if she expected it. Now Will is deep in thought. He puts his cell in his pocket.

Jerry cocks an ear to Simon's distant singing, "Wow. Hey, I gotta go. I think my Jolene is birthing our baby soon!" He disappears.

Then they hear it. Tentative at first. Way under everything. The drumming.

⁂

Will settles, somewhat, deeper into the bench.

She turns to him, "You okay?"

"What?"

"This. Pretty spooky, eh?"

"Why is it you Indians always think things Indian are 'spooky' to us non-Indians?"

"You been talking to Frank, uh? Well, when I look at you, I see someone a little spooked. That's all. There's a sadness here, right? A tension, okay? You're probably not used to this kind of thing."

"I know Simon's in trouble. If there's a medical component to it, I'm responsible."

"Medical component?"

"Aach, I know that sounded cold. It's just that—."

"But he's happy. And so are the people here—in a way."

"Happy? I don't see nobody laughing and smiling and—"

"Trust me, Will. Something's happening and it's good."

"But there's a life at state!"

"There's always a life at stake. We just don't see it."

"Yeah, and the Council just passed the goddamned MRS."

"It's not like this is the first time something stupid, corrupt, or potentially dangerous has come up. But we have our ways of making them right—if only, if we would use them! This is why I was brought back here."

"Huh?"

"By Mirriamma."

"What are you saying?"

"To see these old connections arising again."

He looks at her with deep yearning, deep questioning.

"Will, I'm not going back. I'm not leaving here. I'm not going to take that fellowship in Cambridge."

"You what?!" he asks suppressing his voice into a rough whisper. "C'mon now—that was a dream come true, not just for you, but for your people."

"My people? Are we talking about the Pueblos, the Sioux, or Native peoples in general? There's only people, all different kinds of people, each one a piece of humanity—." She stops herself to sort it out. "I know now what I can uniquely do that will be of some practical use. We'll talk about this later." She looks around the Plaza in awe of what she sees. "You're a doctor, so you should know that this—this is a healing. They all know that Simon is dying, that's he's picking his time—"

"Unless he's committing suicide, nobody knows his time."

"Will! Listen. Open yourself. The healing comes seeking out the disharmony, a sense of dark powers or unrest that has risen among us. The singing—listen now, it's just beginning—the singing wants to restore the harmony."

"The singing? You mean the song? What song is it?"

"The singing is what's happening. The song is what's sung. It's not an intellectual thing. It may not even be conscious. You're forcing this consciousness in on me right now—but here, among the people, it's spontaneous." She takes a deep breath. "Night is falling, but this moment seeks a light, an inner light, not just for Simon, but for everyone. I don't know how to explain it any better than that."

They withdraw into themselves.

Then Wynema speaks again: "There are only a few medicine-people left, across the country, among the Indian peoples. Mirriamma is one of them. They're here, all around the Plaza now—and I'll tell ya, I don't even know who all of them are. I'm too new here. And I wouldn't be surprised if there aren't other tribes elsewhere, at others Pueblos, other medicine-people—who knows how far away—somehow feeling the urge to sing right now, to focus their intentions into a community space—I don't know. I think I feel it. I do feel it."

"You mean there are a lot of medicine people here? Right now? From this village and others? How'd they learn about this and get here so quickly?"

"No. No. That's not what I mean. I'm sorry."

Both of them drift again for while.

Then Will softly, "This is why you think we as a couple won't work—because you think I can't understand these things."

"I don't know. But you think of sick people as being sick, isolated in their sickness, sad, tragic, alone, in trouble."

"I'm a doctor. That's how I have to come to it. To be effective. To bring them back to health. For as long as possible."

"In Diné land, the Rite of the Blessing Way might last eight or nine days."

"One healing ceremony lasts for that long?"

"Think of it as a surgery that last for ten hours."

"I'm serious."

"So am I."

⁂

The last outsiders are guided off the rez. Young men and women wearing orange traffic vests place red cones and sawhorses with signs at the two entrances to the Pueblo. If you listen carefully, you can hear the drumming from here.

A large van picks up two more villagers from their outlying houses and drives towards the plaza.

A woman takes the last of her laundry from the clothesline and hurries inside with the basket.

A father stops his son he sees driving past in his car. The amplified hip hop from his powerful woofers immediately ceases. The son shakes his head and pounds his fist on the steering wheel and just sits there. The father just stands there. Finally, the son nods. The father walks away.

Two women carrying two *luminarias*, one in each hand, set the paper bags half-filled with sand on the edge of the plaza. A boy with a fire-brand follows and quickly lights a candle and thrusts it into the middle of the bagged sand.

≈

Simon lets loose with a new song. Completely different from the last. Only Will is arrested. Everyone else takes it in stride, welcoming it.

"What's happening now," asks Will.

"Same thing as before only different."

"You ever study ancient Greek drama?"

"Sure. Why?"

"A lot of the things that go on here seem like ritualized dramas."

Wynema taps his head with her middle finger. "Get out of your head, Will. Or go home."

≈

Simon's song softens, but it's picked up by others now around the Plaza, perhaps not singing the same tune, or the same words, but it's clearly the same song.

Simon suddenly stops and though his eyes are closed he moves his head about as if looking at something, trying to see it clearer.

He sees himself and Dahyanee, each on a horse, loping up a gentle hill. Now their horses are close, near the top, stopped, side by side, facing in opposite directions. He hears himself, much younger, ask, "*Why'd you run us all the way up here?*"

"*To tell you something.*"

"What is it?"

"We're gonna have a baby."

"Yeah! How'd you know that so soon?"

"Mirriamma told me. And it's a daughter."

"Aw-w...how's she know?"

"Can we call her Louisa?"

Simon stops swaying, smiles, and shakes his head at his own skepticism. With his eyes still closed, he says, "What a fool I been. Sure glad I knew *that* before I died—."

Suddenly, his eyes go wide. Something soft slowly explodes within him. He bends forward and grips his side. "Ai!!!"

Looking down at his chest, he says, "I think you just gave way. Hey, when is Feast Day, anyway? Is it today? Okay, tomorrow. Tomorrow is close enough."

Simon's head bobs and weaves; his hands grip the bench harder. "Ah, there goes the pulse. Running away with me. Light-headed, light-body, not dizzy, but—drum-beat inside, nice. Ha-hah—I come in with a dance and go out—Ai! Cold, sweaty, tingly—oh, very cold, but a fire in the belly, cold in the heart—yes, Dr. Will, what you call the aneurysm comes on of its own now. I'm not ready—but I'm willing."

Simon gives a little twitch and closes his eyes and appears to have died sitting up.

Not far away, in a darkened window of an adobe bordering the plaza, Mirriamma sits looking out, silently watching. Another old woman stands in deeper shadows behind her. Infinite mirrors.

Less than fifty yards away, Will is straining to see, to understand, to connect. His body has become alert, his legs tense, his feet wants to move. Wynema places her hand on top of his. He can't move. He turns to her, panic rising. She's calm and, with a look, tells him to let it be.

"The man needs a doctor right now," he says under his breath. "I swear to you."

"No, Will, you are not what he needs right now. He will tell you when he needs you."

"As doctor or friend?"

Wynema smiles. "Is there a difference?"

Dayone slides onto the bench next to his grandfather. As they touch, the old man's head falls lightly onto the boy's shoulder. The boy doesn't look, doesn't move, just sits there waiting for his grandfather.

Simon slowly opens his eyes and sucks in a huge breath. He smiles, touches his own chest. Very softly, he talks to his own heart. "There are things for you to do." As if in another world, "Got to get my bag and get my horse ready." He straightens up in his seat and closes his eyes. As he starts to chant or sing softly to himself, he's also laughing.

The faithful warrior rises now inside of Dayone. Making sure his grandfather is balanced, he stands carefully, take a step away, then another—now he's sprinting, away from the plaza, up a narrow alleyway, until he disappears flat-out running, his feet barely touching the ground.

Dayone flies across the field next to Simon's corral and vaults the gate that separates the paddock from the tack shed and stops abruptly before the door to the cabin, thinking—.

—A few minutes later, he's tying two bags to the pommel-horn of Simon's saddled horse. As he's about to swing up, he remembers something. He flies into the house and returns with Simon's rifle, a 32-40 Winchester carbine with saddle-ring, at home in its battered sun-yellowed leather scabbard. He thrusts it into its place under the stirrup-strap. He grabs the horn with his left hand intent on swinging his right leg up over the saddle in one smooth movement, but his leg catches on the saddlebag and he falls onto the ground. He laughs at himself then uses the stirrup to mount.

65

YOU LOOK BUT DO YOU SEE?

Victor steps out of the Council Hall building dialing his cellphone. "Hello, Jim? ...Yeah, it's done, we're good—" He looks up and stops dead in his tracks. "Hold that thought." He looks up the short road to the plaza where he sees people converging. "Hey, I gotta call you back." Shoving the cell into his pocket, as if picked up gently by some current, he moves with mounting curiosity towards the plaza.

Dayone stops at the river to let the horse drink. He cocks his head, listens. "I can't lose him. Not yet. We need him." He looks up river, past the Pueblo, to the water's source on the flanks of their sacred mountain. He looks in the other direction, following the water all the way to the Rio Grande Gorge. Horse and rider are tiny next to the great cottonwoods that line the banks.

When Victor reaches the plaza and sees the *luminarias*, he grasps what is happening—things he himself did not set in motion. Either he has to distance himself from it or figure out a way to control it or take credit for it. His head stutters as he sorts through his options.

Louisa steps up next to him. "I gotta go to Teo and Tessie's. Jolene's water just broke."

"Okay."

"I don't want to, but I gotta go."

"I know. Okay."

"Victor."

With difficulty she makes him look into her eyes. She touches his hand with hers. "You see what's happening?"

He looks but says nothing.

"Victor!"

"I see."

"But do you see?"

"I see, yes."

Dayone enters the plaza area at a gallop and immediately pulls up to a walk.

Louisa is surprised. "Look, Victor, your son."

He pulls away from her and looks where her lips point. Dayone steps off the horse in one fluid movement and walks up slowly next to his grandfather.

Father and mother see their son hand Simon the reins to his horse and pull out the medicine bag from his shirt and hand it to him.

"Victor?"

But the governor says nothing. His head nods, his jaw muscles pulse. He's feeling behind the curve. A little panic is rising. He doesn't know why. He's having a hard time catching up. Louisa touches his arm and starts to leave. He puts his hand on her. "Wait. Stay. Just a few more minutes—."

"You stay. I gotta go."

"Okay." But he looks off, as if searching for someone.

"You stay, Victor. This is your place."

"Okay. But wait, just a little longer, with me."

"Just a little."

Now, no matter where one looks, it seems that more and more *luminarias* are lit and placed around the plaza. The sun may be fading, but the community still finds a way to keep itself in light. Used mostly around Christmas, now in window sills, in open doorways, next to the drying racks, on top of parked cars, on top of the beehive ovens—all around the outside of the plaza, candles flicker softly. To keep the paper-bags open, their tops are rolled down once or twice.

"Whenever I go to the synagogue," Will confides, "which isn't very often, mostly on the big holidays, there is ritual, a set service that the rabbi and cantor and everyone follow. Maybe there's one or two Hebrew prayers that are so "holy" that everyone knows them by heart—but you know, there are probably very few in attendance who

throw themselves into those prayers so deeply that they disappear in
it."

"That's when we find ourselves."

"Huh?"

"When we let ourselves disappear."

They become quiet and give themselves to the moment, within and
without themselves.

After a while, she leans over and speaks softly. "I didn't know you
went to church—I mean, to synagogue."

"My battle with my own culture has been pretty heated and nasty,
I'm sorry to say. Not like Frank. But, in a way, yes, like Frank. Jesus!
Anyway, it's something that I've been able to keep down to a soft,
seething, inconspicuous boil."

"You suppress it? Why? For yourself—or for whom?"

"I suppress it, I suppose, because I'm supposed to. And because
there's no percentage in letting it out. And it's immediately suppressed
by most Jews whom I challenge or just want to get to talk to about
it." He pauses for a moment. "Ya know, there are very few topics
that Jews won't talk about or even debate. But they're there. They exist. Oh, yes. And they are *verboten*—spit upon thrice."

"I don't understand."

"It's a cultural superstition, a gesture of denial or protection, spitting three times off to the side. To ward off the demons."

"But what are the forbidden topics you were referring to?"

"Oh, like whether or not we're the Chosen People, or what it
means to be that. Or, how and why the Holocaust happened—no, no,
you do not question the holy Holocaust. Oh, we argue like hell about
whether there's a God or not; that's easy, abstract, fun. But it's not
okay to argue about whether Israel has a right to exist as a Jewish
state. I find it disgusting and embarrassing and ironic that in *spite* of
the Holocaust, perpetrated by the those who called themselves the
"master race", there are Jews today who down deep inside consider
themselves to be superior. My grandfather, he—."

"Go on."

"I asked him once. Maybe I was eighteen or nineteen. But he just
shrugged and raised his eyebrows and pursed his lips and tilted his
head just a little. So I asked him again: 'Are the Jews a superior peo-

ple?' And again he said nothing, just raised his eyes and nodded as if he understood why I had to ask the question. 'But I'm serious, Zeyda, are they? Are we?' He raised his hands as if asking God how he should answer such a question. And this is what he said: 'I'm not saying no. But it's a question I'll never say yes to, no matter who asks me. *Ferstaist?*'—which in one word means 'Do-you-understand-what-I'm-telling-you-And you better understand!'"

He touches her hand again. "Dayone has issues. Frank has issues. Simon has issues—or at least he did up till today. I have issues." He turns to her until she looks at him. "Do you have issues?—"

Suddenly, Simon is saying something else. The moment continues, but the music has changed—the singing, the chanting, the praying—the sounds, the voices soften. The drumming softens.

Wynema and Will turn and listen carefully to Simon.

"...and to the Councilmen, the big shots, *you know their names,* Great Spirit, give them ears to hear the Grandmothers and Grandfathers, give them the courage to step aside and let their people hear. I know it takes great strength to do this, Great Spirit—."

Louisa pulls Victor slowly with her, towards her father. They stop four yards away. With humble eyes that quickly look down, they greet the Bernal family standing next to them, Gladys plus ten.

In a soft, quiet reverie, Simon is praying in Pueblo and English. "—and the Mendozas, Herman, *he's a good man,* works hard for his family, his son, Pete, recovering from that accident, *make him strong,* Great Spirit—and don't let Herman worry so much, Great Spirit, You know what's best. And Louisa, my only daughter, always there, so good, so kind, *bless her, Great Spirit,* and give her again the hope she had as a young girl—"

Coming up slowly and soft, as if the ground of the plaza were the drumhead itself, the sounds of the drummers and singers rise up the legs and lungs of the listeners.

⁓

Victor and Louisa squeeze hands once and pull away, each in their own direction.

⁓

"—and my good friend, Great Spirit, Teo, *and his new baby,* Great Spirit—give him many years of joy to watch his new son grow into manhood, *Great Spirit, and let him give thanks to You, Great Spirit, for all our ways which You gave us so long ago—*"

A few more villagers find a spot to stand or sit around the plaza—on benches, low adobe walls, a plastic milk crate.

Sotero, fingering a small stone in his hand, bends down and places it on the ground just in front of him, then starts a soft prayer of his own.

Wynema bends, finds a stone, then walks to the invisible circle begun by the Cacique and, brushing smooth the ground with the backside of her hand, places her stone with reverence on the Earth. Will tries to fathom all this. She comes back to him.

More and more villagers place stones and stand behind them, a big circle forms around the plaza.

In a window, in the shadows of an unlighted room, but part of the circle, Mirriamma sits quietly, her eyes open or close. She, too, is praying.

A woman in a blanket, with both stone and luminaria, places them in the circle and sits on Will and Wynema's bench. She pays them no mind and begins praying to herself. A man, not far away, moves forward and places a stone and a prayer stick into the ground next to her luminaria.

"What's Simon's saying?"

"He's asking for good things for all his relations, for all of us."

"—and for Jerry's little boy, Rio, *who can run fast, Great Spirit,* with always a smile for everyone, keep him that happiness even when he becomes a teenager—and Wynema Mondragon, *let her learn well the ways, Great Spirit, of healing and balance and teaching the young ones to walk in balance*—and Mary Archuleta, let her husband, Bernie, understand that this is a difficult time for her, Great Spirit, going through her change, so not worry and be kind, as is proper, Great Spirit, after so many good years, *and let them feel good again together, Great Spirit*—." And with that Simon closes his eyes and disappears again.

Will squeezes her hand. "All right, but, shouldn't I—you know, as his doctor—find the right moment just to check—"

Her looks quiet him instantly. Then she turns to listen, as does he, to the drumming circle softens but becomes more incessant. When one

drummer steps out, another takes his place. More people bring luminarias into the plaza circle, or place them on the ledges of the tallest
buildings. Teo sweeps by quietly and quickly.

"Okay," she says, "as his doctor, go place a stone. But that is all."

Will looks left and right. He doesn't see a stone. But she has two
extras in her hand, and offers them. He picks one and hefts it in his
palm.

"Don't weigh it—feel it," she whispers. Then with great affection,
"How beautiful the *luminarias* and candles and *farolitos*."

But Will closes his eyes, as if he doesn't want to see this. But then
he places the little stone. He reaches deep. "You're going to learn a lot
from Mirriamma."

She comes to him. "I will be a fat old woman."

"I hope I still know you." He shivers, inhales, shifts, "Still, you do
know, Simon doesn't have to die right now."

"Only he knows what he has to do right now. His father and all
his grandfathers want to be with him right now."

Something washes over Will. "I can feel my zeyda, my own grandfather—I miss him." As she leans over and puts her head on his
shoulder, he continues. "You and I—I hoped you and I could form a
bridge and—"

"Not in that way, like that." She pulls him closer. "But we love
each other."

"You're a piece in my puzzle all right, but not in the way I
thought you'd be."

"We seek the same thing, Tall Man."

"And when we find it we will share it."

"What we share is everything. When you doctor at your best, it's
a gift—and giving is what it's all about. And it's not that the old ways
are better—though in some ways they may be. No, it's what I have to
bring to my life that's changed. 'It may be the devil, it may be the
lord, but you're gonna have to serve somebody'."

"I beg your pardon."

"Just another song running through my head."

"But I wouldn't have stopped your work, or gotten in the way.
No more than you would have mine."

"Could Mirriamma be married to a non-Pueblo and do what she does for her people?" Off his sigh and silence, "It's not easy in these times to hold on to the old ways."

"My grandpa said something like that just before he left for Israel."

"That fire-pit in the middle of the room—. Just think about that for a few minutes."

And, after a few minutes, Wynema reaches out to him again. "No, don't think about it—"

"I know, don't think about it, feel it!"

"Even more. Become the fire-pit and feel what it is that native peoples come to the fire-pit for."

"Out of fear, confusion, hope, togetherness."

"Good abstract concepts, Will."

Simon erupts into intense but not loud wailing grief. Will is startled, but Wynema's touch assures him that it's natural and necessary. The woman next to them echoes Simon's grief with her own, even louder.

All the small lights the villagers have brought, standing or sitting behind them, make the villages shimmer in the night. All night long, they will come and go. But the the circle around the plaza will not be broken tonight. If becomes too thin and threatens breaking because others have left, they will adjust or somehow communicate with others to join them.

The shared grief, the mourning, the release—the sounds of villagers rise and reach for a peak...and then fall. And so it will go.

The cries of a young woman in labor fill the inside of Teo's house. Teo stands in the doorway to the living-room listening to his daughter in labor. Behind him women's voices. Mirriamma appears out of the night and enters, followed by a younger woman carrying a large basket filled with things needed tonight.

66

Memories of Her in These Stones

Frank sits on his Harley a mile away on a ridge overlooking the Pueblo—he and the moon looking down. "It's good. It's crazy. At last. You'll probably live longer than I. See you soon, Papa."

Simon sits on his bench, gently ecstatic, softly praying. Sotero sits with him now, holding a cloth-wrapped bundle—he's rocking gently back and forth with Simon's song. Behind them, standing quietly, three elders wrapped in their blankets. Dayone, not far away, stands holding the reins to the horse.

Simon continues his prayer. "...Not I, not nobody, I guess, knew how to tell him. Strange, like that. But let my son find his way and bring some happiness to his life—he deserves it, Great Spirit—*thank you, Great Spirit.*"

Simon ends his prayer with a sigh. He looks and discovers Sotero there. The two men simply look at each other and smile.

Sotero hands him the bundle. "Your father gave me his medicine bundle to hold many, many years ago. I couldn't give this to you before today."

"I understand, Grandfather. All these years, yes." Simon takes it, smells it, closes his eyes....

Sotero waits, then, "After they took you away from us, your father's grief was loud and unstoppable. He quit eating and would have died if your mother hadn't promised that you would return stronger and wiser, and someday be a leader to our people. She was wise."

Tears falling, Simon hands the bundle back to Sotero. "I have felt its power. Give it to my son, Frank, when he is ready."

"I will. It'll be good. Walk in beauty, my brother."

As Sotero rises, Simon sighs a great sigh of relief. Sotero, accompanied by the three men, leave.

≈

Louisa has returned as soon as she could. She draws near. She carries a nicely folded shirt.

"Papa—." She sits down next to him, lays her hand in his, sits proudly, on the verge of tears. Simon, without hesitation, opens the bag and extracts a tattered sketch book. He opens it, takes out a photograph, and hands it to her.

"This photograph of Mama is for you. And this sketchbook—she drew for me, you know—early on." He tries to laugh, but something catches him in the ribs. "It's you touching a skunk."

"Oh, Papa. You goin', uh?"

"It's okay."

"I know. I'm happy for you, Papa." Her next thought makes her cry. "But Dayone—what if I—and Victor—"

"Oh, no, no, no—he'll be okay."

"Yes, yes, okay. Thank you, Papa."

They both take a deep breath—and then relax into the night.

She places his shirt on his lap. "Good powwow tonight. Let's change your shirt."

At the perimeter of the plaza, Lola and Rebeca step into the circle, placing stones.

≈

A few moments later, Louisa is buttoning Simon's new shirt for him. Simon turns, beckons into the night—and Dayone is right there, standing next to him. Louisa steps away.

"The older you and your dad get," he says to the boy in a whisper, "the closer in age you grow together. Pretty soon, he'll be like an uncle to you, ol' Victor will, then like a brother, and when he grows very old, your dad, he'll be like a child maybe—and you'll just let him go, back to where we all come from—and join him yourself someday on the other side. Who knows? Where's my horse?" He becomes aware of the reins in his hand.

"Grandson—Dayone—this horse is yours now—because you know how to protect this great animal. In his veins runs the blood of many fine horses our people have known since the animal came to us.

It's no secret that our clans have the best horsemen of anyone. That's just true. The Apaches will not always argue with this. Ha! We always had a way with horses. Ummm, I could ride once. The Apache and the Pueblo, always jealous of each other on the horse. Damn jealousy, damn jealousy. Oh, by the way—." He coughs and clears his throat and laughs once to himself. Dayone bends closer. "Would you do me a favor and teach my sons, Frank and Will, to dance a little more—yes? It is really the Way of our lives, these dances we do: connect us to the land. We are grateful for this, okay, because we don't want to fall apart and blow away in the wind. You're a much better dancer than Frank or Will."

Yeah, Frank's still there, all right—up on the ridge-line, in the dark. He's been crying, too. Now, throwing his bike into neutral, pushing off, he coasts down towards the Pueblo.

Simon watches Dayone stroke the horse. "Go take your place with the drummers."

Dayone drops the reins and goes.

Victor, accompanied by Louisa, steps up next to Simon, sits.

Simon turns. "You have helped me, Victor, to get back on that road I fell off of. You know that, Victor? The strength of both of us is in Dayone."

Somewhere in the circle of people ringing the plaza, Armand's father, Ron, an alcoholic, is as sober as he's been in three months. He turns to his son, then both bend to place a stone in the circle. He remembers something his grandfather taught him. "*Our memories are locked in our bones. But the memories of the Earth are in all these stones. My grandfather told me that. I remembered, Armand. I remembered.*"

Armand isn't sure what going on. He's never seen it before. But somehow a frailty and innocence are there. "Those big stones down by the river. Sometimes they cry in the sun."

The father raises his eyebrows and acknowledges the boy warmly.

Wynema leans forward a bit, sensing. Her eyes narrow. Will notices. Tentatively, she turns to Will. "I think you—we should go to him now."

Will is perplexed, but willing. They slowly rise, and he follows her as she walks clockwise around the circle of people gathered. Halfway around, as they pass Will's truck, "You go to him. I'll be right there." She disappears into the darkness.

Simon's breathing is labored. As Will approaches, his concern grows.

Simon raises his finger, closes his eyes, twitches. Will sits and bends to hear. "Velvel, son of Yitzak son of Abraham. I had another dream."

"Just now?"

"It's getting easier. I dreamed about those piñon trees going crazy all last season making too many seeds. Good food for rats and mice, but maybe bad for other things. Not the natural way. The Hopi say: *Koyannisqatsi,* out of balance. The virus you are studying, the one with the Navajos—."

"The hantavirus."

"Doctors say it's because there's too much germs in the air from deer-mice poop. So one doctor told them to stop dancing. Did you know that?"

"Yeah—the epidemiologist—to keep the dust down?"

"Your research, your paper—you tell the Navajo to keep dancing. It's the only way to restore the balance of things. Tell 'em—tell 'em —."

Wynema steps up behind and hands Will his father's *talis* bag. Will looks at the bag, looks into the night, then puts on the *talis,* kissing the *tsitsis,* the fringed corners. He sits down next to Simon and cries quietly. Simon's hand touches his thigh.

"The whites are being whites the best way they can. We should do the same and be Indians as best we can. We are different and this difference makes the land strong. Many different relations living together create a prayer to the Great Spirit that is strong and clear. If the walls of a house or the poles of a tipi are all leaning in the same direction, it will fall over, like that."

Victor walks slowly around the circle of people. As he passes, villagers look at him briefly and communicate their emotion to him.

Simon is having a little difficulty in breathing. "But if we are many and different we make a strength that the biggest wind will not push down. Our relations are many—and this is good. The wisdom of our elders who have now gone beyond, this wisdom teaches all of us—" He looks around until he finds Wynema. He smiles, "—not just government leaders, chosen or appointed, or Presidents, War-Chiefs, Governors—but the people."

Reyna now is standing with Victor and with a look expresses how important this moment is.

"The spirit of the people don't want the MRS," says Victor with a sigh.

"And the grandfathers," adds Reyna.

"I'm canceling the vote," he says, and with a wave of his hand changes his future.

Simon's eyes are closed. Will watches him.

Without opening his eyes, "Nobody is born a grandmother or grandfather. You gotta earn it by living it out, passing on the ways of those who came before." Simon opens his eyes. "Hey, Will?"

In Pueblo, Will answers. *Grandfather*?

"I never would have figured this out without you—"

Will bends his head, almost overcome with emotion.

"—or Dayone, or even Frank."

He takes Will's hand, puts the arrowhead he's been holding in it. "Found this arrowhead the moment I first found you. Kinda reminded me I was wounded. All healed now. Thank you."

His eyes close and open slowly again. "My father was a healer like that there." Pause. "Like you will be—to your son."

Simon resumes praying in Pueblo.

Two hundred feet away, lost in the darkness, Frank lies on his stomach, spread over the largest kiva mound, embracing it like a baby on his mother's breast. Tears on his cheeks, he faces toward the lights of the Plaza.

Simon's head is still, but his eyes, bright in a placid face, look to Will. Will breathes erratically, tears streaming silently.

"The son must not carry the father's pain. I do not want it for you. We already know these things about ourself. And God knows these things about all of us, so you don't have to struggle with these things all the time. They are old ghosts. Let them go, son, and the father's pain-of-so-many-years can be released like that. And he can rest. Your grandfather Abraham tells you this, Will. I know."

A soft wail comes from Will as he rocks back and forth. Simon's eyes flare, then close, and he begins praying in Pueblo again. Out on the llano, a pack of coyotes tells us the rest of the world is there.

67

Her Definition of Cure

Frank has climbed to the tallest rooftop now. He's been here before, oh yes. There are others there, but they're not concerned about him. He's silhouetted as he steps into the moon.

Dayone is drumming, containing his pride and his sadness. Victor stands nearby, deeply moved. Dayone offers his father his seat at the drum. Victor takes the drumstick and joins the men at the clan drum.

Will and Wynema step away as Teo and Mirriamma approach.

Simon stops praying. He reaches into his bag, draws out a small cloth bag. Simon turns, smiles, and gives the bag to Mirriamma. "Seed-corn. The best."

Mirriamma takes it, touches Simon, then moves off. But as she passes Will, she pauses long enough to say: "'Old Lady Sickness is hurrying away with slobber on her mouth. It's running down her jaws. Her clothes are in tatters'."

Will is almost frightened by the strange non sequitur. In a hushed voice, "What did she mean by that!?

"Her definition of cure."

Teo sits down. Simon gives him two pieces of silver-and-turquoise jewelry. "One for you, one for your new son. Where's Will?"

Teo motions to Will, then touches Simon's ear and takes a step away. Will sits down quickly.

"I'm gonna make the rain come soon."

"How soon?" asks Will with a soft smile.

"Wanna feel something strange—my pulse."

Will gently touches Simon's face and slowly, affectionately lets his hand reach the carotid. Will feels it, it's faint, fast—then it stops. It just stops. Simon smiles, inhales for the last time—. "Feel that."

Simon exhales—and dies. Will knows it. He takes a hard breath, rolls his eyes, and smiles and lets it out. As Will rises, Teo sits down next to his old friend. Will quietly walks to Wynema.

The villagers know the moment, too. Mirriamma returns and, opening another small leather bag, pours some corn pollen in a steady line from Simon's feet towards the west.

The drumming like a heartbeat stops for a second, and then starts off again. Something gathers in that beat of silence.

Mirriamma speaks softly, as if to herself. "Teo, his daughter, Jolene, just had a nice girl—wants to know if it's okay to name her Dahyanee at the naming ceremony?"

In her head, she hears Simon answer. 'It's okay.' She nods then breaks into the proper prayer for laying the Corn Pollen Road.

No one looks, no one stares. But everyone feels the road being laid out before them, everyone this night in the medicine wheel circle. They might stay here an hour, perhaps all night. The singers and dancers and drummers will be the last to leave. They all know when it's over.

Wynema walks by herself around the circle. For her, it is a spiral. Each circuit winds tighter all the threads of her being—the logical, the emotional, the physical, the cultural, the spiritual. With each circuit, the spiral she travels wraps itself closer around her, more deeply alive at the center of her being. Each time she passes Will, whether he sees her or not, she smiles and tears flow. She knows a part of her is pulling away from him. One part of her understands this. Another part of her won't let him go. And yet her feet walk, around and round. She knows she's not walking in a circle.

Will tracks her. He watches everything he can of her. As she approaches him on the right and moves away on the left. Her right side when she's on the opposite side of the plaza. Her left side when she passes close by. She doesn't smile. Or maybe just a hint, to comfort him.

His cell vibrates. "Hello."

It's Abraham. "Favileh, is that you? I can feel you already."

"Yes, Papa, I'm fine. I was missing you. I'm glad you called. The last time I called you, I couldn't—you weren't—."

"I know, I know, I wasn't home. I was out to lunch. I was in a coma. Not alive. Not dead. But the tumor is stilling working for me. We're getting closer to an answer. You?"

"Um, it's kinda hard to talk to you right now. But I really want to talk to you."

"So talk. Gimme a little. You were telling me about this girl—excuse me, this woman, this lovely Indian woman. Does she think she's one of the Twelve Lost Tribes? Because if she does, this is good!"

"How you doing? Dr. Grossman sends me your charts. Some things better, some not."

"Doctor, doctor, I don't want to talk about that. I just want to be with you."

"I wish I could be with you, too, Grandpa."

"You're so close to me, my beautiful boy. You're right here with me, right now. I'm telling you. Whoo-boy. I'm telling you, Favileh. We are more than grandfather and grandson. We are brothers, you know what I'm saying? I'm almost sorry Yitzy and Debbie didn't name you Yakov. But never-mind—Abraham, Isaac, and Jacob—it's too obvious, I know. Because then—then you would go out and find your uncle Ishmael. That's right. And you would find him and you would tell him that I am sorry for sending him and his beautiful mother, Hagar, out into the desert. It was an egotism on my part. It was jealousy. Sarah's jealousy got the better of her. And so she sent her sister away. But now I know that there won't be peace until all my sons are friends and family once again. If we can't be Jews and live with our brothers and sisters the Arabs, then we don't deserve to be Jews. It's as simple as that. One country. One beautiful together country. That's the answer the tumor wanted to tell me. Now it's time to go, Favileh. I'm tired. Doctors say I have a week, maybe a month, they say. But I told them, I'm not going anywhere until I hold you in my arms again. And that's a promise. You believe me?"

"I believe you."

"Then give me a kiss. I'll see you soon. *L'hitra-ot.*"

"I'm coming, Zeyda. I'm coming tomorrow."

"The day after will be fine."

"Hey, you know why the *Chasidim* are always dancing around? So happy. I'll tell you. To remind them of the beginning. *B'reisheet ha-rikud.* That's how it all started. And that's how it's going to end."

"I love you."

"Come here and say that."

"Okay. Day after tomorrow. We'll dance."

Wynema draws away from the circle and rejoins him, and sits and lays her head on his shoulder. "Talking to your Zeyda?"

"How'd you know?"

"Who else?" She sits up and looks at the stars.

Will puts his head in his hand and rubs his own forehead. He begins to sob quietly to himself, covering his face with his *talis.* And he gives himself over to it. Pure grief releases itself. Tentative at first, but then unstoppable. Unalloyed to anything except the moment, his moment, right here, right now.

Wynema, relaxed, takes hold of his hand, without a fear, without a thought. For connection, nothing more.

But she is *not* in the moment. She is very aware of herself. She is thinking of the Universe and her relationship to it. She is in *more* than the moment. A true mystic tonight.

"'Feel that,' he said. Was he talking about his pulse I felt? Or what did he mean?"

"Just what he said. Don't think about it, just feel it. That's what he wanted to pass it on to you. Just that." His mind takes control and drills deep. She grabs his chin. "No, I'm serious. That's what he wanted you to do: feel it, don't think about it. Feel him and you'll understand why he got sick, and about his place in all this."

"I'm going to Israel."

"Tomorrow?"

"Day after."

"Wish I could go with you."

"When I come back, let's dance together."

She looked at him—and finally smiled.

∿

Victor, Dayone, and Sotero stand close by as two elders wearing traditional blankets gently lay Simon on a blanket-covered ladder and cover him with his own blanket. They carry Simon slowly all around the plaza.

Will moves gracefully to stand next to Simon's body. He's not a doctor now.

Not until the Tribal Police Chief steps up next to Will and waits for the doctor to see him. When Will turns, the Police Chief, notebook in hand, asks him to call the time of death. "I don't know," Will says. "I suppose he died exactly when he wanted to."

Mirriamma sits down next to Wynema. "He should go visit his grandfather."

"He's way ahead of you."

"Good. Smart boy. You okay?"

Wynema turns and with the faintest of smiles. "Oh, yes."

Mirriamma touches the back of Wynema's hand.

Suddenly, she remembers. "I wonder if Will left a pass at the gate for Alána and Jahbig."

Old woman smiles and removes her hand.

∿

Wynema stands before Will. "Jahbig and Alána!"

He grabs his cell. "I put mine on vibrate and I didn't hear it. You, too? I'm sure they called."

"Put it on ring, but don't call. Let's go to sleep. I don't want to talk to anyone tonight. Not even my best friend. They're fine."

"But—."

68

IN THE HEALING GARDEN

Early next morning, Wynema and Will are in bed at Will's. He's awake and faces the wall. She's awake and looking at his neck and the back of his head. They're relaxed, but lost in thought. Will is covered by the sheet; Wynema has one leg under it and the other flung across his thigh.

Jahbig and Alána step into the room, stirring the two.

Jahbig is dancing from one foot to the other. "We tried to drive onto the Pueblo last night—you know, me at your place, Alána with Wynema—but they wouldn't let us on. We called you but—."

Alána says "Wyneeeema," but her tone clearly means 'I'm gonna get you'.

Will is embarrassed. "I'm sorry, Jah. I forgot to call in a pass for you at the gate. Where'd you stay? I'm so sorry."

Jah, "No worries, fool."

"They closed the pueblo last night. Shut it off from the world. Because, well, Simon, my patient, my friend—he died last night. It took a long time. We were up most of the night. I'm sorry for your trouble, my brother."

"My condolences, eh. We took a couple of rooms at one of the casinos. Nice rooms. Totally fine. Gives you guys some space in your grief."

Alána inclines her head off to one side. "No, we took one room. And I learned something about myself. I can share a space of prayer with a man."

In one fluid motion, Jah kicks off his shoes and sits cross-legged in a reading chair. Alána sits on the bed and leans over for a hug.

"Simon was really your friend." Jah says with deep affection.

Will nods slowly.

"Sorry, mon."

Wynema gently squeezes Alána's hand. The faintest of smiles in the corners of their mouths.

Jah stands and pulls Alána up. "C'mon, get up! Let's be together. I'm gonna make some coffee."

All four on the roof holding hot coffee—the women on one side looking up, the men on the other looking down.

"I really thought she was the one," says Will softly.

Jah, quietly tickled, "She might still be, in ways you've yet to discover."

Will double-takes, then slowly considers.

Both women are looking across with admiration at the men talking.

They turn to each other. "If actually you got him to see you," says Alána, "you know, the woman in his life, in a different way, then you did good, gal."

"We'll see. I don't have much objectivity right now."

"This one has possibilities."

"His intimacy is good."

"That's what counts."

Wynema sincerely, nodding her head towards Jahbig, "You like him?"

"As far as men go, he's a good man." And Alána, of course, could mean this in a numbers of ways.

"Men are part of the healing."

"In the Healing Garden of Dance."

"Dancing.... Speaking of dancing, today's is San Lucas' Feast Day. Every pueblo's feast day is different, but the one here is pretty special. I want you to dance with me."

69

IN THE BEGINNING THE DANCE

A few days later, at sundown—at the mouth of a beautiful, steep-walled canyon—Will stands next to the little cedar tree he's just planted next to Simon's grave, freshly dug, piled, and decorated. He's wrapped in his father's prayer shawl, reciting the Kaddish in Hebrew.

When he's done, he steps away but quickly returns. "Simon, you'll meet my Zeyda soon. I'm going to see him in a few days. I'm going to work here for another year, and then, who knows? Maybe I'll get a job over there, in his hospital. Maybe I got to work in Israel, too. Lord knows they need a healing. Okay? And just in case you don't know, a couple of other docs from some of the other pueblos—we're going to do whatever it takes to get Indian docs working here. If there aren't any available, we'll train them ourselves. Pretty good, huh?—like that."

With that, Will scrunches up his arms and shoulders...and starts dancing.

ACKNOWLEDGEMENTS

There are many people to thank. Most of them don't want public thanks here or anywhere. Just know that I am grateful and couldn't have completed this without you. There isn't one of you I don't hold dear in my heart with profound gratitude.

I must, however, mention five.

Steve Cotler, Big Mama, and Dayla Hepting helped me seriously with Frank's performance rants and poetry.

Without the love and support of my beautiful bride, Karina McAbee, OMD, L.Ac—endless wandering and depleted chi.

And Carl Hammerschlag, M.D.—Carl was the initial and continuing inspiration for this story. His writings and personal guidance gave me the confidence to throw myself into the process. His magical book of memoirs, *The Dancing Healers*, was the springboard. Look on the back cover of this book.

꙳

The native Pueblo language you find transliterated herein is not real. It is made up. The real dialect, *Tewa*, does not want to be written here. I can only respect that.

ABOUT THE AUTHOR

ABOUT THE AUTHOR: Lanny Cotler was born on the Fourth of July. He was an Eagle Scout, arrested in the Free Speech Movement, a Vietnam vet (USAID/CORDS) and taught Classics at St. Johns College, NM. He lived in San Miguel de Allende, Mexico, for two prime years, then spent an energetic decade in Hollywood writing and directing feature films ("The Earthling" and "Heartwood").

He adapted for the screen both Frank Waters novel, *The Man Who Killed the Deer,* and Carl Hammerschlag's *The Dancing Healers.* Both of these projects brought him into contact with the people and culture of the Pueblo nation.

He is an activist member of the Grange Movement and lives in Mendocino County, California.

www.lannycotler.com